TREAD SOFTLY IN THIS PLACE

'Brian Cleeve gives his characters flesh
and blood and gives their movements
meaning, and he has wit and
understanding and a gift of phrase. He
moves effortlessly, from mood to
mood, from the tender and the true
to the comic, from a calm view of the
past to a sharp view of the present.'
– *Sunday Independent*

'The work is given added dimension
by a credible interfolding of past and
present . . . the imaginative mixing of
allegory and reality, and the hint of
further sacrifices to come. *Tread
Softly in this place* is by no means a
cool book. It's written with a certain
passion, it has guts, wit, tenderness
and quite a few astute asides. The
author has a good ear for colloquial
speech and a sharp eye for the small
hypocrisies which oil our daily lives.
It's a piquant comment on life in
provincial Ireland today.' – *Irish
Independent*

Also by Brian Cleeve

VOTE X FOR TREASON
THE JUDAS GOAT
VIOLENT DEATH OF A BITTER ENGLISHMAN
EXIT FROM PRAGUE
CRY OF MORNING

and published by Corgi Books

Brian Cleeve

Tread Softly
In This
Place

CORGI BOOKS
A DIVISION OF TRANSWORLD PUBLISHERS LTD
A NATIONAL GENERAL COMPANY

to EDMUND FISHER
with thanks

TREAD SOFTLY IN THIS PLACE

A CORGI BOOK 0 552 09376 9

Originally published in Great Britain
by Cassell & Co.

PRINTING HISTORY

Cassell edition published 1972
Corgi edition published 1973

This book is set in 10pt Plantin

Corgi Books are published by Transworld
Publishers Ltd.,
Cavendish House, 57–59 Uxbridge Road,
Ealing, London W.5.
Made and printed in Great Britain by
Cox & Wyman Ltd., London, Reading and Fakenham

**N.B. The Australian price appearing on the
back cover is the recommended retail price.**

CHAPTER ONE

THE two old men crouched for a half minute in the black shadow of the hedge. Their breath rattled in their bony chests and their hearts thudded with fear and excitement. Beside them the road ran white and dusty in the starlight and the first beginnings of the moon. Everything else was black. Black hedge at their backs, black velvet sky with its pale swarm of stars, black mountain, black sea. Although the sea was out of their vision, beyond the hedge, beyond the flat rows of fish ponds. Even their hands and faces were almost black, not by design but from the turf smoke, and indifference to washing.

'What do we do now, Peadar?' the younger whispered. He was seventy-eight and deferred in almost everything to his brother, who was eighty. Peadar cocked his big, gnome ear to the light movement of the night air; not even a breeze, only a soft stirring.

' 'Oo follow me, boy,' he said at last. His voice cracked with nerves and they held each other at the sound. Ooh God almighty, Jesus and Mary and Joseph save them, if they were caught, if they were catched inside there, ooh ooh ooh. Their bent old fingers dug into each other's arms, bone into bone, threadbare sleeves rustling together. They wished in sudden, telepathic unison that they were back up the mountain side, in their cottage, in their big double bed in the inner room, piled high with old coats, army blankets, the patchwork quilt, the cushions stuffed with chicken feathers; sleeping soundly there with young Jamey snoring in the box bed in the outer room, beside the red ashes of the fire. And Jess the sheepdog, and the cats, and the donkey, and the chickens, and the five cows scattered round the cottage in their various sheds and lean-to corners like images of safety.

It crossed Matty's mind to say, 'Why don't we go back, Peadar?' but he was afraid of the shame of it. And God above, wasn't it right what they were doing, wasn't it justice? Peadar, creaked his knees upright, turning his big, furry head left and right, for all the world, Matty thought suddenly, like the blessed donkey aself. He suffered at times under Peadar's domination and had his own secret life of the mind.

'Follow me now, boy,' Peadar hissed through his gums. They were almost beside the gate, white painted iron piping, the latch and the hinges oiled and silent. And somehow that fact alone gave them the necessary inch more of courage, of anger. Oiling a gate! The divils, the foreigners. On their land! That hadn't had a gate to oil since the memory of man. Only a furze bush dragged across a gap, or a couple of tree branches. And now look at it! They trod on gravel and then, crunching off it, on to mown turf like a lady's lawn. Away and away to the right the rising moon showed them the long buildings of the hatchery, the round roof over the big round pool for fingerlings. Through another gate, wooden this time but also freshly painted and oiled, another hedge, and they were looking down at the ponds. Like twenty swimming pools, big swimming pools although that simile could never come to the two old brothers. Big pools with corners and straight sides, like nothing that they had ever seen until they saw these being dug a couple of years back. Four terraces of them, five ponds to a terrace, stepping down towards the sea, the edge of the bay no more than fifty yards away from the lowest terrace. And out of the hollow waters, a dark whispering of fish, a strange, eery slithering sound of fishy movements, thousand upon thousand of rainbow trout, ten, twenty, thirty thousand to a pond, the youngest fish on the high terrace, the big fish, ready for table, ready for flying to London and to Paris and New York, packed in ice, slithering their half pound bulk in the lowest pools.

They had finished their night feed hours before – the liquid fishmeal and the dried insects sprayed from hosepipes on to the surface. Now they drowsed, but always moving, endlessly restless, fish body rubbing against fish body, and the stench of them rising into the soft summer night as their backs broke the surface of the water, rippled it like moving silk, like the writhing souls of the damned.

'Ooohah,' breathed Peadar. 'Will 'oo look?'

They stood looking and both of them saw not what was in front of them, but what had been there only three years ago. Nothing. Inimitable, irreplaceably beautiful nothing. Reeds and rushes, swampland with runnels of muddy streams slowly

6

moving, scarcely moving towards the sea. Their cows knee deep in it, mud to the udders, flicking their tails at summer flies. Beyond the swamp, the muddy, shingled beach, mud giving way to shingle, to stones, to seaweed, to the clean sea, to the great path of the bay leading out between the headlands to the ocean. Although the old men had never thought of the ocean, had never gone the ten miles down the shore of the bay to see the ocean. It had never occurred to them. Out there was the Head, and the kind of people that lived on the Head. And here was them. The Powers. Their land. Their swamp. Their cows.

And then the foreigner had come and offered them so much money for the swamp land that they had been stunned. Fifty pounds an acre for thirty acres. They had sat by the fire night after night looking at each other, turning the figures over and over. Fifteen hundred pounds! They had sat so long that the foreigner had come back and offered them eighty, and then a hundred and at that after another week of thinking Peadar had looked at Matty – not at young Jamey who was not yet seventy, merely a boy, a child – had ordered Jamey to mind the fire, and Peadar and Matty had gone down to Ross Harbour to sign the papers. Three thousand pounds.

'What'll 'oo do with it?' Matty had breathed.

'Keep it safe, boy.'

Matty had only seen the money once, in bundles of new pound notes in the solicitor's office – Peadar had refused to accept a cheque and had stuck out for a long time for sovereigns, until Father Culhane had been mentioned as a man whose word might be accepted that no such things existed nowadays, or at least not for buying and selling land.

'Arragh damn,' Peadar had said. 'It isn't a thing to be worrying the Father with,' seeing visions of God knew how many pound notes finding their way into the Church's pocket in return for being called on. And Martin O'Loughlinn, the solicitor, who had known what the reaction would be, had stiffened his thin mouth against smiling and pushed the piles of notes forward again. That had been the last Matty had seen of them. Where they might be now – in the bank, in the mattress, in the thatch, in a hole in the field stuffed into biscuit tins – he had no idea at all, and it had crossed his mind many times that if anything happened to Peadar, God between him and all harm, it would be the devil's own job to find the money, together with

7

whatever it was that their father, God rest his soul, had left. All that he had ever known about that was finding the upholstery of the armchair ripped open and the flock all over the floor.

'What 'oo find, Peadar?' he had said eagerly, to be crushed with the answer, 'Enough for masses, boy, and no more. Yerra 'tis a wonder what he did with it all, and the mother God rest her bringing him a big dowry aself. Oh 'tis woeful hard to be orphans and me to have the care of both of ye.'

For a year after they sold the land it had been as if nothing had happened at all. No one came. They went on driving their cows down to the swamp all through the summer, so that they could cool their legs. Then they walked them into the sea to clean the mud from them. And back home up the mountainside. It was still their land. They almost forgot the money. Matty did forget it. Until the beginning of the next summer they found the fence blocking them off from the sea. They simply took it down and went through.

They went on doing that even when the men had begun digging the pools. Their cows ate the tender shoots of the young green hedge, trod great divots out of the delicate new-laid turf, dropped great steaming pats of manure on the raked gravel, and the big blond Norwegians cursed and shouted, tried to drive out the cows, threatened, begged, fetched the guards, and finally had the two old men dragged into court to have an injunction put on them.

'A Junction?' Jamey had asked them, amazed. 'What is it, lads?'

'Arragh damn them,' Peadar had said, aiming a kick at the old dog and missing her by a tail's length. 'Foreigners! Junction!'

Night after night by the fire, turning the injustice over in their minds, over and over. Their land. Their cows. The swamp gone. The sea. The junction. The court. And the image of that lost paradise with the cows standing, and them standing, and the sea quiet and shining and the slow rivulets of yellow water wandering between the reeds and the sedge grasses and the little blue flowers. It was past all bearing. Now and then they went down to stand by the green hedge that had grown quite thick and tall and they would stare over it at the lawn and the long white building and the queer round one with no walls and the men with rubber boots and hosepipes. A few times the biggest Norwegian came out and tried to talk to them and the third time he urged them to come inside and see what he had done. That was when they got a proper look at the pools with the fish in them. Half a million fish. It didn't mean anything. Three thousand pounds. Thirty acres. Twenty pools. It didn't mean anything at all. No figures meant anything except their five cows and the swamp and going down to the sea. But something had stayed in Peadar's mind.

The little gates. The little sunken wooden gates between the pools that a man in rubber boots and a long brown coat pulled up while they were there. When he had pulled up one of the gates all the fish from the upper pool went slithering down a narrow channel into the lower pool that had already been emptied of its big fish that were ready for the market. And at the far end of that pool was another gate. And beyond that gate another channel, curving away below the lowest terrace to join the small river that had once fed the vanished swamp, and that now travelled between dredged and disciplined banks down to the beach and the sea. The water for the fish ponds came from the river, travelled from pond to pond through the narrow concrete channels, dropping from level to level, controlled at each pond entrance and exit by its elm-wood sluice gates, and finally returned to the river, burdened with its stinking silt of fishdroppings that would spread out into the bay like a milky cloud, to be eventually cleansed by the healing of the sea.

' 'oo saw what I saw, boy?' Peadar said that night to Matty. 'If those little gates were taken away in the dark with nobody knowing, what 'ould happen?'

'The fish 'ould escape, Peadar.'

'Yerrah, boy, you're right, they would.'

Even so they had brooded on it for a long time, turning it round and round, over and over. The danger, the rightness, the justice of it, the danger, the rightness. If they were catched? Would it be against the Junction? Would they have to give back the three thousand pounds? But the money had been for the land, not for building fish pools and taking away the swamp that God had put there, and yerrah, had they wanted the damn money? Hadn't the tall divil pressed it on them, begged them and chased them like Jess chasing Jamey's ould ram on the mountain? It wasn't right. As sure as there was a tail on the cat it wasn't right, they had been done and right done. They had been robbed of their own land and God would mind them.

9

But each night they put the plan off on one excuse or another. Young Jamey was lying awake coughing and it 'ould never do if he heared them. The moon was too bright or the night too dark or Matty had seen a devil's coach horse in the hearth and failed to get his thumb on it in time. 'The divil break your legs, boy, you're the slow one.' One night they had got outside the house but the goat had been there and had looked at them and they had gone back inside again. ' 'Twas a warning, boy, 'twas his way of telling us never to go down this night or we'd be cott.'

They never would have gone down if it hadn't been for the Public Meeting. They didn't go to it. It wouldn't have crossed their ancient minds in a thousand years to go to it. 'Yerrah man, meetings!' they said, but they would have been heart stricken with fear at the thought of going to it, into the town with all the people and the young gerruls looking at them, their souls to the Devil. Yet if they didn't go to the meeting itself they heard of it, and the reasons for it, and out of all the talk they absorbed one thing; that there would be more buying of land by incomers, more changes. And they saw in their minds' eyes the hundred mountain acres that they lived on taken from them, turned into sleek fishponds, lawns and hedges. They saw their low cottage taken and rebuilt into a house for fishes.

'Yerra manalive no,' Donal Carmody the roadmender had said, leaning on his big broom by the pile of chippings, 'it isn't that class of a carry on at all. It's – it's factories – 'tis chimneys and smelters they do be after.'

They hadn't believed him. And if they had believed him it would have made no difference. They wanted no more changes. Now they were by the outlet gate of the first pond. ' 'oo do it,' Matty whispered. 'I'm feared.' His legs shook and he held on to his brother's arm. The fish sensed a presence above them and swirled in the dark water, hungry for the hose-shower of food that they associated already with any movement near them. 'I'm feared of the fishes,' Matty croaked aloud. 'Ooh God, if afell in?'

Peadar bent slowly, knees creaking, gums locked. He had his hand on the upright wooden handle of the sluice-gate when he stopped. ' 'tis at the bottom we need to begin, boy,' he said. 'Nearest the sea. Let them out first to make room for these.'

'Do 'oo hear them talking?' whispered Matty, his eyes fearful, looking at the glistening movement of the pond, a boiling, moving mass of fish that looked so solid in the moonlight that a foot could walk on it. 'Íosa Críost Peadar, let's get out of here.'

'The devil fire you, boy, come on down.'

They went down to the last gate. Peadar knelt by the sluice. 'Out 'oo go, lads,' he whispered. He pulled up the gate. For a long moment nothing happened. The fish seemed to hesitate, to hold themselves back in the mouth of the sluice as though an invisible dam still held them from freedom. And then one nosed his way into the channel. Within a breath the channel was full of trout. A brown and silver stream of fishes, the fish smell breaking up in waves, pulsing up from their bodies, from the teeming, flooding mass of them as they swam over and under one another, writhed and shimmered through the channel. A hundred, a thousand, ten thousand fishes, ten thousand full grown trout slithering towards the sea. And still and still they came, pressing on to nowhere, mindless, blinded, driven by nothing but the need to swim, to nose through water, to follow others, to hunt for food.

'On 'oo go lads,' cried Peadar, delighted. He clambered to his feet and lifted his cap, feeling that such a great mass of nature needed respect.

'Are we for home now, Peadar?' whispered Matty.

'The devil be from me we are. Aren't there more ponds in it? 'oo take that one and I'll do the one beyond. 'tis great sport, boy. There's fishermen their lives long 'ouldn't see the like of this night's work. 'twill go into history.'

He ran to the farthest pond, bow-legged, furry headed, like an old gnome in a cap, sucking his gums with joy. Matty trotted after him in terror of being left behind. It took them barely a half-hour to pull all the gates of the ponds.

A quarter of a mile away, beyond the place where the small winding river emptied itself into the bay, a young man and a girl lay on the bank of grass above the narrow, stony beach. An old white mare cropped the turf behind them, its teeth crunching, every now and then a hoof stamping, solid and re-assuring.

The boy was thin and dark, with a pale, gaunt face that seemed permanently hungry, and eyes that seemed always to be thinking of something else. Even now. It was a look that had annoyed a succession of employers, and the magistrate who the previous year had sentenced him to six months for assaulting a

11

policeman, and the warders in the prison where he had served the sentence. Most recently it had been annoying the girl's father, Hubert Kershaw, proprietor of The Old House Hotel, and the boy's present employer. It made Hubert Kershaw think, as it had made all the others think, that the boy was regarding him with disrespect; that he found other things more worth his attention than whatever it was he was saying to him at that moment. Sometimes, when his mouth took a particular shape to it, he thought he might even be laughing at him.

'If your father finds out we're here—' He was sitting up, hugging his knees, staring out across the stillness of the bay at the lights of Ross Harbour. But even as he said that his mind seemed to be going beyond what he was saying, as if in that same moment of saying it he was no longer thinking only or even mostly of her father finding them, but of something quite different. But where this quality infuriated Hubert Kershaw, it was the very thing which had first attracted Jennifer Kershaw to the new barman-cum-handyman her father had employed a few months earlier. If he had looked at her as though he was interested, as though he was a young man looking at a girl, she would have treated him as she would have treated any other barman, as she treated Fish Doyle's son when he delivered fish and blushed from the collar of his shirt up to the thatch of his head if in signing his book she accidentally touched his hand. She might have been polite to him, might have been scornful of him, might have teased him or laughed at him or ignored him or been arrogantly indifferent to him. But he had looked at her sometimes as if the sight of her started a train of thought that swiftly took him far away from her, and she had begun by being annoyed and ended by being enslaved.

When he played the guitar on Friday evenings in the bar and other girls looked at him it was all she could do not to be rude to them there and then and to him afterwards, and she had finally, tonight, reached the point where she knew that if she could not make him fall in love with her she would do something terrible. And so she had gone to his room over the stable and told him that the horse, the old mare Coca who had never got lost in her life, had never willingly strayed a foot beyond her own field, was lost and gone and that he was to get up and help her find her.

'The Gallaghers must have her,' she had said in a trembling, unnatural voice as he sat up in bed startled and still half asleep. 'The Whisperer must have taken her.'

She hadn't expected to be believed. She had thought he would be angry, that he would – she hadn't thought what he would do – but he had simply asked her to turn her back for a second, and she had turned it, the skin of her shoulders alive with fright like electricity, thinking that the next second, the next second – already sorry for what she had done, half terrified, half hysterical with laughter – and he had said 'All right', and he was dressed in jacket and trousers and old shoes and was buckling his belt. Did he believe her? She had not known, she had still been afraid and at the same time electric with excitement and they had gone softly, quietly down into the courtyard, down the outside ladder-stairs from his room into the courtyard and the moonlight and out through the stable archway on to the drive; through the few trees and over the wooden fence, and Coca had been standing there under her own tree like a grey ghost, like an illustration from a children's book. And Michael still said nothing as the old mare, surprised, ambled towards them. He merely looked at her, one eyebrow tilting upwards, not even smiling, not frowning.

'She must have come back on her own,' Jennifer had said, her face flushing dark. How dare he say nothing, how dare he look like that? I must be mad, she thought, suddenly humiliated, furious. She wanted to order him to go back to bed. But as soon as she thought of it she was afraid that he would go.

'Let's walk down to the shore,' she said distantly. 'There – there might be someone prowling about still.'

'Then they'd be near the road,' he said.

She didn't answer, but strode away from him towards the shore of the bay, crossing the drive. Coca ambled behind her, amazed at so much activity at a time when no activity ever was. Jennifer went one stride beyond the edge of the drive, two. If he stayed where he was, turned back to the house, she would die, die, die. But she heard him follow, knew in her bones and blood that he was following before she heard the rustle of his clothes, the light crunch of his foot on the dusty, sparse gravel of the drive that had not been renewed since Grandfather's time and was now no more than earth with pebbles here and there. He was following, following. She felt her blood sing.

They came to the shore of the bay and he was almost beside her and when she sat he sat next to her, so close that their hands in the grass almost touched, and she knew that she had been right, that everything she had done was right and wonderful and he was going to belong to her. She was so sure of it that she had felt, she had begun to feel condescending about him. It was not a very great conquest after all, her father's handyman, the boy who served pints and swept the bar and cut the grass and touched up the paintwork and saw to Coca as far as she needed seeing to and washed the cars and cleaned out the stove and hefted the crates of beer around. The son of Donal Carmody the roadmender. The grandson of old Michael Carmody who had also in his time been a roadmender.

Except that he was also a little more than that. Two years in University. Four months in gaol. She imagined describing him to her friends in England who until last year had been her friends in school. They would be more impressed with the gaol than the University. She was herself. A Communist! He said he wasn't, but what else would he say? Leading a strike, hitting a policeman, going to prison for it. Was that what he was thinking about when his eyes had that strange, far away look in them? The things he had suffered in prison? The wrongs of the working class? The Revolution?

'What are you thinking about?' she had whispered because even though he was sitting there his hand had left the grass beside hers and was clasped round his knees, and he was staring away across the water at nothing. She could feel, actually feel his mind going away from her. And what had started as a playful, half provocative question took on an edge.

'If your father finds us here—'

For a second she was furious again. How could he think of anything like that at a moment like this? But then she knew that he was lying, or at least that he was not telling her the real truth; that he hadn't been thinking of that at all, but of something quite different that he wanted to keep secret, and even if it was not about her, even if it was a million miles away from her, it was a secret, something that made him different, worth bothering about. She lay back, content.

'Are you afraid of him?' she said. Her voice smiled, teased him, caressed him like a kitten caressing skin with half unsheathed claws. She had him to herself, to herself, out here in the moonlight, and she didn't care what he said, what he was secretly thinking in his far, far away mind. Another time it might matter but this first time it was enough to have him there.

She lay on her back, the grass cool damp against her shoulder-blades through the cotton of her shirt. When she stretched her arms over her head the bottom of the skirt came away from the band of her jeans and left her stomach bare. The night air touched her skin and she half closed her eyes, stretched up her chin and throat, smiled like a kitten stretching, like a leopard cub, its claws going in and out unconsciously, the whites of its eyes showing with delight.

She rolled her head sideways smiling very slightly, her mouth invisible. She wanted to touch him and at the same time not to touch him, to let this stillness of their bodies continue, his curved body, chin resting on knees, arms locked round his shins, making him like the shadow of a rock, jutting up from the ground. A rock that someone had begun to shape, half shape into the body of a man. A man sitting with arms locked round knees, head bent. She put out a hand and touched his back, the denim jacket stretched tight on the thin muscles. Her fingers traced the muscle ridges, the bones of the spine. When her fingers reached the bottom of the jacket the band was for some reason looser than the cloth above it so that it gave under her fingers and she was suddenly touching bare skin. The whole palm of her hand rested on bare skin before the edge of her little finger touched the edge of the leather belt that he wore. Part of his flesh was warm, and part quite cool, like ivory. He reached behind him and took her hand away, not roughly, but firmly enough to show that he was angry.

'What are you trying to do?' he said in a hard voice. But he didn't get up and leave her there.

She rolled on to her stomach on the grass. Lying like that she felt at once more protected, and more intimate, closer to him. 'Don't you ever feel like doing mad things?' she said. She pulled a blade of grass and began to suck the end of it, feeling the small instant of sweetness on her tongue. 'I didn't mean any harm.' She looked at him sideways.

'Your father wouldn't think that. At least he wouldn't think that I didn't.'

'Did you never have a girl-friend?'

He seemed to think about that for a long time and again she had the maddening sense that his mind had gone far beyond the question, far away from her. He said slowly, 'I came here to be left alone. Is that too much?'

She took her own time to answer. 'Yes,' she said, 'it is.'

'Why?'

She had the sudden, warm sense that at last they were on even terms, that he genuinely wanted to know something that she could tell him. But she took her own time answering and her mind drifted, over the last year since she had left school; the coming home with five O levels and a warm report on her character. 'A splendid prefect.' 'Qualities of leadership.' 'A fine sports girl, the best Captain of netball for many years.' 'Might well make a good Domestic Science teacher.' Mrs. Randall genuinely crying when she left. 'We shall miss you.' Pippa saying, 'Why don't you come out to Bermuda for the Vac?' Geraldine asking her to the Argentine, to the ranch. The others talking about summer courses in Geneva, or hitch-hiking to Turkey, or sitting for Cambridge scholarships. Mummy had already had her down for the Boulanger School of Cordon Bleu Kitchen Management in Highgate.

'What do you think it's like for me in this place?' she said pulling another long blade of grass, the stem coming pale and delicate from the sheath, sweet on her tongue. 'I'm sick of the kitchen, and the hotel, and the bar, and Colonel Mace getting drunk and trying to grab me, and Mrs. Mace looking at me as though I'm trying to seduce him and – and – everything, everything.' Of her mother, her father, herself. 'I'm sick of being solid and reliable and responsible and helping out and being a good sport and dear stupid Jennifer. Of course she's not an intellectual, the poor sweet, but *so* sensible. I'm sick of being sensible!' she cried, her voice rising with a sudden ferocity of anger. She brought down her fist on the grass with a small thud.

'You've little to worry about,' he said, 'if that's all that's worrying you.'

She came up from the grass like an eel curling, until she was sitting back on her heels, facing him, the moonlight falling between them so that half of each face was dark with shadow and the other half ivory. 'They make it all seem so pointless,' she said. 'Drinking every night in that awful phoney Copper Room, and telling lies about what they did in the War, and how rich they used to be and how frightful things are now and talking about how ungrateful the poor are not wanting to be servants any more. *I'm* a servant. And I hate it, I hate it. Why did they bother to send me to school?'

'Why don't you go away?'

'Why don't you?' she said bitterly.

'I've been away. I wanted to come back.'

'What could I do? Be a servant somewhere else, cook Sole Bonne Femme in someone else's horrible kitchen?'

'People do.'

She pushed her fingers between her thighs, looking down at the smooth cotton of the jeans. 'You despise me,' she said.

He shook his head. 'You interest me,' he said.

She looked at him, coldly angry. 'Class of spoiled girl, sub class Anglo-Irish decayed gentry? Who do you think you are to judge me?'

'I don't judge you,' he said, refusing to get angry in return. 'And I don't know who I am. I suppose that's why I came back.' He smiled slightly, almost invisibly in the shadow. 'Apart from having nowhere else to go.'

'It's strange,' she said. 'We were both born here, we're both of this place, and we know nothing about each other, nothing at all. And in a way I have everything here and I want to go away, and you have nothing here and you want to come back. You'd say that's because I'm not really Irish.'

'I wouldn't say anything.'

'It's nothing to do with being Irish or Anglo-Irish or – or – It's just – I want something more out of life than this. There has to be more. I don't mean money and cars and ski-ing holidays, I – I don't know what I mean. Just more. The other night when you were singing, that was more – at least – it was like looking out of a small window high up somewhere and seeing – like seeing the moon on the bay – you know the way it makes a path and you think, if I could get down to the shore very quickly, now, this second, I could walk on that path, it would be a road and I could – and then daddy and the Maces came in and started sounding all patronizing and I could have killed them—' She had bent her head so far down that her eyes were hidden from him, all her face in shadow. Her hair that was dark red by day was black by moonlight, like carved ebony, short curls and tongues of dark hair round her head. As he looked at her he found himself wanting to touch it, and the careful barrier he had created and maintained between them for these months seemed to be falling, seemed never to have been there at all.

'I didn't mean any harm bringing you out here,' she was saying. 'I'm sorry – if—'

'I needn't have come,' he said.

'Why shouldn't we?' she whispered. 'Why can't we just talk

if we want to? If it wasn't daddy's hotel – if it belonged to someone completely different, and I was the cook and you were the barman, wouldn't you talk to me?'

'I do talk to you.'

'But really talk. About – about things that matter.'

'I don't know what does really matter,' he said. 'That's half my trouble.'

'What's the other half?' She looked at him, waiting, but his face had not closed, simply gone away again. She put out a finger and touched his knee, prodding it gently as if she was waking him up.

'How could you understand?' he said.

'I do,' she said. 'You don't know what matters, you don't know who you are, or why. Your father works on the road, and you went to University, and you've been in gaol and you think and you read and you have to earn your living as a barman and it doesn't seem just—'

'It isn't that.'

'It is, and I do understand. I'm the same, no, not the same, but in a kind of way. Can't you understand that? My father and mother talk like country gentry and they run a rotten pub that doesn't even make money and they use me as an unpaid skivvy. And I went to school too. I wasn't as clever as you, I didn't win scholarships or anything, but I was with girls who were collected in Rolls-Royces at the end of term and had their chocolates sent to them from Paris and other girls who were going to be doctors or journalists or go into the Foreign Office or marry boys they loved. And I had to come back to this. And all you say is, "You've little enough to worry about".'

'Isn't it true? Have you ever gone hungry? Not known where you'd sleep?'

'You don't understand anything,' she said, angry again. 'If I needed to go hungry do you think I couldn't? If I'd wanted to I could have – could have just gone out with bare feet and a headband and slept in the Park, or hitch-hiked to Afghanistan or killed myself. It isn't that I'm afraid, or soft, or . . . If there was a reason for doing any of those things – if they – if they led anywhere – I want a reason.' Even as she said it she wondered if it was true. As though she had surprised herself by saying it, had made a discovery, and she thought of herself with a new respect and at the same time felt infinitely lonely, even lonelier than before.

18

She found that she was crying. The tears fell on the tight-stretched cotton of her jeans and made damp patches.

'I'm sorry I woke you up,' she said. She knelt upright. In another second she would be standing up and she would walk away, back to the hotel and her bedroom and her closed life and when they saw each other in the morning – she felt sick with anger at herself for being there at all. And at the same time the things that had driven her there had in a way been made much worse.

He saw her face close to his, the tear tracks like silver, her eyes lowered, mouth locked and what was left of the barrier fell completely, vanished, and he saw her as close as if she was a friend. As though he was inside a locked room that he himself had locked, and the door was being opened; and he was desperately afraid of it opening, leaving him unprotected, and at the same time desperate for company, for human contact. For this human contact.

'Don't,' he said, not knowing what else to say, what to do. As long as he was indifferent he knew exactly what to do. Was this what had held him back from her, from letting himself be friends with her? Not sense, not caution, wisdom; not even fear. Just ignorance, not knowing what to do, what to say. Because she was a different class. Not like the shopkeepers' and doctors' daughters he had known in College. Not like the girls he had known in London. Something quite different. A lady. The roadmender's son and the lady. The thing that everyone laughed about, that wasn't supposed to exist. That didn't exist, unless you wanted it to. What was her father, except the left-overs of the Ascendancy? An amateur hotelkeeper who'd be bankrupt in another couple of years. If he had met her in London he might have liked her or not liked her, but he wouldn't have given a damn who her father was or what her accent was or—

He put out his hand to touch her face. It was a lie, he would have been frightened of her anywhere, she was in his blood, in the bone of his tradition, the lady and the roadmender. And yet his people had held this land when hers were pirates, sea rats out of Bristol. As though his mind had been crippled by generations of slavery. Had his great-grandfather the Fenian felt like this when he went out in '67 with his pike and his long gun? Afraid of the landlord he was going to shoot? He had her cheek cupped in the palm of his hand and for a second she leaned her head sideways so that the weight of it was on his palm and both of them felt that the gesture and the moment were important, that it was a seal of friendship. And half of her wanted to stay like that, resting her head on his palm, waiting for him to move, to—

And the other half of her shivered suddenly, afraid of what might happen, of not being able to stop it happening. She let the shiver become more obvious. 'I'm cold,' she whispered. 'You must be cold too. We ought to be getting back.' Behind them Coca stamped and shifted, tossing her great bony head. She smelled a strange scent floating towards her from the river, the smell of the fish, the first comers of the great shoal released by the two old brothers a few minutes before; a blue steel and silver torrent of rainbow trout slithering and tumbling towards the bay and the open sea. The smell of their vast, unnatural numbers stirred wild senses in her, as if Pan was loose, and she pawed at the ground and felt vaguely that she should be away from that place. But her mistress still knelt quietly, apparently unafraid, and the old mare hesitated, torn in mind, blowing and snuffling.

'Coca's feeling cold as well,' Jennifer said, as though she needed more arguments for going back. But still she didn't move. The strange, Pan-scent of freedom reached her too, reached her senses, shivered them with ghostly urgencies of fear. And for a second she was not Jennifer Kershaw of The Old House Hotel, she was one with the ground she knelt on, the grass, the shadows of the trees. The night, the moonlight flowed through her body like a powerful, steady current. She was on the point of knowing something and the knowledge would be terrifying. She shivered in earnest, her whole skin pricked with gooseflesh.

'I'm frozen,' she said. She stood up and almost fell, one of her legs gone half to sleep under her, but it seemed to her as if the ground was pulling her back and she was touched with panic. 'If they find I'm gone,' she whispered.

They began walking back to the hotel, Coca ambling after them, pleased to be getting away from that unnatural smell and yet still disturbed, blowing through her velvet nose, her black, rubbery lips. Jennifer put her hand in Michael's, for re-assurance as much as friendship. She felt as though something was happening, had happened, that she could not control, that she had not meant to happen; that what had begun as a game

20

had become serious, adult. She felt a grave seriousness in her mind, even in her walk, so that she was quite different from the girl who had left her bedroom an hour or two earlier for the kind of adventure that schoolgirls undertake. All that had been safe and dull and unendurable now seemed unsure, like things seen through water or rainwet windows, changed out of recognition.

She held his hand, not talking, not sure enough to talk. What could she say to him? She felt humility, a serious gratitude that he allowed her to hold his hand. 'Am I in love?' she wondered in amazement. An hour earlier the thought would have been so ridiculous she could not have entertained it, and now she was afraid to entertain it. She wanted to look sideways at him, she could not remember what he looked like, wanted to remind herself of the line of his chin, the curve of his eyebrow, the shape of his mouth. But she was afraid to do that, afraid to make any move like someone watching a strange and wonderful bird from a distance, frightened to move closer in case it flies away.

And he held her hand with something of the same strangeness, the same unexpectedness of feeling. Of all the things that could have happened between them he had least wanted this. For three months he had treated her with an almost hard indifference, making it clear that there was a fence between them and that she had no right and no invitation even to look over it, let alone cross it. Almost ostentatiously he had talked in front of her in a completely different, casually intimate tone to Eileen Hegarty who helped in the kitchen and did the scrubbing, and to Teresa Mullen who did the dining-room, underlining that he and they were of a common understanding, and that she, Jennifer, the owner's daughter, did not share it.

He had expected her to answer indifference with arrogance, and then they could have been comfortably hostile to one another whenever they needed to meet. But she hadn't reacted like that. She had been humble instead of arrogant, and had seemed never to notice the difference between his manner to her and to the two other girls. She had worked as hard as he did and far harder than the girls did, when he had expected her to be as lazy as her mother was, and as idiotic as her father was, and gradually, gradually, from being an embodiment of prejudice, daughter-of-the-gentry, daughter-of-the-owner, she had become a person, and he had had to be rude to her to prevent himself from being polite.

But since it was not in his nature to be rude to women, she had never noticed that he was being rude, and one by one his prejudices had fallen, until all that was left between them was his need to be left alone, and above all by her, who could destroy his refuge, make it impossible for him to stay here. And if he had to leave here, because her father threw him out, where could he go, what could he do? A police record trailing him from job to job, the Special Branch calling on his employers with 'a word of advice about that fellow you've just taken on'. They had done that with Mr. Kershaw and it hadn't mattered because he had already told him the truth, and there wasn't a chance of Mr. Kershaw finding another man in mid-season at the kind of wages Michael was working for. But if there was a question about Jennifer as well—

And yet he went on holding her hand and every second that he held it he knew that he was sealing a bargain that he shouldn't make, that he could not unseal again without doing the kind of harm he did not want to do to either of them. Her hand rested in his, thin and warm and dry, a working hand, but with the long bones of fineness. His sisters' hands were square and fat and his mother's were calloused like a man's from carrying buckets and scrubbing and the ferocious handling of her broom.

Why had he let her call him out tonight? He had known she was lying, playing a game with him, but he hadn't let himself know it, and even when the horse came towards them the second they stepped out of the courtyard, he had followed her down to the shore. And he had to recognize that it was because he wanted to, that he had wanted to follow her more than he had wanted to save his privacy, the mental refuge that he had constructed round himself when he came back to The Ross.

But if he asked himself why he wanted to, there was no answer at all.

They separated in the entrance to the courtyard, under the high brick and stone arch. She went very quickly and lightly over the cobbles, her shirt a pale shape in the dark that already had a faint suggestion of false dawn about it, a lightening of black shadows, a dullness of the stars. He saw her stop by the drainpipe at the far end of the yard, under the low roof of the old gun room that was now an office. The rolled sleeve of the shirt lifted, she was climbing, going up hand over hand like a sailor climbing the rigging of a mast. On to the roof of the gun room, then up again, perching for a second on the windowsill that served the upstairs passage window. She had left the window open and in another moment she was gone. The shadow of her hand waved from inside, or perhaps that was his imagination, but he lifted his own hand in answer.

He climbed the wooden stairs to his room slowly, suddenly bone tired. What had he done? He lifted the latch and went into his room, not bothering to turn on the light. He didn't need to turn it on to find his way back to bed. But after he had closed the door he stood for a second with his back to it, leaning against the wood and the cloth of his good suit that hung from a nail in the door, his eyes shut, still feeling the print of her hand in his, the thin, long bones, the warm dryness. He put his own hand up to his face and held it there for a moment, like a man listening to a seashell, hearing the roar of the sea that lives in the shell.

Far up the mountainside the two old brothers climbed wearily towards their cottage, through familiar gaps in familiar stone walls, now and then up stretches of the cart track that served as a road to their farm, now cutting the short way again across hummocked fields full of gorse and boulders and ancient rabbit warrens where no rabbit had been for fifteen years since the 'tosis. They came at last to their own fields and felt a weight of fear fall off them. The goat was not there to greet them but the donkey had his head across a wall, scratching his long rough throat on a stone. A chicken squawked under a bush, its minuscule brain dreaming of foxes. A broken harrow lay like a skeleton, reassuring as their own hearth. The bitch Jess barked one sharp bark of welcome and came out whining and wriggling her spine and feathery tail, reproaching them for not letting her go with them that night.

'Yerra bad luck to ye, ye divil,' Peadar said, aiming a friendly kick at her. ' 'tis done, eh, boy, 'tis done and well done. They'll be leaping with rage surely down below in the morning.'

'Hush Peadar,' Matty whispered, 'ye'll have Jamey waking on us.' As Peadar had become the father of the family Matty had become the mother, worrying about Jamey, and cooking the potatoes. It was he even more than Peadar who saw to it

23

that Jamey didn't smoke. They crept into the cottage, into the familiar dark and smell: turf smoke and dirt and boiled potatoes, dog and chickens, cats and old age and mouldy thatch. An eye of turf still burned in the grey ashes of the fire. The cats lay in their cardboard box. Jamey snored in his box bed under the army surplus greatcoat they had bought for him in nineteen and forty-six, his hat on his head and his socks on his feet, the basin of milk for breakfast on the bench beside him with a cracked plate over it to keep the cats away. If they tried to get the plate off in the night he would hear them.

'All safe and sound boy,' Peadar whispered hoarsely. He took his feet out of his boots, leaving the boots by the fire, and more quietly Matty did the same. Then they went, Peadar first and Matty after him, into the inner room and their own brass bed. Peadar got in as he was, pulling the heaped coats and blankets up to his chin. Matty knelt down by the side of the bed.

'Our fader—'

'Yerra damn you, get into the bed boy. Is it religious mad you're going? God knows you're there without you telling Him twice in one week.'

Shamefacedly Matty climbed into the bed and sank into his own worn hollow. 'I'm feared for tomorrow, Peadar.'

'Divil a fear, boy.'

'I heared there was a feller in Dublin beyond that could look at your fingers and see what you'd been at, if it was thieving or murder.'

'The seventh son of a seventh son maybe?' Peadar said scornfully.

' 'tis all done with ink this feller was saying to me.'

'He must be the right scholar. Will you let me sleep, you divil.'

'Will you not hold me hand, Peadar?'

'Agh damn and blast,' Peadar said. But he took Matty's hand and the two old men fell asleep as they had fallen asleep in any times of danger for seventy-five years and over, since they were two and four years old and had first slept together in a box on the floor of that same room. Within a minute they were asleep, dreaming of the great flood of fish, of vengeance, of their land, of the cows knee deep in mud and reeds, of summer days by the shore.

CHAPTER TWO

THE next morning, a few minutes before five o'clock, the sun rose over the shoulder of Slieve Clogher like a great cry of golden joy on the empty stillness of The Ross. Nothing stirred. The long, broad fjord of Ross Bay lay like a steel mirror between the dark Peninsula of Ross to the east, its rocky, heathergrown sides and small valleys still partly in shadow, and the slender peninsula of Lir to the west, the gentler, grass grown hills of Lir Head, and the low isthmus of the Swan's Neck pale green and beautiful in the sunlight.

In the Bay itself shoals of rainbow trout swam here and there, attempting to adjust themselves to salt water and to freedom. The gulls had not yet discovered them, nor the catfish, and for these few hours they had enjoyed a fishy Eden, a primal innocence of swimming and feeding and exploring, and already the packed miseries of the fishponds were gone out of their collective mind. Not many of them would survive to see another sunrise turn their water from darkness to silken bright. Some would die of the salt, and some by the beaks of gannets and cormorants and skua and herring gull, and some to bigger fish in the deep. But a few would survive. Indeed one shoal, already acclimatized to salt water in the brackish ponds of the lowest level of the farm, was nosing its way towards the narrows between Lir Head and the Head of Ross, the gateway to the south.

Even now the first swimmers could sense the vastness of the sea beyond the headlands, the mass of its moving waters. Fine shivers of excitement ran through the shoal, and by an instinct its leaders tilted downwards, looking for protection from the sun, their shadows flying over still deeper levels, where the wrecks lay, piled about the rock foundations of the headlands, a Frenchman from Bordeaux in 18 and 71, carrying silks and brandy and claret wine and two stowaways fleeing from the Commune; a French cutter from the Napoleon War, that had been bringing messages from Wolfe Tone to the United Irish-men; a barquentine from Britanny, sunk by the navy patrols in 1710; older wrecks without names or surviving memories, back and back into the past until their timbers were crumbled into seaweed fodder, held together by barnacles, grown into the living rock; a norse long ship, the tall skeletons still lying at the thwarts, held there by the heavy sand, a woman's skeleton among them. A girl of the Carmodys' who had been washing clothes by the shore and stolen by the pirates. A Roman galley with great jars of oil from Spain. And still older ships, back to the beginnings of history and far beyond, the ghosts of their masters like shadows in the dark currents of the water gap, as the fish shadows sped over them, fleeing over the sudden patches of pale, shelving sand, blending with the dark weed forests of the rock, here where the bay and all the small world of The Ross ended, and the great world began. Out through the gap with them, and into the huge Atlantic, Biscay before them and the coasts of Lusitania, and the far Azores. What fish of all those tens of thousands would ever reach them? But neither would any of them reach the frying pans of smart hostesses in Cork and Waterford and Dublin; nor the chefs' kitchens of Parisian and London cafés. They would surely die, but they would die in freedom. Rainbow trout abú, my loves, swim-ming for liberty, for death and glory.

Far above them the sun rose higher, falling on the rooftops of the dwellers in The Ross. On the thatched cottage roofs of the Irish-speakers out by Ross Head, that last handful of families that stood so handsomely in Government statistics as a Fíor-Gaeltacht, Gaelic-speaking, glory of Ireland, justification of Easter Week 1916 and the long centuries of suffering and fierce rebellion. Each grateful family receiving a £10 annual bounty for each happy Irish-speaking school-going child; looking with blank and cunning eyes at itinerant inspectors who tried to trap them into speaking English. In the Government maps the Fíor-Gaeltacht spread proudly to the outskirts of Ross Harbour, and many enthusiasts in the Department planned to include Ross Harbour itself in the next edition of the map. Hadn't eighty-four per cent of the adult inhabitants of Ross Harbour signified on the last census form that they could speak and understand Irish? A breac-Gaeltacht at least, an almost-area won back from the tide of foreign speech. Reclaimed, reclaimed.

The reality of course was slightly different, as it tends to be when measured against any Government enthusiasm. The Irish-speakers consisted of eleven families, most of whose children had emigrated to Birmingham where they met on Saturday nights to talk among themselves. Little of their talk was in praise of the Irish government, or even about it. Mostly they talked about football and going home for Christmas.

At home, the survivors woke and turned on their transistor radios to listen to the B.B.C. and to decide whether to go fishing or stay at home. Very often they decided to stay at home, and with the price they got from the Doyles on the quay-side of Ross Harbour for anything they caught, it was no wonder if they did.

Between those eleven families, loosely scattered about Lir Head and in one or two of the more fertile valleys behind it, and The Old House Hotel, there was almost nothing. Small, rocky bays like bites out of the steep side of the headland, each with its new moon of sand, a few ruined cottages high above them, surrounded by what had once been fields, now no more than squarish patches of grass, the rushes or the gorse invading them.

In The Old House Hotel, the Kershaws, Hubert and Angela, lay asleep in their modernized four poster, the morning sun bright through the flowered chintz curtains, falling gold on the uneven, black oak floor with its threadbare Persian rugs, and on the whitewashed walls. Floors and walls and ceilings and mullioned, leaded windows met at odd, irregular angles and the big, curtained bed needed a small block of wood under one foot to keep it level. In the bed the Kershaws slept decently apart, Mrs. Kershaw in a good, sensible nightdress that preserved something of the atmosphere of the fine, games-playing English school in which she had once been a happy boarder; her husband Hubert in well-cut striped pyjamas, a clean handkerchief in the breast pocket. His bony nose and long narrow chin jutted up from the pillow, and he snored, slightly and evenly. Even asleep there was a look of haunted stupidity about his face, of a furious refusal to accept that life had not allowed him even to be clever, let alone wise. His red leather slippers lay side by side on one of the rugs, waiting for him to wake up and go and make the morning tea.

In the next bedroom Jennifer Kershaw was already awake and at the window. Her view was across the Bay towards the Swan's Neck and Lir Head, where she could just make out the small square shape of their rival hotel, The Angler. But she was not aware of it. She had been awake for an hour and for most of that time she had been standing by the window staring out of it, seeing nothing, thinking of what had happened last night – not last night, this morning, only a few hours ago – and what it meant. What was she going to do? What would she say to him when they met downstairs in an hour's time? What would he say to her? What did she want him to say, to think? She felt as though a portion of her life had ended and something new and frightening was about to begin. She tried to recapture the strange, floating feeling, a kind of dazed wonder, that for a few minutes she had felt as they walked back from the shore to the house, holding hands. But that was gone and what was left was a coldness about the heart, fear of what was coming.

'For seven years I have been one kind of person,' she thought, 'and now I am another.' Seven years of being a schoolgirl, a boarder, the Irish girl, the stranger. Covering her real self with layers of protection, camouflage, until the camouflage had been, had seemed to be, her new real self. So reliable, so sensible. And yet such a *strange* girl. So – so *withdrawn*. Upper Fourth. Remove. Five B. Lower Sixth. The netball team. The swimming team. Her own self crushed inside, silent, invisible. Almost forgotten, lost. And now?

What would she say to him? She wondered if he was awake, if he was thinking of her.

He was. But not by the window of the loft. And if he had been standing by it he could have seen almost nothing out of it, for it was coated on the outside with a thick layer of dirt. It would have taken no more than a ladder and half an hour's work to clean it, but since Michael was almost never in the room during daylight he had never bothered. His room, the 'staff' bedroom over the stables, had been done up in a great rush of enthusiasm for the first barman, three years ago, and had had nothing done to it since except the most basic cleaning. There was a very worn strip of carpet on the floor that had spent the previous thirty years in an upstairs passage outside the maids' lavatory. There were large nails driven into the back of the door to take whatever clothes the barman might wish to hang up. There was a white-painted deal chest of drawers from the old nursery, with one leg missing and replaced by a book. (None of the other barmen had touched the book, but Michael had fished it out the first night in the hope that it might be interesting. It was volume two of the collected sermons of a Doctor Nehemiah Gwynn, D.D.) There was a rough shelf above it that had once supported bottles of harness oil and various horse medicines and now supported Michael's own books. There was the round window with a cobweb on the inside and the dirt outside. There were two brick walls, white-washed, and two timber partitions with the door in one of them giving on to the stairs down into the stables proper.

And there was an iron bed with a set of springs that twanged like a harp in the night, and a coir mattress, a flock pillow, two ex-army blankets like thick grey sandpaper, two ex-army sheets like thick whitish sandpaper, and a faded patchwork quilt made by Hubert's grandmother's housekeeper for the head parlour maid as a Christmas gift in 1913. There had been a bedside chair but one of the legs had been worm-eaten and the whole thing had collapsed under one of Michael's predecessors. Now there was a wooden butter box covered with oil cloth. The only other decoration in the loft was a wooden crucifix. It had been there always, or at least since long before the conversion of the loft into a barman's bedroom. Mrs. Kershaw had discovered it there when she had been deciding where their barman should sleep, and having been baptized a Protestant she had had a superstitious tremor about removing it. It was an extremely ugly crucifix, or so she had thought, and she had the unpleasant feeling that the carved eyes in the tiny, tortured head were following her about as she walked over to the round window and tapped the partitions with her knuckles. But if the barman was to sleep here that might be no bad thing.

It had in fact given the first two barmen extremely un-pleasant dreams, both of them being Catholic alcoholics, and the second had got pneumonia because of doing an Easter vigil on his bare knees in front of it, two years ago. But no one liked to do away with it and even Michael had left it there. He was rather fond of it and was now lying looking at it, his hands linked behind his neck, the lumps of the coir mattress more or less worked into a convenient shape by his night's sleep and a pleasant warmth in the rough sheets against his bare skin.

Straight above his head, if he lifted his eyes to look, were the beams and joists of the stable roof, and the undersides of the slates, not much insulated against the cold by applications of cement on their inner joints.

And he too was feeling the thought of what had happened

between himself and the girl those few hours before as a weight, a kind of threat. But in his case the threat was obvious.

He got up unhappily, pulled on his trousers and went down to the yard to wash under the cold tap. The thought of providing hot water for 'the staff' had occurred to Mrs. Kershaw, but the problem of doing so had seemed so complicated, and the need for it so small, that she had dismissed the thought again. People didn't appreciate these things anyway. One of the barmen had actually smelt, particularly in winter.

Michael had brought his other clothes down with him and when he had finished washing he dressed in the shadow of the stable where Cocà was housed in winter – her dreamy existence allowed the Kershaws to advertise 'Riding and pony trekking – have an adventure holiday in luxury surroundings'; fortunately no one had responded to the call – and when he was dressed he went to the archway of the courtyard and stood with the house and stables at his back, looking down the gentle slope of grass and occasional, aged trees to the edge of the water, where they had been last night, and beyond it, across the bay, to Ross Harbour itself, and the rising ground behind it, where the white ribbon of road curved up towards the Gap and the world beyond. It was eleven years since he had first taken it, to go to secondary school, and four years since he had taken it in full earnest, school and two wasted years of University behind him, and the new world of revolution in front of him. He had never meant to come back at all, except perhaps for a week's visit and even that not until the revolution was begun. Not the futile, essentially bourgeois revolution of The Soldiers of Freedom whose ranks he was leaving, but the true and inevitable revolution of the working class, whose coming day would transform the world. He had climbed that road singing the Red Flag at the top of his voice, glory in his heart that an Irishman had written it, the ring of his steps on the road crying Marx, Engels, Marx, Engels, a parcel of sandwiches and curranty brack, and a clean shirt and spare socks in the bag slung over his shoulder, and no day, no moment in his life had been so full of joy, in spite of his arrest for illegal, subversive political activities on University property, his consequent expulsion from College, his mother's pitiful and bewildered weeping, his father's mute heartbreak.

'Then raise the scarlet standard high!
Beneath its shade we'll live and die!'

It had carried him a long way, that song. Over the Gap, to Belcorrig. Along the main road to Dublin. On the boat to Liverpool. To London. To the whole miraculous, heady world of Camden Town and politics and strikes and demonstrations, of a love affair with the proletariat. 'Oh, when I was in love with you, Then I was clean and brave.' The frank and fearless eye, the open heart, the singing throat of Labour. Oh my love, my sweet, my darling, marching to tomorrow's world. A world for children, without fear or hunger, a world of beauty, a world of honesty. And the Song had taken him into sullen, venomous strikes on building sites, to ferocious in-fighting with strike leaders who thought that Marxism was about power rather than freedom. It had seen him driven from one job to another as a Trotskyite wrecker, unemployed, kicked senseless. It had seen him marching on Trafalgar Square, fighting with Empire Loyalists, with the police. It had seen him into gaol and deportation. A thin, dark, passionate boy in the dock, passion cooling slowly in the cell.

Out of gaol again he could have headed in a dozen directions. But something had happened to him in prison, that he himself had no name for, could not yet describe. As though the cooling passion had crystallized inside him and the emotions, the qualities that until then had burst out of him in revolutionary idealism had become caught and concentrated and were now held in his mind like diamonds waiting to be discovered and cut and polished. Except that he didn't so much as know that they were there to be discovered.

All he had felt was tiredness. Men in prison get tired because of hunger, and after a while the hunger sinks into the bone and they become so tired that even thinking is too much effort and sleep makes no difference. And he had been tired before he went to prison. Not only in the physical sense, but mentally, from the constant effort of believing what was obviously untrue; that the men who were working effectively for revolution were also working for human happiness. And he had begun to fall asleep at night thinking of The Ross, and his childhood there, and the road outside his father's cottage and men going by, or stopping for a chat; he had dreamed that he was there again, that he was a child going to school, that everything was to do again. He dreamed of his father or Peadar Power telling stories by the fire, of his mother making bread. He dreamed of the grey horse that lived in the field opposite.

He dreamed of his sisters. And he would wake and wonder why he existed, what he was doing, what meaning any of it had.

So that when he was deported he was glad. Many Irishmen are deported every year from England, and half of them are back the following week since there's nothing to stop them except the mild fear of being deported once more. But he had come gladly back and even now he was still glad. Where else in the world had he any meaning at all? Merely to be here was to have some kind of meaning. He had grown in this landscape, it had shaped him, made him. If he read the words Bay, or Sea, or Rock, or Mountain; Town or Harbour or Boat or Seagull, this landscape came to him like the scent of grass in darkness, filling his mind instantly with the entire vision, the whole reality.

What would he do with it? What would it do with him? He didn't know. He scarcely asked the question in a conscious way. And yet something in him asked it. It was inconceivable that he could have no meaning, no purpose, except that of a blade of grass that dies to make way for another blade. There must be reason, must be purpose. At times he felt that he was on the point of knowing what his purpose was, like a child stirring in a woman for the first time, a warm darkness inside him, and in it, movement. At times even feeling the hold of religion again, or at least a longing for the certainties it gave his parents, and his sisters.

The blind love for the working class of the world had faded, without driving him back into the even blinder semi-religious nationalism of his adolescence. He had no longer any feeling that he had been born to liberate The Ross, or transform the lives of the small farmers and the labourers of the Peninsula and the valleys of Slieve Clogher. And yet he must have been born to do something, and where else could he do it? Or perhaps he had only come back here to draw vitality into his bones again before – before what?

He looked at the folded flank of the mountain and imagined a boulder broken loose from it, waiting to be carved. The first work of art he had ever consciously seen, knowing it to be a work of art, had been an engraving of one of Michelangelo's studies of slaves, the body still half buried in the stone from which it was carved; as though the stone itself was becoming man. The schoolmaster had brought it in to school with a dozen other cheap prints of World Masterpieces of Art given away free by a fertilizer manufacturer as a calendar, the previous year, and had pinned them round the walls of the schoolroom. But only that one picture had stayed in Michael's mind. Perhaps because his own name was Michael, or because his great-uncle, his legendary great-uncle Patrick Carmody, had been a sculptor. And the image had grown with him, of the slave half-freed from the rock that was himself, the living man out of the living stone. Sometimes he had thought of the slave as mankind itself; sometimes as the working class. And sometimes as himself. In prison he had felt it most heavily to be himself, as though the prison walls were the rock.

But all these thoughts, if they were continuous, conscious enough to be thoughts, were no more than shadows drifting over the surface of his mind. In reality he was thinking of nothing, only feeling, as if he was waiting for something to happen, as if he was realizing slowly that he had come back exactly for this unknown thing to happen, had been drawn back. And the thought of the girl weighed on his spirit. Was it her? He could go away again. It wasn't impossible. Nothing is impossible if you want it enough or fear something else enough. What was there to fear? A row with her father? It was laughable to think of it, that poor fool of a man with his eyes too close together and his adam's apple jumping and his play acting the squire. Not that. Then what was he afraid of?

Simply of getting involved? Of caring about something? But that was why he had come back, to care for something, to be able to care for something real, something that had meaning. He stared at Ross Harbour, across the corner of the bay, and felt a strange, close, and yet detached affection for it, as though it belonged to him, like an old toy. But old toys have no meaning for a grown man except nostalgia. Was that all that there was for him here? And he began again to feel the same slow smouldering of rage that he had felt long ago whenever he thought of The Ross, of Ireland; rage for the waste, the smugness, the death-in-life of the place, where nothing happened, nothing would ever happen, where those who stayed home rotted before they were ripe. And yet he loved it.

And it had no place for him. Nothing for him. No place, no job, no need. Even this job was an accident, a temporary thing that wouldn't last beyond the tourist season. And then? Nothing. There was no shop that would be willing to take him

33

in as a shopman, no office as a clerk. 'Arragh yes, Micky Carmody isn't it, Donal's son? And how is your father, the decent man? Well as ever I hope? Ah sure, the road is a great place for health, hard and all as it is, and me here behind the counter dying of the asthma. What wouldn't I give to be out and about under the sky like your good father. I'll keep you in mind, boy, but times is hard you know, there's little enough money about and that's the truth of it. Maybe when this great Development comes that they're talking about—'

Maybe. Maybe. And when his back was turned the finger alongside the cunning nose and the hard smile. Employ him? That bolshy that was in gaol the other side? Sure, who'd be safe in his bed and him about?

And yet he loved it with the kind of hatred that grows out of love, and the kind of need. Like a man whose lover is a hopeless slut, and yet she's beautiful, and his, and he sees her asleep on the broken couch with her stockings twisted and the washing up from yesterday still piled in the sink and something about her clenches at his heart and he thinks what she might have been, might still be, and imagines her in silk and diamonds.

Bad luck to you, he thought. What did you ever do for me, or for anyone else that was born in your lap, unless they were born rich? What did you give to me as my birthright? Not work, nor even the hope of work; not even my own language to talk as I went looking for it, or stood in the dole queue. Much sympathy I'd be likely to get from the clerk inside in the Labour and I asking him, ''ere a job I don't suppose?' in the first official language.

There were men working for the government who thought the day of the Tally Stick was still here, and a child to be thrashed for speaking Irish and his father reported to the R.I.C. Oh my free, my Gaelic Ireland. The right rose tree you've grown into.

And indeed there was little enough about Ross Harbour that early morning to call up images of rose trees and a noble freedom, even in the mind of a romantic. Its old, grey-walled houses and slate-grey roofs, leaned and clung close to one another across the narrow, twisting lanes, like grey-shawled old gossips on the way to market; the lanes themselves, cobbled, granite-stepped, slippery with mud and dirty with uncollected refuse, lurched down towards the Harbour, where much of the refuse would eventually be tipped into the long-suffering water.

34

The two principal streets, High Street and Knuckle Street (the latter known since 1966 and the half-centenary of Easter Week as Patrick Pearse Street to officialdom, but still Knuckle Street to every other living soul in the town), these two principal streets were not much more grandiose or noticeably cleaner than the twisty lanes, and even less interesting. Except that they did meet at the Square (still known simply and obstinately as the Square in spite of its new official name of Eamonn Ceannt Square), and in the Square there were not only the traffic lights, but the Protestant Cathedral, founded in 1201 by a grand-nephew of Raymond le Gros and completed in 1346 by Murtough Eagan.

The pale grey tower of the Cathedral and the darker spire of the neo-Gothic Catholic Church of St. Finbarr rose over the town to give it some kind of dignity, and in front the two unequal arms of the harbour curved forward and inward, like a tray on the knees of an old man in bed. An almost empty tray. Three or four fishing boats. John Mulcahy's deep sea motor cruiser with its dinghy behind it. A couple of other dinghies. No more than that in a harbour that had once sheltered men-of-war and three-masters and a fishing fleet that moved out on a summer's evening like a flock of dark red birds.

Under the roofs of the town there was hardly a soul stirring. Glennon's Hotel lay dead as an abandoned barracks, even the maids still fast asleep in their attics; Mrs. Glennon asleep like a Roman matron in her mob cap, her false teeth and her false fringe on the night table beside her, ready for instant action if the hotel should catch fire or burglars break in. The space of a garden away old Aloysius Mulcahy, 'Gombeen' Mulcahy, lay in his brass bed with his old yellow hands on the counterpane, the Rosary beads from the Holy Land wrapped round his rheumatic, grasping fingers with their thick blue nails, his wrinkled eyelids and the stretched skin of his cheek like yellowed wax, his head already a skull. He had been asleep for more than an hour and would soon wake again, to draw in a breath of piteous relief that there was sunlight beyond the thick, dusty curtains and that the night-dark and its shadows and its terrors were gone for another day. In a few minutes he would wake, his heart starting with fear, would see the filter of light and say three pious ejaculations and five decades of the Rosary. Then he would call his niece Mary to lift him on to the commode. She slept on a narrow bed in the dressing-room next door, ready wrapped in her dressing gown for when he would call her in the night.

At the far end of Knuckle Street in the Catholic Presbytery of the Parish of St. Finbarr Father Culhane was asleep, his old terrier Jim snorting in the basket under the bow window, the decanter of whiskey, the soda siphon, the Waterford tumbler and the digestive biscuits on the side table under the picture of Our Lady of Lourdes, where he had left them last night. Down the corridor and up a narrow flight of stairs, in what had been the cook's room in the good old days, the curate, Father Paddy Cooney, was on his bare knees on the linoleum, preparing himself for early Mass.

Half a mile outside the town, in their ranch-style bungalow, with its patio and its lawns and its ornamental pond with pottery gnomes fishing from its edge for pottery frogs on artificial leaves in the middle, John Mulcahy and his wife Clara lay side by side in their large, expensive bed; John Mulcahy with his mouth open and a thin stubble on his double chin, his plump, soft stomach swelling the bed clothes, his breath rasping shallowly in his fat throat, while his wife lay awake, staring at the play of light on the ceiling, her mouth already sullen with the beginnings of the day's boredom and discontent.

It was a magnificent mouth, above a magnificent bosom, but no passion had yet shaped the mouth, nor throbbed inside the white breast, and the black wealth of silken, raven hair lay on the pillow like a spoiled child's. She did not know why she was bored, nor what was the reason for her discontent, nor what there was in the world that might happen to her to make life seem worth living. Even her waking dreams were colourless and genteel, convent-bred, fed on romantic novels from the lending library in Mr. Carney's Chemist Shop in the High Street, made occasionally drunk by thoughts of film stars, by the sight of Hubert Kershaw vrooming past in his Bentley, by strange, inexplicable pulses in her blood. But never by the belated comings-to-bed of her husband. She lay at the moment wondering if she would have one egg or two for her breakfast, and if Mr. Carney would have any new novels in, and if he had not, how she would get through the afternoon. Her husband stirred on his side of the wide bed, his arm fell sideways on to her arm and she drew away with a quick shudder and a catch in her throat. And yet when she had done that she looked at him swiftly from the corners of her eyes, almost held her breath

36

waiting for something to happen, for him to move again. But he was sound asleep.

She thought of Clark Gable whom she had seen the previous night in a film on television, his chest bare, his smile wickedly knowing. Her heart beat like a bird trying to escape from a net. If she was married to someone like Clark Gable she wouldn't be bored, she wouldn't be lying awake like this thinking about breakfast. What would she be doing? She would be asleep herself, locked in his strong arms, so strong and yet so tender, and she would wake to the warm touch of his lips upon her fluttering eyelids while his hands – at the thought of his hands, her own plump little Spanish hands like warm white doves fled up to her bosom, drawing the flowered nylon nightdress more safely over it. She felt her cheeks burning, strange shivers in her stomach. Mrs. Clark Gable. A waiter bringing their breakfast on a silver tray. Clark opening her egg for her, spooning the yellow yolk for her on a silver spoon, sprinkling it with salt, holding it up to her ruby lips.

'Clara my love, let me feed my little bird!'
'Oh Clark!'

She was very hungry and it was going to be hours before Nanny had their breakfast ready and she would have to watch John getting dressed and cutting his toenails and have him sitting on the side of the bed belching and telling her about his indigestion and what he was going to do in the Supermarket. And there would be nothing, nothing to look forward to. Nothing at all. A huge tear slowly gathered at the corner of her left eye, swelled, hung for a long moment and ran down like a great pearl into the perfect shell of her ear. Please, please God let something happen. Something. Anything. Oh Clark.

A mile up the hill from the Mulcahys' bungalow the Georgian mansion of Eaganscourt stood tranquil in the sun. Its grey park wall curved and rose and fell over the gentle contours of this first foothill of Slieve Clogher, enclosing deep green fields and paddocks, huge chestnut trees spaced with eighteenth-century art to grow to their full splendour and throw down great circles of shadow for horses and cattle in the summer heat; stone terraces with urns and statues, fine lawns no longer quite so well tended as they should have been; two walled gardens of old red brick, one for flowers, and one for fruit and vegetables with medlar trees and nectarines growing on espaliers, and red-currant bushes and gooseberry brambles and trim rows of lettuce like pale green favours on ridges of chocolate earth.

The house itself presented tall, flashing windows like old silvered mirrors towards the morning world. French windows on to the terraces, long Georgian windows almost to the ground on either flank of the front door with its fine, arching fanlight and its pillars and its portico. Within the house Sir Philip and Lady Eagan slept in their respective bedrooms, both bedrooms large, both pleasant, both airy and filled with morning sun, each with its bathroom and its fine windows overlooking the terrace and the park. Lady Eagan's was cool and controlled, with a faint suggestion of no one living there, of the unlived-in Stately Home; a suggestion that no one ever sat, ever would sit on the chintz-covered couch that faced the windows, that no cigarette would ever be crushed out in the cut glass ash trays on the dressing table, or on the pedestal table beside the bed; that no head would ever lean against the padded backrest covered in a flowered chintz that matched the covers of the couch and the big armchairs.

Even with those large chairs and the couch, and the wide bed, and the dressing table, and the occasional table by the bed there was room and to spare for anyone to walk about the room thoughtfully, or lost in abstraction, without any sense of being confined. But nothing suggested that Lady Eagan, or anyone else, walked in it like that. Even asleep she lay as still as a waxwork figure, her faded fair hair and aristocratic nose giving her a look of well-bred dignity. She seemed *like* a wax figure and the bedroom like a bedroom from a museum of how people of different classes once used to live; 'The country house bedroom of a gentlewoman, England, circa 1925.' Except that the description, to be accurate, would have needed the additional words 'Anglo-Irish survival of – 1971'.

There was not a great deal more evidence of individual choice or of living presence about Sir Philip's bedroom. Ivory backed, hog's bristle hair brushes lay on the masculine dressing table as they lay in ten thousand rooms of the same type, ready to brush the sparse grey hairs of elderly gentlemen of the same background as Sir Philip's. The Persian rug, the brown leather armchair, the copy of last year's best-seller got from his daughter for Christmas lay by his bedside as it did by ten thousand other bedsides. He read a page or two of it each night and had been doing so for several months in order to fall asleep tranquilly. The half dozen twenty-year-old tweed suits and the two dozen vintage, striped linen shirts in the mahogany wardrobe – all these and almost everything else in the room and the adjoining bathroom belonged to the category 'Separate bedroom-cum-dressing-room of elderly English landed gentleman, circa 1910.' And here again one would need to add the rider 'Anglo-Irish survival of – 1971.'

Only the blanc-de-chine statuette of the Goddess Kuan Yin was evidence of some kind of personal choice, of some kind of individuality in the man who lay rather stiffly in the narrow, somehow military-seeming bed. Evidence supported by the small piece of pale, grey-green jade, carved in the shape of a fish, a Chinese fish of longevity and good fortune, which lay on the mahogany bedside table along with his key-ring, and his gold chimer pocket watch and his worn, calf-leather wallet with his initials stamped in gilt on one corner.

Now, in this moment between sleeping and waking, he was dreaming of China, of a woman's voice calling to him across the thousand noises of a Chinese market place, with its sellers of crimson melon slices and its squawking chickens tied by the legs and hanging from the pole of a booth; its piles of fruit and vegetables, its fortune tellers and its ragged soldiers; its half-naked craftsmen beating copper or heating silver wire; its beggars crying their sores and its coolies shouting 'Shao Lai! Shao Lai!' as they ran with bent knees and bare feet through the jostling crowds, their bamboo carrying poles bending on their calloused shoulders, nets of melons at each end, or big pottery jars of oil, or three sewing machines tied together.

'Pi Li, Pi Li,' she was calling. He tried not to wake so that she would have time to find him, so that he could have a chance to see her in the swarm of people, see her and push his way through to her and touch her hand. But he was already awake, and there was no one calling him.

Two storeys below his bedroom, Kathleen the cook who had bad legs and was therefore excused from climbing too many stairs, slept in the semi-basement beside her kitchen. One floor above him Maureen Carmody, the indoor parlour maid, elder daughter of Donal Carmody the roadmender and sister to Michael Carmody now temporary barman of The Old House Hotel, slept in a small clean attic under the roof, with the twitterings and high-pitched screams of swallows and swifts to greet her in the mornings. Abby MacDonnell and her daughter Sarah, who between them did the rough cleaning and the washing up, slept in the main gate lodge with her husband Seamus MacDonnell, odd job man and gardener, and his father, Rory MacDonnell who had once been head gardener. A slightly retarded boy, Billy O'Loughlinn, came up from a nearby cottage at nine o'clock every morning except Sundays, to work under Seamus. Old Mrs. MacDonnell was bedridden in the County Home this ten years past.

There was about Eaganscourt and its surrounding park, its greenness, the size and spread of its trees, the rich appearance of its horses as they stood in the deep grass greeting the day with slowly moving tails; about the seemingly endless length of its outer wall, and the satisfying shapes of its clumps of woodland in far corners of the park; there was about all this – and its tranquillity – something that set a tone on the entire district, even against the district's will, and against the centuries long failure of the family to fulfill its true purpose in the scheme of things. If it was failure it was still a handsome failure. Like the old tower of what had once been Eagan's Castle, a short half mile away from the present house, its ruined windows and doorways now blank archways open to the birds of the air, its stones half-covered with ivy, its dungeons half-filled with fallen masonry and rubble, its secrets hidden.

The two buildings, house and tower, looked down on the town with quiet ease, even in failure and in ruin breathing a kind of permanence and authority. Both of these qualities were illusions, but no one looking down on the park and the Palladian dignity of the house that early morning could have guessed how close the end of these illusions was; that already the fuse had been lit for the mine that would destroy it all.

Three miles to the north west, and over the crown of a ridge that ran down from the western shoulder of Slieve Clogher to the beginnings of the peninsula of Lir Head, so that it could not be seen from Eaganscourt, and even less from the town, stood the Bishop's Palace.

The Bishop was long retired from Pastoral work, and the Palace, once a country house of the great Ascendancy family of the Clarkes, Earls of Medmenham, might easily now have been mistaken for a large but dilapidated farm house. Its front door stood open as it always did, and chickens, already awake and urgent to be fed, were running in and out, adding new splashes of white droppings to the near-carpet of old droppings that almost covered the worn slate floor of the passage.

Upstairs, at the back of the house, Matilda Carmody, younger sister to Maureen, the Eagans' parlour maid, and to Michael, snored in her sagging iron cot, one arm hanging over the edge until it touched the bare, dusty boards of the floor, her red, healthy face like a smiling apple as she dreamed of dances and of the trumpeter of the Steeplejacks who had winked at her twice last Saturday night between blasts on his trumpet.

The strictest of Catholic eyebrows might once have been raised at the idea of so young a housekeeper even for so old a Bishop. But when Matilda's maternal aunt Chrissie had been forced to retire the previous year, because of varicose veins in her legs and rheumatism in her hands (both almost certainly deriving from the slate floors of the kitchen and the passages and the damp, icy cold that rose up from them in winter) – when she retired there had been no one else available and willing to take her place except her niece. Either the Bishop must go into a home to be cared for by the Poor Sisters of the Crucifixion, which the old man would not hear of, or he must live alone, which no one else could think of, or he must be entrusted to Matilda. Very sensibly Father Culhane and Father Conroy of Belcorrig, who had promised the new Bishop to keep an eye on him, agreed to this last. And in these new, liberal, post-Vatican Council times, no one had given the matter another thought. Often the old man himself called Matilda by her aunt's name and complained that she seemed to have forgotten how to make caramel pudding, which he had used to love.

The old man wheezed and coughed himself awake to realize once again that he was still alive, that God had not yet shown him the mercy of an easy death. In the name of the Father and of the Son and of the Holy Ghost. His bony hand like the skeleton of a bird's wing crept across his sunken chest, up to his ivory forehead, slowly down again. In a little while he would get up and say his prayers at the Prie-Dieu. In a little while. When he had his strength. He turned his mind away from the waking pains in his bones and joints. Most merciful Saviour, look down on your poor servant, pity him, forgive him.

Outside the palace in the stone courtyard the hens pecked and clucked, three or four of them dashing towards this doorway or that as they prepared to lay eggs, one in a disused stable, one in the kitchen under the table, another on the kitchen steps on a pad of convenient moss. It was that same stable that housed the Bishop's secret, Pat Carmody's statue of Christ the Sufferer that had been lost and hidden for more than thirty years, boarded up at one end of the long stone building, behind the collapsing remains of a ponytrap and a carriage, and the worm-eaten wheels of an old farm cart.

But if both the Eagans' mansion and the Bishop's Palace were hollow at the heart, what could be sound about The Ross? Where could it find its strength? Not, surely, in Gombeen Mulcahy's sick-bed? Nor the trout-farm of the foreigners? Nor even The Old House Hotel, nor Glennon's? Yet there must be a centre, there must be a well-spring.

I would suggest a strange place. Swinging back eastwards from the Bishop's Palace, north of Eaganscourt and above it along the massive side of Slieve Clogher, ran the road from The Gap to the Head of Ross. And about half-way along it stood Donal Carmody the roadmender's cottage, square and pawky, with small windows and a slate roof, built by the County Council in 1887 to be let, with its half acre of garden, for 1/– a week to Donal Carmody's great-grandfather, who had gone out with the Fenians in '67 and escaped to America, but had come back to become a roadmender when all was quiet again and forgiven if not quite forgotten.

There, already, Mrs. Carmody was up and clattering, drawing water from the roadside pump a hundred yards down the hill towards the bridge. If she looked straight down the road beyond the bridge she could see the trees surrounding The Old House Hotel. If she looked left, up the mountainside, she could see, very far away and high up, the yellow-grey thatch and whitish grey walls of the Powers' cottage. If she looked right, straight down towards the bay, she could see the rectangles of the fish ponds and the long white buildings of the fish farm. But she looked at nothing except her slowly filling bucket.

'Wirrah damn you will you never fill up, the devil mend you. The fire will be out on me.' Curses and water flowed together, the one as slow and easy as the other. When the bucket was full she trudged back up the hill in her short rubber boots and her black skirt and her brown jersey fastened with its large safety-pin across her flat chest and her black hair escaping from under Donal's second best hat. 'Blast every step of you, bad end

42

to you and you getting steeper on me every day of my life. Oh says he in his bed, is me tea ready says he, is the fire lit? Oh Jesus Mary and Joseph 'tis the women's liberation coming, I can tell him that, the great ugly galoot. The blacks of Africa first and the women of Ireland after, I can tell him, I can promise him.' Slop of water in the white dust of the steep narrow road between green hedges, with birds singing, and a hawthorn tree leaning over the ditch, and the glory of the summer sky above. 'Liberation is coming, and the women of Ireland lying in bed and the men up betimes in their socks and trousers getting us tea and toast and we lying easy. Oh the devil is weighing the bucket and my arm out of my shoulder with the pull of it. Bad luck to you bucket.' A small black-haired bony furious woman grumbling her way home from the pump in the early sun with all the beauty of Ireland spread before her like a Queen's cloak, green brocade and velvet of the fields and silver of the sea and the twenty fish ponds like twenty diamonds cut and shimmering.

Out of one of the white houses Per Olafsson came, stretching himself and yawning, holding up his blond face to the sun. He already wore his big white sweater and black leather knee boots, laced up the front, grey flannel trousers tucked into their tops. His blue woollen hat was perched on his straw-coloured hair like a blue pimple and he was huge and young and happy and thinking condescending thoughts about this country where no one ever got up in the morning. Already it was half past six and no one was stirring, not a living soul except himself, and Åke Jenssen whom he could hear singing as he shaved in the next small bungalow.

'Good day Åke!' he called out and Åke pushed his face through the small window-opening of his bathroom, one cheek pinkly shaved, the other froth-white like half an ice cream.

'Beautiful, beautiful!' Åke carolled. 'How are the fish?'

With that question something strange pushed its way further into Per Olafsson's consciousness. Something strange. Not quite as always. He stood thinking, his pale blue eyes with their invisible lashes like the eyes of a puzzled baby, the somehow childish, almost infantile forehead knitted in thought. Not as always. He moved on slow, unbelievably long legs towards the ponds. Not— The fish. He moved faster, the frown deepening. The fish so quiet. He began to run.

He stood by the first pond, staring down at it, not crediting what he saw. Nothing. The surface still as steel, as a mirror. No ripple, no movement, no urgent shadows moiling below the skin of water, no sudden flash and leap as his own shadow fell on the pond. Nothing. Gone. He didn't believe it. He rubbed his eyes and looked again. Ran to the next pond.

'Åke!' he called. 'ÅKE! THE FISH! THE FISH ARE GONE!'

Within moments they both stood beside the fourth, the fifth, the sixth and seventh ponds. Not a fish left of all their half million. Nothing. Åke put up his hands to his hair and tugged it as if somehow this would let reason into his head.

'The old men!' Åke shouted, 'The old men have let them out!'

'Impossible,' Per Olafsson said slowly. 'Im-possible. No one could do such a thing.' He looked down at the pond at their feet as if expecting a veil to clear from his sight and reveal the fish. 'The old men are too stupid,' he said, more to himself than to his assistant. 'They would be afraid.' If he allowed himself to believe that the old men were capable of such a thing too much would follow from it. That it could happen again. And again. He did not put this thought into firm shape in his mind, or even acknowledge its existence. It was as though he still half-hoped that in the eighth, or the ninth, or tenth, or eleventh, or for God's sake at least in the twelfth pond, all the lost fish would miraculously be found collected. It was not possible that twelve, fifteen, twenty sluice gates could have lifted themselves all in the one night. Or not been put properly back by one of the Irish labourers after clearing some of the ponds. None of the ponds had needed clearing last night. Not one.

All the possibilities revolved themselves inside Per Olafsson's head. And to each he had to say, 'Im-possible'. It was not possible that the fish were gone. They might have died of disease in the night. Of poison even. But they could not have gone. Suddenly, like a stepladder taking life, he ran to the seaward gate of the enclosure, flung it open, and hurled himself towards the river, where the concrete channel from the last of the ponds curved towards it and emptied itself into it. He flung himself down on his knees and peered down into the muddy water. Pushed his arms into it to the elbows. Nothing.

Åke came up behind him. 'We must tell the police, Per.'

Per stared at him, distraught, sinking back on to his heels, his arms dripping. 'The police—?' Quite suddenly he realized that for all of the eighteen months he had been in this country he had hated it with a deepening passion. Its laziness, its inefficiency, its incomprehensible customs. The way a workman would disappear for days at a time and turn up smiling one midday to say he had taken the time off to go fishing. Fishing! When there were half a million fish needing to be fed, changed to another pond. The hatchery to mind, the fingerlings to be transferred to the round pond. Empty ponds to be cleaned. Grass to be cut, gravel to be raked and weeded, walls to be whitewashed, metal food drums to be scalded, fish to be packed in ice for export, cases and cases of fish to be packed. So much work that the day was not long enough. And the man would say with a happy smile that he had gone fishing.

And the old men driving their cows through the hedge, over the grass, the lawns, the gravel, even into the empty ponds at first. And the other man walking through with his fishing rod to go fishing off their part of the shore. As if their gravel paths were the highway. And the police sergeant saying in a strange voice, 'Was he doing any harm? Any damage, now?' As if there was no such thing as property, as if they did not understand that a business is a business, that when a gate is shut it means 'Keep out until I invite you in.'

'The police,' he said again. 'Yes,' he said heavily, 'we must tell the police. And we must cable to Norway. They will be very angry.' He got to his feet and went with Åke back to the office building to telephone. It was almost seven o'clock.

Sergeant McMenamin took the call. He was still half asleep, having stumbled downstairs in his bare feet and his pyjamas, and he made the Norwegian repeat the story twice.

'Ah,' he said, to gain time.

'Can you understand me, Sergeant?'

'You say the fish have escaped?' Sergeant McMenamin said. Seven o'clock, he thought. God of Mercy. If they were escaped they were escaped. What did he expect the Gardai to do about it? Swim after them? 'Would you be suspecting foul play, now?'

'Play?' cried Per Olafsson, his face beginning to burn pink with temper. 'I tell you this is serious, this is a crime! My fish, all of them, they are worth fifty thousand of your pounds and they are all gone!'

'You say a crime has been committed? Is there a witness?' The Sergeant moved from one bare foot to the other to warm himself and stood on a drawing pin that had fallen on to the

45

floor the evening before. 'Oh, oh, oh, oh, God's curse on it,' he shouted, 'God damn it to hell and beyond, my foot, I've stood on a bloody nail.' He had let the telephone receiver fall to the end of its cord and was jumping about behind the counter holding his wounded foot in both hands. From the receiver the tiny Norwegian voice was calling 'What? Are you there Sergeant? What did you say?'

It was not a conversation destined for a smooth course or a satisfying end. But an hour and a quarter later Sergeant McMenamin, accompanied by Garda Constable Phelim O'Neill, drove out in Sergeant McMenamin's car, an oldish Ford Cortina, to inspect the scene of the crime. 'If it is a crime,' the sergeant said to the constable. 'Bloody foreigners. Always complaining about something. Carelessness more like.'

'It's the two Powers,' the constable said sombrely. Like the sergeant he came from Donegal, but whereas the sergeant had been long enough in the far south to become acclimatized and even tolerant, the constable looked on all around him with dislike and suspicion. In this of course he was a far better policeman than his superior, and it is exactly in the hope that its members will distrust all the inhabitants of a county different from their own that the Garda Siochana sends them to serve in places as far as possible from their homes. 'Without a doubt in the world,' said the constable, 'it's those two old imbeciles.'

'The policeman's worst enemy,' the sergeant said, 'is making his mind up in advance of the evidence.' He said this in a pawky, putting-down tone of voice that, if he kept it up for more than a minute or two, drove Constable O'Neill into a white rage, and made any rational conversation between them impossible for the rest of the day. They arrived at the fish farm in a taut silence. Per Olafsson was pacing up and down by the main gate. Åke Jenssen was scouring out a metal forty-gallon drum. None of the Irish workmen had yet arrived.

The four of them, the two policemen and the two Norwegians, went to look at the ponds. Constable O'Neill lifted the sluice gates one by one, squinting his eyes narrowly and with professional zeal. Sergeant McMenamin looked down at his squatting blue figure with tired dislike. It seemed to him at times that nothing had gone right in Ross Harbour since the constable had arrived. For ten years it had been the pleasantest station of his entire twenty-seven years of service. From one year's end to the other nothing happened. Sometimes one of the

Walshes or the town O'Loughlinns got so drunk that they had to be locked up for their own good, in case they fell into the harbour. Or the tinkers came into town and got into fights. Or a drive was initiated from Dublin about unpaid licences or bicycle lamps or poteen being distilled out on the Head or up in the valleys of Slieve Clogher. But a man had to do something to justify his pension. It was only in the past year that things had become unpleasant.

Starting with rumours about the factories. The Development. God in His mercy, who'd want to develop a place like Ross Harbour? Talk about a smelter, whatever in hell that might be, and a deep sea dock, and oil tanks and God knew what. And people coming in wanting to buy land and other people making speeches that Ireland was being destroyed by foreigners, agitators no less, coming down from Dublin to make trouble.

None of this had a bit of connection with Constable O'Neill, except that he had added his own contribution to the changed tone of Ross Harbour. He had his eyes fixed on Dublin and swift promotion and he brought a cold eagerness to his work that had upset everybody; Sergeant McMenamin, Mrs. Walsh the cleaner, almost anyone in the town with whom he came into contact.

'What do you think?' Per Olafsson said.

Sergeant McMenamin cleared his throat. 'Have you any reason to suspect anyone?'

'The old men,' Åke said. 'The old brothers.'

Constable O'Neill allowed himself to smile coldly at his superior. Sergeant McMenamin cleared his throat again, his face flushing slowly. The two Norwegians and the constable looked at him. 'We'd better go up and talk to them,' the sergeant said heavily. He started back towards the car without waiting for an answer, and with Constable O'Neill in triumph at his side, drove up the lurching track to the Powers' farm in complete silence except for the occasional scrape and thud of the underside of the car on a stone or a hump of turf, and the clatter of the engine.

The sheepdog bitch came out of the yard and barked at them. Constable O'Neill kicked it efficiently, feinting with his left foot and catching it under the tail with his right. It ran howling round the corner of the house and from behind the low, greyish-white building with its collapsing roof of mouldy

47

thatch a goat and a ram scrambled and galloped away up the mountainside towards 'The Queen's Road' and 'The Queen's Fort' that crowned the summit. Hens clucked and squawked. Constable O'Neill rapped on the door. Nothing happened. A cat peered at them round the gate pillar. The yard was full of mud and manure and smells. A cart with one wheel lay tilted against a wall. The mountain above them was green and gold and purple. Far up, a few sheep of Jamey's nibbled and moved slowly across a stretch of turf. A cloud drifted. Below them the bay, the headlands, the distant sea. The constable knocked again and then kicked the door until it rattled like a broken drum.

'Open in the name of the law!' he shouted. Sergeant McMenamin gazed over the constable's head. Something stirred inside the cottage. A sound of muttering, a voice grumbling to itself, the scrape and clatter of boots being put on. Very slowly the door creaked open. A strong smell of old men and cats and turf smoke billowed out. Sergeant McMenamin and the constable both stepped back a pace, catching their breath. An ancient, lined and dirty face peered out at them, like a troll from a cave, old blue eyes, stiff grey hair under a grey felt hat so crushed and slept in that it seemed to have become part of its owner's head.

' 'oo ah,' Jamey said. His body began to shake and he tried to shut the door again. The constable kicked it open. The sergeant drew in his breath, started to duck inside the doorway and changed his mind.

'Tell your brothers we want to see them,' he said. But the constable had already gone in. The sergeant heard him cough and then choke. He came out, his eyes red and beginning to run water.

'God Almighty,' Constable O'Neill croaked. They stood waiting in the sunlight and the comparatively harmless smells of the yard for nearly ten minutes. Twice the constable went and kicked the door. From inside a voice said, 'Yerrah, be easy now, Sergeant darling. Amn't I getting dressed for 'oo?'

Until at last Matty opened the door and Peadar came out, bow-legged, his cap perched on his furze bush head, held on by the spikes of dirty white hair, all his buttons undone, the laces of his boots undone, great bulges and folds and corners of grey flannel shirt falling out from his trousers front and his waistband and from beneath the tail of his coat.

'Is it the licence, Sergeant darling?' he said winningly, screwing up cunning eyes at the sergeant, at the sun, at the constable, at the cat on the gate pillar. 'Yerrah, didn't I tell Jamey—'

'It is not any licence,' the sergeant said. He felt stricken at the idea of what they had come up to do, and what must follow.

'What were you doing down by the ponds last night?' the constable said.

'The ponds?' Peadar said in wonder as if he had no idea what ponds they meant. Behind him Matty clung on to the latch of the door for support. Invisible behind him Jamey was telling his Rosary, on his knees by the fire. 'Hail Mary full of Grace – ooh ooh—'

'You were seen,' Constable O'Neill said.

'Íosa Críost,' Matty whimpered.

'Ooh ooh the Lord be wid you.'

'And who would be seeing me down anywhere in the middle of the night and I in my bed beside Matty?' Peadar squinneyed his eyes at the constable. But his face had lost a fraction of its colour under the dark, turf-smoke patina and the brown wrinkles. And if the constable had been alone he would have had his victory. He would have invented a witness's name and then he would have caught the old man by his flannel shirt collar and shaken the truth out of him in a couple of hard minutes. But with the sergeant watching him his nerve failed.

'Never mind who it was,' he said. He switched the attack to Matty. 'Tell the truth now. You let the fish out didn't you? Come on, we know the whole story. Best tell us everything and make it easy for yourselves.'

'Ooah, I never wanted—' Matty began. And then as Peadar kicked his ankle, 'agh agha agh, the divil mend you.'

'The fish is it?' Peadar said. 'Out of the little ponds? Mwirra and all the saints, but that was an unnatural class of a thing to happen. And 'oo would be wanting to do that now, Sergeant dear? Maybe they just 'scaped away into the sea?'

'Blessed is the fruit of thy womb, Jesus,' Jamey whimpered, his voice rising. He saw himself orphaned, alone in the world except for the bitch and the cows and the goat and the ram and the hens and the donkey, with Peadar and Matty taken below to be hanged. Maybe they would hang him too. He began to cry so loud that he couldn't pray.

'Hould your whisht, boy, blast you,' Peadar shouted.

'How could they escape away into the sea?' the constable said, feeling the investigation beginning to lose shape and firmness. If only he had been able to come up by himself. The sergeant was watching him, not openly smiling, but a hint of hostile amusement at the back of his eyes.

'Yerrah but you'd be surprised at the things that creatures can be doing and they with no natural right to be doing them. The divil blast the lie it is but the grandfather of that cat on the wall behind you spoke to me twice out like a Christian.'

'I'm telling you you were seen!' the constable shouted.

Peadar hitched up his trousers and great handfuls of spilling shirt tail.

'Yerrah but what wonder if it did speak to me,' Peadar said. 'Didn't all the animals have the power of speech once, and they losing it for the sake of one of them betraying Our Lord to the heathen Jews?'

'Let me take him down below,' the constable said between his teeth.

'On what charge?' the sergeant said. He had made up his mind about two things. That beyond question the two old men had done it. And that equally beyond question he was not going to have them arrested. At least, not now, by Constable O'Neill. He didn't even know why he had decided that he would not let them be taken in. He had no particular affection for Peadar Power. Only for the rightness of things, for things as they were against the threat of things as they would be if new ugly-minded men like Guard O'Neill had their way.

'What charge?' the constable said, stupefied.

'We'll be back later,' the sergeant said. 'I may want to take a statement from you about your movements last night.'

'Divil a movement,' Peadar said. 'But what am I at not asking you if you have a mouth on the pair of you and you coming up the hill in the heat of the morning? Will you step in till I get Matty to wet the tea? And a cut of the sody cake Matty is after making a week ago only?'

'Not now, thank you,' the sergeant said. The constable simply looked away with a locked face. He'd have the old bastard's stripes off him before another year was out, or die for it. What charge! Take a statement from him! Two good thumps with a fist and he'd get all the statement he needed.

50

The two men got into the sergeant's black car and the sergeant turned it down hill. Chickens ran from under the wheels. The donkey brayed.

'Glory be,' whispered Matty from behind the door.

'The Divil fire him,' Peadar said, staring after him.

CHAPTER THREE

FATHER PADDY COONEY had the story of the escaped fish from the Presbytery housekeeper, Mrs. Cleggan, as he ate his boiled egg after first Mass. Father Culhane, the Parish Priest, had it from Father Cooney. And it was Father Culhane who saw, as though by a lightning flash, what depths of meaning there might be hidden in it. He was an old man who had lived his whole life in Ross Harbour, except for his early youth, and his years in the Seminary. And during that long adult life he had seen almost all the storms of the world pass by The Ross, leaving it untouched. What interested The Ross, what moved its passions, was not the rise and fall of Empires, but the rise and fall of prices; of cows and young heifers at the cattle mart in Belcorrig beyond the Gap; of a cran of herring down at the quayside, or potatoes in Dublin market, or boots in one of Gombeen Mulcahy's shops, or porter in any of the forty-three licensed premises of the town, or whiskey, or tobacco.

And this to Father Culhane was a wholesome and praiseworthy state of affairs. Men who darken their souls with hard bargains six days a week go to Mass on Sundays to ease their consciences. They give at least some part of the fruits of their bargains to Mother Church. But men who concern themselves deeply with politics and what they are pleased to call political ideals are only too likely to spend their Sundays learning how to shoot other idealists or blow them up with gelignite, and they often do not consider that their consciences need easing. They may even begin to tell Mother Church that She is the one in need of Reform and repentance. And whether they go so far as that or not they certainly have few fruits to share with Her. For Father Culhane, in his private heart, the most desirable parishioner was not some latter-day Patrick Pearse, such as Michael Carmody had promised to be before he ran away, but Gombeen Mulcahy, a man who knew beyond argument that he was a sinner, and was prepared to make substantial amends for his sins. And it was Gombeen's name and interests that came into Father Culhane's mind on the heels of his first reaction.

'This is bad news you are giving me, Father,' he said, stopping short with his hand over the silver-plated cover that was keeping his pair of smoked kippers warm on his breakfast plate.

'Of course I'm sorry for the poor Norwegians,' Father Cooney said. He had thought the news extremely funny and was cast down, although not much surprised, by his senior's gravity. He had long learned that Father Culhane had no sense of humour.

'*I* am sorry for The Ross,' Father Culhane said, filleting his first kipper with an expert knife point. 'There's politics behind this.'

'I'd have thought it was the Powers,' Father Cooney ventured.

'The Powers!' Father Culhane said angrily. He had not thought of them at all and, although as soon as he did there was a plausibility about the suggestion, he was no more inclined to accept a suggestion from his junior than Sergeant McMenamin had been. 'The Powers are a decent God-fearing family. They'd no more think of an act like this than – than – damn these bones, I wish she wouldn't give us kippers. Hand me the sausage dish.' He heaped his plate moodily. 'Politics, that's what's behind it. And I think I know why. As a warning to the Mulcahys.'

'A warning? To the Mulcahys? If you said to the Norwegians, Father—'

'I said to the Mulcahys. Pour me some tea, Father, if you please. To the Mulcahys I said. And to the Mulcahys I meant. Because of the Development.'

Father Cooney suspended his tea-pouring. 'The Development?' The idea sank into his mind more slowly than it had entered Father Culhane's because he had thought much less about it. But for close to three years it had hung in the air like an echo, a rumour, now almost certain, now receding into nothing; now contradicted, now repeated, then half-forgotten again. Beginning with the two men who had come one week in September three years ago to stay in Glennon's. They had had a small green motorvan with bits and pieces of equipment in the back and they had spent days together scouring the roads of

53

The Ross, climbing the sides of Slieve Clogher, bumping out beyond The Old House on to the farm tracks of the Peninsula or down the swan's neck of the other headland, past The Angler. And for the last two days of their week they had hired one of Jim Hardy's dinghies and an outboard motor and had puttered across and across the Bay, pretending to be fishing, but every now and then taking notes and measurements and dropping a weighted line over the side as if they were checking the ninety-year-old charts of the Bay for accuracy.

For weeks the town had buzzed with theories about what they had been after, and every one who had had the slightest contact with them, from the old waiter in Glennon's dining-room, to Jim Hardy, had been pumped and wrung out and pumped again for any titbit of information he might have forgotten to deliver. Until finally the judgment was reached that it was a 'factory'. That at long last, thanks to the efforts of Benedict Mulcahy, younger son of Gombeen and younger brother of John, and now a Minister no less up above in Dublin, Ross Harbour was going to be awarded a factory. Savage arguments began to develop about whether it would be a knitting factory, which would take wool from the mountain farmers; or a shirt factory, which would employ the town girls; or a fishmeal factory which would take the waste fish from the fishermen; or a boot factory which would employ the unemployed men of the town.

But autumn passed into winter and winter into spring, and nothing happened, and the arguments gave way to the old familiar arguments about the prices of fish and cows. Then there was a by-election, and Benedict Mulcahy came down to support his party's candidate and the rumours started again. There might be more than a factory in it ... it might be a real Development. Great things might happen if the party's candidate was elected. He was elected, but still nothing happened. And hopes which had risen as high as a cold storage plant added to the fishmeal factory, or spinning mills allied to a knitting factory, or even the reopening of the branch railway line that had been closed in 1964, faded again.

To be revived, and lifted to an even higher level, by the news two months ago that solicitors from Dublin had written to Mr. Kershaw of The Old House, now The Old House Hotel, asking him if he would consider selling his property, consisting of seventy-two acres on the shore of Ross Bay, for the purpose of a major industrial development. A major industrial development! Solicitors from Dublin! With foreigners behind them no doubt. Americans. Germans. Englishmen. Japanese even, like the ones by Limerick. Pucks of money behind it, mountains of money. It wouldn't be one factory or two that would be in it, it'd be three or four. There wouldn't be an unemployed man or boy or school-leaving girl in the town or the two headlands. There'd be a Gaeltacht grant for speaking Irish in the factory. It'd be opened by the Taoiseach. By President Nixon. Mrs. Kennedy was coming to live in The Ross. Aristotle Onassis himself was going to start building ships in the harbour to spite Belfast. There'd be rivers of money in the place.

And then, like the first touch of mildew on a fruit that was not yet ripe, a white rash of printed posters had appeared on walls and hoardings, and in the broken windows of abandoned houses, announcing a Public Meeting for the following Saturday evening in the market square. 'Irishmen! Irishwomen! Wake up to what's happening behind your backs! Your birthright is being sold. Join THE SONS OF IRELAND and protect your HERITAGE! Hear the price you're going to pay to be EXPLOITED BY FOREIGNERS! SATURDAY 8 P.M. THE MARKET SQUARE.' More than half the posters were printed in Irish, but enough had been in English to ensure a small crowd of fifty or sixty townspeople, and a number of children that altered by the minute, but that swelled the total to around a hundred.

At ten past eight a small green mini-van arrived and four Sons of Ireland, and one Daughter, got out and erected a portable podium. The Daughter, a small, stocky girl in a belted raincoat, climbed on to the podium and launched into a fierce speech in Irish. The four Sons stood round her like the angels on the O'Connell monument in Dublin, or the Landseer lions round Nelson's Pillar in Trafalgar Square, and stared intimidatingly at the crowd. They wore black berets and battle jackets and had a certain stamp, a common denominator about them; a pale passion as if much of their lives were spent in candlelight quarrelling about the millennium. The crowd stared back in tolerant curiosity. Everyone was used to politicians making ritual speeches in Irish before they said what they had come to say in English. It was usually divided on a common-sense basis. Thirty or forty seconds in Irish talking about Pearse and Connolly and De Valera and thirty or forty minutes talking about the farm subsidy and the rates and street lighting and the price of pigs and the old age pension.

But this girl with the black hair and the white face and the worn raincoat had apparently never heard of the rules. She passed a minute, two minutes, five minutes and she was still talking Irish, and already the fringes at the back of the crowd were breaking away, and deciding that even staring at the Harbour was better than the Sons of Ireland. The children had more patience and also more Irish, but since they had been taught Ross Irish, by edict of the Department, which believed they already knew the dialect from their cradles, and the girl spoke Dingle Irish because she had spent all her summer holidays there since she was thirteen, understanding was limited.

Even so a few words that the girl said floated into the crowd's collective mind. Capitalists. Exploration. Judas Iscariot. Slaves. Purity. Ideals. Gaelic. Free.

'It's the Jehovah's Witnesses,' someone said.

'Adventists.'

'Communists.'

'MOWSY TUNG!' a woman shrieked suddenly. 'LOWSY MOWSY!' The children took up the cry, 'LOWSY MOWSY LOWSY MOWSY!'

The white-faced girl looked momentarily staggered. One of the young men put his hand inside the breast flap of his battle jacket.

'We are for Ireland!' the girl cried. 'Ireland free, Ireland Gaelic.' She had changed to English, some instinct telling her that what she had been saying for the past six minutes had not been completely understood. 'We are for an Ireland where the fruits of the soil belong to the tillers of the soil. Where wealth belongs to those who make wealth possible. To you – and you – and you. The workers of Ireland. Are you willing to sell your birthright? Are you willing to give your heritage to foreigners in return for a starvation wage?'

'We've got no wages,' a man yelled. 'We're unemployed.'

'And why are you unemployed? Because the capitalists in Dublin want to keep you quiet and frightened. They want to make you grateful for crumbs.'

'A bloody Communist!' the same woman shouted. 'We don't want your kind in The Ross. Throw them in the Harbour.'

'LOWSY LOWSY MOWSY TUNG,' the children chanted delighted with the growing excitement and their own wisdom in staying through the dull part. The four young men closed tightly round the podium. They looked as though they had faced situations like this before. The crowd might believe for the moment that they were looking at a handful of long-haired deviationist adventurers with Little Red Books between their ears, and that they could throw them in the Harbour at their ease and pleasure, but the first man to try and lay hands on them was going to get his skull laid open with the butt of a Webley ·45.

'STAND BACK!' the leader of the Sons roared, and the crowd of part-time fishermen, unemployed labourers, clerks, counter hands, small shopkeepers, small farmers' sons in for an evening on the town, housewives, shopgirls, maids and other young women waiting for the dance in St. Finbarr's Hall to begin at nine o'clock, recognized something in his face, in his tone, in the trained and urgent stance of his body and that of his companions that stopped them in their tracks. They had had no experience of it themselves. Not even the oldest man or woman in the crowd had seen it. And yet they knew it instantly, as a puppy that has never seen an adder knows by the shiver of its blood that here is killing, as it sees the diamond head creep through the summer grass.

When he had his silence the Chief Son shouted, 'We are here to warn you. There is a plan in Dublin to rob you. It's going to be presented to you as a wonderful gift from the Government. There are going to be jobs for everyone – they'll *say* – there'll be a grand development for the town – they'll *say*. What they won't tell you is what that development will do to the town – what kind of jobs they'll be—'

'Get out of here you dirty reds,' a man shouted. Within the few seconds of the Chief Son's speech a subtle but definite change had come over the crowd. The simple jollity of proposing to throw unwanted strangers into the Harbour had vanished and given place to a mood that would throw stones. From the shadows of two doorways Sergeant McMenamin and Constable O'Neill drifted slowly forward to stand on either side of the man who had shouted.

'Move along now,' the sergeant suggested to him pacifically. The two Guards worked their way through the tightening crowd, teasing it out like an old flock mattress, a friendly touch on the arm from Sergeant McMenamin, a harsher grip from Constable O'Neill, a word here and there. 'Get along with you all now, the meeting's over, you'll miss the dance if you don't hurry, Lily, go along with you, Jim, you don't want any trouble now – get along, get moving,' until they reached the Four Sons and the Daughter and the collapsible podium.

'I'd be getting along if I was you,' Sergeant McMenamin said.

'We've a right to be here.'

'You're causing an obstruction and under Section—'

'Fascist pig!' the Daughter said in an almost friendly tone of voice, in Irish.

'I'm no relation of yours thank God,' the sergeant said. 'Are you going to collapse your wee stand and take it away with yourselves, or not?'

The Sons and Daughter hesitated, looked at each other and decided to obey. 'We'll be back,' the Chief Son said. The two Guards stood between them and the crowd until the green mini-van was loaded, and driven out of the Square. The children cheered. Some of the crowd booed. Then the young ones went off to the dance, the men with money went to the pubs, and the ones without to look at the Harbour and talk about what had happened, and nearly happened, and by God, if it had been them that had been standing at the front instead of trapped at the back behind a lot of cowards and slieveens it would have happened, and double fast. The children ran about the Square sticking their hands inside the flaps of their jackets, if they had any jackets, shouting 'Fascist pig!' in Irish and English.

Not much of this had penetrated into the minds of the well-to-do and well-intentioned of Ross Harbour. People heard of it as they heard of everything, but it meant no more to the substantial classes of the town than the news of later that night that one of the O'Loughlinns had fallen into the Harbour in a disgraceful state of intoxication. In fact it meant less, because Tim O'Loughlinn was known to everybody, being the son of Paddy O'Loughlinn foreman to Mr. Seamus Doyle the Jobbing Builder. Some strange trouble-makers from outside had come, and been very properly sent about their business by the Guards before they were able to make their trouble, and that was that. Except to someone as long-sighted as Father Culhane.

'It's that damned Public Meeting of the other week that's behind this, Father, mark my words,' he said to Father Cooney. 'Would you mind troubling yourself to pass me the marmelade? I've never found a priests' housekeeper yet who managed to master the simple art of making toast that didn't turn into burned leather inside five minutes. I'll have the brown bread, Father, the wholemeal. Thank you. Yes, that meeting is behind it. It sowed the seeds.'

'But the crowd refused to listen to them, Father.'

'Seeds give the impression that they have vanished from sight, Father. It is often a substantial period of time before they reappear.'

'Heaven forfend.'

'Amen,' Father Culhane said ironically, buttering his brown wholemeal slice and marmelading it with care.

There was a knock on the door and Mrs. Cleggan the housekeeper came in, or at least half of her came in. 'It's Mary Mulcahy, Father. He's taken a penitent fit again she says and will you come at once.'

Father Culhane sighed and put down his tea-cup. Father Cooney looked reprovingly at Mrs. Cleggan. 'Father has not even finished his cup of tea.'

'I'll come; tell her I'm coming.'

'You allow yourself to be made a martyr by that man, Father.'

Father Culhane sighed again, levering himself up from the table, unable to restrain a small smile of pleasure at the flattery. 'You needn't keep lunch for me Mrs. Cleggan. I may have to stay with him for the length of the morning and no doubt Mary will find me a crust of brown bread and a corner of cheese.'

'Never fear, Father,' Mary Mulcahy said from behind the housekeeper's substantial back. 'I've a grand saddle of mutton in the oven already, only come quick, he's heard about the fishponds and he's terrible bad, he thinks he's going to be murdered in his bed and he wants to confess. And didn't the string of the Sacred Heart come astray in the night and the picture fell down behind the chest of drawers and he has it for certain sure that Our Blessed Saviour has abandoned him. "Why else would it break?" he keeps crying, and he's alone there in the house now and I'm afeared he may try and get out of the bed behind my back and say his prayers on the floor. Please come Father and I'll have the grand breakfast for you the minute you draw up your chair by his bed.'

'What breakfast would he be wanting and he after finishing one this minute?' Mrs. Cleggan cried in a fury. She was long and long tired of Mary Mulcahy and her terrible old uncle, and although she knew very well why Father Culhane allowed himself to be put on night and day by the pair of them and even approved of it in logic, emotionally she found it undignified, a kind of diminution of the Church's grandeur. So that she herself felt humiliated when she saw Father Culhane get up from the table, or from reading his office, to go stumping down Knuckle Street to the big Victorian house, there to reassure Gombeen Mulcahy that he was not damned, that God in His infinite mercy and gentleness loved all His children; that in the sight of Our Saviour Gombeen Mulcahy, with the sins of eighty years crusted on his soul, was as dear a child and as much a child as the urchins playing hopscotch outside his windows.

The two priests saluted each other, and with Mary Mulcahy tugging ahead of him in impatience, and falling back in respect only to tug ahead again, the old parish priest went down Knuckle Street still adjusting his black hat on his head and buttoning his black raincoat over his comfortable stomach. But his heart was heavier than it usually was on that particular errand.

CHAPTER FOUR

MICHAEL forced the polishing cloth deeper into the glass and the glass seemed in a moment to relax, and fell into two neat halves in the cup of his hand. He dropped the two halves into the waste bucket and took up another glass to polish. What was he going to do? Go away? He blew on the glass, pretending to himself that the decision was still his to make. That he was still as free as he had been this time yesterday, or even a few hours ago, when he woke and washed himself and stared across the fields at Slieve Clogher.

But he had seen her again since then. And the thing had happened to him that he had always been certain could never happen, that no girl could do to him. He had been caught. Caught in a silver net, Micilín the Idealist, the thinking man, the boy who came home for privacy and the quiet life and restoration of the mind, and a chance to find a meaning in life. He had seen a girl with long legs and red hair and after three months of shutting his eyes to her and pretending that she wasn't there, his head had been jerked and his eyes opened and he was like a fish gasping on the bank.

'You are not only stupid, Michael Carmody, you are pathetic, ridiculous, you are a pitiful idiot. She fancied you a small bit because she thought that you despised her, and now, the second that she guesses that you're gasping and panting after her like a little dog with its tongue hanging out she is going to despise you in her turn, she is going to have her revenge, and well she might, and well she will, she that for weeks past must have had her arrogance crucified every time she failed to get you to smile at her. By God, it may take a fool a long time to fall over his own feet, but when he does he'll truly hurt himself.'

He took another glass and blew on that. 'Dialectical Materialism, my dear, no less, and the Theory of Surplus Labour and the Role of Trotsky in the Development of Revisionist

Economics and The place of Connolly in International Marxism and the Economic Foundations of Partition. Where are your great thoughts now, Michael, and you with nothing in your head but a grey eye and a slender neck and her fine hand? Arragh, God be good to you and mend your mind.'

He did not know that he had inherited his mother's habit of talking to herself in a streaming monologue. He had only thought of it as a weakness and most times since his childhood he had suppressed it as unworthy of a serious mind. But this morning he was no longer capable of restraining himself. What in the name of Hell was he going to do? 'Oh Mr. Kershaw, I'm in love with your daughter. I think she's a beautiful girl. Would you mind – would you think – Mrs. Kershaw ma'am, you wouldn't have the slightest objection now, would you agradh?'

He had a temptation to hit himself on the front of the head with the heavy heel of the glass. 'Of course I can't offer her a great deal of luxury just this minute, but there's a spare bed-room up in my father's cottage now that both my sisters are working and my mother'd be delighted with a helping hand, especially getting water from the pump down the road and feeding the hens—'

He stopped himself, furiously. A slieveen even in his private mind, touching his forelock and making a mockery of his family. What in hell was the girl doing now? If she wasn't feeding the hens she was cooking for the English visitors and washing up after them and making beds after them and listening to them saying that the Duck à l'orange flambée wasn't quite up to what they had expected and they'd have Escalope de Veau Milanaise instead if she didn't mind. Oh no, not at all, a pleasure, may Christ carry them off with perforated ulcers. While her big ugly slug of a mother lay upstairs reading the *Observer* and eating *marrons glacés* and dropping little hints that of course usually they had a more experienced barman who knew how to make White Ladies and their last barman mixed a Rum Punch that Colonel Mace said was the best he'd ever tasted east of Jamaica. Of course, not that we're criticizing *you*, Michael, we know that you're doing the best you can. And at the back of her English eye little glass splinters darting looks at the till, wondering if he was going to make off with the takings, or murder them in the night, or both. That must have been an interesting half hour when the Hubert was persuading the Hubertess that even a chap that had been in the bally jug was better than sweeping out the jolly old floor oneself and heaving the dashed crates and pulling pints for the locals, by Jove yes, and jolly lucky to get him this time of the year, especially at half wages. The last barman had gone off with a slipped disc and a severe shortfall in the bar takings.

He realized that she was in the doorway, looking at him, and he felt his face go a dark red, and his throat tightened. They had seen each other half a dozen times that morning, but they had had no chance to talk, not even the chance to look at one another without someone else there to see them. He stayed with the glass held in his two hands, the polishing cloth half in half out of it. She opened her mouth to say something.

'Yes?' he said after a long wait.

'I – nothing,' she said. She held a cookery book in one hand and a wooden spoon in the other. There was a smudge of flour on her forehead and on the roots of her hair where she had wiped her wrist across it a moment ago. 'I just wanted—'

He waited. How had he not seen how beautiful she was? Her skin was very pale and smooth, stretched almost, over high cheekbones so that her cheeks seemed hollow and her mouth full of longing. Her hair was dark copper red and sometimes her eyes were grey and sometimes green and it gave him a weakness about the legs to look into them. 'I'm ill,' he thought. 'Something has happened to me.' How many times had he seen her and not turned a thought towards her? Seen her with butter on her mouth from tasting the pudding and an apron twisted round her waist and – if I could untie that apron for her, he thought, smooth that flour away from her forehead, walk her out of here.

'What did you want?' he breathed. And 'I am a bloody idiot,' he still had the strength to think even as he breathed it.

'Just – I was looking in this book and—'

They looked at one another across the bar of the Copper Room, that ridiculous fake Home Counties Tudor Bar, with its copper warming pans and horse brasses on the walls, and its holograph letter from Wordsworth to his sister telling her how he had hoped to visit the little town of Ross Harbour but had been prevented by the rain and the state of the road, 'if anyone were so bold as to call it a road' – they looked at one another and thought that it was a miracle that they should be standing there and alive, and in love, and it seemed to both of them that this, exactly this, could never have happened to anyone before. For if it had happened people would have heard of it and made a fantastic commotion.

'You aren't – angry?' she whispered. 'About—'

'Angry?' he breathed. The glass dropped slowly from his hands and fell in the bucket, with a pleasant, musical sound of breaking. Automatically he picked up another glass.

'About last night.'

There were steps in the corridor outside, the hard, firm, heel-clicking steps of her mother in a hurry and Jennifer said quickly in a loud, casual voice, 'I want some Advocaat and some brandy, please. I'm making a new pudding.'

Her mother came into the Copper Room sharply, managing to convey in the hurried sound of her steps, the forward tilt of her head, a suggestion both of injury and suspicion.

She was a tall woman and had been handsome in her time, and her figure was still capable of catching at Colonel Mace's imagination if not her husband's. But her hair, from its original nondescript brown, had become by alchemy a hard, metallic gold, and there were tell-tale traces of too much gin in the yellowed whites of her eyes, and the small blue, broken veins of her cheeks. In another ten years they would give her face a purplish, 'hunting' colour even under make-up. She carried her shoulders slightly drooped forward as though she was about to swing a golf club or a hockey stick, and her mouth had an echoing droop of discontent suggesting that she knew that it was pointless to contemplate the stroke; that the malice of things had already taken away the ball.

She took in everything about the pair of them in one irritated, suspicious glance. Their faces, the distances between them, what they were holding. Michael's face had already gone unnaturally blank. Had they been? Could they—? What were they—?

'What's broken?' she said sharply.

'Broken?' Michael said in amazement.

'It sounded like half a dozen glasses being smashed all at once,' Angela Kershaw said. She put her hand to her forehead to emphasize the burdens under which she was surviving. They hadn't, they couldn't have been, it was ridiculous of her to worry so much, Jennifer would never, the boy was almost an imbecile, but a mother can't help, if only Hubert... She had gone far enough forward to look into the waste bucket at Michael's feet. 'What are those?'

Michael looked down. 'Oh those?' he said. 'I broke a – two glasses.'

Mrs. Kershaw didn't bother to comment, turning away with a long sigh of resignation. Behind her back Michael felt the blood coming up from his shirt collar, burning his face. Jennifer looked away. 'I'd better get back to the kitchen,' she said. 'If I could have the Advocaat. And the brandy.'

'I'll bring them,' her mother said. 'I heard something boiling over as I passed the kitchen. I hope it wasn't important.' Jennifer ran. Michael slowly finished polishing the glass in his hand and put it under the counter. Mrs. Kershaw had turned her back to him and was staring abstractedly round the Copper Room, looking for something to criticize. There were a dozen sharp phrases on the edge of her tongue, but the only one that would truly have satisfied her – 'Pack your bags and be out of here before lunch' – was the one she could least afford to say.

She stared at the larger of the copper warming pans as if she was attempting self-hypnosis to calm her nerves. It wasn't fair. She had created this room above everything else in the hotel as a bastion of civilization, a defence against the whole damp, lack-lustre inefficiency of Ireland. It had taken her years to bring Hubert to the point of turning The Old House into The Old House Hotel, and through those years she had dreamed of what this room could be, would be. Like a fragment of England. Where their own kind of people would feel instantly at home.

And that was exactly what she had made it. It gave her a sense of achievement every time she looked at it. Except, and from the beginning, the man standing behind the bar. She imagined to herself the kind of man she had dreamed of getting. White coat, pink, smooth, friendly, anonymous face. The kind of man everyone calls 'George' whatever his real name might be. A man like a rock in the centre of a sure world. There had been a barman exactly like that in the Golf Club bar at Sunningford. Ten years after she had married she had gone back there and he had remembered her. 'Welcome back Miss Angela. Excuse me, Madam, Mrs. Kershaw now, isn't it? Your usual, ma'am?' A gin sling. Deep leather armchairs. The eighteenth fairway through the window. The *Bystander* and *Sketch*. The *Tatler*. The *Field*. Members' own silver mugs hanging behind the bar. Gold trophies in glass cases. England. She had wanted to cry. And then she had lifted her chin and thought, I'm going to do it, I'm going to bring something of this over there.

Until that visit she had still thought of bringing Hubert and Jennifer back to Sunningford, or at least to London, of getting Hubert to find something or start something in England. But there had been no money, and except for oases like Sunningford, England in 1962 was worse than Ireland. Strikes and taxes and a Conservative Government that was as bad as a Labour one and everyone predicting that there *would* be a Labour one after the next election. No servants. At least in Ross Harbour you could get some kind of servants. Although not a George.

She tightened her mouth, coming back to reality. 'The windows are filthy, Michael,' she said. 'If you could possibly find a minute—'

'I'll see if I have time this afternoon,' Michael said. 'My mother-in-law,' he was thinking. 'Jesus.' She stared at him sharply, trying to convey that that was not the proper way to answer her, but he looked so peculiar that she gave up and went back out into the corridor and towards the kitchen. As she went out she heard the outer door of the Copper Room opening and a customer coming in. She wanted to go back and see who it was. If it was one of the locals she could give a nod to Michael to get him into the Public Bar. But she didn't feel able to cope with Michael twice in the one minute and she went on towards the kitchen. She was getting one of her headaches again. And with guests coming it might be best if she went and lay down. She changed direction and went upstairs.

In the Copper Room the newly arrived customer had already crossed from the outer to the inner door, opened it a crack and looked with one narrowed eye into the corridor beyond. He came back to stand with elaborate casualness by the counter, his shoulders against the wall, his eyes more on the two doorways than on Michael.

'And how is it with you after this long time, English Michael?' he said in Irish. He was the same age as Michael, twenty-four, and the same height, but where Michael's face was thin, and tanned, the newcomer's was pale and packed with muscle so that at first glance he seemed fat, his narrowed, dark eyes like dates in a round white pudding, and because he had been walking fast in the sun, wearing a type of battle-jacket and

66

carrying a heavy gun in a shoulder holster, there was a film of sweat on his white skin like the suet shine on a pudding. But a second glance would see the hardness of the cheeks and the thick jaw, and the rubbery, bouncing way his body moved. He was Seagrun Ó Maelchonaire, one of the four Sons of Ireland who had guarded the platform at the public meeting in Ross Harbour. Until four years ago he had been Michael Carmody's closest friend.

'Well enough,' Michael said. He had been waiting for this meeting, or something like it, for the three months he had been in the Hotel. He saw the bulge of the gun butt under Seagrun's arm. The last time they had talked Seagrun had threatened to use a gun on him if they ever met again and against his will and his common sense he felt the nerves of his stomach tightening. He had dropped one hand beneath the bar counter and was holding a bottle by the neck.

'I like to see both a man's hands when I talk to him,' Seagrun said, his eyes restless, moving from doorway to window to inner door to Michael's face to the counter that hid his right hand. Michael brought up his hand, still holding the bottle, and rested it gently on the bar. Seagrun stared at the bottle for a second that seemed to stretch out for a long time, a corner of his tight mouth quivering slightly, his nostrils tightening. And then with a curious, high pitched cackle of laughter he flung his arms wide across the bar.

'Your sould to the Devil, boyeen, but it puts ease on my heart to see you, and you still the same fighter that first blacked my eye in the schoolyard in Belcorrig.'

And Michael, who had indeed for ten years of his life loved this madman like a brother, and played his own unwitting part in turning him into a madman, sent the bottle spinning to the far end of the counter and answered the outflung arms of renewed friendship with his own, the two of them clasping each other's shoulders across the counter, laughing with a kind of hysterical joy because they were not killing each other.

'How are the Soldiers?' Michael said, shaking his friend affectionately so that the leather of his shoulder holster creaked under his outstretched arm.

Seagrun stiffened and drew back, his almost invisible eyebrows drawing down over the dark slits of his eyes. 'Do you not know even that?' he said. 'Íosa Críost! you are a long time gone from us, Micheál Ó Cearmada.' But then his face melted again and he renewed the clasp of friendship. 'We are the Sons of Ireland now. And there is a place for you in our ranks. In the front rank of all, Michael of the Silver Speech that was my teacher and my comrade and then my enemy but will again be my friend.' He pulled Michael towards him until their faces were almost touching. 'Did you hear of the blow that some patriot struck last night against the foreigners?' His eyes searched Michael's, his mouth twitching with laughter. 'Or did you maybe strike it yourself?'

'The fish, you mean?' Michael said wonderingly.

'The fish? he says!' Seagrun mimicked him. 'Yerrah, the close divil you've become, and more power to you. It's a lesson we in the Sons are also learning. But that was a great stroke whoever struck it. Set up a tomato juice and whatever you'll have yourself and let me tell you all that's happened since you left us for — since you went away.'

CHAPTER FIVE

THEY had met first more or less as Seagrun Ó Maelchonaire (then plain Johnny Conroy) remembered it, in the schoolyard of Belcorrig Secondary School; a school that the parents
of neither of them could really afford. Johnny's father a clerk in
the Belcorrig Flour Mill. Michael's a roadmender. Both of
them on scholarships that still meant sacrifices for their families down to the amount of bread on the supper table. Their
parents praying for them to get taken into the Civil Service,
and they themselves staring at the school, at their new school-
mates, and at the future, with a tight hostility. To be without
the right kind of shoes, to have no proper shorts and jerseys
for games, to know that to buy them a future their sisters were
going to bed hungry. They had stared at each other in class,
insulted each other in the playground, fought, and become
friends.

From the beginning it had been a revolutionary friendship,
aimed at the Establishment of the school, in so far as they could
reach it. One after another they had demolished the senior boys
who until then had enjoyed a kind of tyranny over newcomers.
They had developed an ambush technique, one of them saun-
tering in an apparently exposed place doing something for-
bidden by class protocol like having both hands in his pockets
or all his coat buttons open. A senior boy would swoop down to
punish the new rat and find himself taken in the rear, from
behind a hedge or a wall or the corner of a building. They never
used stones, and they never hit an enemy in the face to let him
carry a black eye or a split mouth to one of the Brothers. They
always went for the body or the legs, having discovered that a
head butt in the stomach or a strong kick to the side of the knee
was far more effective and left no evidence. Within a month
there wasn't a senior boy in the school who would go near them.
An attempt by three seniors together to turn the tables had
ended in disaster. The decoy senior had been crippled in the

first few seconds, before his reinforcements arrived, and these, faced with two small savages who had obviously never heard of fair fighting, hesitated for a crucial moment. Johnny Conroy put down his head, charged like a small fighting bull and hit one senior full on the mark, knocking him unconscious. Michael, swerving in like a dancer, kicked the other boy's ankles together and when he had fallen, jumped on his stomach.

The three seniors reported the matter to a Brother. The Brother punished all three of them for attempted bullying, and then punished them again for failure and cowardice. Johnny Conroy and Michael Carmody became heroes to the juniors. But heroes of the kind who are more admired and feared than liked. Small boys appealed to them for protection. Larger boys offered them sweets. But only the most slieveenish kind of boy offered them company, and this they rejected with contempt. They walked by themselves, like two lean wolf cubs in a world of pet dogs, despising what they saw, wanting no friendship other than their own.

Each of them brought to that friendship a quality that joined to the other would make a dangerously explosive mixture. Johnny Conroy brought a rage for social justice inherited from his long-defeated father. Michael brought the Irish language. Not the school Irish that they were both enduring in Belcorrig, but Irish that sprang out of a way of life two and three hundred years dead; the Irish of the Ross Peninsula, learned from his grandmother; which in its turn was the Irish of the old order of the Gaelic world, an order of aristocracy and earthiness, of a high contemptuous courage and of peasant cunning; a world of beauty where women were loved for being beautiful, half of that love as chaste as a monk's love for Our Lady and the other half as full of lust as the King of Ulster's love for the girl Deirdre. A world of concubines and rape and killing, of vengeance and sacrifice. A world half pagan, as far from the Irish schoolbooks of the Department of Education as it is possible to find. Like laying down a sword among propelling pencils and bicycle clips.

A large number of the stories his grandmother had told to Michael were about his ancestor, Seán Dubh Ó Cearmada, the poet, and she had taught him his poetry and songs; love songs and drinking songs and prayers that enemies might die in agony for having touched the honour of the poet. Seán Dubh, who died by hanging in 1770 or thereabouts, had himself been a man born out of his true time, his life and his poetry echoing a still older world than the sullen, beaten, peasant Ireland of the Penal Laws and the Ascendancy and the Squireens with their loaded whips, in which he was condemned to live. So that the Irish which Michael Carmody taught to his friend was heady stuff.

Mixed with Johnny Conroy's own contribution it became like dynamite. Johnny's father was already old when Johnny had been born; fifty or more. He was forty-three before he could afford to marry and sixty-five when his youngest child, Johnny, won a scholarship to the Secondary School. By then he was a thin, bald wisp of a man with a celluloid collar too big for his neck, his shoulders bent permanently from crouching on a high stool over the Flour Mill's ledgers. He looked at his young bull of a son with dim amazement and at the same time with faint flickerings of hope. If he himself had suffered continuous defeat there yet might be some kind of victory for this changeling child of his. And he began telling him, with quick, frightened glances over his stooped shoulder, in case someone, his wife, a superior, anyone, might overhear him, that once there had been a man called Connolly, who had taught that there was Injustice in the world and that a man's whole duty was to fight it. 'Never give in to them!' the old man whispered with trembling lips. 'Don't let your life be like mine!'

At thirteen Johnny Conroy believed that he was a Marxist and that the high point of Irish history had been reached in Belcorrig Creamery in 1922 where, for one heady month, there had existed a Workers' and Peasants' Soviet. He was determined that as soon as he was grown up, say when he was fifteen or so, he would take over the Creamery again, and the Flour Mills as well, and they would hang the managers on the new street lamps in Art Ó Griofa Street. But it was his friendship with Michael Carmody that gave to this simple vision its peculiar and lifelong twist.

It began very innocently, with Michael's offer to teach him real Irish. Johnny Conroy went quietly mad in those first months of the friendship and never really regained his sanity. Ever afterwards his world was the world of Gaelic visions, of the Aislingi, of the woman Ireland stepping like a goddess from the snow-foam of the sea, sword-light in her eyes. All the gross side of Michael's Irish he rejected with a shudder of disbelief, convincing himself that lust had been introduced into Ireland by the Normans and the English, and he became so passionate about it that for the sake of peace Michael began to apply an automatic self-censorship in what he said and taught to his friend.

For Michael, his friend's madness was half amusing and half catching, and he himself caught from Johnny the feeling for Class war, and the fight against Injustice. It was a curious thing that although his own family's poverty was even worse in its way than that of the Conroys, it had given him no feeling of social injustice. The wrongs that he had learned to see through his grandmother's eyes and in her stories were not ones of class, but of race and family and breeding. She had never taught him that it was wrong in principle for one man to be too poor while another was too rich. She herself had never thought about that at all. She had simply taught Michael that it was a sin against the honour of God that a Carmody should be poor, at least her branch of the Carmodys. His grandmother and grandfather were third cousins and both of them Carmodys by birth, but she had despised her husband heartily for having given up his language and even more for having given up his pride, and she had seen from the beginning that their son Donald was of the same despicably contented stamp. Only in her grandson Michael had she seen the hallmark of the old race of Ó Cearmada; the searching, ironic eye, the narrow, high-boned face, the independent mind.

She had made him her pupil as soon as he could talk, filling the small, dark kitchen with stories of fine castles and pillared halls that Carmodys had held, from the times of the Tuatha Dé Danann down to the fallen days when the upstart Eagans had torn away their last lands. (To her hooded glance the like of the Kershaws were no more than thieving tourists and not worthy of discussion.) And before she died of a stroke, at eighty-nine, just short of his tenth birthday, she had given to Michael a cast of mind and thought, an attitude to the life around him, and to the pretensions of the rich and powerful, that would never leave him, although it might take many forms that his grandmother would never have recognized as created by herself. For one thing, it left him very ready to believe his friend when Johnny told him that no rich man had any right to be rich; that all property was theft; all privilege injustice. His grandmother had already taught him this about the Eagans. Johnny extended it to everyone who drove in a motor car and could afford bacon every day for breakfast.

These two fixed ideas, of a magic, golden past, and a grimly unjust present, might have been harmless enough if they had been kept separate. Unfortunately for the friends' health of mind they infected one another, and out of two obsessions they created one near-insanity which they greeted as a revelation. It seemed to them that destiny herself had brought them together to save Ireland. For a long time they believed that they were of one combined mind about everything, creating in long sessions of passionate talk a Gaelic Ireland that was at once Marxist and aristocratic; where old wrongs would all be righted, where old legends would come true.

From secondary school they both won scholarships to University and there discovered with amazement that they were not alone; that there were others of their own age and older who thought very much as they did or seemed to. Within three months of going to College they had joined The Soldiers of Freedom. This was, historically, a splinter group of the Warriors of Macha, which was, at several fissions removed, a descendant and collateral relative of fragments of the I.R.A.

As Soldiers of Freedom they had, for the first time, come to the notice of the Special Branch. Several of the Soldiers were in fact undercover agents of the Branch, that long suffering body of policemen whose business it is to keep the destiny of Ireland safe from men like Johnny Conroy, now calling himself Seagrun Ó Maelchonaire, and Michael Carmody. Both boys, and their professors, began to get quiet warnings that they were entering on a path that had no good end. The warnings merely drove them down it at a faster pace. They organized a student strike, a boycott of two of the professors, a sit-in, and a demonstration against a visiting Fianna Fail Minister. It was this last that was the point of no return. There was serious fighting, two Soldiers and four members of the College Fianna Fail society were taken to hospital, a Garda Sergeant had to have four stitches in his scalp and an assistant Lecturer in Zoology only saved himself from a severe beating by hiding in the women's lavatories of the Lecture Hall.

Michael and Seagrun were arrested on charges of disorderly conduct, breaches of the peace and obstructing the Guards in the course of their duties, found Guilty, fined £10 apiece and bound over to be of good behaviour for two years. The College authorities simply expelled them, having already warned them that this would happen if they were in trouble again. But whereas for Seagrun this was no more than a baptism into serious revolutionary activity – the Soldiers immediately picketed the Lecture Halls in protest against the expulsions – for Michael it was like a release. For months he had felt less and less at ease with the Soldiers and less and less at home in the College. The Marxist infection that he had caught years earlier from Johnny was turning to fever and the Green National Socialism of the Soldiers and the narrow middle-class provincialism of the College seemed the one as unreal and meaningless as the other. In the world outside there were Famine and Exploitation; Vietnam and South Africa; neo-Colonialism and the volcanic happenings of the Cultural Revolution. In College the Soldiers were fighting to have the Canteen menus written in Irish.

He had come home to The Ross to say good-bye to his parents and his sisters and after two uncomfortable days and tormented nights had escaped towards Dublin and London and World Revolution, and finally, disillusion. During the three and a half years that he spent in London only the faintest of echoes had reached him from the world of Seagrun and the Soldiers. Of splits and quarrels and betrayals, like the squabbling of rooks in a distant tree. 'The bloody bastards,' Seagrun was saying about one of those betrayals. 'No better than Fascists, either of them. I told them I wouldn't dirty a bullet by firing it into them, and the two of them so frightened they couldn't say a Hail Mary between them. Íosa Críost!'

It was a long and involved story, and Michael listened to it with less than half an ear while he looked at this man who had once been closer to him than any brother, and now seemed like a ghost out of another world. And yet he found that he still loved him in a strange, astonished way, his voice waking echoes in Michael's mind, recreating pictures in it so that he found himself leaning closer and listening no longer with condescension but with a real interest.

For several years the Soldiers had been splitting not only into Right and Left wings, but also cross-splitting into those who believed in Physical Force and those who thought that the State could more easily be brought to its knees by Civil Disobedience and Street Democracy. At the last Annual General

74

Congress of the movement there had been a dozen rival groups whose beliefs ranged from the Theocratic State to the necessity of a Popular Front, to Connolly Socialism and the Workers' Republic. Fighting broke out on the platform for control of the microphone, spread to the floor of the hall, to the street outside, and ended with several arrests and the final collapse of The Soldiers as a recognizable movement.

Seagrun Ó Maelchonaire and four of his friends fought a rearguard action against a momentary street alliance of the Theocrats and the Civil Disobedience faction, found themselves cut off by a flanking attack of eight Gardai, and escaped into Grafton Street and the tranquil, bourgeois safety of Bewley's Café. There, after several cups of strong coffee and a plate of currant scones, they created from the ashes of the dead Soldiers a new Movement, The Sons of Ireland. Helped by more coffee, they drew up a Manifesto in Irish, with versions in English, French and German (these latter to be sent to Leinster House, the Westminster Parliament, and the E.E.C. Commissioners in Brussels as a warning not to take Ireland's future for granted), and after a certain amount of quarrelling about the exact translation of this word and that, signed all the copies (having gone across the street to buy stationery for the purpose).

It was a good Manifesto.

'We the SONS OF IRELAND (a motion by Eibhlín Ní Laoghaire to have the word DAUGHTERS incorporated in the title was defeated four to one) on behalf of THE SOVEREIGN PEOPLE OF IRELAND, hereby PROCLAIM THAT SOVEREIGNTY INVIOLABLE and declare null and void all past and future surrenders of any portion or aspect of the Sovereign People's INALIENABLE RIGHTS by any so-called Irish Government.'

As well as being a good Manifesto it was also rather a long one, with the more striking and significant ideas expressed in capital letters.

'... RESOURCES OF IRELAND ... DEDICATED OUR LIVES ... TRUE IRISH REPUBLIC ... RISEN PEOPLE ... IMPERIALISTS AND THEIR GREEN TORY LACKEYS ... USURY AND RUTHLESS PROFITEERING ... A NEW ERA IS BEGUN.'

Seagrun recited the whole text to Michael, his voice shaking with emotion and rising to a near shout to express the capitals.

'I recognize the Conroy hand in that,' Michael said, only half jeering.

Seagrun blushed. 'We sent it to all the Seaneen papers,' he said, 'but only the *Irish Times* had the guts to print it and they stuck it away on the inside with the cattle prices, God's curse on them. We're thinking of starting our own newspaper to tell the people the truth. Like about this that's just happened down here.' He bent his pale eyebrows at Michael in a fond frown. 'Arragh, don't be acting the astonishment with me. If you recognize my hand in the Manifesto, do you think I don't recognize the hand of Big Michael in the emptying of the ponds? I wept tears of laughter and I hearing about it in Ross Harbour this morning while I struggled to keep my face straight.'

'I suppose it's no use telling you I had a lot else on my mind last night than a farm full of trout?'

'Divil a bit of use, boyeen. By God, in all the months we've been organizing we've done less than you did in the one night. You have to come back to us, Micilín. Soul of my soul you have. Little I thought when we came down here to organize the Meeting against the Development that you were already here and planning this stroke.'

'How did you know I was here?'

'A man told me. A little ratty man with a dripping nose who seemed to know a great deal. There was a group talking and I listening and he gave my sleeve a tug. "Why don't you ask your friend Michael Carmody," he said, "that's barman in The Old House Hotel? I hear he does sometimes walk about in the fields at night and maybe he might have seen a bit of it happening?" If he's a friend of yours, Micilín, I'd ask him to be more careful what he says.'

'He doesn't sound like any friend,' Michael said. He felt himself flushing.

'I thought he did not. I gave him a sight of my gun butt and he scuttled for his life. But damn your soul, Michael, what are you doing buried in this place?'

'What are you doing?'

'I have my Headquarters in Belcorrig.'

'You mean you're still living with your mother?'

The warm affection in Seagrun's face died as though winter had struck it. 'Be easy, boyeen,' he whispered.

They stared at each other, of a sudden the same naked anger between them that there had been at their last meeting and one or two meetings before that. And again it was Seagrun who threw his arms wide and laughed his strange, cackling laugh.

'By God we're the touchy pair. The one of us will kill the other if we're not careful.'

'Not me,' Michael said. 'I'm looking for peace and quiet.'

Seagrun curled his thin lips. 'We'll soon change that.' His eyes turned cunning. 'If any change is needed. There's peace and peace, and quiet and quiet, and maybe it was peace and quiet that was all someone wanted to bring to the fish farm this past night?'

'Will you listen to me?'

'I will listen to you when you tell me that you are coming back to the ranks. Michael, Michael, it isn't with one man's blow struck in the night that we're going to bring down the System. Nor even the Development. We need to stand shoulder to shoulder.' He held himself at arm's length from the counter and fixed Michael with that mad stare of his that at the same time had a wild and burning innocence.

'What Development?' Michael said, trying to bring him back to firm ground.

Seagrun turned his head from side to side in pitying reproof. 'Do you not know anything? Did you not even hear that they are going to destroy this place? Your own home, Micheál? The foreigners are coming, boyeen, and not in their ones and their twos to build little ponds for fish or bungalows with barbed wire across the public beaches, but in their thousands, like the Huns of Attila, to turn this countryside into a concrete desert. Coming with their money bags and their bribes for this one and that one; for the Green Tories above in Dublin who'd pawn their mothers' souls for a block of shares.

'Oh mwirra, a great bounty they're promising you, with jobs and benefits for all, moyah! Factories and Smelters and Oil Terminals and the Devil have me if I know what else. A new Birmingham no less.'

'That might be no harm,' Michael said.

'No harm?' whispered Seagrun, shocked for a second out of the rhythm of his rhetoric that was in fact part of the speech that Eibhlín Ní Laoghaire had tried to deliver at the Public Meeting. 'Have you turned into a slave across in England? Who will own this new Birmingham of yours do you think? The people of The Ross maybe? The people of Ireland? God mend your head if you think that, or the tenth part of that.' He had recovered his rhythm and set his face in the sarcastic mask of a

revolutionary who is insulting his audience for the audience's
benefit. 'It is the foreigners who will own it, who else? The
foreigners will grow fat out of these factories, and the gombeen
politicians above in Dublin will scamper round their shoes like
little mice after crumbs. What harm! And the people of this
place begging for slave work in factories where they should be
masters. While if a man or two comes back from Birmingham
or London to work in this wonderful gift of the foreigners the
Green Tories will be screeching out on the Television in their
Party speeches, LOOK AT US! WE'RE BRINGING BACK THE EMI-
GRANTS, RE-PEOPLING THE LAND!

'For what, by God? To be helots to the foreigner here, instead of overseas, to be exploited in their own land instead of
the exploiters' land. Unless we fight them, unless we create a
land where the fruits of our labour—'

'You've recited the Proclamation already,' Michael said. He
was suddenly tired of Seagrun, not with the tiredness of
affection, the way one might want to stop a child who has gone
on too long with a game; but with the grey, sick tiredness he
had felt in prison, and for a long time before he went to prison;
tiredness from endless listening to the passionate voices of mad
idealism; to the husky, cellar voices whispering of the day when
there would be an English K.G.B. to protect the rights and
freedoms of the workers; to the shrill cries of the Trotskyites
and the Maoists; to the sullen hatreds of the Works' Committees and the ad hoc Strike Committees, and the Shop Stew-
ards' Committees; to the mindless chanted slogans of the
Demos. Until his nerves screamed for quiet. And even more for
reason.

He had come back from England in the hope of finding both,
and here was this poor maniac like a reproaching echo gibber-
ing out of his past. Had he talked like this once himself, thought
like this? He imagined for a mad second trying to tell Seagrun
what the world was really like, teaching him economic reality
as he had once taught him Irish. And as he thought of that it
flashed into his mind that this man in front of him was his own
creation, that out of his grandmother's legends he had created
The Sons of Ireland and their Proclamation; with Seán
Dubh's poetry he had driven poor Johnny Conroy mad. But as
soon as the idea came to him he refused to accept it. He had
enough weighing on him without adding Johnny Conroy's
sanity to the burden.

'I'm sorry,' he said. 'I'm not in the humour for speeches and heroics.'

Seagrun had fallen half a pace back as though Michael had struck him, and he actually put up one hand to his cheek. His nostrils were wax white and his forehead burned a delicate pink. At that moment there was the sound of footsteps coming quick and light down the corridor. Seagrun's hand went to the butt of his gun and he moved sideways, putting his shoulders flat against the wall of the Copper Room, beneath Wordsworth's letter to Dorothy, in its glass frame.

Jennifer came into the bar, checked for a second at seeing a stranger and said, 'Sorry, I – mummy must have forgotten about the – brandy and – the Advocaat.' Something about the customer leaning against the wall embarrassed her. She looked at Michael and quickly away again, making a small performance of seeing where the two bottles might be. They were on the counter. She glanced again out of the corners of her eyes at the customer. He was staring at her and she caught up the bottles hurriedly and went out. When she was gone there was a lengthy moment of silence.

'I see,' Seagrun said at last.

'And what does that mean?' Michael said, trying to make his voice sound natural. To his fury he felt the blood coming up into his face like fire.

'There are many reasons for a man betraying the truth that he once held,' Seagrun said in a low, cold voice. 'But that is as pitifully vile a reason as I ever heard of. Unless I would be wrong in thinking that that was the owner's daughter? Is it her lapdog that you have become as well as her father's potboy? You that threw my mother in my face just now.'

Michael leaned over the counter and caught Seagrun by both lapels of his battle-jacket, pulling him round so that they faced each other. Seagrun did not try to resist, and in the lack of resistance there was more insult than in his words and the expression of his face.

'What has anyone said to you?' Michael whispered.

'What would they need to say? It is in her eyes that she owns you, and in yours that you are owned. Take your hands from my coat, Michael of the pots.'

Michael let go of him, opening his hands as if he was disengaging them from something unpleasant. And yet in a most strange way he felt a sense almost of guilt, and at the same time

79

of pain that his meeting again with Seagrun should end like this. Both feelings made his face and his voice still harder.

'Go away from here,' he said. 'Don't speak about her. Don't speak about me. Can you remember that?'

Seagrun walked to the outer door, and even in doing it his eyes glanced quickly at the window, at the inner door, his ears seemed visibly to listen. 'Yes,' he said very softly. 'I can remember that. I wish that I could remember nothing else about you, you that were my teacher.' He went out, closing the door so softly that it made no sound.

In the Copper Room Michael leaned on the bar with both hands as if he needed to support himself. He stared unseeingly at the warming pans. 'Why did I come back?' he whispered. Even the thought of her had been damaged, like the glass smashed over a photograph in a frame.

CHAPTER SIX

FATHER CULHANE spread his napkin under his chins and across his black and ample front with an inward sigh of pleasure and relief. It had been a long morning with the old man, and threatened to be a long afternoon. Mary Mulcahy put down the plate of smoked salmon and sliced tomato in front of the parish priest, bobbing her grey ringlets and one knee as she did so, like a practised acolyte genuflecting as he tos and fros before the alter and the Blessed Sacrament.

'A slice of lemon, Father? Or a touch of vinegar?'

'The lemon, child, God love you. Ah, he's in a wearing mood this morning.'

'You don't need to tell me, Father. Will you take the wine with the salmon or wait till the next course?'

'I'll take just a drop now, since you have the bottle in your hand. Lord save us, Mary, you've filled the glass.'

'No harm to you, Father, and the hours you've spent with him. I thought he was gone on me and he hearing the news. His face looked like a piece of dough out of the ashes and his heart pelting in his poor body so you could see it leaping against the ribs. It was a fright.'

'It'll take more than that to put R.I.P. on your uncle, child. There's years of life in him yet with the kind of nursing you give him, God preserve him to us.'

They both crossed themselves. The priest emptied the glass absentmindedly and Mary Mulcahy filled it with equal lack of attention to worldly things.

'He has it fixed in his head it's the I.R.A.,' Mary said. 'And that the next thing is they'll be burning the house over our heads. "Who else'd be letting the fish out that way and they knowing I have shares in the farm?" If he said that to me once he said it twenty times and I getting my coat and hat to fetch you this morning. "Lord save us," I said to him again and again, "what for would the I.R.A. be wanting to burn the roof over respectable people like ourselves, uncle, and we never speaking a word of politics against a soul in our lives?" But right nor wrong he wouldn't heed me.'

'Ah, you do your best for him, no doubt about that, and it'll stand to you when you need it, child. A slice more of your excellent brown bread if I may. A splendid piece of salmon, smoked to perfection.'

'And he up there not able to eat a crumb, only tell his beads. He'll have Our Lady worn out with listening to him.'

But at that the priest looked rather grave. 'Nothing wears out Our Lady's patience, Mary. Your uncle's long penitence brings great joy to Heaven, have no doubt of that.'

'And he struggling to get on to his poor knees on the cold linoleum of a morning and a night, it'd break your heart to see him, Father,' Mary said, carried away by womanly compassion to a height where the Church's gravity could not check her.

'He is a good man, a true child of his Holy Mother the Church,' the priest said, placing the last fragment of smoked salmon on a corner of his bread and anointing it with a drop of lemon juice. 'If only all of us had the Grace to prepare ourselves for our latter end as well as he is doing—' He popped the bread and fish into his small, rosy mouth and wiped his lips with the napkin. 'A feast fit for a king,' he said.

'A feast, Father?' cried Mary, scandalized. 'Don't tell me you're not going to try my saddle of mutton and I all morning over the stove with it thinking how well you'd like it.'

'Oh Mary, Mary, the temptations of luxury. But if you have gone to so much trouble—'

'And just a small slice of my special paté to keep you from wall-falling while I fetch it. As plain as plain. Just chicken livers with a touch of onion, and butter of course, and maybe I showed a finger of garlic to it from a foot away.'

She refilled his glass with one hand and laid the generous plate of chicken liver paté, lettuce and beetroot in front of him with the other. It was the sorrow of her life that for ten years past her uncle had lived on gruel and broth with an occasional rice pudding, and whenever the priest came to lunch, or supper, which was often enough, she blossomed like a retired soprano trying out arias in her bath.

'It wouldn't be Mrs. Cleggan would spoil me like this,' Father Culhane said, squaring his elbows at the paté and leaning forward for the first bite. 'And just as well for me if she doesn't.'

'What spoiling?' Mary said triumphantly, whisking herself away from the table with an almost coquettish toss of her head. 'I'll get the mutton, Father, and not the smallest piece of that paté to be left on the plate now, or I'll think you don't like it.'

She paused at the door as if it was the wing of a stage. 'And if I run up to himself for a moment to see if he's eating his gruel and not spilling it on the sheets, don't let yourself be going dry, Father. The bottle is by your hand.'

'Child, child!' Father Culhane reproached her, but she was gone, scurrying up the stairs.

In the big, dark, Victorian bedroom, full of brass glimmers and mahogany shadows that defied the daylight, old Gombeen Mulcahy lay with his spoon in his knotted fingers, his tray balanced on his lap, and his eyes fast on the re-established Sacred Heart above the big chest of drawers. A large black crucifix with a silver figure of Our Lord hung over the bed, mercifully out of his vision, but he was conscious of it there.

'God be merciful to me a sinner,' he whispered. He wished he had his Rosary beads in his hands, but she had taken them away so that he could feed himself. He wished that Father Tom was still in the room, but she wouldn't have that under any conditions or threat or pleading. The place for the parish priest to eat was the dining-room, and flesh could have been torn from Mary Mulcahy's bony breast with red hot pincers and she would not have surrendered that conviction.

She came back into the room, rustling and creaking and he turned his head at her with embers of resentful anger. 'I thought it was Father Tom,' he whispered. 'What's keeping him all this while?'

'Can you not let the poor man eat his boiled egg in peace, uncle? Hasn't he spent enough time with you for one day?'

'Isn't he coming back up to see me?' Gombeen lifted himself suddenly in the bed as if his skeleton body had suffered an electric shock. 'Is he gone?'

'Never fear. He'll be up just as soon as he's finished his sup of tea. And you've spilled your gruel again. What will I do with you at all?' She righted his spoon and scraped up the warm gruel with the napkin. Gombeen watched her with nervous hatred. He couldn't cut her out of his Will because he had done that already, but she didn't know and he could at least frighten her. He thought of telling her to fetch Martin O'Loughlinn, the solicitor, but the multiple terrors of the day pressed too close on him to allow for pleasure and he only mumbled under his breath, 'There's some that thinks they'll be glad to see me gone, and maybe they'll get a great shock when the time comes.'

Mary Mulcahy crossed herself but gave him no other satisfaction. She knew exactly what he had done in his Will, or rather, what he thought he had done. She had her own understanding with Martin O'Loughlinn and between them they had taken care to see that neither of them would be completely unrewarded when the time came. 'And well you might look for something, Miss Mary,' as Martin had said when he added in the paragraph in the blank space above the old man's shaky, spidery signature. 'Twice as much would be little enough for all you've put up with these thirty years, and you like a living martyr to him. God between us and all sin, but his two sons and Holy Church won't miss the little bit I've put down to you, and sure when you're done with it won't you be leaving it to the Church anyway? What is it but a class of a loan to keep you from starvation when himself is gone? And since he always had it in mind when he was in his health to leave you comfortably, why, amn't I only doing what his true self wanted to do, and what would weigh on his soul if it wasn't done?'

'It will indeed be going to the Church,' Mary had said with a tight mouth. 'Not a farthing would I leave in any way that that one would lay her hands on it.' That one being Clara Mulcahy, the wife of her cousin John.

The thought of that providential and certainly justifiable paragraph in the Will had strengthened her through many moments like this one. Her one fear was that the old man might ask to have the Will back so that he could read it again and maybe cut out John, or Benedict, or add something insulting about Clara, or delete the Sisters of the Crucifixion in favour of the Poor Bernardines, or add another few hundred masses for the repose of his own soul, or alter the legacies to Father Thomas Culhane and St. Finbarr's, according as his fear of Hell was on the wax or the wane, that particular day. But she had made up her mind that if he demanded the Will she would contrive to step on his glasses before he could read it.

'Finish your gruel now,' she said, 'and Father will be up to you in a minute. Although Heaven knows what more he can do for you than he did this morning.'

'What do you know about it?' Gombeen said, but in mid-snarl his voice changed to beseeching. 'Give me my Rosary, put it close to my hand.'

She gave it to him and went out and he clutched the beads like a lifebelt. He had said the five sorrowful Mysteries twice over before Father Tom came up to him again, his face comfortably flushed by the wine and saddle of mutton and peach flan and cream and cheese and digestive biscuits and coffee with just the smallest dash of brandy in it – sure Father why shouldn't you, just this once? – and another thimbleful of brandy in a big, balloon glass.

'Well, how are we now, eh, 'loysius?' the priest said in a cheerful voice and Aloysius Mulcahy looked at him from the bed with miserable reproach.

'You'll stay with me a bit, Father?'

'Be reasonable, man. You're not the only fish in the frying pan.'

'Oh, oh, oh,' Gombeen cried in the agony of fear brought on by that unhappily chosen image.

'Oh be easy, be easy, I'll stay with you a bit. But only a bit now. It isn't healthy the way you're carrying on. Sure, aren't we all sinners? Isn't it flying in God's face to doubt His Mercy the way you're doing? And as for the I.R.A., what would they want with you and you not stirring out of this bed this ten years?'

'I hear them creeping about the house at night and whispering.'

'Fiddlesticks, man. Imagination and nothing but.'

' 'tis easy for you to be talking, Tom, and you prepared to meet your Maker day or night. But what about me? Suppose they were to come and kill me this night and I in mortal sin?'

'Yerrah, what mortal sin? Haven't I given you absolution till you could wash your socks in it, and then given it you again? It's a heretic you're becoming, 'loysius, a heathen heretic.'

'How can I believe in any absolution and I with that on my soul?' And his eyes burned in their hollowed sockets with such a hellfire of torment that it touched the priest as it always did.

'Wisha, 'loysius, are you doubting God's strength? It was sixty years ago, man, and haven't you shed blood from your feet for it since? 'tis other sins than the old Jew man you could be

85

remembering, and sure aren't all of them gone out of your heart? Have trust in God's gentleness.'

'If I could,' the older man whispered, knotting the Coronet of beads between his yellowed hands. 'But how could He forgive me and I selling the Images of His Blessed Mother, and the Cross of Christ Himself, and the beads and the Holy pictures, along with the Jew man, as if I was a Jew aself?'

'Didn't you leave him, didn't you put an end to it?' Father Tom said irritably. He wanted to sit easy and digestively by the window and think of nothing, or even catch a minute of a snooze.

'But the money, Tom? The money that started everything? It was Jew money, like the Thirty Pieces that bought Our Lord. The bed I'll die in, the gruel in that bowl, wasn't it all got from that beginning?'

'Stuff and rubbish. 'tis gone and long gone. Haven't you given me alone ten times over what you got for his rickety bits and rubbish?'

'But it left its taint on me, Tom. I tell you I see Judas himself at times, hanging in that corner by your head.'

'Jesus, Mary and Joseph,' Father Culhane said, jerking his head sideways in spite of himself. 'Don't be saying such blasphemy.'

'The last time the Bishop himself was here I offered him money for a new car and he wouldn't take it. He knew—'

'Yerrah damn. What would he be wanting with a new car and he as near ninety years old as a kitten to a cat? It's a coffin he needs.' The last was said with more feeling than decency, for Father Tom had waited on the Bishop's funeral for ten years and more, before the old man retired, only to see a younger man than himself win the purple. He had grown too old waiting.

'Don't be talking of coffins, Tom, and I so close to mine. And the Jew man waiting for me below.'

As he said it he saw the small red flame of the Sanctuary lamp wink and waver below the Sacred Heart. Like an eye in the dark, like the small, jetty, burning eye of the Jew man staring at him from the pillow in Clonmel. The grey, dirty pillow, in the grey dirty room of the back street boarding house, sixty years ago, and the old Jew man dying in the bed, only his eyes still full alive, bright with fever, his voice like a ghost's already, whispering in the shadows.

'Don't leave me 'loysi, stay with me. I'll give you an extra

86

pound, I'll raise your commission. Don't leave me to die here with strangers.' The boxes of samples under the bed. Our Lady of the Seven Dolours. St. Bernadette. St. Catherine. Our Lady of Lourdes. The Sacred Heart. Rosary beads. 'Real Mother of Pearl, my dear, got from the Holy Grottoes of the Land of Our Lord, from Bethlehem. Maybe Our Saviour's own Blessed baby eyes rested on these same pearls in the cave of Bethlehem itself. Would you think of that now and grudge five shillings? Never your life long my dear will you see a crown of beads like that. Such a value! Such prettiness my dear! Ach, Gott! You can only lay down a shilling? Well well, times is hard, eh 'loysi? I tell you it's two days we haven't eaten a decent bite nor seen hot food in front of us. A shilling is a shilling, eh 'loysi? If we came back next week for the other four shillings? With another sixpence for the time? Eh? Oy, oy, a shilling every week? It would have to be seven shillings we'd charge you then, a shilling now and seven weeks at a shilling each Friday, when you have the egg money? Ach, I don't know when I met such a clever bargainer, eh, 'loysi? This is my apprentice, my dear, and such a hungry boy to feed I have to let the hard ones like you take the blood out of my veins so that I can feed him.'

That was how it had begun. Tramping the roads with the old Jew man, carrying his pedlar's pack, farmhouse to farmhouse, sleeping in sheds, in ditches sometimes in the summer, eating scraps and leavings, the straps of the pack cutting the young bones of his shoulders like gallows' rope, his feet bleeding. The old man walked as if he had no feet, as if he trotted on cushions. Mile after mile. Now a lift on an empty farm cart, now a climb up the rutted mud and stone of a boreen to a lost cottage that owed them sixpence. The old Jew's ragged coat tails, flapping round his heels, his flattened shoes like flippers, his knees bending, his shoulders stooping, his hair in grey ringlets and greasy strings on his greasy collar. Sixpences, shillings. On wonder days a half sovereign, even a sovereign, for a statue of Our Lord, a Crucifix with a silver figure – 'as true as I stand here in the dust of the road that is true silver, isn't it, 'loysi? The best German silver, better even than British may God's curse fall on me if I tell a lie. Only a sovereign to look on the Blessed Face of Our Lord, day after day till the end of your life and He gathers you in His arms. Could you grudge a sovereign for the Lord God?'

Sometimes there had been an ugly moment when the man of

the house came suddenly on them and shouted, 'By God it's the Jew man! Get out of that you dirty rapscallion heathen, robbing poor people!' And the woman of the house would shriek, 'A Jew? Is it a Jew? Oh Mother of God have mercy, a Jew man? God save us!' But often enough Moishe talked even that to advantage, wept and prostrated himself, poured dust on his head, spoke of the Cossacks who had murdered his mother and his brothers, his sisters and his nieces, cried up the Faith of Ireland that might – that might – one day bring him to its blessed embrace. Sometimes they had simply run.

There was the time and more than one time they had run for their lives, a yelling crowd behind them. 'Who killed Christ! Get the Jew men! Head them off, head them towards the river!' Stones flung after them, and the pair of them panting like coursed hares down the laneways, over ditches, into woods.

And the time the lodging house keeper whispered that if Aloysius would contrive to give him a sight of the old Jew's tail he could have his dinner for nothing. There had been scarcely a day of all those years that the work hadn't worn its grooves in Aloysius Mulcahy's soul, like mortal sin repeated and repeated. But how could he stop? What else could he do? Until the time had come in Clonmel with the old man dying and he had found the courage to take the pack, and the box from under the bed, and leave him. What had screwed up his courage to the last notch had been the knowledge that at the moment of the old man's death the Devil would come for him, and for any Christian in mortal sin who might be near him at that hour.

The old man had tried to lift up in the bed as Aloysius dragged the black sample box from under it. 'You can have it,' he whispered, his breath rattling. 'Everything, only don't leave me now. If I had someone to pray with me.' His bent claw fingers went to his phylactery and Aloysius had backed away in terror, a sweating terror that he might hear the old man's whispering blasphemies, that the old man might die that moment with heathen prayers on his lips and the Devil would come leaping in a blue flame of sulphur, summoned up from Hell by the words. He had backed away across the floor dragging the box in one hand and the pack in the other, like an animal tugging meat, gabbling an Act of Contrition. 'Most merciful Saviour—' 'Oh Christ protect me from the Powers of Hell—' 'Oh loving Father I have sinned—'

Out of the door with him in a swim of sweat as if he had fallen into a river, and down the narrow stairs. 'Christ have Mercy, Mother of God look down on me with pity.' Into the hallway, out into the street and the evening dark. Hoisting the pack on to his shoulders and running, running, staggering out of the town and up the hill, blind to where he was going so long as it was away from the jaws of Hell. 'Tower of Ivory – Queen of Heaven – St. Patrick and all the Saints protect me.' Until he fell into a ditch by the roadside with pack for pillow and box for comfort and slept exhausted. He woke screaming of hell-fire, with a sheep looking down at him out of its amber, hellish eyes, and the sheep galloped off in fright and Aloysius thought that he was in rigor mortis, his jaws locked with terror, his body numb with cold and muscle-pain and hunger. 'Jesus, Jesus, Jesus. If I live this night out I will crawl to Knock on my bare knees, and then to Croagh Patrick. I'll have masses said for the conversion of the Jews. May the Curse of Judas fall on them for tempting me into sin. O blessed Mother of God I repent, I repent.'

In a way his whole life had been a repentance, of his own rather peculiar kind. And there had been many times when he was quite sure that his repentance had been accepted, his soul had been washed clean of the sin of trafficking with the heathen, of selling holy things for profit, of Simony and Blasphemy and the corruption of the Spirit. Hadn't he prospered? Hadn't he sold the old man's stock at a handsome figure, and washed his hands of that kind of business for ever? Hadn't he taken the money he had gained and gone back to Ross Harbour with it, and begun a Christian business, buying the allfalls cheap from the market, meat that was a bit off, vegetables that had got trodden on but could be shaken good again, bruised fruit, fish that only needed a touch of vinegar and seawater to give them back their freshness, and with an old wooden barrow taken them round the back streets selling them cheap; trundling the barrow up the hills to the farmhouses and cottages to sell the remainder there and save the housewives coming to market? God in His Mercy had smiled on him. The past was surely forgiven.

But the past had slept in his soul like the spirochetes of a vile disease asleep in a lecher's blood. And as the years of prosperity accumulated, the sleeping past gathered its strength against him, until there were times when he woke in the night in a cold sweat believing himself back in a ditch with his head on the pedlar's pack of holy objects and only a crust of bread in his aching stomach. There were times when he dreamed of the ashen moors of Hell, and a cold wind whistling about his skin and that cursed pack like a sack of stones dragging his shoulders down, breaking his spine, and his naked feet torn by the sharper stones of the ground. Hell closed round him like the walls of his bedroom and he poured out money into the laps of priests and Sisters in a golden stream. But faster than he poured it out his businesses poured it back again. Supermarkets and travelling shops. Money lending and mortgages. As a friar might be going out of the front door carrying money for a dozen masses for the donor's intentions a scruffy man in a raincoat and a trilby hat pulled down over his eyes might be coming in the back way, carrying a greasy notebook and wads of bank notes. Or his son John might come with the lists of the day's takings in the shops, or Doyle or O'Loughlinn to report to him about mortgages fallen into arrears and ripe to be foreclosed or Muldoon from the bank about his investments, or the postman with letters from his Dublin broker, or advice from Benedict about some piece of land that ought to be acquired.

Money spouted out of the ground, heaped itself in golden piles, and with the Development that Benedict was planning the heaps would become hills, would become mountains. Nearly all the land that would be needed for the sites and roads was his or John's or Benedict's or Clara's already. Only the Kershaws' bit of land and a few other plots here and there were still needed, and there was no problem about any of them. And over and above the profit on the land they would have shares in the companies, in the factories and the oil terminal, the docks and the smelter; they would build the houses for the workers and make their profit on those; they would have government grants and ground rents; they would be building new shops to sell every mortal thing to the inhabitants of what would grow into a whole new town, a city almost; they would sell them groceries and clothes, furniture and refrigerators, motor cars and petrol and wireless and television sets; fish fingers and bicycles; beer and stout and whiskey and cigarettes and tobacco. A dozen more scruffy men in raincoats and trilby hats would lend them money at a shilling in the pound a week, and God in His wisdom knew that there were many who would charge them four times that and not think it a sin. But if there was one thing that Aloysius Mulcahy would never countenance it was usury. A shilling in the pound and not a farthing more.

At midday when he thought of the Development it was with a warm joy, like pulling a soft, luxurious lamb's wool blanket up to his chin. But with the dark it seemed to take on an almost threatening shape, just as the furniture did, and leaned and moved, as if it was creeping towards him to bury him under a weight of gold; gold that carried with it the curse of Judas. The dreadful taint of its origin in the Jew man's pack.

And since the Public Meeting he had become possesed by a new terror. Of the I.R.A. That they knew that he was behind the Development, and that they would come one night and kill him in his bed, without giving him so much as time to make an Act of Contrition, let alone send for Father Tom and the Blessed Sacrament. With each dawn the terror had receded as the light grew. This dawn like the others. Until with breakfast had come the news of the fish ponds emptied, and it had been like a bone hand on his heart.

He could feel it now. Like a hand. A skeleton hand. Tightening on his heart.

'Tom,' he whispered.

But the old priest was fast asleep.

CHAPTER SEVEN

HUBERT KERSHAW arrived at Eaganscourt with the usual
tremendous vrroom of exhaust and scatter of gravel. He wore
driving gloves and a tweed cap and a Leander scarf wrapped
twice round his throat, the ends flung dashingly over his shoulders. Behind the big wheel and the long, green, high-bridged
bonnet of the vintage Bentley his usual anxieties about what
impression he was making vanished, and he felt completely
confident, as if the three and a half litres and the six cylinders
and the thunderous exhaust (his silencer was broken and he had
somehow managed never to get it replaced) as if these were his
true self. He switched the engine off with a physical sigh of
regret, swung the small, thick door open and stepped down on to
the gravel sweep as if he was returning to earth after flight.
Instantly, even before the Eagan labradors reached him, or the
maid. Maureen Carmody, Michael's sister could open the
inner door of the porch, his confidence and air of certainty had
given way to a self-conscious jauntiness. As Lady Eagan had
said, long ago, with the eye of a general's daughter trained from
girlhood in judging subalterns, Hubert Kershaw was irre-
trievably second class.

There was no earthly reason for it to be so. The Kershaws
had held their land in Ireland since the time of the first
Elizabeth. For a hundred or so years, until the Eagans took the
Oath of Allegiance and abandoned Catholicism, they had been
the leading, or certainly officially the leading family of the district, and had remained important. If they had lost most of
their money and their land during the last fifty years, so had the
rest of the gentry with a few exceptions like the Eagans, and
even the Eagans had had the bulk of their land taken. But
where other men of Hubert's standing drank and hunted and
shot and went to London and to Paris on their overdrafts as
happily and arrogantly as their ancestors had done on their

rackrents, Hubert faced life like a coloured man trying to pass as white in Georgia.

'What ho, Maureen,' he said as the girl opened the glass panelled inner door. 'Sir Philip in?' And to the dogs, 'Down fellows, there's good chaps.' His father, for some quirk, had disapproved of dogs, and Hubert had never got over the suspicion that any dog which approached him intended to bite.

'I'll tell the master you're here, sir,' Maureen said, although anyone within half a mile could never help knowing when Hubert arrived anywhere. Hubert touched the underside of his moustache with his knuckle brushing it upwards. Oddly enough this nervous tic seemed to Maureen Carmody the most gentlemanly gesture she had ever seen and like a number of the sillier girls of Ross Harbour, she thought Mr. Kershaw infinitely more a real gentleman than her employer was. She found Sir Philip too quiet, too strangely remote and detached. In her heart of hearts she was frightened of him. 'He'd look at you half the time as if he didn't see you at all,' she complained long afterwards. Even his continual politeness frightened her. Whereas with Mr. Kershaw, she felt, life would be jolly and noisy and the way life ought to be in a gentleman's house, with the master shouting and the dogs hiding under the table if the kippers were burned. Sir Philip wouldn't even notice a thing like that. All he thought of was his old book and his bits and pieces of Chinese stuff, so that her heart was in her throat when she dusted them, and even then she knew he wouldn't shout if she broke the lot. He made her shiver sometimes, he was so unnatural.

Which was bitterly unfair, and yet it had its perverse element of truth. Sir Philip himself sensed it in his relations with Maureen, and cook, and almost everyone else in Ross Harbour below the level of his equals, and even with them he felt constraint so that he seemed to walk through life like a stranger, carefully polite, made more careful still by their carefulness of him. A stiff, military figure, not tall, but so spare and straight that he seemed tall enough; grey hair, trim grey moustache, old, expensive tweeds, and old, expensive, beautifully polished shoes that still looked as if there was a batman somewhere about to polish them. Almost a caricature of a retired military gentleman of ample, country means. Until one looked into his eyes and found there, instead of the expectable fierce military directness, an abstracted thoughtfulness, as if he was constantly absorbed in some scholarly problem utterly remote from his surroundings, as indeed he was. It was this remoteness which worried Maureen and everyone else who might have been inclined to look to Sir Philip for some kind of leadership.

It worried Hubert Kershaw as well, but there was no one else he could turn to. And so he brushed his moustache with his knuckle and straightened his tie while Maureen knocked on the study door.

In the study Sir Philip had already put away his pen, cursed under his breath, and prepared himself to be polite. He had promised himself three uninterrupted, perfect hours with his manuscript between lunch and drinks and he had had barely twenty minutes. Nothing would get rid of this fool in less than an hour and if it was anything of significance that had brought him it would stretch out to two, or more.

'Jolly good,' Hubert was saying as Maureen showed him in. He waited until the door closed behind him, and then, lowering his voice dramatically, allowing his look of meaningless good will to vanish, and glancing over his shoulder to make doubly certain that the maid had gone, he said, 'Have you heard?'

Sir Philip clenched his teeth. Three hours at least. He cast a longing look at the pile of manuscript pages on his desk. 'You mean about the fish?'

'Worse than that,' Hubert said. His eyes wandered round the room and his knuckle went up to his mouth again. The old fellow was so damned smug, as if he thought nothing could ever happen to *him*. Perhaps it couldn't, but they weren't all so jolly sure they were safe, not by a long chalk. 'Much worse. It's what's behind it. And old Mulcahy – you've heard about him of course?'

'No,' Sir Philip said. He sat down, suddenly interested. 'Sit down, man. What about Mulcahy?'

Hubert sat, folding himself down into the big club armchair with its leather upholstery and velvet cushions, and brass ashtray held on the fat arm by a weighted scarlet strap. He gnawed his finger. 'He's had a stroke.'

'Serve the old villain right,' Sir Philip said. 'What's that got to do with anything?'

'It was the shock. The fish. And – and the politics behind it.'

'Politics?'

'The I.R.A.,' Hubert said solemnly. 'And one of them was

out at my place just before lunch. In the bar. I tell you Philip,
I'm damn near out of my mind with worry. And that fellow of
mine, Carmody – he was talking to this chap. Having a real
confab.' He rubbed his fingers over his mouth to hide its shaking.

'How do you know he's in the I.R.A.? This other man, I
mean, the one in the bar?'

'Doyle told me. He was bringing some fish in the van, and he
saw this chap leaving and recognized him. He was at that damn
meeting they had. One of the thugs.'

'And your fellow was talking to him?'

'I tackled him about it and he said, "Oh, that was just an old
friend of mine." I didn't say anything about the I.R.A. of
course, just asked who the feller was and what he wanted.'

'I see,' Sir Philip said. He sat at the desk for a moment
longer, staring at his manuscript and the small Ming blue and
white jar that held his pipe cleaners, and then got up and went
over to the window. Behind his shaking fingers Hubert almost
smiled with satisfaction. Let him chew on that for a bit. And
yet even at that moment of minor triumph he felt his own
inadequacy and Sir Philip's effortless superiority. Even with
his back to the room Sir Philip dominated it, and not for the
first time Hubert wondered why, what it was that men like Sir
Philip had, that had been left out of his own make-up. Arrogance? Self-assurance? These things were merely descriptions,
epithets. What was the reason? A small, elderly man, in his late
sixties, with thin grey hair and a red, wind-burned face like a
farm-labourer's, and queer, vague kind of eyes. And yet where
he was was the centre.

It was a large part of Hubert's pathos that he was not, in
reality, quite the fool he looked, nor half the fool he managed to
behave like. At some moments, he could achieve an almost
complete detachment from himself as though behind the caricature 'gentleman' mask, the upward curving moustache, the
bouncing adam's apple, the carefully brushed wing of greying
black hair, the jutting nose and weak, handsome chin with its
cleft, there was quite another face, a different, sharper, classless
intelligence, wincing with pain at the mask's 1920ish postur-
ings and charades. And yet the observer was incapable of cor-
recting the observed. In any crisis, and for Hubert almost
everything was a crisis of one kind or another, he could only go
further along the known path like a runaway tram, or a dog

faced with disaster that knows only one trick. The dog may know the trick is useless, and yet panic forces him to tumble through it once more. And while his own innermost mind cringed at his folly, Hubert found himself willy nilly tumbling once more through his 'inarticulate subaltern' act for Sir Philip.

God blast him, Hubert thought, and at the same time clung to the thought of him and knew no other way to cling except by presenting his act. And indeed, by the age of forty-seven, the act had very nearly become the man. Hubert stifled the inner voice, along with his rebellious spurt of anger at Sir Philip's calmness.

It was too serious this time for things like resentment. They had to hang together or they'd bloody well hang separately. He gnawed his knuckles one by one, remembering Carmody's face, the false innocence, the big eyes. Why in hell had he even taken him on? He hadn't liked the bloody fellow from the beginning, not really, there had been something about him, a kind of cheek. Only he had to have someone.

'I haven't told Angela yet,' he said. 'No good frightening the women.' She'd be saying 'I told you so' all damn night, and wanting to throw the fellow out. And *then* the fat would be in the fire. 'M' first thought was to throw the chap out on his neck,' he said.

'Better not to,' Sir Philip said, still staring out of the window at the terrace and the park, or at least as much of them as he could see from where he stood. He saw the trees like great pagodas of chestnut, one here, one there in the wide, falling apron of green parkland, sweeping down to the grey stone wall of the boundary. And beyond the wall the haze over the roof-tops of Ross Harbour, and the broad, dark mirror of the bay. With the news that Hubert had brought he felt the scene tighten round his heart. 'Not yet, anyway. No good asking for trouble before you need to.'

'Just what I thought myself.'

Sir Philip went on staring, half unseeingly, at the trees. There had never been surety about this scene, not for any man who ever stood at this window, or any window like it in Ireland. The gun behind the hedge, the flaming torches in the night. Long before there was an I.R.A. there had never been surety, never been certainty of tomorrow. Ride out at morning, and ride home at night to find blackened ruins and women dead.

Since history began it was a blood-stained countryside. Until uncertainty of the future was bred in the bone of families like Sir Philip's, and Hubert's for the matter of that, and they rode through life with a soldier's arrogance and watchful eye, expecting violence even from men who touched their hats to them by daylight. No common interest had ever linked landlord and peasant since the Gaelic world broke down and the gentry had grown used to hatred from below and living with pistols by the bedside. For fifty years now there might have been some kind of quiet but it was uneasy quiet; a truce at best, and a truce broken by fearsome incidents. Old Admiral Charlemont shot in his dining-room in '31, in front of his wife and son. The Breakspears' place burned over their heads in '48, for nothing on earth that John Breakspear had done, but as far as anyone could tell for something his grandfather had done in the 1890s.

That was the really frightful thing about all these incidents. There was no rhyme or reason to them. Two chaps getting drunk in a pub, and remembering something that happened to one of their great-grandfathers God knew when, and the next thing was a bomb through your letter box, or your ricks on fire.

The Carmodys for instance.

'What d'you think?' Hubert said, made more nervous by the long pause in the conversation.

'They always have been a damn queer family, the Carmodys,' Sir Philip said. 'You know what Donal Carmody said to me once?'

'Donal Carmody?' Hubert said vaguely. The Ross was full of Carmodys and he had never been interested enough to disentangle them.

'Your feller's father. The roadmender chap.'

'Oh, him.'

'He said to me once, "Yerrah, your honour," he said, "if things had gone different between the Eagans and Seán Dubh, it might be me riding in that big motor car and you sitting here with the hammer and the ring breaking stones for your living. Isn't life the queer parcel to be opening?" That's what he said to me.'

'Bloody cheek.'

'Seán Dubh was hanged in seventeen seventy or thereabouts. But to hear old Donal talking about him you'd think it was last week.'

'It's a damn pity it wasn't last week.'

'And I could see in the back of his eye that some way or other he held me responsible. I was an Eagan and he was a Carmody and the feud was still there.' He leaned his forehead against the glass, seeing shadows. His old nurse, Sarah, who had first told him the story. She was a Raftery from the town but related to the Carmodys and she had told him the story one dark winter Sunday afternoon with lip-smacking relish, after extracting a dozen promises that he would never tell his father or mother that she had told him the story. Crouched on his favourite cushion by the schoolroom fire, ten years old, and already feeling that he had long outgrown Sarah, but willing to condescend, to be made to shiver pleasantly at ghost stories.

' 'tis no ghost story I'm going to be telling you Master Philip, not a ghost in it unless Seán Dubh himself walked after he was hanged down in the square below.' The old, fat, breathless woman with her white apron and her frilled cap, her voice whispering and the evening darkening beyond the windows. The fire throwing long shadows on the schoolroom walls. The shadow of Seán Dubh Ó Cearmada the poet, press-ganged into the English navy from one of the drinking dens down by the harbour.

'Such beauty on him that girls peeped out of their windows to see him pass, and he stepping in buckled shoes like a gentleman. And the Carmodys had been gentry in times gone by, chieftains they called themselves, but by that time all their grandeur was gone and your own family had put them down and well down and so had the Kershaws, until they were little better than farm people, and bitter enough about it. But Seán Dubh hadn't a care in his head for bitterness, or family feuding, or anything in the world but pretty girls and drink and poetry and singing at parties and the like. They say he had a voice that was like a lark singing, and would charm the heart out of your breast to hear him.' She took a long, anticipating breath. 'Whhhelll now—'

A long story, winding through the evening, Seán Dubh's father owning a black mare that one of the Eagan brothers wanted, and claimed for five pounds.

'That was his right, being a Protestant and the Carmodys Catholics. The Penal Laws they called them. Oh they were a fright, those times. And old Micheál Ó Cearmada wouldn't give up his mare, right or wrong, and said he would shoot the man that came for it, if he had fifty soldiers with him, for it was soldiers the Eagans threatened him with.'

Until the Eagans came for the mare, not with soldiers, but with their own people, and Micheál Ó Cearmada was as good as his word and shot George Eagan full in the breast with a fowling piece and killed him. Three minutes later he was dead himself, his body flung into the first flames licking about his farmhouse, and his wife and his small children driven out like foxes to live or die as they could. Any man or woman that sheltered them the Eagans said could look to his own house being burned. And Seán Dubh had been at sea, in one of Keppel's ships that took Belle Isle.

He got back to The Ross in 1763, to find his family vanished and the ruins of his home with weeds growing from the walls. It was then that he wrote the poem by which he is still best remembered, 'A dark curse on the Eagans'. He went and recited it in the market square, and six of the Eagans' men attacked him and beat him senseless and tied a warning round his neck that if he was not gone out of town by daybreak he'd be joining his father. Indeed, when Sir William heard he was back he was for hanging him then and there, senseless or not, and sent men to do it, only Seán Dubh was already escaped.

'It was a young girl saved him, and she lifting him out of the gutter where he was lying with the blood gushing out of his head, and she hid him safe till he could walk and then didn't she follow him out of Ross Harbour and up into the hills and he without a roof nor a table to offer her. But sure, there was never a girl cared for a sensible thing when Seán Dubh was in it, only that he'd smile at her.'

After that, seven years wandering, until the poet heard that Sir William had been killed falling from a horse on to his head, and he could come back to The Ross. And then a new quarrel breaking out, and one of the Eagan followers stabbed in a brawl in a tavern down by the harbour – the tavern was still there, still owned by a Doyle – and Seán Dubh had been hanged. He had almost escaped again, but he had been wounded in the tavern fight, and the wound had festered while he was hiding up in the folds of Slieve Clogher, and he had been taken by the redcoats.

'And his body left hanging in chains to frighten the people! Oh the terrible times those were, Master Philip, and if you breathe a word to your mother now that I told you such a story she'll have the ears from my head and you'll get no supper for listening to me.'

'And did he hang in the chains until he was a skeleton, Sarah?'

'He did not. For didn't three girls come in the night and charm the men away that were guarding the body, promising them bottles of brandy and a fine dinner and more besides that it wouldn't be proper for me to be telling you about—'

'What did they promise them, Sarah, tell me, tell me.' Pulling her skirt and apron and the ribbons of her cap until she got angry and threatened not to finish the story at all. 'Will you be good now?' 'I will, I will.' 'Well then, when the men got back in the small of the morning wasn't the body vanished away? And not a living soul in the world knew where it was gone beyond the men that took and buried it. But they say—' the old woman lowering her voice, whispering, the firelight dancing shadows on her pink apple face and her wide blue eyes full of ancient innocence – 'they say they buried him above on the mountainside standing upright in the ground with his sword beside him that he'd used to kill Diarmuid Ó Loughlinn, and a book of his own poems in his pocket, and he looking out from his grave across the Eagans' land to the bay, and the wide sea beyond. And if they did, then he's there yet.'

He had seen an engraving of him once. God knew if it was from life or the pious imagination of an amateur artist. A man with a thin white face and dark hair, and great luminous eyes. A face that thirty or forty years later would have been dubbed Byronic. Seán Dubh Ó Cearmada. Poet and patriot. And a couple of lines of Irish verse underneath, his own, presumably, or maybe someone else's written as an epitaph.

The story had stayed in his mind like an engraving itself, and when he had been older he had looked back always on that evening of the story's first telling as a kind of watershed, a turning point in his life. Until then he had thought of himself and his parents and the servants and the men who worked on the estate and their families and the people of the district as a continuity, a spreading whole, a world of which he and his mother and father were the centre and of which Ross Harbour and Slieve Clogher were the limits, with the two headlands spreading beyond and the world over the Gap of Slieve Clogher as an outer world of strangers. But that he and his mother and Sarah and his father and Mrs. Coonerty the cook and the MacDonnells down in the gatelodge and Mairtín and the gardeners and Aloysius Mulcahy who had the travelling cart selling vegetables and fish and eggs who sometimes let him ride up the hill beside him on the driving seat of the cart and say, 'Ho there, whoa' to the old grey shambling horse; that he and all these people were part of one tightknit world, that he knew and loved them and that they knew and loved him, he had never for a second doubted.

That they were 'R.C.s' and he was 'Church of Ireland', and that they went to different places on Sundays, he knew naturally enough, but it had seemed no more important than the fact that he ate in the nursery or sometimes in the dining-room, while old Sarah ate downstairs in her own little room and the cook and the maids and John the footman and the Doyle boy who did the silver and the boots ate in the kitchen and Rory MacDonnell and his wife and their children all ate in the gardener's cottage and the two under gardeners went home to their meals or brought sandwiches and ate anywhere they happened to be. All this was as natural as running about. People ate and slept and went to Church in different places according to their station in life, but none of this meant that they were really divided from one another in things that mattered.

Until he heard the story of Seán Dubh. It had sunk into his mind quite slowly. At first only a story, like something in one of Henty's books, or Rider Haggard. And then something deeper. Eagans and Carmodys. Killing one another. Hating one another. Why? A body hanging in chains. Not a fairy story body but a real man. A Carmody. One of the kitchen maids was called Carmody, Janey Carmody. He found himself looking at her with strange eyes. And for a long time he wouldn't go up the mountainside even if Mr. Mulcahy offered him a lift on the cart there and back. The body of a man buried there, standing upright, his sword beside him, staring down on the Eagan land with hatred and vengeance in his dead eyes.

He looked at his father with new bewilderment. Would he hang the kitchenmaid if he felt like it? But Seán Dubh had killed someone. An O'Loughlinn. Like Mairtín. Would Janey's big brother kill Mairtín? But nobody could want to kill Mairtín the handyman, with his whiskers and his pet rabbits and white mice in his pockets and his trousers tied up with string.

He couldn't ask his father about it at all, nor his mother, and cook knew nothing about it, and told him not to be bold and to be worrying her with fairy stories when she had the pastry to make but Mairtín told him more.

'Yerrah they was always fierce people the Carmodys, from far back. Divils for everything. Michael's father now, you know Michael the stone breaker, Janey's uncle, well, wasn't his father out with a long gun with the Fenians in '67, and 'scaped hanging by the breadth of a piece of string. Off to America with him an' didn't come back for nearly ten years till all was quiet.'

Until out of the talk of Martin and Jim MacDonnell down at the Gate lodge, and scraps and pieces from Aloysius Mulcahy riding on his cart, and even from Cook, and again from Sarah, he began to see his world with new eyes. Not a quiet, loving wholeness, but savagely divided, filled with hatred, death and violence, a world with his own kind on one side, along with the 'quiet' people, like Martin and Jim and Cook, and Sarah – people who served his family and loved them and were good and obedient to his father and mother; and on the other side, people like the Carmodys; Fenians, murderers, men with long guns behind walls and ditches, waiting to kill him.

Until even that picture of the world fell to pieces. He had been down in the kitchen, tormenting Janey to play with him or let him make a pie while Cook was asleep in her room. And she wouldn't and he had said jeeringly, although not meaning it, not even knowing he was going to say it – 'We hanged a Carmody once, did you know that Janey?' And she had turned on him with her sixteen year old face suddenly ugly, red and sweating and her hair in damp strings on her forehead as she knelt over her soapy water on the stone floor, scrubbing-brush poised like a stone in her hand. 'Sure don't I know it. And do you think any Carmody has ever forgotten it? One day you may be sorry it happened, all of you.'

Like the floor lurching under his feet. Even the 'quiet' people, the good obedient people, only seemed quiet and good, only seemed loving. He had wanted to run to Sarah and cry in her lap, and then he had remembered Sarah's face and eyes as she had told him the story. Whose side had she been on? Not his. Not the Eagan side. Whose side would Martin be on? Or Jim? Or Mr. Mulcahy? Like walking on the bog, high up on the mountain, and feeling it give under your feet. Thinking of the green bogholes, bright welcoming green where they said a man on horseback could be drowned and not the feather on top of his

hat would be visible and he down there under the green surface and only bubbles coming up to mark the place. Like looking down on the Devil's Pool that his father had taken him to see one day, far up the Ross headland, and looking down and seeing the sand shelve under the water, and then – then nothing. Blackness. The depth of the pool going straight down and down and down. No end to it, so that your heart seeemed to catch in your throat looking down at it, imagining falling in, being sucked down, black and endless.

All his safe and loving world dissolved around him.

After that, maybe the same summer, had come the war, and then two years later the distant news of the Rebellion, the dreadful Easter Rising of '16, and the talk of Shinners, and the bewilderments of a war against England. How could they fight against England? Like the Fenians. But by then he had been at school in England and a good many of the other boys called him a Shinner himself because he couldn't be whole-hearted in cursing the Irish. Coming back on holidays, never quite sure if the house might be burned before he got there. His mother and his father living in the house as if it was a fortress in enemy territory. Two of Martin's sons slipping away to join the Flying Columns. One of Tom Doyle's sons going. Talk of arms being landed in the Bay.

Until miraculously war and civil war were over and men who had been gunmen and guerillas came back smiling and telling jokes and stood at the same corners and drank in the same bars they had stood at and drank in years before. And it seemed after a while, that nothing, almost nothing had changed. Except that what had been a childhood fear had proved itself an adult reality. The long gun behind the hedge, the burning in the night, the shootings and hangings and murders for revenge of ancient hatreds, all these things were real and had come. And could come again. There was no more safety and surety to life than the green scum over the boghole.

It was a conviction that had grown into his bones like an axe head driven into the trunk of a tree and left there, to be grown over by new bark and hidden, but still there, the mark of the enemy. And now, fifty years later, an ageing man looking out from his quiet window over his quiet land, such of it as the Land Commission had left to him, there was no flicker of surprise in his mind that the threat was come again. And that a Carmody should be behind it. Or mixed in it. With fifty years

and a lifetime of other happenings, the images of that ancient story had lost their sharp edges. What remained was the feeling of insecurity, the sword hanging over his head, over the collective head of his kind.

In a way it was that constant feeling that had drawn him to the subject of his still unfinished book, unfinished after ten years of loving labour. The Fall of the Chinese Feudal Systems, in the time of the Warring States. How many Chinese noblemen, Chun Tzu of the old kind, had looked out from the windows of their mansions as he was doing, on gardens as quiet and far more beautiful than this, and known that that summer, or the next, some cavalry patrol of a Ch'in army would sweep through the district and destroy everything, mansions and gardens, culture and tradition, all that made life endurable? Automatically Sir Philip felt in his pocket for the jade finger piece that he always kept there. The small, carved green fish, smooth and cool and restful as the giver had been. Kim Suan. In the narrow Hutung in the Old City. Almost forty years ago.

'Please, Pi Li. Accept this small gift so that you may remember this day with happiness. It is a fish of good omen. Linghsiu wan sui.' Joining her hands together, bowing her head a little. Her hair cut short like a boy. In the small, dark, stuffy hole of a shop in the Lane of the Beneficent Tiger in Peking. Further down the lane they had found the body lying against the wall, stiff and bent. A beggar who had died of the cold, during the night.

'We gave him money yesterday, do you remember, Pi Li? But it must not have been enough.'

He had thought then that she was indifferent, her voice was so controlled, so flat. But there were so many dead bodies in the lanes of Peking that winter.

Behind him Hubert Kershaw cleared his throat. Sir Philip came back to the origin of his train of thought with a sense of shock. 'Sorry,' he said abruptly.

'What ought I to do?' Hubert said, his voice growing plaintive on the last word.

'Nothing,' Sir Philip said tiredly. 'Except see that your insurance is tip top. Although I doubt if they cover that kind of thing.'

'I don't suppose they do,' Hubert said, sucking a knuckle that

he had chewed too hard and had hurt. 'Damn and blast the Mulcahys,' he said. 'Them and their damn' Development. Why the devil couldn't they leave things alone?'

'You said the old chap had a stroke?'

'A couple of hours ago. I was on the 'phone to the Supermarket and they told me. It must have been fright that brought it on.'

'Poor old devil.' Big, bony hands lifting him up on to the seat of the vegetable cart. The smell of fish. The *tchock* of the gaunt old horse's hooves on the dusty road. Sunlight. It'd be difficult to find a single redeeming thing to say about the man and yet he was sorry to hear of it. The door opened and Lady Eagan put her head round the edge.

'Hullo Hubert. They told me you were here.' One of the Labradors nosed past her tweed skirt into the study and Hubert forced himself to smile encouragingly at it as he unfolded himself, rising up from the depths of the armchair like a telescope.

'Ho, Lady Meg. Just havin' a chinwag.' A kind of added silliness came over his conversation whenever he was talking to Lady Eagan as if he was endlessly trying to conform to what he imagined to be her standard of English aristocratic breeding; as if he felt that he must not only play the inarticulate, respectful subaltern to please her husband, but a half-witted one to please her, the belief remotely based perhaps on some nineteenth-century theory of drawing-room etiquette that had laid down that no lady could ever support hearing any gentleman speaking seriously about anything, except possibly romance. And in this instance he had the added purpose of showing Sir Philip that he would not for the world let any woman, let alone Lady Eagan, guess that there was any cause for alarm. Even though while he was unfolding himself, putting on his jolly, vacuous guardee expression, he knew what a spectacle he was making of himself; worse still, knew that Lady Eagan despised him for it. Yet he could not help himself.

Lady Eagan kept herself from catching her husband's eye. 'Did you hear that poor old Gombeen has just had a heart attack? Mrs. Mahoney was telling me on the 'phone. Apparently he thought the I.R.A. were going to blow him up.'

She ignored Hubert's efforts to shepherd her into the chair he had been sitting in himself and went to the window seat, where the light would be behind her. She was tall and thin with the remains of an English prettiness that had left her with faded fair hair and hollowed eyes and cheeks and overlarge teeth. But for Hubert she was neither pretty nor plain nor anything physical at all. She was calamitously the standard by which he judged his own life. Instinctively, without thinking about it, he judged the things that he himself did, or that his family did, or that happened round him, by whether or not 'Lady Eagan' would approve. Long before he had so much as met her or heard of her as an individual, he had had in his inmost mind the image of a Lady Eagan who acted as his judge and touchstone, an image compounded of Headmaster's wife and the mothers of the more aristocratic boys at school; women with angora sweaters and real pearl necklaces, whose husbands governed colonies or had large estates, or both.

'What did the Mahoney woman want?' Sir Philip was saying, trying to sound civil.

'Oh, flowers of course. What else does that woman ever want? I've a good mind just to give her the pinks. I really don't see why I should ruin the roses—'

'Oh, for this bally Fête of theirs,' Hubert said, 'theirs' referring to the Catholics. 'They were on to Angela too.'

He said it eagerly, out of ingrained habit become a reflex, trying to set up all kinds of kindred vibrations; that he and Angela were just as badgered by the Catholics for small favours as the Eagans were; that Angela was really just the same kind of woman that Lady Eagan was; that both families were cut from the same straight-grained timber. As he said it the whole pretence hung in front of his mind's eye like a line of ragged washing, old socks and underclothes with holes in them and greyish shirts. He felt himself flushing.

'And how *is* Angela?' Lady Eagan asked ritually.

'Oh, right as rain. A bit moithered trying to cope with visitors and sudden lunches and what all, but thriving.'

'And Jennifer? John and Sue ought to be home together soon. We must try and organize some kind of hooley for them.'

'Jenny'd love that.'

The line of washing flapped in his mind. Dear God why did nothing ever go right in a man's life? And he had tried so hard, so bloody hard. Even Angela. Her father had been a brigadier. He had had a gentleman's farm in Berkshire and a house in the right part of Kensington and she had been to Roedean and in the WRNS for the last part of the war; she had the right accent. And yet Lady Eagan only had to ask how she was, and he was obliged to remember all over again, his teeth clenched, that Brigadier Crampton had never been a real brigadier, only a wartime sort of chairborne type, a stockbroker with a red hatband. That his farm had been a tax-loss racket and that he had bought the Kensington house cheap during the war from a German Jew refugee who had been interned on the Isle of Man and was getting out to Mozambique.

Twenty years ago when he had first brought Angela back here, like a trophy; an English wife; the right kind of English wife with a rich father and a hard bright confidence that he thought of as 'aristocratic' with an almost sensual joy; twenty years ago when he had brought her to call on the Eagans, Lady Eagan having broken her leg hunting and being unable to pay the first welcoming visit, he had realized within five minutes that nothing was as he had thought it would be. Lady Eagan had asked pleasant questions and Angela had given pleasant answers and on the surface they were obviously going to be the jolliest of friends, never out of one another's houses. But he had known with his desperately alert antennae, like radar for disaster, that this *was* disaster. He never knew in advance. He could never sidestep social catastrophe. But he always knew within seconds that the catastrophe had happened.

'What a dreadful woman,' Angela had said on the way home. 'If *she*'s the local Queen Bee—' And his soul had twisted in pain. He had done it again. And although he would never have admitted it even under torture, he had never thought quite in the same way about his wife ever since. He admired her in many ways, he loved her even, he allowed her to organize his life. But she was not another Lady Eagan, and he had once hoped that she was. As he had once hoped that by some Protestant miracle his father's debts would translate themselves in his father's Will into gilt-edged assets which would permit him to keep on The Old House as a gentleman's estate. It had taken Angela three years from the time of his father's very nearly bankrupt death to make him face reality and, since it couldn't be profitably sold, at least turn the house into a Hotel. And the unadmitted reason that had stiffened his resistance most was the fear of what the Eagans, of what Lady Eagan, would think.

The same fear had plunged him into an indignant rejection of Alloway, Barnacle and Truett's offer to negotiate for his land two months ago. He had not even been tempted. Gentlemen didn't sell their homes, even if their homes were now unprofitable hotels. He had brought the letter hot-foot to Sir Philip to tell him about it, to explode about the damned cheek of these solicitor chappies, and to tell him that never in a thousand years would he sell an inch of his land for any figure on earth. And had known even as he was saying it that Sir Philip was hearing him with something between amusement and derision. He had thought then as he had thought many times, that there was something – something not quite *there* about Sir Philip. All the damn Chinese books he was always reading, and the frightful history thing he was writing. He sometimes *looked* Chinese. It was a real agony of mind to Hubert to feel, to know even, that the things, the values he held dearest, were far less important to Sir Philip than they were to him. And yet the very reason that Hubert held them dear was because they were Sir Philip's values, the values of men like Sir Philip. It was so complicated that he sometimes felt like chucking everything; like an ardent courtier forced to realize that his king has no real belief in monarchy. To stop kneeling and bowing and crying, 'God save the King,' and become a bloody Republican.

'You must have some coffee,' Lady Eagan said, without making any visible effort to send for it.

'No. No, no thanks,' Hubert said, flushing again and for a second time making unfolding motions that indicated how determined he was not to allow Lady Eagan to put herself to the least trouble. 'Just leavin', Lady Meg. Just – well, I er–' He went on unfolding and stammering, balancing a need to have more reassurance that he was doing the right thing about Michael Carmody by doing nothing, against a determination not to appear ready to upset Lady Eagan with rough men's talk about danger. The fact that Lady Eagan already knew everything there was to know had nothing to do with it. It was a principle. He looked beseechingly at Sir Philip, willing him to come to the rescue, either by accompanying Hubert to the front door out of Lady Eagan's hearing, or by reopening the subject himself.

'Well, if you have to go, my dear chap,' Sir Philip said.

It was Lady Eagan who saw him to the door. He shook hands with her, miserably aware that his hand was damp. 'You must drop down and see us more often y'know. Can't think how long it is since you and Angela had a get-together.'

'I know, isn't it awful of me?' Lady Eagan said. 'Angela must think I'm a complete hermit. When John and Sue come I must bring them down to one of your ballad sessions. Such a wonderful idea.'

'Yes – I mean – would you? That'd be marvellous,' Hubert said with increased unhappiness. He stood awkwardly, casting about for the correct degree of respectful jolliness. Lady Eagan watched him, satire hidden in the shadows of her rather sunken eyes.

'Well,' she said helpfully, at last, 'see you tomorrow for the D-Bs send off?' And then, anxiously, 'Angela *is* coming, isn't she?'

'Oh yes, rather,' Hubert said. Lady Eagan smiled with relief. Hubert smiled as if his upper lip had a twitch. He shook hands too heartily and said, 'Well, what ho,' and flung himself into the Bentley. The battleship engine coughed and roared into life.

The faulty exhaust shot one of the Labradors amidships, sending it cowering for cover, the tyres turned, crunched the gravel, spat stones as he swung the wheel, accelerating, and he at once grew powerful and devil-may-care on the high leather seat. With one hand he twisted his pink Leander scarf round his thin, long neck, crash-changed upwards, and sped away, cavalier, knight, eternal horseman. Lady Eagan put one hand to her forehead protestingly at the noise, comforted the Labrador, and went round to the walled flower garden to think about flowers for the Catholic Fête.

In his study Sir Philip was thinking about Michael Carmody. He wouldn't have recognized the boy if he had seen him in the streets of Ross Harbour. And yet it was as though he knew him, as though instantly, hearing his name, he had recognized it as the name of his destroyer. It was curious. He had spent the best of his adult life as a soldier and had never been consciously afraid of anything. Yet now? No. He was not afraid now. Sorry. Sad. He had gone back to his desk automatically, not thinking of what he was doing, as if that was the best place to be at critical moments. He picked up the thin bronze mirror that he used as a paperweight and looked into its green surface, the patina so smoothly, beautifully green that it was like a disk of spinach-jade. It was of the third century B.C., from Shou Hsien in the country of Wu, and he had sometimes imagined that he could see a great deal that was hidden in its smooth and enigmatic surface. It had been almost the first thing of true value that he had bought in China. Professor Khoo had found it for him, and then helped him to bargain for it.

'It is our vice,' the Professor had said, with his smile that seemed to contain within it layer upon layer of irony. 'Nothing in China is as it seems, not even the price of an object in a shop.'

Afterwards he had invited the young soldier in civilian clothes to come to his house. 'The friend of my brother is already a member of my family,' he had said. And there had been the house, a few rooms and two courtyards, very simple and rather poor because the Professor was no longer a Professor after the purges of the Universities in Peking; nothing more than a provincial schoolmaster and only by courtesy still called 'Professor'. And there had been Madame Khoo. And there had been Kim Suan, the Professor's youngest daughter.

'My brother has been indiscreet,' Lieutenant Khoo had said in Shanghai. 'But for your purposes of gathering information and forming an opinion of what is happening in China he may be helpful to you. And also the Communists are not a great distance from Changsha.' He had made the last statement as though it had nothing at all to do with his brother. Perhaps it had not.

And as far as Lieutenant Eagan of the British Military Mission in Shanghai was concerned, it was of no importance at all whether Professor Khoo was a Communist. All that he had wanted had been information. Not the 'official' information distributed by the spokesmen of the Kuomintang. Nor the 'inside gossip' of the Europeans safely isolated in their Concessions. But real information, of what was really happening, going to happen; what the Chinese themselves were thinking; of the Japanese, or the Communists, of Chiang Kai Shek, of the foreigners. That was why he was in China. That was why he went to Changsha.

'But I'm simply an observer,' he would say long after that first meeting with her, when she had become angry with him for looking at China with dispassionate eyes.

'You are a landlord,' she had said. 'How could you care what happens to poor people?' It had given him a strange sense of shock to think that that was how she thought of him, saw him. A landlord! And he felt so unlike a landlord that it seemed ridiculous and at the same time hurtful, as if she had just made an unkind joke. But that first day she had seemed much too timid, too courteous to quarrel with him, even if there had been anything to quarrel about with her father's guest.

'I am Third Daughter,' she had said, not looking at him. Looking down at the ground, in the garden.

There had been nothing distinguished about that garden, nothing. A few willow trees, a few flowers, some water, a painted wooden bridge with a roof, a stone dragon. He had asked her if she was still at school and she had looked at him for the first time. Her face like ivory; eyebrows, eyes, the line of her hair brushed on to the ivory with charcoal, with the blackest ink; a look of stilled quietness, and he had realized that she was not timid at all. He had sensed even then the strength in her, her certainty.

'I am soon to study at the University of Peking,' she said. 'I begin the next term.'

He had shown her the bronze mirror and she had held it for a moment in her hands, as more than twenty-two centuries earlier its first owner must have held it.

'It is very beautiful,' she had said politely. And these past years, when he did not so much as know what had happened to her, where she was, whether she was still alive, it was that moment of her that he remembered. Not their time as lovers. Nor of separation. Nor the last time in Canton. None of those times. But this first meeting. As if in his remembering he wanted to think only of a moment when everything had still been possible, when every choice had been open. Although even then there had really been no choices open except the one that he had made.

'You are a landlord, Pi Li. How could you care what happens to poor people?'

He had tried to say, 'I care what happens to you.' He had said it, and she had shaken her head without answering, as though it was not possible that he should care for her if he did not care for all the things that she cared for. And yet she had permitted him to love her. Had loved him. He tilted the small round mirror in his fingers, as if he hoped to catch in it a reflection of her face.

Love? It was a strange thing. He had not known that he loved her. The word 'love' has so many meanings. Had she loved him? She must have done. She would not have given herself to him if she had not. He thought of the hotel, the enormous carved bed, the white silk hangings, the black and crimson lacquer. As though they were making love on a throne of dragons. It had been the next morning that she bought him the small jade finger piece, the carved fish with its omen of 'Ten Thousand Years'. Life, Happiness. All fortunate things. And the beggar lying dead, bent with cold against the grey brick wall.

'I must be getting old,' he thought angrily. But he went on looking in the green surface of the mirror, seeing the past. As though it would save him from seeing the future. A future of being driven out of this place, this house, forced to sell up the last of his land so that there could be factories built on it. Or burned out of it by Michael Carmody and his friends. Where would he go? Dublin? London? To a strange house. An old man walking in unfamiliar streets, waiting for – what? Nothing. Nothing.

'Why couldn't they have waited?' he thought. 'At least have let me die here in peace.' To be buried beside his father, his mother, all the Eagans who had died in Ireland.

'Why are you here if you do not care what happens to China?'

'It's not that I don't care,' he had said, trying to explain. 'But I'm an observer, simply an observer. I can't allow myself to care in the way you want me to.' He had guessed by then that she was a Communist, that she was working among the students in the University. And that too he had to observe. In Shanghai they were interested in knowing what the students were thinking, what they were doing.

'Oh my poor Pi Li,' she had said at last. 'I do not think you know how terrible a thing that is to say of oneself. That one is only an observer. Why is one alive, if not to act? Are you no more than that mirror that you brought when you were with my father, reflecting what passes before your eyes? Why do you think you were put into this world?'

'You don't understand.'

'Even in your own land you have told me, you do not act, you do not take part. What will become of you, Pi Li?'

What had become of him? All his life observing. Why not? What more could a cultivated man do in times like these? What could any of his kind do? What part had there been left for him to play?

No more than for the man of old family of the feudal age, sitting among his trees, his manuscripts, hearing that the soldiers of Ch'in were approaching, destroying all in their path. What could that Chun Tzu have done? What act would have been worthwhile?

A time comes when the world changes, when old values are no longer held. Then for the man who still holds them, there is nothing to do but wait with dignity for the end. But she would never have accepted that. Was she pleased now with the China that she had helped to bring into being? He wondered what she would have thought of Michael Carmody, and it was like receiving a wound.

CHAPTER EIGHT

THE news of the emptying of the fishponds and of old Aloysius Mulcahy's stroke reached last of all the Bishop's Palace. It was brought on the wheels of the King Gallagher's scrap-cart, iron banging, brass glinting, pots rattling, the piebald pony with his shaggy coat trotting between the shafts as if he knew that on this call above all others the King's dignity must be upheld. The cart swung and swayed up the rutted drive that was no better than a farm track and crashed to a stop. The half-bred Alsatian sitting beside his master eyed the chickens with a hungry lick of his lip, and then looked at the King as much as to say, 'God between me and harming a feather of their blessed bodies and they belonging to Holy Church.'

'Whoa dere,' the King cried, and to the dog, 'Stay there you shcoundrel.' He threw the reins down on the pony's back and heaved himself off the seat. He was a broad, stocky man with bowed legs and a royal face, carved out of teak, nose jutting, eyebrows black and heavy over glittering brown eyes, a man as sure of his role in life as the Bishop of his. More certain, for no intellectual or spiritual doubts had ever troubled the King.

Matilda Carmody came out of the front door in a red rage. 'Will you take that old cart out of here this instance? What for do you think you're leaving it there in the front door? Is it a parish priest you think you are? And himself too soft to say a word to you. Get yourself round to the back.'

'Arrah whisht, child, don't be vexing me. Tell himself that the King is here, and with news, terrible news faith that will startle His Honour out of his standing.'

'His Grace, you villain, you. GRACE. GRACE.'

'Grace or Honour, Honour or Grace, damn the bit of difference it makes to himself.'

She had half turned away, flouncing her skirt. 'What news?' she said, turning back.

'News for His Honour, you sthrap. 'tis your mother forgot

114

the better end of your education and that's for certain. It isn't people live in houses always have the knowledge of how to rear children.'

'Don't you dare speak of my mother.'

'Will I go into the old gentleman myself then, and tell him I'm here?'

But the old gentleman had heard them and had come out. He had been reading a book, or had thought that he was reading a book although all that he had truly been doing was to stare at a page and remember the last time he had read it. From which his mind had drifted to other things. He came totteringly, his hand on an ivory handled stick, his black slippers shuffling in the chicken dirt of the stone hallway, his clothes greenish-black, small whitish stains on the purple of his vest where he had spilled his hot bread and milk.

'Yourself, King.'

'God save Your Honour.' The King knelt with a quick flourish to kiss the beautiful topaz in the heavy gold ring on the old, leaf-thin hand.

'Grace, Grace, Your Grace,' Matilda hissed from the background like a furious goose, or gosling, for she was only sixteen.

'Calamity on you girl, get back to your business,' the King whispered in a voice pitched below the old Bishop's threshold of hearing. And louder, 'Is Your Honour for a step in the air, seeing the fine day that's in it? I've brought a bit of news up with me from below.'

The old man felt to see if his shawl was round his shoulders, but already Matilda had gone to fetch it, grumbling as she went. ' "Your Honour," he says! The dirty tinker.'

She came back with the black shawl, knitted by the Sisters of the Crucifixion with pious, loving hands, and laid it on the old man's pointed bones of shoulders and patted it round his chest. 'Not a moment over five minutes, now, or not so long.'

When she was out of earshot the King paused solemnly in his steps, turned to face the Bishop and said, ' 'tis murder and destruction come below. Isn't every fish in the Norway men's little ponds let out into the sea by rebels? And isn't the Gombeen struck by a stroke in his heart and he lying paralysed in his own bed, like a stick. The terror of the rebels was on him so that he couldn't breathe nor move, and the stroke up and struck him like you'd fell a bullock with a hammer.'

The Bishop said nothing, his lips alone moving a little as if he was testing an unfamiliar flavour in his bread and milk. 'Rebels?' he said at last, gazing out over the blue distance of his bishopric, that God had entrusted to him. 'Rebels?'

'Aye,' said the King, who had hoped to learn himself what kind of rebels they might be. It had been the Fish Doyle who told him the news, as cart and van passed one another on the road below, and he hadn't liked to ask the Fish, and reveal ignorance. 'Aye,' he said again. 'Terrible men with guns.'

'God between us and evil,' the Bishop whispered. He put his leaf-hand to his heart, barely protected as it was by the thinness of his bones. 'And the Gombeen, you say? He's not dead?'

'Divil a bit dead that one,' the King said, on surer ground than with the rebels. 'Lying in his bed like he'd be drunk to the world on whiskey, parlatic with it and just his two eyes moving in his head, this way and that way, like his soul trying to escape out of his skull.'

'The Lord save us,' said the Bishop. 'May God treat him gently.'

'And he in need of it I'll tell you. There's not many will cry tears when the Devil takes him in the end.'

'God has more charity than men,' the Bishop said, not bothering to contradict the King. He crossed himself. Rebels? All the world seemed in a rebellion. Why should this small corner escape? He looked into the milky haze as half an hour before he had looked at the page of his book, not seeing anything truly, but remembering. The fold of each hill, each valley of the mountains, the curves of the white roads, the long headlands sleeping like the paws of a lion stretched out on a marble floor. And his heart filled with such wounded love for his countryside and people that it was like a spearhead in his side, turning against bone. He had heard echoes of coming changes and had heard them like warnings, like the croak of the Morrigan the night before battle. All the innocence that he had loved and guarded, the souls for which he must account to the Saviour of Mankind. 'What do you have to tell me of my sheep, son John?' And the bronze and silver voices of the angels crying out like trumpets, 'Bishop John, what answer for Our King?'

'I have loved them,' was the only answer that he would have to offer. Would it be enough? If he could lay his heart between this countryside and the wheels of change.

'You are a good and simple man,' he said to the King Gallagher, 'and you mean well. But you must not judge as the world judges if you wish to escape judgment. Pray for the Gombeen. He needs your prayers, and I will pray for him too.'

'Yerrah was it not full in my mind to be saying a Rosary for him this night?' the King said, whose actual mind had already advanced to other matters. 'And didn't I haste up to you so that you'd be puttin' in the Holy word for him as quick as possible in case he slipped away on himself between this and nightfall?' The King screwed up his bright eyes at the afternoon sky as if watching for the Gombeen's escaping soul.

'But,' he said thoughtfully, 'wouldn't it put you in thought of the chanciness of life and the sudden things that do be happening?'

'It would indeed,' the Bishop said, crossing himself again.

'And there's none of us would like to be taken off and we leaving unfinished business behind us.'

The Bishop looked at him sideways, sensing the drift of the King's thoughts.

'Now take yourself, Your Honour,' the King said. 'And that bit of a stachy you have back there in the barn. Wouldn't it be a great wrong to all to leave it there for the like of that sthrap of a girl to be dealing with and you – God between Your Honour and every harm but even a Bishop is mortal flesh, God protect Your Honour – wouldn't it be the Devil's own joy and she showing that stachy to the world and telling them you had it hid on them since the time it disappeared? Wouldn't it now? And I with a fistful of money to give you for it. Think of the great charities you could be leaving behind you with the money, and what is the statue but only old metal and no good to God nor man? That girl would be giving it to the first traveller that passed the door, maybe the Knocker Connolly or some feller from Cork that wouldn't give her half its value and she only a child.'

He said all this in a smooth rush, just as he had said much the same speech fifty times before. It woke him in the night, sometimes, to think of the painful waste of that great lump of bronze, the best of a ton of it, hidden away in the Bishop's disused stable, hidden under bales of mouldy hay and broken carts and God knew what. And the price of bronze up beyond in Dublin, a right *tom tul* he'd get for it, *nus a Dhalyon misli.*

'King, King,' the Bishop said in a piteous voice. 'Don't be

tormenting me.' He could see, as if it had happened this past hour, Pat Carmody's eyes the day the statue disappeared. He had not seen such depths of pain in a man's eyes in all his priesthood. And yet he had been right to have it taken away, to have it stolen – no, not stolen, for how can one steal from God *for* God? Not stolen but only taken, taken into safety, taken to protect the souls of men who might be led astray by that work of – what? Could the devil have portrayed Christ in any way at all, even like that? And if not the Devil, had it been God who moved the sculptor's hand? For what end? For what end? That Face. He had not looked on it for thirty years and it still burned in his soul.

'Do not torment your friend,' he whispered to the King. They had grown true friends since the Bishop had become old, as if his increasing gentleness and self-questionings needed the King's strength and certainties. From the house came Matilda's scream:

' 'tis five minutes and more than five minutes! D'you want to be killing His Grace? His GRACE I say, d'you want to be murdering him? Bring him back here this minute! I'll tell Father Cooney when he comes up, I will so. BRING HIM BACK HERE!'

'Jasus,' the King said, 'if she was mine I'd sthrike her.'

But the Bishop had not heard her. He allowed the King to turn him round and lead him back to the Palace.

'Ye'll have to decide what ye'll do,' the King said urgently, feeling death in the thinness of the Bishop's arm. ' 'tis unreasonable to be leaving it there any longer, and all them bar yourself that cared one way or the other about it buried and dead. What harm would you be doing any living creature and you selling it to me? I'd get the Whisperer and his big lorry and a sheer-legs, and my sons and the Whisperer and me would have it away from you in a flea's hop and the weight would be off your mind for ever.'

'No, no, no,' the old man begged.

'And we'd have it carved up nice and easy and not a soul would recognize a bit of it, and the Black Men themselves wouldn't get it out of us where the bits came from.' In his urgency he shook the Bishop's arm like a stick and the old man stumbled.

'What are you at, you big villain?' Matilda shrieked. 'Is it for killing him you are? Give him here to me. God and the Saints protect him from heathens like you and he the age he is. Come away in Your Grace and have your tea and you get out of it with your dirty cart and your dog and your old horse, you thief.'

'Arragh Jasus,' the King said, to the closing door. 'The Seven Curses of God on that child. DON'T BE FORGETTING WHAT I SAID NOW!' he shouted. 'I'LL BE BACK UP IN A DAY OR SO.' The door closed with a slam. A chicken shot out from under it in fear of its life and the pony stamped its feathery feet, raising the dust of the drive. The Alsatian yawned. 'Giddap, giddap you divil,' the King cried, swinging the horse and cart about to ride to another corner of his kingdom.

CHAPTER NINE

PATRICK CARMODY'S 'lost' statue of Christ the Sufferer, Christ Crucified, had been first commissioned in the 1920s by a pious Committee to which the young Gombeen himself had belonged, and the Committee had dreamed of setting it up on the quayside of Ross Harbour as an indication of the holiness and purity of the town. It would have had, in a discreet place on the back of the pedestal, a bronze plaque with the names of the Committee set down in handsome lettering, followed by a request to passers by to Pray for their Families and Intentions. On the front would have been the names of those townspeople who had given their lives in the Struggle for Independence.

The project had not been without its opponents, some on political grounds, because they belonged to the Opposition of the day and wanted a quite different list of names on the front of the pedestal; some on moral grounds, because they knew that Pat Carmody was badly lapsed from his religious duties and drank too much into the bargain; some on basely practical grounds, claiming that if the town was to spend money on anything it should be on something like a Public Convenience which was badly needed on market days and the lack of which led to scandalous exhibitions; and some on aesthetic grounds, that what was needed was not a little small ordinary statue on the side of the Harbour, but a grand tremendous statue like the one at the entrance to New York Harbour, with a lamp in its hand and a staircase inside for visitors, and it should be out on Lir Head. This faction was very small, consisting solely, in fact, of the family that happened to own a suitable piece of land in that place which they would have been willing to sell to the Committee for a modest consideration.

But all these objectors together had been no more than a minority, and the Commission had been given to Patrick Carmody, who had begun his working life in a stonemason's yard in Belcorrig, cutting the letters on gravestones, and had graduated through the carving of angels to a London foundry that cast bronze statues for sculptors, to pre-World War One Paris and a modest reputation as a follower of the great Rodin. He never made much money in Paris, but he never starved, and it was on a holiday visit of his to Ross Harbour in the early 1920s that the idea of a statue on the Harbour site was born. The Committee was born soon afterwards. Two years and many Committee meetings later, both site and artist and size and cost of statue were agreed on. Pat Carmody was asked to submit sketches and if possible a model.

The original idea had been an angel. She would have had many meanings for the town and district. An Angel of Victory and Peace and Death for the tragic heroes commemorated on the pedestal. An Angel of Welcome for homecoming fishermen. An Angel of Protection for those leaving the Harbour's safety. An Angel of Purity casting her benign influence on the entire population.

But as soon as Patrick Carmody's first sketches began to arrive, it struck the horrified Committee members like a revelation that Angels are not only feminine in ordinary grammatical thought. They are *physically* feminine. Patrick Carmody's Angels had bosoms, clearly defined under the drapery.

'It won't do,' Henry Carney the Chemist had said indignantly. 'It would be putting bad thoughts into the heads of every young person that was frequenting the Harbour.'

'I never did like the idea of that man,' Walter Doyle the Fishmonger said. 'Why can't we just order a nice saint from Dublin? We could have St. Patrick, or St. Finbarr, cast in cement—'

But Father Thomas Culhane, then curate to Father Pusey, and Father Pusey himself, together with most of the Committee, clung to the idea of something more exceptional than a cement statue the like of what any village in the country might have at its cross-roads, and they had sent back a request for a male angel, St. Michael, say. But when sketches of St. Michael came back, killing the Serpentine Devil, someone – possibly Aloysius Mulcahy, youngest but most politically alert of the Committee – pointed out that this might easily be confused with St. George and the Dragon, with all that *that* implied. And so St. Michael, and with him all ideas of Angels of either sex, was abandoned, and the Committee gradually came to the conclusion, over many acrimonious meetings, that after all tradition was the best guide, and they should content themselves with either a Saint, or Our Lady, or a Crucifix, or Christ the King.

No two members of the Committee could agree on the same saint, and Our Lady was feminine and Patrick Carmody evidently was too carnally minded to be trusted with the portrayal of Sacred femininity (this was never spelled out in words during Committee meetings, the whole subject being too delicate for overt expression. It was absorbed and digested by means of nods and expressive frowns and dwellings on the word 'Lady' – 'Our *Lady*' – the *peculiar* temperamentality of artists, don't you know? until Father Culhane settled the matter briskly by saying that everyone would agree that Paris wasn't a place to be having statues of Our Lady made, was it? No, of course it wasn't). As to Christ the King, Aloysius, exalted by his triumph over St. Michael/St. George, simply said that they hadn't been giving their blood and lives a few years before to get rid of King George, to be bringing back the idea of Kings in the shape of a stachy on the Harbour wall.

This brought such a storm of abuse, accusations of blasphemy, reminders of the time when he was selling stachies of Our Lord for a Jew man, and threats of fisticuffs, that all meetings of the Committee had to be suspended for several months and factions developed in the town between the followers of Christ the King and those who owed Aloysius Mulcahy money, or hoped to owe him money, or to get a job from him, or sell something to him. Until Father Pusey summoned a further meeting of the Committee at which he announced that he had consulted with the Bishop and the Bishop had decided that in view of all the circumstances what the town needed was a nice Crucifix. The Bishop had no doubt, and he, Father Pusey, shared His Grace's certainty, knowing as he did the obedient and loyal hearts of his parishioners – obedient and loyal, he hastened to say, not to him, unworthy shepherd that he was (cries of No! No!) but to His Grace, and to Our Holy Father the Pope, and Mother Church – (Hear hear!) – that everyone present would agree—

A contrite Committee voted unanimously for a Crucifix. It had spent four and a half years and fifty-one meetings reaching this decision, but once it had been reached, all concerned felt that they could relax. Even the influence of Paris could not turn a Crucifix into anything but a Crucifix, and within a year or whatever time it took, Ross Harbour would be the enchanted possessor of a real work of religious art; not just a cement statue, but a bronze Calvary. People would come from far and wide to see it. It would be in the papers. Mention might even be made of it in Dail Eireann and Maynooth. Future ages seeing it would know that in 1928 no common type of man had sat on the Special Committee of the Parish of St. Finbarr in Ross Harbour. Dublin might have its Senator W. B. Yeats and his old coins. Ross Harbour had Bishop Mulvaney and Father Pusey and Father Culhane, and Mr. Walter Doyle and Mr. Henry Carney and Mr. Aloysius Mulcahy and a dozen others of equal sense and sensibility and religious integrity. If the furious quarrels of the past four and a half years had left their smouldering enmities, they smouldered beneath a surface of pious content in work well done.

The year of expectation went by. More money was requested by Patrick Carmody, and it was, with no more than normal difficulty, collected and sent to Patrick Carmody's Paris bank account.

A second year went by during which two further requests for money were received and ignored. Father Pusey dictated, and Father Culhane wrote out in his Maynooth copperplate, a stiffly courteous letter saying how eager the entire parish – the entire Parish AND the Bishop – were to see the physical realization of all their hopes. Sketches came back which caused Father Pusey some stirrings of alarm. A further Parochial letter was sent to Paris with requests for clarification of certain details. This was in its turn ignored by Patrick Carmody who in fact had left Paris with a Spanish woman for a prolonged bout of lechery in the south. This ended with severe dysentery after eating a dish of Moules Marinière, the Spanish woman left him to go to the then unspoiled beaches of Majorca with a Uruguayan painter, and it was a debilitated and bankrupt Patrick Carmody who limped and hitch-hiked back to Paris in the chill autumn of 1930.

He was a small, twisted, hunchback of a man, with big hands and a big head that was thrust down and forward by the lift of his left shoulder; the runt of a Ross litter who had been put to work in a stone quarry because he was not big enough to work on the roads. And from the stone quarry, as has been said, to the Belcorrig stonemason, to London, and to Paris. His reputation had reached its modest peak about 1912, when he had won a prize in a competition for a monument to honour Joan of Arc.

It was the echoes of this small triumph that, reaching Ross Harbour ten and eleven years later, had prepared the way for the great Commission.

But at that moment in 1930, his money spent, his health ruined, his crippled body feeling every one of its fifty-three years twice over, nothing seemed less likely than that the Commission would ever be completed. And yet it was. Slowly, between drinking bouts, and interrupted by one last splendid fling with a voluptuous Russian Jewess who believed in God and Art and Giving, the Crucifix took shape. He borrowed, begged, cajoled; bombarded Father Pusey and the Committee with letters that swung between furious denunciation and winning blandishments, and now and then managed to wring another thirty or fifty pound money order out of them, although at longer and longer intervals.

In 1934, faced with one more 'final' beseechment for money to pay a vital debt for materials which, if unpaid, would lead to the loss of all the work done to date, the Committee decided that nothing but a personal inspection by a delegate of the Committee would meet the case. So much money had already been spent, so many expectations had already been roused, that it was not possible simply to cut their losses.

It was thought at first that Father Pusey was the obvious person to go. Chairman of the Committee, a man who had already travelled, having been to Lourdes twice with invalids, not to speak of Dublin, Maynooth, Knock, Croagh Patrick and Liverpool; conversant with foreign languages such as Latin and Greek; trained in Theology and with long experience of Judging Art from having lived with Church Statuary since his youth, he seemed designed by Fate to be their delegate. But he was eighty-four, and stone deaf, and much troubled with arthritis, and some felt that the rigours of the journey and foreign ways and food might be too much for him.

Father Culhane was the clear second choice, but here a matter of some delicacy obtruded. Father Culhane was only thirty-two years old. And Paris was Paris. It was not to be thought that Father Culhane would succumb to temptation. But it was equally clearly not right that a young and innocent curate should be submitted to it. Much deliberation went into the ways and means of avoiding the choice of Father Culhane without referring to this particular difficulty.

At last it was decided that the delegates should be chosen by

Lot, and since it was clearly improper that a Priest of God should take part in a Lottery, Father Culhane would not be involved, except to draw the tickets out of Henry Walsh's black hat.

The Lot fell on Aloysius Mulcahy. Patrick Carmody was told of the visitation, and in due time and with some ceremony Aloysius set off, with a new suit and a new suitcase, and several scapulars to protect him from foreign evils.

News of the visit threw Patrick Carmody into despair. He had several times sold his necessary supply of metal in order to buy drink or pay for something more immediately necessary, like a woman. The rent of the cellar where he worked and lived was eleven months in arrears and his landlord was threatening to evict him. The clay model of the Crucifix was almost finished, and there was absolutely nothing that could be put before this terrible delegate of the Committee which would show him cause why more money should be sent before the Crucifix could be cast. Worse still, it now occurred to the unhappy sculptor that the Crucifix bore almost no relation to the sketches he had long ago sent to the Committee in the first flush of mutual enthusiasm.

There was no trace in the almost finished work of art of the conventional Christ on the Cross to which Ross Harbour was happily if impatiently looking forward. No trace of the head of the sorrowing Madonna and consolatory St. John who were supposed to figure at its foot. No gleam of that Divine Message of Hope and Victory over Death which the tranquil Saviour had been supposed to show in His quietly patient face and decently disposed limbs. What stared back from the squat and ugly Tree of Execution was the face and body of Patrick Carmody, tortured by lust and unfulfilled desires, by a crippled back and weak and aching legs, by a bad stomach and a worse conscience, and beyond all, by that agony of the artist that cries out for wasted years, for ruined talents, for that glimpse of Eternal God that could never be translated into stone or bronze. What looked back at Patrick Carmody in that dark, damp, unhealthy cellar was the face of despair. He fell on to his knees and leaned his big forehead on to the clay feet of his work. Oh Christ forgive me, he wept in his drunkenness. Send me to Hell. And then, because he was drunk, he passed out.

It was in that exact situation that Aloysius, carrying his fibre suitcase and wearing his practically bullet-proof Irish overcoat, found the sculptor. He was deeply impressed. A handsome young woman of the quarter had guided him down the street to the correct house, and with that casual friendliness which no doubt was common in foreign parts she had come down the cellar steps with him to make sure he was not lost in the last moments of his search.

'Voilà, Monsieur Patrice!' she said, returning to Aloysius the luggage label on one side of which was written his own name and home address, and on the other, Patrick Carmody's. Seeing that Monsieur Patrice didn't stir from the foot of the Cross she went and shook him awake.

'I'm dying,' Patrick croaked. 'Get me some Calvados. Anything.'

'Is he ill?' Aloysius asked nervously, and on it being made clear to him that money was urgently needed to prevent death, he very reluctantly took out his purse. At home nothing on earth, not ranks of artists dying at his feet would have made him allow a woman to stick her fingers into the very heart and soul of his being, but here, abroad, with the sounds and sights and smells – most especially the smells – of Paris surrounding him, the rules of life seemed suspended, all logic and reason banished and he let her rummage for a full two seconds before common sense triumphed and he looked to see what she was taking. What she showed him was a franc piece, having already safely palmed two ten franc notes, at that period enough for a substantial blind.

She was a more or less honest whore who had a fondness for Monsieur Patrice and she spent at least half the money on a kind of Calvados that was only about fifty per cent adulterated with wood alcohol. She also, because she was hungry, bought bread and sausage and pickled herrings and two bottles of Algerian red wine, and came back with her shopping to find Monsieur Patrice lying on the floor groaning, and the ugly stranger walking up and down in his overcoat reciting prayers.

An hour later they were all on the floor. Two days later again Aloysius came to something approaching his senses, lying on a flock mattress in the whore's attic, indescribable sensations churning in his stomach, his head chiming like Big Ben on the radio, and an unbelievable taste in his mouth. There were a lot of empty bottles around, a number of fish heads, some wooden boxes, and a cat. The cat looked at him with hatred, threatening him with ripped eyeballs if he tried to take the fish heads.

Nothing was further from his mind. What he wanted was water, buckets of cold water to put out the fire that seemed to have been burning in his stomach for weeks. He saw a cretonne curtain sagging from nails in the sloping ceiling, and thought he might find a washstand behind it with a jug of water. What he found was the whore, locked naked in the hearty arms of a porter from Les Halles, both of them soundly drunk and asleep.

In horror Aloysius clapped his hands to his eyes to shut out that vision of entwined bodies, brawny legs and snowy buttocks, and staggered back to realize that he himself was naked. Stark. A piece of broken mirror fastened by nails to the wall showed him a sight that he scarcely dared to look at in his monthly bath in the kitchen (he had not yet moved into the big Victorian house on Knuckle Street, with its real bath and splendid Victorian geyser, although he already owned it). But although his nakedness was unfamiliar to him it had a wastedness, a strickenness that seemed to him even less familiar, as though his poor body had been through hard times since he last laid eyes on it.

'Sacred Heart of Jesus have Mercy on us,' he whispered. 'What have I been doing?' He looked at the mattress on the floor, the cat, the bottles, the fish heads, his clothes heaped in a corner. What he had been doing might not be obvious but the possibilities were frightening. He pushed tottering legs into his trousers, felt for his purse. It was as flaccid as himself. Empty. ROBBED!

Jacket? Jacket pocket? Overcoat pocket? Both jacket and overcoat had disappeared, sold in fact to provide brandy for the porter, who was Mademoiselle Honoré's regular.

'My money!' cried Gombeen in despair. 'My new overcoat!' Little did he realize how lucky he was to have his trousers. A girl of less conscience than Honoré would have left him in his drawers, and not on a spare mattress in her room either, but in some distant gutter.

He went in to shake her awake, averting his eyes as he did so. His fingers touched a warm shoulder and shuddered, some faint memory of the last days and nights being stirred by the contact. Had he? Of course he hadn't. Drugged and robbed. Kidnapped. The word 'murdered' sprang of itself into his mind. In foreign parts people, travellers, were always being murdered for their money. He looked at the porter's sleeping face. A murderer's

face a dozen times over, flushed with lust and drink and atheism, bulging with flesh and muscle, he was obviously a man
who would not only not think twice about assassinating a kidnapped stranger, he would enjoy it.

Never had Aloysius regretted anything so ferociously as he
regretted having voted against having the Statue represent St.
Michael. What he needed now was not the gentle protection of
Our Lady, or the probably overworked attention of Our Lord,
but that of a saint usd to tight corners and hard fighting, such as
St. Michael himself, armed with a large sword.

He left off shaking Mamselle Honoré's slightly sweaty, but
beautifully modelled shoulder, averted his eyes not quite
quickly enough from a bare bosom and coral pink nipple nes-
tling in the black hairs of the porter's rhythmically heaving
chest, and stole back to his corner on stockinged feet to look for
his boots. Gone too.

Nothing but Yiddish learned from Moishe Gavron could
meet the case and for a long minute he stood cursing with the
richest stream of ghetto blasphemy that had ever startled the
musty rafters of any attic in that quarter of Paris. Until, head
bursting, stomach queasing, feet tiptoeing unsurely on splin-
tered, filthy floorboards, he crept out of the room and down the
endless flights of stairs to find himself in the slightly more
familiar hallway above Patrick Carmody's cellar.

Patrick, having no mattress, was stretched on the floor. He
showed some surprise at seeing Aloysius leaning over him,
dressed in a dirty vest and trousers and shaking with rage. He
had forgotten who Aloysius was and it was some time before
they came to an understanding. When they did, Patrick Carmody advised Aloysius to bid his overcoat and his jacket
and his boots and his shirt and the contents of his purse good-
bye. The *flics* might indeed arrest Mamselle Honoré. They had
often done so before. But that wouldn't get back Aloysius's
clothes or money, and how would he explain to the Committee
at home how he had ever become involved with the lady?

'I was kidnapped,' cried Aloysius.

'Do you think Father Pusey will believe that? Or Father
Culhane? Or Mr. Walsh? Or the Bishop?'

Aloysius did not answer. He did not need to.

'On top of which,' said Patrick, 'that porter is a very bad-
tempered man, and he would not care for being deprived of her
company for the period of the case.'

'Again there was little need for Aloysius to say anything. It was too clear that that might well be so.

'But how can I go home without my money?' he shouted furiously after a further moment's pained thought. The shout did terrible things to the inside of his head and he clutched it hastily.

'You'd better have a drink,' Patrick said kindly, offering the dregs in the bottom of a bottle of Calvados.

'Water,' Aloysius whispered. 'Water.'

Patrick went and filled the bottle from the tap in the yard and brought it back. Even diluted it was powerful stuff and it made Aloysius feel slightly better, if only for the moment.

'What you must do,' Patrick said, who was used to roughly similar situations, 'is to send for more money.'

'But how can I explain—?'

'There's no need to,' Patrick said. 'Send for it for me.'

'For you?' screamed Aloysius, and then, 'Oh my head!'

'For me,' said Patrick. 'Then we'll split what comes.'

It took no time at all for this suggestion to penetrate Aloysius's wounded brain, and not much more for him to accept it. There was really no other course open. And so, after scraping sous from here and there so that they could obtain another bottle of Calvados to heal the effects of the last dozen bottles, they wrote out a telegram to the distant Committee. 'Overwhelmed by beauty of Crucifix. One hundred pounds urgently needed for furnace. Work at crisis point delay disastrous. Remaining to oversee completion. A. Mulcahy.'

'How will we pay for sending it?' whimpered Aloysius, most of whose mercantile genius had evaporated in the air of Paris and the Calvados hangover.

'We'll get an advance from Honoré out of the money she knocked off from you,' Patrick said. And so they did. The money came, accompanied by furious instructions to A. Mulcahy to see the spending of it himself; it was split; and Aloysius tottered home, trying to blot from his fevered mind the memory of a passionate farewell kiss from Mamselle Honoré. No sooner did the pure sea airs of the Channel blow over his prematurely balding head than he knew with religious certainty that none of the past seven days had happened. It was all a nightmare brought on by foreign food and French atheism. It would not even be necessary to confess any of it since it had not really happened. He hesitated about that last kiss for a quarter of an hour's Examination of Conscience, but since he had neither invited it, nor been an active partner in it, nor had he admitted to enjoying it, nor taken sensual nor mental pleasure in it at the time or afterwards, he thought that it would be unnecessary to confess even that. He felt better already, and as for his share of the hundred pounds, it was no more and in fact much less than was due to him. As to what would happen when the Committee discovered that the casting had still not taken place, let that bridge be crossed when they all came to it. No one would be more surprised than he. In fact, why should it not take place? Patrick Carmody had fifty pounds. No question at all but one could buy a great deal of scrap metal for fifty pounds in a place like Paris, where old motor cars, broken machinery and burned-out saucepans could surely be bought for next to nothing. No doubt but that the casting was at that very moment going ahead.

And so he informed the Committee.

Eight months later, in answer to a fourth, furious and menacing letter from Father Culhane on behalf of Father Pusey and the Bishop, threatening excommunication and legal action like a right and left from a shotgun, one barrel marked Heavenly and the other Temporal, a pained postcard came back saying that cooling a statue took a long time if the perfection of detail was not to suffer. A week later, a further postcard said that because of imprudent haste inspired by the Committee's cruel and undeserved threats, the entire casting had been ruined. It was the winter of 1935.

At this, the Committee did not so much acknowledge defeat as tacitly accept it. Father Pusey retired to bed, and not long afterwards to a pleasant and sunny Home for Retired Clergy. A new Parish Priest was appointed. The Committee wrote to its subscribers telling them as much of the tragic story as it was thought proper to tell, asking their forgiveness and announcing a General Meeting at which subscribers might express their thoughts and wishes. But since the Meeting was to take place in Ross Harbour on the fourth Wednesday from the date of the letter, and most of the subscribers lived in America, being emigrants there from the town or district, there was a thin attendance, and those who were there, faced with the choice of subscribing further funds to take legal action against Patrick Carmody (Mr. Aloysius Mulcahy spoke very strongly against this course of action, the *South Munster Gazette* reported, showing true Christian charity and a deep understanding of the artistic temperament, as well as the wide knowledge of the world and the pitfalls of going to law in foreign places that one would expect from Mr. Mulcahy); faced with the choice of paying in more, or writing off what they had already subscribed, the Meeting almost unanimously decided to call it a day. The only objector was a man who turned out to be drunk and not even a subscriber. He was ejected, and the motion that the Committee be absolved from all further responsibility in the matter and therewith dissolved as a Committee was declared passed nem con.

And then, miraculously, in the spring of 1939, word arrived on expensive notepaper with a crested envelope addressed to Father Pusey that the Crucifix was ready. A second, equally expensive-looking letter to Mr. Aloysius Mulcahy, Ross Harbour, The Ross, Ireland, explained what had happened. Patrick Carmody had fallen in with a Portuguese Princess. She was not really Portuguese, being American by birth, and perhaps not strictly a Princess, her husband's family having been by some malice left out of the Almanac de Gotha, but she was very, very rich, and she loved Art and she was crazy about Artists, and she had installed Patrick Carmody in a Château on the Loire, one of several that she owned for similar charitable purposes, and commanded him to do some Art. He had done the Crucifix. It stood now on the terrace of the Château ready to be transported to Ireland. And even the transport would cost the Committee nothing. The Princess, with her mind on Papal recognition of her title, was willing to pay all costs, provided only that the Bishop would meet her and himself unveil the Crucifix in her presence, and afterwards convey to Rome the delight of Catholic Ireland at the artistic generosity of the lady who by every religious and philanthropic test had an undoubted right to call herself a Princess.

The Committee was hastily reconstituted, Bishop Mulvaney was approached and his agreement in principle secured, a letter of congratulation mixed with only the gentlest note of fond re-proof was sent to Patrick Carmody Esq., c/o Her Highness at the Château, the long neglected and overgrown site on the quayside was cleaned and once more prepared, and everyone waited with breathless piety for the work of Art and Faith that would distinguish Ross Harbour as it deserved to be distinguished.

Three months went by (during which the poor Princess had to pursue the errant Patrick Carmody to Malaga and have him dried out in a Spanish Sanatorium) and just as the Committee at its third monthly meeting was beginning to say Aha, and start fresh quarrels, further word arrived, this time from the Princess herself. She and the Crucifix, Patrick Carmody and her chauffeur, her lady's maid, her hairdresser, her masseur, her secretary (male), and her bodyguard (also male), would be arriving in Ross Harbour on August 29th at about four o'clock in the afternoon. She would appreciate it if the ceremony could be scheduled for midday the following day, preceded by an open air High Mass with choir. The Committee need not trouble itself about providing her with a Throne, as she was bringing her own, and would be delighted to present it after the ceremony to the dear Bishop for his own future use. All she would need would be simple accommodation for the night. A suite of five or six rooms for herself; smaller suites for Patrick Carmody and her secretary; large and pleasant bedrooms with bathrooms for the hairdresser and the masseur; and plain bedrooms for the chauffeur and the lady's maid, naturally not adjoining one another. If her own suite contained a private chapel so much the better, but she realized she was travelling to a delightfully simple country town and she would quite understand the absence of a real chapel. An ordinary room set out as a chapel and consecrated in advance by His Grace would do. She was bringing several seventeenth-century Prie-Dieux of her own and the Committee could spare themselves the trouble of finding any if none were immediately to hand. She would expect Benediction at four thirty, Vespers at seven, and would be ready to make her (and her staff's) confession after dinner, at say ten o'clock. The Bishop would be welcome to join her at dinner. The Parish Clergy and the Committee would be equally welcome to join the party after dinner for coffee.

As might be imagined this letter, arriving on the 27th, caused the Committee some anxiety. Glennon's Hotel, then the only hotel in the district, let alone the town, was full of Commercials and it took the combined efforts of the Clergy and Mr. Glennon himself (at that time still happily alive), aided by the commercial pressures of individual members of the Committee, to clear them out. They went eventually, threatening never to return, and the Committee and Father Culhane and Mr Glennon were left with thirty-six hours in which to do whatever might be done to reshape Glennon's Hotel to the exacting requirements of the Princess.

Since it was only eleven or twelve years since the whole hotel had been tastefully repainted in chocolate and green, inside and out, there were not many fears on that score. But the suites? The rooms with baths? There were only three bedrooms in the hotel. A chapel?

In the event the first floor in its entirety was declared the Royal Suite, and the Commercial Lounge was declared the Chapel. Since the Bishop declined to consecrate it even for a Princess the religious aspect had to be taken care of by Holy Pictures and Statues borrowed from the Committee Members' own homes. Rows of Bernadettes, Little Flowers, Infants of Prague, Sacred Hearts, Our Lady of Sorrows, Takings down from the Cross, St. Patrick, St. Finbarr, St. Laurence O'Toole, St. Brigid, and the Christmas Crib out of the Parish Church's storeroom, surrounded and interspersed with lilies, paper flowers, wax fruit, coloured candles, and several crucifixes, contrived an atmosphere that was almost overpoweringly religious. But as Mr. Carney wisely said, 'Ye can't have too much Holiness.'

And when the Princess arrived, if nothing was quite as she expected or had requested, she was too good natured to make a great fuss about it. Since she had brought her own Renaissance Four Poster bed Glennon's best double bed and real hair mattress were not put to any royal test. And since she had also brought her own food, and drinkables and intimate necessities, including large supplies of bottled water in which to wash her silk underwear (carefully labelled in green as opposed to the purple labels on the bottles of Jordan Water for her portable Holy Water Stoup), no great extra strain was placed on the Glennon's kitchen.

In fact, almost nothing went wrong.

Except the Crucifix. It arrived, accompanied by eight workmen hired in Waterford, on a large lorry, carefully and totally swathed in sacking, and by nine o'clock that evening it had been placed on its waiting concrete pedestal, Father Culhane and Patrick Carmody supervising the operation. And then, Patrick offered the good Father a preview.

An hour and a half later Father Culhane was closeted with the Bishop, His Grace having just finished the hearing of Her Highness's confession, which somehow managed to contain one or two allusions to her future requirements, vis à vis the Vatican, and recognition of her title.

'I think that Your Grace should see it at once,' Father Culhane said, forgetting protocol and the niceties of phrasing such suggestions in his anxiety. 'Far be it from me – but – no judge of art – a poor curate unversed – no doubt a well-intentioned – I have not said a word to the man Carmody – no – not to anyone – the only word that one could charitably apply would be startling—'

Bishop John Mulvaney, at that time a vigorous and forthright prelate approaching sixty, went to see for himself. For once he totally and unreservedly agreed with Father Culhane. The thing was monstrous. Incredible. Blasphemy. It would corrupt the Parish. It would bring a curse on the district. It must be taken away at once and destroyed, or at least removed from all contact with simple and susceptible members of his flock. But how? If the Princess had not been involved. If the newspapers had not been advised. If the whole Parish had not been agog with expectation.

There was only one answer. The Crucifix must be stolen during the night. By? Even that problem was not long in being solved by that strong mind. By the tinkers. Father Culhane was despatched on his bicycle to find the Gallaghers and their allies. Eight of them, with a strong cart and three hardy horses, were rounded up from the boreens between Ross Harbour and the Gap, promised money, whiskey and a Full Dispensation, and told what they had to do. By three in the morning they had done it. With the help of a sheer-legs and much sweating brawn, the Crucifix was loaded on to the creaking cart and the horses, with muffled hooves and whispered urgings (the whispers from the mother of the Whisperer now practising) the whole cortege moved out of the little town like shadows. Its goal was the Bishop's Palace, where the Crucifix would be temporarily stored and hidden until the Bishop might consider what should best be done with it.

It's easy enough to imagine the general consternation the following morning. Who ran here, who there. The Princess told. The Committee bewildered, furious, incredulous. Patrick Carmody demented. Father Culhane blandly astonished. (In his superb assistance to the Church and his Bishop in that small crisis, Father Culhane removed all doubts about obstacles to his succeeding in due time as parish priest of Ross Harbour.)

The Princess, who was five feet tall and rather stout – in fact an unkind observer of her arrival had described her as 'like a pat of butter in a fur coat' – the Princess threatened to have a heart attack. The Bishop, under guise of concern for her health, had private words with her, in which he explained under oath of secrecy what had happened. What had had to happen, my dear lady. But rest assured, my child, Holy Church and Our Lord are concerned not with the imperfect fruits of our actions and intentions, but with those intentions themselves, and those alone. The world judges the act. The Church judges the heart, and that only with Charity and Love and utmost Compassion.

From fury, the Princess descended to grudging acceptance, to obedience, to humility, as became a simple Catholic girl from Montana, and as even more became a Princess whose late husband had (almost) royal blood, brought down the ladder of wounded pride rung after rung by the Bishop's exquisite tact and holy understanding. The Bishop made discreet suggestions about the expense to which she had been put, coupled with even more discreet and loving reproofs at her impetuousness in setting off with a statue which no competent person had seen or approved.

'But your Mr. Mulcahy!'

'Ah yes,' the Bishop sighed. 'Our Mr. Mulcahy.'

But in the upshot the Princess most graciously waived all claim against the impoverished and now doubly deluded parishioners. As for Mr. Carmody, Patrick Carmody Sculptor, she did not wish to see him or hear his name spoken again. By three o'clock that afternoon Her Highness's entourage, repacked into three Rolls-Royces and a van for the luggage, had left for Cobh and the next suitable ship for the United States.

Patrick Carmody, who had found two bottles of whiskey unattended, woke to find himself bereft of patroness, masterpiece, means of subsistence, or even the wherewithal to pay for the whiskey. The Bishop discreetly arranged for the whiskey and one or two other small items like bottles of brandy the previous night to be paid for (the Princess having had them struck out of her own bill in a fit of moral indignation) – and summoned Patrick to the Palace. The Bishop fully expected the interview to follow much the same course as that followed by his talk with the Princess. High rage leading gently down to low humility and obedient acceptance, a pattern that interviews between laymen and bishops in Ireland often follow. And this one ran true to form to about the half-way mark. Rage, shouting, curses (these last unusual, but much is forgiven to artists), and then quietness.

But it seemed to the Bishop a strange, and rather terrible quietness; this hunchback with the big head and the bloodshot eyes and trembling hands. His coat stained with drink and spew, his hair jagg'd sideways and everyways like a bush in a gale.

'My soul is in that Cross,' Patrick whispered.

'May God forgive you for it, my son.'

'What do you know about Christ?'

The Bishop did not answer. But after a pause the Bishop said again, as he had said earlier when Patrick was not really prepared to listen: 'The work is a blasphemy. If it was shown to untried minds it would do them great harm. Perhaps this is the measure of your art. I cannot judge that. I judge it as a work of Catholic truth, and this it is not. It is a lie. God could not seem like that. It would not be right that any simple heart should be led to believe that He might. Patrick, whatever your faith now you were brought up in this parish as a child of Holy Church, obedient to Her wishes. The Church does not wish that – that statue to be shown. And it now belongs to the Church. The Church, through Her instrument, the Committee of this parish, has paid for it. Do you deny that?'

'You paid for it to be put up in a public place.'

'Lawyers might argue many ways, my son. But we are not lawyers. Do you deny my rights in this – work?'

'I deny any man's right to take it away from its rightful place.'

'I want more than that, Patrick, my child. I want it to be destroyed.'

'NO!' Patrick screamed.

'It must be destroyed, my child. Give me your consent. Although I do not believe that any court would consider your consent to be necessary.'

'I will never consent.'

'Then I must do what I think right.'

They looked at each other, Bishop and hunchback artist, both much of an age, but the Bishop smooth in flesh as a man of good conscience deserves to be, poor Patrick tortured by ill-living, by long periods of hunger and even longer periods of excess, by nights spent sleeping on stone floors in damp cellars. Patrick knew that in any contest between the two of them he must inevitably lose.

'Please,' he whispered.

The Bishop sighed.

Patrick looked down at his hands that had made the Crucifix, and that would never make much else that would be of account on Judgment Day. 'I will give you the Crucifix,' he said at last. 'It is not important that it is mine. Or my work. Or even that it contains my soul. What is important is that it is the true image of God and of mankind. God and man, suffering one agony in one flesh. When you go to destroy it, think of that. Look at it carefully.' He hardly knew why he had said the words, or even what he had said.

'I will give you some money for your journey,' the Bishop said.

'I do not need it,' Patrick answered. 'I have reached the end of my journey. Only let me see my work once more. We could look at it together.'

They went out to the stable and looked at it. Patrick touched the bronze. 'I know more about Crucifixion than you do,' he said. 'Much more.' He took a last look at his own face on the Cross and went away, but the Bishop remained there for a long time. And he did not destroy the Crucifix. He had it carefully hidden and boarded up and for the next thirty years it was to grow greater in his dreams until it seemed to lie on his breast at night and he would have given a great deal never to have heard of it or seen it or had it in his unwilling possession. While Patrick Carmody took to the roads like a tramp.

Now and then houses took him in for pity or cousinship or so that he might repair a kitchen table or a stone wall. Sometimes he slept in ditches or a tinker's tent, sometimes in the cell of the police barracks in the town for being found drunk and incapable and without visible means of support. A few times he went to gaol. But in his wildest bouts he never spoke about the Crucifix. He kept that inside him like a private wound that would gain nothing by exposure except shame. Other people spoke to him about it, because for years it was a famous story, how the Ross Harbour Crucifix had disappeared the night before its unveiling. The most incredible stories circulated – how it had been made of gold and the Germans had stolen it. How it was in America. How it was in the Harbour. Some people even knew that the Bishop had it, and this few included naturally enough the Gallaghers and their allies of the night of the Disappearance. But to all queries and invitations Patrick Carmody turned a closed face and an unhearing ear.

' 'tis all past and gone,' he said. And yet now and then, out of old habit, he carved something, or moulded a head out of clay. One time, when Hubert Kershaw's father allowed him to sleep for a few nights in the stables of The Old House he carved a crucifix, in what he thought might be an acceptable style, forgetting that the Kershaws were Protestants. And since Hubert's mother was at that time thinking of teaching pottery-making to the ladies of Ross Harbour (she was a woman of sudden and rather unstable enthusiasms), Patrick Carmody showed her something about handling clay. In the course of it he modelled two or three heads, of herself, of old Mr. Kershaw, and of a servant girl, and even cast them in plaster which Mrs. Kershaw obtained for him. He himself disappeared soon afterwards on another of his journeys about the south, and it must have been not long after that that he died, in the winter of '44, of exposure and malnutrition and advanced cirrhosis of the liver. He was found in a ditch somewhere north of Belcorrig.

For years the three heads he had made and the crucifix he had carved for the Kershaws remained about the place, as curiosities. Until first one and then another of the heads got broken and the maid's head was tumbled into a corner of the storeroom. The crucifix was nailed up in one of the stable lofts by a pious stable hand who found it lying on the storeroom floor. And that was the end of the artistic career of the local boy who had once made good, winning a competition for a monument to Joan of Arc, in – was it 1911, or 1912? Art is a hard career.

CHAPTER TEN

THE Public Bar of The Old House began to fill up by nine o'clock and Jennifer came in from the kitchen to help Michael serving. Pints of draught mostly, with thick, creamy heads, and stone cool from the cellars.

'What's the matter?' Jennifer whispered.

'Nothing,' Michael said. But his face contradicted him. He served people without looking at them, without laughing or answering their jokes and when Jennifer tried to stand beside him so that they could talk he moved away to the end of the bar and made himself inaccessible, crouching to open a case of lager, or going down into the cellar for something, disappearing through the trap behind the counter. Until in the end when there was a minute's lull in the ordering she followed him down the ladder. The cellar was huge and low and musty dark, smelling of age and mould, with pillars like a Cathedral crypt and shadows vanishing away into black arches. He was standing by an untapped barrel doing nothing, merely standing there with his face to the dark.

He often stood like that, for minutes at a time, as if he was lost, and if they had been above, in the Hotel itself, she would have turned away and left him because the way his face looked at those times frightened her, made her feel suddenly childish and inadequate, and that he could never belong to her. Even down here she was afraid that he would turn on her, humiliate her. But she touched his arm. 'Michael,' she said, 'is it me? Have I done something?'

He looked round at her as if he was coming back from a long distance away and she was a stranger. It was this that frightened her, this sense that the boy she knew was not real, was only a mask over someone else, and that sometimes she was talking to the empty mask; that the real person had gone. And when he came back he had forgotten who she was. And of all the things in the world that she wanted, the one she wanted most was someone who knew who she was. Not her father's imaginary Jennikins, not her mother's inefficient cook-parlourmaid who was also a shameful social disappointment, not Kershaw, J., Captain of Netball and House Prefect, Miss Beal's 'really reliable girl'. None of those imaginary, invented Jennifers. Someone who knew her and accepted her for what she really was. She wanted to say, 'Don't look at me like that, don't hurt me.' And she knew that all he was seeing was his employer's daughter playing games in the cellar. He was going to say something so cruel and filled with misunderstanding that they would never be able to look at each other again.

'Please,' she said.

But he hadn't been going to say anything. He saw her face in front of him in the yellowish, misty, mote-filled light falling from the open trap above her head, and tried not to see it, not to let it touch him, not to let her become real. He had been making up his mind to go away. All afternoon and early evening he had felt things closing on him. Nothing rational. Only a premonition. A kind of shadow. Seagrun's stupid talk, and then Mr. Kershaw, and finally Sergeant McMenamin coming out to the hotel and sniffing all round him like a mournful foxhound in a wood. And all the while the thought of Jenny, like a warmth. But he daren't let it warm him.

'I want to go away,' he said. He had meant to say, 'I'm going away.' What had stopped him?

She put out her hands very quickly, feeling her chest tighten as if someone had caught a loop of rope round her ribs and was twisting it like a garrotte. 'No,' she said. All their talk seemed to be jerky sentences that never told what they meant. He saw her face beginning to break, the smooth, childish face that was still a schoolgirl's.

'I'll do you harm if I stay.' He tried to make the sound of his voice tell her what he felt. And simply by trying he made it worse for himself and still told her nothing.

'You won't. What's wrong?' She had her two hands on his arms. A voice shouted from above, 'Where's the barman? Where's Michael, damn you Michael, we're dying of thirst!'

'Promise me you won't go.'

'I can't.' Her face was so close to him that he had to shut his eyes to prevent himself from kissing her, and if he kissed her he was lost, lost for ever.

He tried to move towards the ladder and she held him.

'MICHAEL!'

'Your father'll hear.' Like a man escaping. And yet from what? Why did he have to escape?

'I don't care,' she said. 'Please—'

She saw again that strange expression in his eyes as if he was not seeing her, was looking at something, someone else, at nothing. But not at her. As if she was not there, had never reached him with any word she had said. Like a raft floating away from her in the sea and she was drowning. There were a thousand, a million things she wanted to tell him, explain to him. That she was alone and lost and afraid in the dark and wanting someone to – to – to talk to – hold her by the hand, make her feel not afraid. Not love, not sex. All right, a little love, kiss her, make her feel like a – like someone that was wanted, loved; touch her skin, stroke her, like a cat. Anything. He could believe anything he liked, only not to go away, not push her off as if she was last night's left over. Listen to me, listen, hear me. If he left her now, this second, she would die.

But he had put her hands away from his arms and was already at the ladder. She watched him going, her face stiff as though it was frost-bitten, numb with cold. Up the ladder. Head gone. Dark, beautiful head. As if she would never see it again, never come up from this cellar. How much better if she didn't, never came up. The light came down, misty yellow, unbroken by his shadow. Shout of people, calling for pints, for songs. She stood still, holding her misery like a doll to her breast, her arms close against her body where he had put them. She could feel the print of his fingers on her wrists.

She turned round and leaned her forehead against the stone of the heavy, outspreading pillar, cold and mildewed. She used to play down here as a child, climbing down the ladder with a shiver of terror in her throat, her legs shaking. The room above just a junk room then, the tower, filled with bits of harness and broken furniture and trunks and boxes and bundles of news-papers and magazines.

The years stretched back like a tunnel, opening suddenly on a golden time of childhood, before she had been sent away to school, when her grandfather was the most important person in the world, and grandmother; and she had walked out on to the grass lawns like a Princess in a story. And this cellar had been part of the same story. Like the threat that hangs over

Princesses' heads and that at some hidden moment will strike them with a terrible reckoning.

She had been afraid of it then and forced herself to go down into it against her fear, the terror. Ghosts and skeletons and the sounds of chains creaking.

She moved away from the pillar, going deeper into the shadows. There was a light now but she didn't switch it on. So long as no one called her, not Michael, not daddy. Just stay down here. The light faded behind her. Suppose he forgot she was down here and closed the trap? It didn't matter. Better if he did. A bottle rolled in front of her foot as she kicked it. Something scurried. The smell of damp and mould grew stronger and the arch of the stone vault lowered over her head, brought the darkness thicker round her. She put out her hand and found the low archway into the further cellars. All this was part of the old castle. From the time of the Fitzwalters who, although she did not know it, had taken this part of the Head of Ross from the Carmodys, almost eight hundred years ago, and built a square stone tower on the site of the Carmody Dun. Two hundred years later they in their turn had been driven out by the Eagans. No one knew how far the cellars extended. Further in stone had fallen, blocking another archway. No one ever came here. Her father said the vault was dangerous and could collapse any time, just someone talking could make it collapse. He was always meaning to get the vault shored up.

'Michael,' she said aloud. Her voice seemed to come back to her from the walls, distorted. 'MICHAEL!' Nothing happened. She remembered hiding down here once, when Susan Eagan and her brother John were coming to tea. Susan six years older and patronizing and clever and 'so good at managing Jenny. Sometimes I don't understand that child at all. Such a secretive little thing. We'll have to send her to boarding school I'm afraid.'

She had thought that Susan was going to take her away to boarding school that same day, after tea, and she had hidden down here until it was dark outside and it would be too late to take her. She had never told them where she had been, even though she was sent to bed early every night for a week. 'I'm absolutely in despair about her. She looks at me in such an odd way sometimes, just like a little grown up.' And, 'Boarding school for you, my girl, that'll make her into a proper child.'

This was the place. Sitting here hour after hour, playing with the head. She knelt down on the rough stone and felt in the dust. It was still there. Only shrunk, grown small. She picked it up between her hands and fondled it. She had brought it down with her from the junk room up above, the first time she came. Damp and cold. Poor head. Perhaps it was only that she had grown. She used to talk to it. A woman's, a girl's head, the mouth open, as if she was saying something, or singing, or shouting. She had called her Deirdre. Once she had told her mother that she would never go to boarding school, that Deirdre would save her, they would run away together, and live somewhere where there were no schools, where no one had to learn anything.

'Who is Deirdre?'

'She's a lady. She sings.'

She had never explained that either. She held the head in her hands and wept for her own childhood. A voice shouted, 'Jenny, Jenny, where are you?' His voice. And she thought for a fantastic second that he had come down again, that he was looking for her. She put the head down where it had lain for the past how many years and almost ran back the way she had come, holding her hands out to protect her face.

'Can you look after the bar? They want me to sing a bit.' His head leaning forward, his face framed in the yellow light like a halo. Trying to sound as he had always sounded. She went up the ladder and he reached down his hand to help her. She looked at him, begging him to say something, that it was not true, that he'd stay. He only smiled, his mouth stiff, as if there was nothing to say, nothing to contradict.

'Miss Jenny herself!'

'Venus out of the waves!'

'Three pints of draught stout.'

The Public Bar had been least touched by her mother, and perhaps was no worse for that. The stone walls of the tower had been whitewashed, and draped with fishing nets and coils of old rope slung from rough wooden pegs, driven between the stones. Long benches, a few tables made out of rough timber by a local carpenter, the bar itself made by the same carpenter out of planks from the deck of a wrecked fishing boat, still with a smell of tar and fishscales hanging about it, mixed now with spilled porter. Hanging lanterns from the same fishing boat, and her port and starboard lamps, gave what light there was for thirty or forty people, all with glasses in their hands, all talking, shouting to each other, shouting to Michael for a song, for a different song, to Jenny for more drinks. It was the only part of the Hotel that had ever succeeded. And they were not only what Angela Kershaw called 'local people', which included in her mind anyone from Ross Harbour as well as from the farms, outside of the Eagans. People came from as far away as Belcorrig. Strangers and tourists came, hearing in Glennon's or Hardy's or anywhere that there was great singing and crack at The Old House of a Friday night. In the last few weeks, since Michael had begun the ballad singing, the Public Bar had almost threatened to become profitable, and support the Hotel.

She drew the pints, one after the other, foam rising, slopping, spilling into the zinc trays, smell of porter like a fog, more voices shouting. Then everyone calling 'Ssssss, he's going to sing.' 'Let the man be heard, will you?' as Michael climbed on to an old Guinness barrel, cradling his guitar across his knees, head bent to listen for the key as he tuned a string.

'Give us The Holy Ground!'

'Spanish Lady!'

'Holy Ground!'

'The Boys of Wexford!'

'The Bold Fenian Men!'

'HOLY GROUND! HOLY GROUND!'

He began singing and the room hushed. He had a voice that seemed at that time no better than a hundred ballad voices and he played no better than he needed to play to give himself accompaniment. And yet they listened to him in a different way, once he began, once he caught hold of them. She stood very still behind the counter, a cloth in her hand that she had been using to mop up spilled beer. He sang very low and softly, so that a few people talking could have drowned his voice. And for that reason no one talked, everyone sat or stood as if they were afraid to move, afraid to rustle so much as their sleeves. He was singing *The Castle of Dromore*, the northern lullaby.

'Take time to thrive, my Rose of Hope,
In the garden of Dromore,
Take heed young Eagle – till your wings,
Are weathered fit to soar;
A little time and then our land,
Is full of things to do.
Sing hushaby, lul, lul, lo, lo, lan,
Sing hushaby, lul, lul, loo.'

His voice soft as the nurse's voice as she lulled the small infant Prince O'Donnell; his face bent over the strings as if the guitar were a child, his own small child, and he sang as though the words were coming to him fresh that moment, as if only then he had thought of them, to tell what was inside him, that no other words could say. It may be that this was the secret of his hold on an audience. That he always sang as though he was discovering something. And perhaps he was, particularly then. Perhaps there in those Friday ballad sessions he was already discovering himself, his reason for existence, that hidden self inside him that he had been blindly searching for. And although they could not know what they were listening to his audiences were already held by the promise of what he would one day become. Already, out of the most banal words, out of the most clichéd song he could bring welling up a pure spring of sweet, cool yet faintly stinging water, like a pure champagne, so that even the notes of the guitar seemed charged with meaning, with a strange, bewildering freshness. His shadow moved and curved on the whitewashed wall; there was mystery, and yet the promise of a solution to every mystery, until the people listening thought that they knew much more than they did, that the world was wonderful and that they were on the very brink of understanding it, had understood it, grasped its inmost meaning and were filled with happiness, a kind of drunkenness of the spirit, and while they listened they loved. Loved what? The world, each other, the singer, the foolish song, the fact of being alive.

Only Jennifer listened to him with a sharp pain of unhappiness, and the deeper his singing touched her the worse the pain. He would never love her. And she stopped still behind the bar as though her muscles had suddenly become cramped with agony. Love? Love him? Not just loneliness? Looking for a friend? He was going away. She knew it in that second with total certainty. He would go away. She would never see him again and it would be like having a piece of flesh torn out of her body. How could it have happened? Until yesterday it had been a game she had been playing. Even last night. And now ... She bent over the bar as though literally she had a cramp, trying not to hear his voice. She was mad. He doesn't love me, she thought, and I love him, and those simple statements seemed so profound, to pierce so deep into the heart of things, that tears came into her eyes. His voice reached her, very low, whispering, caressing, touched her skin like a physical sensation. The fine, soft hairs at the narrow nape of her neck lifted and the skin felt cold. 'Michael,' her mind whispered. 'Be kind to me.'

Someone called for 'Scarborough Fair' and he sang them that, and they began calling for new songs, or what Ross Harbour thought was new. 'A New World in the Morning'. 'Love is Blue'. After half an hour or so they wanted songs for which they could sing the choruses, and the tower filled with noise until her head was bursting. And she could think of nothing except the immediate moment, the work, the pain in her head, in her feet. Five pints. Seven pints and three Jamesons. Four halves and three full ones. A visitor wanting gin and tonic. Club orange. Harp. Two Smithwicks and a Beamish. Four pints. She seemed to have been soaked in porter, to her elbows, to her knees. Smoked and soaked and wrung out, her feet hurting until they burned like raw flesh on coals and she kicked off her shoes and deliberately poured slops over her feet to cool them. People kept asking her to have one, one on me, one on us, one on us, Miss Jenny. She had a pint of porter and a Club lemon and a gin and orange lined up on the shelf under the counter and she took alternate sips to clear her head and make her feel less miserable. Her father and mother were in the Copper Room, with the 'regulars'. Colonel Mace who had the fishing lodge on the far side of the Head, and Mrs. Mace, and a houseguest; and the Sandersons, and someone else, she hadn't seen who it was, and the American woman who rented a cottage half-way along the Head, and the American woman's 'friend'. They both worked in television. They'd all be in the Copper Room listening to the natives. She thought of them with a sudden, even sharper hatred.

'That's my chap singing. Not a bad voice, eh? People come from miles away to hear him. Extraordinary, isn't it? But you see there's absolutely nothing to do in a place like this. People are simply starved for a bit of entertainment.'

Of course, her father didn't need to explain that any more to the regulars. They just sat and listened and felt they were eavesdropping on the real Ireland and would tell their friends about it. This *remote* place. And this *lovely* hotel. At least, that was what her mother and father hoped they would say. And *superb* meals.

'I'll run away,' she thought. 'If he goes—' She imagined following him, watching him go into the dark. She'd climb out and down and follow him softly, very silent, up the road to the Gap. And he'd lie under a bush to sleep for a few hours and she'd come close and watch over him, watch his face as he slept.

As though they were trying to steal him from her, and at the same time to destroy him, make little of him, like a possession, like a dog that did tricks. And for a second she saw that he was right to want to go, that he had to go. Except . . . She imagined following him, watching him go into the dark carrying his rucksack and the guitar slung over his back like a troubadour. Watching him from the window and climbing down to follow him. Following softly, like a shadow, very quiet, so that he would never hear her, up the road to the Gap in the darkness, under the stars. And when he lay down under a bush to sleep she'd—

'Sing "Lagan Love",' she whispered. He was looking down at her from where he was squatting cross-legged on the barrel top, but he didn't really see her, didn't hear her. He began to sing 'The Boys of Wexford'. They all joined in the chorus, ragged and noisy, then together. It was time, and past time. Her father was trying to catch her eye through the doorway that connected the Public Bar with the Copper Room. She caught Michael's eye in turn and he brought the verse to an end and lifted up the guitar to show that the evening was finished. But no one wanted it to be finished. It always took half an hour to clear the bar on Friday nights. And then another hour to clear up the glasses, sweep the cigarette ends. She was already so tired that she could have slept where she stood, leaning against the counter.

'Miss Jennifer Kershaw, of The Old House, The Ross, at the Horse Show.' Her picture had been in the *Irish Times* last year, and there had been another one, rather small, in *Social and Personal*, with two other girls, standing by the judging ring. Mummy had left both the paper and the magazine lying about in the Hotel for ages afterwards, just casually open at the right pages. 'Oh yes, I believe there is a picture of her somewhere. The photographers never leave her alone, poor child.' It had been the nearest she had come to being a satisfactory daughter. That and her French. 'She speaks it fluently of course. A French woman who was here last summer said that Jenny's accent is absolutely *indistinguishable* from a Parisian girl's.'

Dear God, please let me escape, please please please let me escape.

The bar cleared, the last drinkers turned reluctantly out into the soft, still almost twilight darkness, standing in groups under the archway of the courtyard, making promises for tomorrow, Saturday, freedom; fishing, a hurling match, the Hop. It was over.

In the Copper Room the 'regulars' were still drinking, no longer as customers but as friends of the family if they were questioned. Mrs. Kershaw with one ear alert for what was going on, what might be going on in the Public Bar. Hubert Kershaw slightly sloshed and much too jolly to think about anything like that. Eight or nine gins-and-its under his waistcoat, a bottle of Beaujolais at dinner, a couple of Martini Drys before dinner. A good night, and lashings of the old boodle coming into the Public B. for once, thank God. Has to be Friday, yer know. Saturday is Hop night, can't interfere with that. Sacred rite of the Irish peasantry. Hop on Saturdays.

In the Public Bar Michael was sweeping the floor and Jennifer was collecting tray after trayful of dirty glasses. There was a knock at the outer door and before either she or Michael could answer that they were closed there was a second, stronger knock. 'Gardai. Sergeant McMenamin.'

Jennifer drew the bolts. He didn't often bother them. 'Come in, Sergeant. Are you looking for my father?' But as she said it she knew that he wasn't. He had an odd expression on his face, as though he was uncomfortable about something.

'Ah. Miss Jenny.' And then, 'Michael,' in a slightly different voice. Michael turned, holding the broom.

'Can I give you something?' Jennifer said. She had known the sergeant all her life, or it seemed like all her life, ever since she could remember. Checking her bicycle bell, making a joke that he'd have to arrest her for speeding, taking the details when she lost her purse one Christmas. A friend. But not now. Like a stranger, even though his face was the same, there was nothing to be afraid of.

'You were telling me this afternoon that you went to bed last night as soon as the Bar closed. Is that right? You're sure?'

'Yes,' Michael said. He didn't look at her. She could see his mouth tighten, the corners of it go white. She didn't know what to do, whether to go on collecting glasses or just stand there. Last night. It couldn't – there couldn't – she felt her heart beating, seem to catch and stop and the beat as if it was trying to catch up with its lost moment. Her mouth was dry. She wasn't tired any more, she was so awake that she could hear their voices in the Copper Room, hear her father laughing.

'I am afraid I have to ask you again,' the sergeant said. 'I have received information that you were seen standing outside this hotel at approximately two o'clock this morning. And that you appeared to be returning to the hotel from somewhere else. Is that correct? Did you leave the hotel last night after you first went up to bed?'

'No,' Michael said.

'What a pity,' the sergeant said, pushing up the peak of his cap and scratching his forehead. 'You see, anyone who was out and about at that time might have seen someone by the fish ponds. It must have been just about that time that the gates were lifted and the fish let escape.'

Michael said nothing.

'There could be a lot of reasons for anyone being out at that time of night,' the sergeant said persuasively. 'Innocent reasons.'

Michael still said nothing.

'And according to our information,' the sergeant said, '—it must be all a mistake of course – but according to our information you weren't alone.' He waited this time for an answer. The silence in the bar stretched like elastic. Jennifer found that she was holding her breath. She put the glasses she was carrying down on to the nearest table and began to open her mouth. The sergeant turned to her. 'Yes?' he said.

Her mother was looking through the connecting doorway. 'Hallo Sergeant Mac. Checking up on us? Hubert, the sergeant's here.' Hubert came to join his wife, peering through into the Public Bar as if it was strange territory, the nimbus of the Copper Room about his head and shoulders, the jollity of the evening round him like a cloak. A cloak he had bloody well needed after the events of the day. The cloak slipped, the jollity vanished as if he hadn't had a drink since yesterday. He came further into the space behind the counter, pushing past Angela.

'You go on back inside old thing,' he said to her, trying to sound casually jolly. He came to the middle of the counter and gripped the edge of it with his hands, looking at the sergeant, at Jenny, at Michael. 'Anything the matter, Sergeant?' Fears surged in his mind like the cold sea rising. The horse lamed. Arson. God knew what. He saw Michael looking at him. That bastard was at the bottom of whatever it was. He'd have him out of here so fast his feet wouldn't touch.

'No, nothing the matter, sir,' the sergeant was saying. And then, with a slight hesitation to give it weight, 'Not really.' There were many things weighing on the sergeant's mind. What had begun that morning as a local nuisance, a bit of old men's stupidity that might cause him a few hours trouble to straighten out, had mushroomed through the day like storm clouds. First, Guard O'Neill nagging about the old men. Making allusions to 'local politics', implying while never saying it that Sergeant McMenamin might have his own extraordinary reasons for not wanting those two ancient cretins arrested.

But that had been nothing. The real unpleasantness had begun with the phone call from Belcorrig, from the Super, in answer to his own message of earlier that morning, reporting the affair. From the first words, 'What the bloody hell is happening down there?' it had been a difficult conversation. The sergeant knew the Super very well, and within a few seconds had guessed that this was not simple hangover, indigestion, interrupted golf, an efficiency drive or a quarrel with the Super's exceptionally quarrelsome wife. It was trouble from higher up.

The sergeant had shuffled possibilities in his mind like a hand of cards, choosing and discarding. Dublin had a hangover, indigestion, an efficiency drive or a complaint from the Norwegians. As soon as he thought of it he selected the last. Which in turn made his own answer inevitable. Or so in his innocence he had thought. When he could get a word into the conversation he coughed deferentially and said that while he hadn't mentioned them immediately because there was no hard evidence so far, there were indeed two obvious suspects, the Power brothers, with a long record of petty nuisances perpetrated against the proprietors of the said firm.

'Said firm, said firm! You mean the bloody trout farm, don't you?'

'Yes, sir.'

'Then why the hell don't you say so?'

'Exactly sir.'

'The Power brothers? Who the devil—?'

'Three very old men sir, who live alone. A bit touched in the head. It was them that sold the pieces of land to the—'

The Superintendent made a sound at the far end of the line that conveyed a number of things to the sergeant. The first and most vital of them was that the Powers were not acceptable as suspects, and just as his own junior had done all morning, the sergeant began instantly searching his mind for some reason why they were not. What conceivable internal, or local, or even national political reason could there be for the Super caring a damn whether the Powers went to prison for this, so long as someone did? Some remote in-law relationship that he didn't know about? Some grand-nephew or third cousin of the Powers high up in the Party? Or in the Castle? Some link going back to 1921, or the Civil War? There was nothing. At least nothing that he knew of. His mind working at computer speed, or at least slightly quicker than its usual Ross Harbour, dreamlike gait, the sergeant said, 'Garda O'Neill was suggesting that it was the Powers, sir. He knows them well.'

'Tell that little Donegal shit to—' The Superintendent took a long, deep breath, like a man preparing to talk to a refractory child in plain, simple, unmistakable words. 'Sergeant McMenamin, this is a political case, with political overtones and undertones, and I should have thought, I hoped, that that would have been obvious to a man of your experience and length of service—'

'Political over—?'

'You heard what I said.' There was a sound like false teeth being ground. The Super had himself received a very tough and chilly phone call from the Castle, which in its turn had had one from the Department of External Affairs. Per Olafsson's cable to his owners in Norway had borne rapid and furious fruit. More fruit than even the Norwegian owners of the trout farm could have hoped for, for their stiffly worded telephone call of complaint to the Norwegian Embassy in Dublin, forwarded more diplomatically by telephone to the Irish Department of External Affairs, had been like a pebble flung into an evenly and tensely balanced scale, sending it down on the side marked 'Crisis'. In a period that had already seen enough alarms and excursions to shred the nerves of any government, between rumours of risings, the smuggling of arms and explosives, something close to armed rebellion across the border, talk of civil war spreading to the south, incendiary attacks on foreign owned farms and explosive attacks on foreign owned mines, any act of sabotage aimed at foreigners and their property was certain to strike horrid echoes in Dublin ears. It was instantly assumed in high quarters that some faction of the I.R.A. was behind the matter, so that in the course of a very few hours a number of extremely influential voices had cried SUBVERSION! SABOTAGE! I.R.A.! DO SOMETHING! to the Castle. And since the Castle was filled with human beings and the cries themselves were plausible, the cries were forcefully passed on to the Superintendent in Belcorrig, with the usual polite wonderment that the Superintendent appeared to know nothing about the matter whatsoever. When, for example, did he expect to report an arrest?

The Superintendent, who had at first taken the report of what had happened quite lightly, and in his secret heart had considered the matter almost humorous, had become very upset, with visions of black marks entered in his Personal File. And he regarded all of this as Sergeant McMenamin's direct responsibility. 'When do you expect to make an arrest, Sergeant?'

'We're pursuing our—'

'God dammit man, you're not talking to the *Cork Examiner*. And this isn't a case of riding a bicycle without lights after dark. This is a political crime and it's going to cost you your stripes if something isn't done about it bloody fast. I'll be coming down to you first thing this afternoon and I want—'

'You think it's the I.R.A., sir?' the sergeant said, his tone intended to convey that this had been his own inner and personal conviction from the beginning. Guard O'Neill was standing looking at him across the desk by now, his thin lips shaping the word 'Powers'. The sergeant allowed himself a hard, brief smile. Let him try and sell the Powers to the Super. Let him bloody try. He'd spend the next thirty years on a bloody island off the west coast trying to tell the sheep it wasn't his fault.

'Of course it's the I.R.A.,' the Super was shouting.

'We had The Sons of Ireland down here a wee while ago.'

'The what?'

'The Sons of Ireland.'

'By God!'

'Exactly, sir. The theory that I'm following at the moment is that they're at the bottom of this.' The sergeant's voice began to regain confidence. 'A member of the organization, calling himself Seagrun Ó Malechonaire, has been active in the district for some time and I have had him under surveillance.' Guard O'Neill was looking at him with growing stupefaction. Let him.

'The Sons of Ireland?' the Superintendent was saying, trying the words on his tongue, as if in practice for Castle consumption.

'I wrote you a report about them sir,' the sergeant said, humbly efficient.

'Ah yes, the Sons of Ireland. Of course. Of course. You think it's them?'

'It carries the mark of their type of thinking, Superintendent.'

'Activists, eh? They believe in violence?'

'Destruction of property. Nothing better than Communists.'

'And this man Sea – Seagrun. Do you want a warrant?'

'I'd rather leave him at liberty for the time being, sir. Give him rope, you see. I want to get the rest of the cell.'

'Cell?'

'Communist terminology, sir. The group. I have my informants watching him—' He had been going to say 'day and night' until he thought of the instant answer, 'what about last night?' 'From this day on,' he said, 'he won't be out of our sight day or night.'

This had not been mere boasting. Even in Ross Harbour there were men who thought it worth their while to keep in sycophantic relationship with the Guards, letting confidential word fall as to who was doing what. Without such men, and women, the work of the Guards would have been impossible. It was the reality of that boast, put into action immediately, that had brought the sergeant out to see Michael Carmody that afternoon. And brought him out a second time now. A man going about business he had not been supposed to be about had seen Michael and Jenny walking back to the hotel at two in the morning.

'I wouldn't swear it was the Kershaw lassie, now, I wouldn't swear that on the Book now Sergeant dear, but it was a female he was with, and a young female, and a tall young female in trousis with a great swing of her as she'd be walking, and the two of them goin' in under the arch there like a courtin' couple that'd be after having a tiff, like, and whose else would Micilín

Carmody be courting out of the Hotel except the lassie? It'd hardly be the mother now, although divil take them there isn't a thing you'd put past the women these days, whatever age of their life they'd be at.' A fleeting look out of oyster eyes, and a dirty hand wiping its knuckles under the dripping end of a long nose. 'Now, Sergeant darling, 'tis all I know, and 'tis the whole Gospel truth of it, not a word of a lie. And you won't be holding that little bottle of stuff against me now, will you, not just this once? And the least littlest thing I might be seeing in the future, sure, Sergeant dear, you'll know it as soon as meself, or as soon as I get the means to tell you.'

'Make sure you do, Seamus, or it'll be worse than ten days you get the next time, I promise you that.'

The informer slipping away from him like dirty water down a drain. If the rebel is the oldest political reality in Ireland, the informer is next to him, closer than any brother.

'Not trouble exactly, sir,' the sergeant said to Hubert Kershaw. 'Just a question or two I wanted to ask Michael here.'

'Jenny,' Hubert said sharply. 'Your mother may need you inside.'

'I'm going myself, Mr. Kershaw,' the sergeant said. 'Don't let me disturb you any more.' He turned away to the door. 'Good night sir, Miss Jenny. Good night, Michael. I might be passing this way tomorrow—'

'I'll see you out to your car,' Hubert said. They went outside together. When they were safely away from the door, he caught the sergeant by the elbow and whispered, 'I think I know why you're here, Sergeant. It's about that business last night, eh? Has anything more happened?'

'Just inquiries, sir, nothing to be alarmed about.'

'There was a damn queer fellow out here at lunchtime, I was thinking of letting you know—'

'That's very good of you, sir. But maybe I know already. A pale-faced, rather meaty looking lad? Wears a beret?'

'That's the chap,' Hubert said, with an ugly feeling in his chest. 'Bit of a fanatic by the look of him.'

'You should have been a policeman, Mr. Kershaw. You're a born detective.'

'Oh, I don't know, Sergeant. When you've knocked around a bit you learn to spot the wrong 'uns.'

'Don't worry, sir. No sense in saying anything to alarm the ladies—'

'Just what I was saying to Sir Philip this afternoon.'

'You've told him about – this particular man?' There were gentle, multiple reproaches hidden under the courteous surface of Sergeant McMenamin's tone.

'Oh, just chatting, you know, neighbours and all that. Sir Philip has his head screwed on. Just wanted to ask him did he think it worth bothering you chaps about it.'

'And did he, sir?'

'Did he what?'

'Think it worth bothering us?'

Again the unpleasant, ugly feeling was in Hubert's chest, like a badly digested dinner. These damn policemen were as bad as the fellows they were supposed to catch. Not like proper policemen, English bobbies. You couldn't really trust these fellows, you could never know what they were really thinking. Behind it all they probably sympathized with the I.R.A. He made a gruff, indefinite noise intended to suggest that conversations are private, other people's opinions privately expressed are inviolably secret, but that whatever had been said at that intensely well-meant meeting had been to the best interests of law and order, the State, the Garda Siochana, and the welfare of Ross Harbour.

'I beg pardon, sir?'

'Hrrrm. I mean, well, I pretty much gathered that Sir Philip took a serious view of things too. I was coming to you in the morning, anyway.'

'That was very good of you, sir. But as I said, we wouldn't like you to feel alarmed, sir. Everything will be under control.'

'We don't want any of those jolly old petrol bombs through the windows, do we? Not in peaceful old Ross Harbour.'

'Do you have any reason to apprehend a bomb attack, sir?'

'Reason?'

'Overhearing anything, sir.'

'No.' The ugly feeling had grown, was filling the space where his lungs ought to be. From a faint and unreal bogeyman on the edge of consciousness, 'bomb attack' leapt to reality, to what might happen tomorrow, tonight. 'You think – you think they—'

'Don't worry, sir. And above all, don't alarm the ladies. I

won't go into details, but there'll be all the protection you need.'

'That's very reassuring. But there is one thing. This damn fellow of mine, Carmody. You think he's in it?'

'We're not laying any charges, sir, not at this stage.'

'I can't very well turf him out tonight, I suppose, but tomorrow—'

'If I may make a suggestion, sir, I think we'd prefer that you didn't do that.'

Hubert stared at him, his large adam's apple going up and down with the effort to swallow. Somehow the use of 'we' made everything worse. A vast, indifferent apparatus of State and police in which his personal interests would be crushed underfoot without a thought. 'Wh – why not? I mean, I have to think of the – there's m'wife, and, I mean – Jenny and—'

'I don't think you need apprehend any violence from that quarter, sir. Not at this moment.'

'You know the chap's been in quod, of course. That was for violence.'

'Did he conceal that fact from you when you engaged his services, sir?'

'N – no. No. Grant him that. He was very frank. Trouble is, me and m'wife, we're a bit soft-hearted. Too damn soft-hearted. Chap spun us a sob-story, couldn't get work because of losing his temper once, gettin' a bit mixed up in politics when he was young and foolish, he said. Y'know he went to University, well, that College in Cork. Didn't take a degree of course—'

'We know his record, sir.'

'Well I mean – thought we were doing the feller a good turn, givin' him a chance to go straight and all that. Didn't want to hang a dog just for his bad name—'

'Very kind-hearted of you, sir.'

'Soft-headed'd be a better word. Thought the damn feller might be grateful.'

'He certainly ought to have been, sir. It was a fine chance.'

'And now all this.'

'We'll be keeping a very close watch, sir. Don't you worry now. No need to lose any sleep over it. But I'd be grateful – we'd be grateful – if you'd just carry on normally as if nothing had happened. When we move, we'd like to catch the lot at one swoop so to speak.'

'I only hope you're right, Sergeant.'

The sergeant got into his Ford Cortina and drove away. Hubert went thoughtfully back to the Public Bar. Jenny and that damn feller, my God. He might cut their throats in the night. Except that these devils weren't even man enough for that. Petrol was their weapon. Was the Fire Policy up to date? He should have bought those Fire Extinguishers that chap was trying to peddle last year.

'You cut off to bed, Jenny. Michael'll finish up.'

He stood up and watched him. The worst damn type. A peasant with half an education. The sort of swine that was behind every revolution there had ever been. Rotted with hatred and envy of their betters.

'Mind your feet Mr. Kershaw.' The broom swept the dust from beside Hubert's brogues. Even his damn voice was impertinent. He had been mad, stark raving mad. And all the bloody police were interested in was who else the chap might lead them to. If his house was burned to the ground in the meantime and all of them in it, what would they care?

'Would you like me to lock up?'

'What?' Hubert came back from a nightmare of flames.

'Shall I lock up? If you want to go bed I mean. I'll be another ten or fifteen minutes.'

'I'll do the locking up if you don't mind.' He had said it, and harshly, before he could catch himself. The fellow staring at him, holding his broom in both hands, something very funny in his eyes. He knew. He knew he was suspected, that Hubert suspected him. He had been going to let that fellow back in, the I.R.A. chap. Several of them probably. Plotting. And now he knew he was being watched. Would it drive him to something? Tonight? Should he ring the sergeant? The fellow might overhear. Christ what a mess. The fellow was still staring at him. 'I mean,' he said, smiling so hard that he felt his lips stretching, 'I mean you cut along to bed too. No sense killing yourself. The rest'll do in the morning. I'll lock up. That's all I meant.'

'If you like,' Michael said. He leaned his broom against the bar and took off the apron he had been wearing for washing glasses. He looked at Hubert again, his own chest feeling tight. He knew exactly what his employer was thinking. And that there was nothing, nothing on earth that he could do about it. If he ran for it, if he got away tonight, it would only make them certain that he had done it. Why in hell had Seagrun had to come to him like that? He felt as a fox must feel, when it hears the hounds from the far corners of the wood. Still far away but closing, closing.

'Then I'll go to bed,' he said. 'Good night.'

Hubert stared after him, his expression a mixture of fear and hatred. Only let him survive this, let him close the deal with those Dublin chaps and get out. To hell with Sir Philip, Lady Eagan, with Angela wanting this damn hotel, with everything. Maybe there had been Kershaws here for four hundred years, but it wasn't going to do anyone any good to be the last of them, getting burned in his bed. Let the Development chappies cope with all that. And then it struck him that if there was violence, if there were burnings, more destruction, the Development people might no longer want to come.

Suddenly there was no one on earth he yearned for quite so much as those anonymous Development men hidden behind Alloway, Barnacle and Truett, whose approaches he had furiously spurned as an insult, whose impudence he had derided to Lady Eagan and Sir Philip, to Colonel Mace and the Sandersons, to Mrs. Herzberger, to the Archdeacon, to anyone who would listen in the Club in Dublin when he was up there last. He might get a hundred thousand from them. More. A thousand or so an acre. Forty-fifty for the house, the Hotel. It was a business, a thriving business, not just a house. A hundred and twenty thousand. They could go to Angela's sister for a bit. Find a decent house in Surrey somewhere. Maybe get a little place in Spain. Costa del what not. He had been mad, he had been out of his mind. What in hell did it matter what Sir Philip thought, what Lady Eagan thought? Two antique fossils, bloody snobs. He hated them, he realized he had always hated them. But for them he could be out of this now, a hundred thousand quid in the bank, debts paid, living in a place where you could go to sleep at night and be sure you'd wake up in the morning.

He'd talk to Angela. She'd have to see reason, of course she would, she had always hated Ireland, really, underneath everything. They could get a Spanish couple, or a Swedish au pair, take the rough stuff off Jenny's hands, do the scrubbing and so on. This bloody place would never make anything, even if the I.R.A. never existed. Malta. Torremolinos. Somewhere where the police knew what was what and agitators ended up behind bars double quick. Show Jenny off, too. Find her a decent husband. Lots of English families out in Spain. Christ what a mess. He might give those solicitor chappies a ring in the morning. Or better write. Don't seem too eager. Just a casual letter. Further to yours of the nth ult. Tomorrow. It was damn near tomorrow already. Five to twelve. He went back into the Copper Room for a nightcap.

CHAPTER ELEVEN

IN the dining-room of Gombeen Mulcahy's house the family were sitting round the table as if it was already a wake. They had collected in the dining-room so that Benedict, who had driven down from Dublin immediately his Ministerial offices closed for the day and the week-end, could be given a cold supper by Mary. She might cook hot and succulent dishes for Father Tom, day or night, but the Last Trump could blow before she would cook anything for her cousin Benedict, Minister or no Minister, and on a night such as this night, with that poor saint of a creature lying in his extremities upstairs like a corpse already. Cooking wouldn't have been decent, it wouldn't have shown respect neither for the living nor the dead. Let him have cold meat and salad and H.P. sauce and some cheese, and if he wanted to read her feelings into it then let him.

But Benedict was not a man to read anything into any circumstances unless it was of immediate profit to him. He sat like an oiled, Assyrian bull at the table head, knife in one hand, fork in the other, mouth full, talking now to Clara, now to his brother John, now to uncle Matthew although what in hell that old fool thought it worth his while being here for, God knew, now throwing a word to his cousin Mary to be a good woman and give him more pickle, another whiskey and a dash of soda, Christ the drought on him driving that bloody road. Now simply eating, bending his black, powerful head with its bursting red cheeks close over the plate like a workman busy on a skilful job of work, shovelling in the cold meat, the halved tomatoes, the pickles, the screwed up leaves of lettuce, not that he set much stock by greenery. His head, his massive shoulders, his short, thick, swelling neck, his hands like thick, round, hairy paws, shouted HEALTH, HEALTH! MAKE WAY FOR A MAN!

Clara Mulcahy in her loose, floating summer dress that had cost a fortune in Dublin two years ago when she had been buying her wardrobe for the holiday in Ibiza, Clara Mulcahy with her fine bosom and romantic eyes looked at him as she always looked at him, hearing the shout, longing to answer it, but inhibited by all the things that inhibit good women in a country place. The laws of religion, of family, of motherhood, of ethics and morality. And more inhibiting than even those strong barriers, in her particular case, an almost complete ignorance of what those strange stirrings inside her really meant. She simply looked at him, half-veiling her large blue innocent eyes with their silken black lashes, like pelmet fringes hiding her thoughts. Her cream white bosom, what could be seen of it, which was quite a lot, lifted and fell. Her small, plump hand plucked at the edge of the linen table cloth, the sharp filbert nails gradually picking a hole in it.

'By Cripes she's wasted on John,' Benedict was thinking, wiping his full red lips with his own edge of the table cloth. 'Trouncing twice and three and four times in the afternoon is what she needs to keep her in trim and I'll be bound he doesn't get at her twice in the one week.' He belched with a long gurgling sound, like drains clearing after a stoppage, and threw himself back.

'Well, the old divil is holding out, eh? 'tis hard to kill a bad one.'

'Jesus Mary and Joseph,' cried Mary Mulcahy. Her father, uncle Matthew, crossed himself, not at what his nephew had said because he had not heard it, being deaf, but by reflex on hearing his daughter's voice raised. John looked pained. He was a pale, plump, anaemic version of his younger brother, as though that bull-like baby on coming into the world had sucked the life out of him. Or as if their mother had saved all her wan energies for one tremendous burst of nativity and had let John, her first born, creep into the world on quarter rations. He had the big shoulders and the bull head, the round hands that should have been like carpenter's clamps. But his shoulders were merely fat and his hands were damp, and he blinked from pale, washed eyes at a world that seemed about to overwhelm him at any moment.

Mentally this was not likely to happen. His brain was like a cash register, always taking in more than it let out. He had his father's tenacity at gaining and keeping money, and as shrewd a mind for using what he gained as the old man had ever had. Not a farthing of the housekeeping money was ever wasted, or if it was he knew it the next Friday night. If his wife had an expensive summer dress and had been to Ibiza for a fortnight it was her aunt Mrs. Glennon who paid for both wardrobe and holiday. (What John had done in London during that fortnight nobody knew. At least, nobody in Ross Harbour. The few books and pictures he had brought back he kept under lock and key in his private safe.) And if either Clara or Benedict thought that he didn't know what they were both thinking they were both mistaken. But he was here for more important matters than that. He was here to make utterly sure that no one got to his father without himself knowing about it, and that above all no one sneaked the solicitor Martin O'Loughlinn (only the remotest of connections to Martín O'Loughlinn, the handyman of Sir Philip's childhood. The Solicitor O'Loughlinns had been solicitors for a hundred years and more and had, what is more, been solicitors to Lord Medmenham and his family in the old days); that above all no one sneaked Martin O'Loughlinn in by the back stairs to change the Will.

He had got O'Loughlinn to draw up a very sound Will for the old man that was fair to everyone that deserved fairness – if it left nothing to cousin Mary that was for simplicity's sake, he could see her straight with a job in one of the supermarkets if she minded her manners. She need never starve. And what would have to go to Benedict would not disturb the smooth running of the businesses down here. What could he expect and he making his own fortune above in Dublin? Did he want the shops as well?

Old Matthew took out his beads and began to tell them. Mary Mulcahy went up and down the stairs like a lift. Doctor Lysaght looked in, shook hands with Benedict, had two whiskies, and went away again saying, 'I'd get yourselves to bed if I were you. No sense in sitting up, you know, he can't appreciate it. And nothing's likely to happen during the night.'

But they sat on.

Above in the bed, Gombeen lay like a living, but only barely living corpse. His face and hands were waxen, even the blue veins faded, his nose pinched at the sides, his mouth fallen, twisted down to the left and the cheeks sucked in so that his face was like that of a mummy, a preserved body in a crypt. Death was on it like a pale luminosity, a sheen of candlelight. It was barely possible to hear him breathing. One eyelid had dropped completely over the staring eyeball, the other eye shone with a horrid fixity under the wrinkled hood of the sound eyelid. He could lift that eyelid if he made a tremendous effort, even turn the eyeball. Now both eyelids dropped. The Little Sister of the Crucifixion who had undertaken to sit with him throughout the night so that Mary Mulcahy might attend to the family and eventually sleep, that Sister sat like a black pyramid under the red lamp that burned below the picture of the Sacred Heart. Her prayers breathed into the stillness of the room like incense. 'Blessed be God. Blessed be His Holy Name.'

The old man sank through layers of semi-consciousness, now aware of the shadowy room, now not. Sometimes he slept for a minute or two. Where was he? What had happened? Darkness. Bed.

' 'loysius!'

'Wha? Wha?' he whispered, shot awake, was upright by the bed. An old man stretched in it, a corpse. But that faded, the room faded. Moishe Gavron calling. The dark shivered. They were standing on the road in the moonlight. White road, black hedges, velvet sky. He was stark naked and the chill of the night was on his skin. He held his arms round him. Moishe was very tall in front of him, much taller than he remembered him. Remember? Remember what?

'The state of you,' Moishe said. There was a pile of belongings by Moishe's side, on the road. A wooden chest. A pedlar's pack, big and awkward. A sagging carpet bag. 'Naked to God,' Moishe said. 'Aren't you ashamed?'

Gombeen looked at him, holding his skinny arms round his ribs, shielding himself with his spread hands. 'Someone must have stole me clothes,' he whispered.

'Get more,' Moishe said. 'We've a long road to travel.'

'Where will I get them in the middle of this road in the night? Have you nothing for me in that pack?'

'Only for money. Have you money 'loysius?'

'How could I have money and my pockets gone?'

'Then have you credit?'

'Credit?'

'Will anyone speak for you? You'll need credit, or hard cash, along this road.'

Gombeen looked round him at the darkness as if expecting to find a friendly face, someone who would speak for him, say that he was rich, that he could pay for anything. There was no one there.

'I was kind to a boy once,' he said hopefully. 'I gave him lifts on a cart.'

The boy was there.

'Speak for me child,' Gombeen said. 'Wasn't I good to you?'

'Lift me up by you Mr. Mulcahy,' the boy said. 'Bring me up to the Gap to see the world.'

'Yerrah boy, how can I? The old horse is dead and the cart gone long ago.'

'Lift him up on your shoulder,' Moishe said. The boy held out his hands to be lifted. Gombeen lifted him and sat him on his naked shoulders. He seemed to have no will to resist any order. The boy sat there clasping his head, half blinding him. Gombeen put down his hands again to hide his nakedness.

'Hold me safe,' the boy said. 'I'll fall.'

Gombeen held him again.

'Now the pack,' Moishe said. He slipped the straps over Gombeen's shoulders, took one hand and then the other to fit them through the loops. The pack hung on his bones like coals, like stone.

'Fine, fine,' Moishe said. 'Now just take the little chest by its handle, one of its handles, and we'll be off. I'll take the bag.'

One hand up to steady the boy. One hand for the monstrous weight of the chest. The pack thudding at his spine. The stones of the road under naked feet.

'At least give me shoes,' Gombeen wept. They had gone a quarter of a mile between the dark hedges and his feet were bleeding. Moishe never turned his head, never showed sign of hearing him. The chest bumped and gouged its corners against Gombeen's camel knee. The boy weighed heavier, gripped harder, his hands over Gombeen's eyes. Thud of the pack on his spine.

'I can't go on,' Gombeen shrieked. The black figure of Moishe Gavron strode ahead, coat tails flapping, carpet bag hanging from one straight arm, black, low-crowned hat bent forward, shoulders hunched high like the elbows of a vulture's wings.

'I'm going to stop here,' Gombeen cried. But he didn't stop. His feet continued, leaving bloody stains on the white road. The boy clasped his head like the driver of a horse and cart. The road lifted above the Bay.

'Where are we going?' Gombeen cried. But Moishe had drawn too far ahead.

'Faster,' the boy said. 'We'll be lost, he's leaving us behind.'

Gombeen went faster, stumbling and crying up the road. A dog howled in a nearby farmyard, pushing its muzzle at the moon, ruff of hair round its neck thick and staring. Dogs heard it further off and howled in answer and the sound ran up the mountain side from yard dog to yard dog to mountain sheep dog sleeping on a handful of hay in a broken upended barrel. The Powers' bitch heard it and lifted her throat and howled in a long eerie scream like a lost spirit. In the cottage Jamey sleeping by the fire lifted his old head in its hat and shivered. The army greatcoat fell off his legs into the hearth.

'Oooah, Peadar, Matty!' he whimpered, but they were past hearing him, deep in the twin pits of the big bed, their heads buried.

The howls echoed and re-echoed along the Peninsula, out to the Head of Ross, until the last dog in Ireland howled his unease on the cliff's edge above the sea.

Inland on the mountain road Donal Carmody's old pointer heard the crying and cried in answer. His master woke in the small stuffy bedroom over the garden and thought instantly of town boys stealing his rabbits. 'The villyans!' he whispered, getting his thorn stick from beside the bed. He crept downstairs in his long johns and his grey woollen socks, and out into the front garden to catch them running away. But there were no boys there. The pointer whined in his box.

'Shurrup you divil ye.' He was a big, slow man, with red-brown hair and wind-burned features and every move he made it was as though he had a good hour to make it in, and if need be another hour on top of that. Lighting his pipe or sniffing the wind or putting on his spectacles to read the paper were things he did with deliberation. Even lifting his stick to bring down the length of it on the roof of the pointer's box was done like a man carving an action out of the air with care and thought.

'The divil blast ye for gettin' me out of my bed.' But he stood sniffing the scents of night, the closed flowers of the hedge, the sleeping grass, the onions and the carrots and the potatoes in their neat rows beyond; the rain water in the rain barrel, sweet and soft as liquid silk; the scent of the mountains, gorse and stone and heather and dark water like horse's urine in the bog holes. The scent of the sea lifting up towards him. And the white light of the moon and the pale starlight.

'Whisha it isn't a bad old night,' he thought. ''twill be raining a little before morning.' Which would lay the dust. He had to meet the lorry from Belcorrig at eight up by the Gap for tar spraying and gritting and he'd have a good bit of crack with the lads and hear the town gossip. It would be a good day. They should get down to Juke's Elbow by tea time, or even Gibbet Corner. He stretched his arms wide and yawned. Out of the corner of his eye he saw a shadow moving, like a tall man in black padding along the road, and the pointer whimpered in the depths of his box, afraid to howl again with his master there.

'Who's that?' Donal called out, going towards the gate. But it was only the shadow of a cloud on the white road. It must have been. There was not the sound of a foot, nothing. The hairs on the nape of Donal's neck lifted and pricked and he felt the night chill through his underwear.

'Be quiet ye brute,' he said, and went indoors. It was a while before the next shadow passed. Like an old man bent under the weight of a sack and a child on his shoulders, and a big box dragging him down on the one side. The dog howled as if its heart was breaking.

CHAPTER TWELVE

MICHAEL CARMODY heard the dogs howling, lying in his narrow white bed in the dusty bedroom over the stables, but it meant nothing to him except the vague sound of dogs crying in the night, far away. Hardly touching his mind. He had begun to read, or pretend to himself that he was reading, because he was too tired to sleep and his mind was going round and round, circling the same question, coming back to it from every angle, rejecting every answer. What was he going to do?

On the surface the question meant, 'What am I going to do about staying here or going away, now, tomorrow, this week?' If he went, the guards would think he was running away from them, that it was a sure confession that he had emptied the fish ponds. If he stayed – they could fasten it on to him at their leisure. And if he went, where would he go, what would he do? But if he didn't—

But there could be no answer to the question because the question itself was incomplete, and he knew it, and was afraid to complete it, to add her to it. It was madness to add her to the question. She had nothing to do with it, couldn't have. She was lonely, bored, there was no one to amuse her, she had decided to amuse herself for an hour with him. Let someone of her own kind come by and . . . He kept trying not to think of her, not to see her face, not to remember things she had said. Or to remember them coldly, to think of her coldly, dispassionately. Not as she had been down there in the cellar under the bar, a few hours ago. Not—

It was then that he had got up to put on the light again and find a book, to try to drive the thought of her away. He owned a dozen books and they stood in a dog-eared row on the wooden shelf, most of them picked up for a shilling or two in the Charing Cross Road, but a few of them survivors from his time in College. *Herodotus. The Story of Burnt Njal. Mediaeval Latin Lyrics. Irish Life in the 17th Century. The Hidden Ireland* by

Corkery. Michael Bakunin by Carr. Poetry. History. A life of Tom Paine.

He took the Latin Lyrics because they were cool and distant from Ireland and from his problem. Or if they were not all so quiet at least their passions were a long time dead. 'Estas in exilium iam peregrinatur—' He let the lines drift through his mind like the sound of winter crying softly in the naked wood. 'Summer to a strange land is into exile gone, the forest trees are bare of their gay song.' He had learned that lyric by heart with a dozen or so more when he was on remand, and they had kept him company through the months of his sentence.

The thought of exile brought an added chill to his spirit. And yet what was here for him except another kind of exile? 'Ailill the King is vanished, Vanished Croghan's Fort.' And all with it, all that those names meant, the poetry they stood for, the Ireland in which their story mattered. 'Have you seen Hugh, the Connacht king in the field?' and the hard, perfect answer, 'All that we saw, was his shadow under his shield.'

The poetry gave him an almost painful satisfaction, like probing at a bad tooth. He stretched his arms and put his hands behind his neck to support his head because there was only the one pillow. The Lyrics lay face down on his bare stomach. The crucifix with its pain-twisted features hung on the whitewashed bricks of the wall beside the door, the eyes seeming to stare at him. 'I suffer, yea, I die, Yet this mine agony I count all bliss, Since death is life again—' His mind left out the ending of the line. He would not think about her, she had nothing to do with it, he had nothing to do with her.

He tried to force his mind in other directions. The crucifix sent him back towards childhood, the kitchen, the crucifix that his grandmother kept in her pocket, carved out of ivory. What had become of it? The old woman letting him touch it, her skirt black, crisp and spotless. She had never seemed to belong in the kitchen, nor in the cottage, nor in the world of his father and his grandfather and his mother and his sisters and everyone else he knew. That world was of bread, and bacon sandwiches – fat bacon for luxury – of stolen apples and boiled sweets and sticky mouths and fear of the schoolmaster and washing in a bucket behind the cottage and crying with burst chilblains and trying to lift his father's broom, the huge road-broom that was taller and heavier than himself. Of empty boots by the hearth and his mother's voice threatening destruction on him for forgetting to fetch the bread or losing a sixpence or hitting his sister or waking his grandfather or oversetting a mug of milk. The close, warm world of poverty. And in that world his grandmother sat like a strange statue, never belonging to it, her face carved, her skirt in hard, proud folds hiding her feet. She possessed one fine cup and saucer, and one beautiful small plate, all three painted with miniature scenes of gentlemen and ladies in a wood, and decorated with gold. He had known without being told that she would have died of hunger before she would have eaten from a coarse, cracked plate on a table covered with a sheet of old newspaper, as he himself ate with all the rest of the family.

When her husband had been the master of the house she had never eaten with him. She had served him at the table and gone herself to eat standing by the dresser when he was finished, or was settled with his tea and pipe. But she had eaten from her Meissen plate and drunk from her Meissen cup and it would never have occurred to anyone that things should be differently conducted. Michael did not know how he knew that, it must have been told him by someone, because by the time he remembered her his grandfather had become half helpless and had eaten bread and milk by the fire from a tin bowl. It must be tin because he often dropped it from his old, work-ruined fingers. And still the old lady had eaten apart from everyone. She ate so little, she said, it was not worth troubling the table. But he had known it was pride.

Taking his hand, turning it this way and that to see if it was clean. And if it was, if it satisfied her, letting him touch the crucifix that, even as a small child, he sensed she loved because it was beautiful and rare, as much as because it was the Son of God on His Cross; letting him touch her skirt, smooth the satin that she wore in the evening. How had she kept it through the years of her marriage, of their poverty, of that cottage, the turf smoke and the ashes, and the mud brought in from the roads? Perhaps it was less fine than he remembered it. And yet it had been cool and clean and smooth and beautiful. As cool and clean as the ivory of the crucifix.

'This came to me from long ago,' she would say, holding the ivory for a moment in the palm of her hand. 'It was saved out of the fire when the Eagans burned the last of our houses.' Her eye bright as jet. 'Where my mother guided the work of the servants, the foxes have their young. Only the birds gather the fruit from my father's orchard.' Sometimes she would recite the whole poem that Seán Dubh had written as his curse on the Eagans, and when she came to the heart of the poem, the description of Sir William, her face would take on a look of such hatred that it was frightening. 'The man with a crook to his knee from stooping below the gibbet, tugging the feet of the hanged. May the cry of his widow be all his music.'

In Irish the words had a venom like a poisoned sword.

Why had she done it? What had she thought she would achieve, teaching hatred and arrogance and high visions to a labourer's son? That one day he would avenge Seán Dubh, murder an Eagan? Hardly that. Or make a great fortune in Australia and come back to buy the Head of Ross and build a palace there? Not that. She would have despised an Australian fortune, or any fortune that one could make, or even steal. What had she wanted? To break the mould? The clay mould of serfdom that she had been hardening around her husband and her son? She had done that at least.

Or had she? His father sweeping the road. He sweeping out the bar. And as he thought of that he knew that he would go, that he had been mad, insane to come back, to think that there was anything to come back for, anything in this dank, sodden, grocers' land to call him back. Daniel Corkery's Hidden Ireland, let Christ have mercy on it, it was long, long dead, and nothing in the world would resurrect it. The old Gaelic life like an underground river, running far down through the limestone layers while the Protestant squireens and the half-gentlemen of the Ascendancy rode their Irish horses and shouted their English curses on the turf above. The last of the Gaelic poets slinking like foxes from woodland to woodland – Seán Ó Tuama, Andrias Mac Craith, Donnchadh Ruadh Mac Conmara, Seán Dubh himself or the great Eoghan Ruadh, carrying their schoolmaster's pack of books, or their spailpín's spade, or the empty sack of beggary. 'None, alas! to befriend me – except heather and the north wind.' Carrying their poetry in their heads like a jar of whiskey in their satchel, to give them courage of heart against death. Why had Seán Dubh come back? To defeat, and misery at the best. To the shame of his burned house and his murdered father. There was a story that in the seven 'lost' years of his life he had gone to Russia and fought there for Catherine. Why hadn't he stayed there, become a Potemkin, a Gordon? What had called him back?

Across two hundred years Michael felt a kind of rage at that perverseness that he himself had faintly echoed. What was there here, then or now? The chance of revolution, Seagrun's True Republic? It would be worse than the worst of what it replaced. 'I don't know. I don't know,' he cried as though this ultimate negative was a Credo, a statement of Faith, a challenge. A challenge against all the narrow bigots who shouted that they did know. That they were certain, that they had found the Grail.

He felt something stirring inside him like a child waking in its mother. If only he could bring it out into the light. He wanted to reach out and touch someone, touch not one person but a thousand people, he wanted to hold out his arms and tell them – that there was nothing to tell. He looked at the small wooden crucifix, at the contorted body, the tiny, screaming mouth, and what he had thought seemed even to him, even to his lost religion, like a kind of blasphemy, and at the same time like faith. One day all of that faith in nothing, that reaching out into the dark, that sense of loneliness among too many people, of lost ideals and lost inheritance of greatness, would go into his singing, would become a cry of pain that would wake so many echoes in so many tormented hearts that it would make him rich, and his dark hair and his white face, like a fallen prince, and his eyes that seemed always to be searching, and never to find, would catch at the throats of a million and twenty million lonely girls as here they had caught at Jennifer's. But the journey would take him a long way from The Ross.

At this moment he did not so much as know that he had already begun the journey. He lay miserably in his bed, trying not to think of Jennifer, and thinking of her, and of what a miracle it would be if he heard her foot on the stairs outside that plank door, and saw it opening, and—

He thought of it so intensely that when he did hear footsteps creaking on the stairs he did not believe that they could be real. He thought that he had conjured the small sounds out of his head and went on listening to them as if he was listening to himself. The door opened very softly and she was there, and he sat up in the bed, quite slowly, the book that had been lying open on his chest sliding away and down on to the floor. He heard the sound of it falling with a strange distinctness, as though that sound was part of what was happening, of the dream.

'I saw your light on,' she whispered. 'It shows through the slates.' She was wearing a shirt, loose over her jeans, and her feet were bare. He tried to answer, to say something, but his throat had tightened and he could say nothing, not even breathe. She came into the room and closed the door behind her, standing as he had stood the night before, her back to the rough planks, and his suit that was hanging from the large nail driven into the timber.

'I – just wanted – to talk,' she said. She didn't look at him, and her skin flushed slightly. Her eyes went here and there about the bleak room. 'It can't – be very – very comfortable for you – here.'

'It's all right.'

She stayed where she was, still not looking at him. 'I had to come.' She waited and he said nothing. 'We – can never talk properly – during the day.'

He had drawn up his knees and now he put his arms round them and looked down at the patchwork coverlet that had long ago faded from its chequered multi-colours to subtleties of white and off-white and shadows of colouring like ghosts. He wanted to say many things. That he had been horrible to her. And why. But why had he been? As though he wanted to hurt her, punish her for nothing that she was nor had done, but for what he was, what he had been born. How cheap he had been.

'What would anyone think if they saw me here like this?' she whispered.

'I know.'

'Do you mind?'

'They've seen us already. Someone has.'

She looked at him without any expression. He could not tell whether she cared, whether that was the real reason she had come.

'If we were in London,' she said, looking away from him again, still with her flat, boy's shoulders against the door, her head a little thrown back as if she wanted him to see the line of her throat, 'no one would think anything.'

'But we're not.' His throat felt dry and his voice sounded unsteady. She will open the door and go down again, he thought. The night was round them like the sea round an island. They were nowhere. Not London. Not The Ross. An island. He wanted to say something that would tell her that, that would be—

With a sudden movement she turned out the light. For a few seconds he thought that she must have heard someone coming and he sat holding his breath, sitting as still in the bed as a statue. Nothing. No sound. Had she heard someone? Her father? She didn't move. After a few seconds more he could hear her breathing. She was still by the door.

'What is it?' he whispered.

She didn't answer.

'Did you hear—'

Her 'no' was so softly whispered that he was not sure that she had said it. He felt suddenly ridiculous sitting like that in bed, in the dark, his knees drawn up, her by the door. And yet if he moved – if he – if she heard him getting out of the bed— And as he thought of that he felt angry and got out roughly, throwing back the clothes and standing up. And she said nothing. The room was so dark that he could see nothing, not even the paleness of her shirt. If she had moved from the door—

But she had not moved. He touched her arm. Found her shoulder. He heard her catch her breath.

'Why are you doing this?' he whispered.

'You think I'm mad?'

'I don't think anything except—' He touched her face, brushed his finger tips across her forehead, as though he was trying to recognize her. 'You don't know what you're doing,' he said. In his own ears his voice was completely strange, shaking. She had lowered her head until her chin was against her body. Her hair fell forward and brushed against his hand.

'Be kind to me,' she whispered.

An island.

'How can I be kind to you?'

'Understand.' Although she knew that that was not possible because she did not understand herself, she did not know why she had come, or what she wanted then, or now. Only to be close. To be understood in spite of the impossibility. To be – not anything special. Only to find gentleness, to lie in the dark and be very gentle. Nothing else. Michael the barman wouldn't understand. Michael the Communist. Michael his father's son. But Friday Michael who sang would understand. She put both hands against his chest, not to hold him away, or invite him, but only to touch him, to know that he was there. She found that she was shivering, and yet she had not known that she was cold.

He put his arms round her and kissed her, not finding her mouth, and she didn't help him. He lifted her chin and she resisted. 'You're cold,' he said, and the remark seemed so obvious, so wrong, that he was ashamed. He wanted to tell her not to be afraid, that he would never — but he was holding her body and he knew that it was a lie, that he would, that if she stayed another half minute he would— The dark was like the sea. They would drown. She shivered in his arms, shivered and shivered. When he tried to kiss her again her face was wet, she was crying.

'I won't—' he breathed, and she went on crying.

'I am bad,' she whispered, her whisper broken by the crying.

'No.' They found themselves by the bed.

'Nobody knows who I am.'

He was hardly listening, he thought she said, 'Nobody knows where I am.' He stooped and put one arm behind her knees and lifted her, and laid her into the warm hollow of the bed where he had been lying. She neither resisted nor reacted. Only when he put his hand to the fastening of her shirt she put up both her hands and caught his. 'Please,' she whispered. His hand was against her breast and he could feel the small curve of it, and the warmth, and her heart beating. He knelt down by the bed. His other hand was already behind her shoulders and he put it further round her so that he held her cradled, like a child. She put her head on his shoulder, snuggled it close, into a comfortable hollow between his head and arm, sighed. His other hand was bent uncomfortably and he drew it out from her hands and used it to pull the clothes over her.

'Can we stay like this?' she said against his throat. He didn't answer. He felt the wetness of her cheeks against his skin but she was no longer crying, no longer shivering. He kissed the side of her forehead. One of her arms went round his shoulders, held him. It was as though they had already made love and she was sleeping, fulfilled. After a few minutes of kneeling his knees became cramped and very gently, as softly as if he was afraid of disturbing a small wild animal asleep, he eased himself on to the bed and lay beside her, the thickness of the covers, the washed-out patch-quilt between them. He touched her face and she stretched and then tightened her hold on him.

'I knew you could understand,' she breathed.

CHAPTER THIRTEEN

THE DAWN of Saturday was as splendid as the previous dawn had been. And yet it was cold. Cold rose from the earth like mist as the sky paled above the Peninsula, and the shadow of Gombeen Mulcahy stumbling over the heather and the rocks felt the cold like fire inside his bones. His eyes were clouded with sweat and yet he shivered. The child weighed on his neck like the beam of a cross. His feet bled. For a long time the child had said nothing, as if he was asleep, but his sharp fingers still clasped Gombeen's sweating forehead. Far ahead of them both, far, far ahead, the tall shadow of Moishe Gavron strode over the broken ground like a giraffe surrounded by a black flapping tent. Then his shadow was lost to view against a ridge of rock that lifted to form a low cliff along the crest of the Peninsula.

'I can't go on,' Gombeen whispered, as though losing sight of Moishe had drained his last strength away, or removed his fear enough to let him rebel.

'You must go on,' the boy said, waking sharply, and kicking Gombeen in the ribs, with his stubby heels. 'We have to follow him.' And he kicked again, harder. Gombeen clenched his shadow teeth and stumbled on. Moishe was waiting for them at the mouth of a cave in the face of the low cliff.

'Taking your time, eh, 'loysi'?' he said.

'I can't go on any more,' Gombeen said, his knees folding. He put out a hand to lean against the wall of stone. He was afraid to look down at his torn feet.

'No need to be worrying,' Moishe said with hard cheerfulness. 'With the sun coming we have to stop anyway. We can stop in this cave.' He went in and sat himself down with his back to the rock. Gombeen followed him uncertainly. Inside the cave it was even colder. His teeth chattered although they made no sounds.

'I'm perished with the cold,' he said. 'If we had a bit of wood for a fire. The boy'd fetch it for us.' But the boy stayed on his shoulders even when Gombeen sat down, his knees collapsing.

'A fine idea,' Moishe said. 'But the boy won't do to fetch it. Not here. You need someone else for that. The boy brought you here and that's enough.'

'Brought *me*?' Gombeen cried, feeling the weight of the child as if every bone and muscle in his body had been scourged with iron rods. But Moishe ignored his indignation.

'You need someone else for that, for wood for a fire. Call someone that you warmed when you were able to give warmth. They'll come.'

Gombeen tried to think of someone, while the weight of the child forced his head forward, and prevented him from resting his shoulders against the wall of the cave.

'Kathleen,' he whispered at last. 'She'll come.'

The shadow of his wife appeared in the mouth of the cave. But she was crying with the cold and couldn't see Gombeen where he sat. All of them looked at her and her exhausted face.

'I don't think she'll do,' Moishe said. The shadow went. Gombeen thought again for a long time. At last he whispered, although not hopefully, 'Benedict? John?' And then with a more peremptory note in his voice, 'Mary? Mary! I'm cold, light the fire.' But no one came.

'Tsk tsk, tsk,' Moishe said. 'Families, families. How about some real friend?'

'Father Tom,' cried Gombeen, his face lighting.

The shadow of Father Tom appeared before them like a picture on a screen, transparent, so that they could see the heather of the hillside through his insubstantial flesh, and the Bay below, and the Head of Lir beyond. It made Father Tom look beautiful. He was asleep in his comfortable bed with the quilt and the downy blankets drawn up to his chin and the decanter and plate of digestive biscuits temptingly set out on the night table near his bed. His breathing rose and fell as he snored.

At the sight of the whiskey and the warm bed a kind of convulsion of unhappiness and longing seized on Gombeen and shook his soul. 'Tom,' he called, 'for the love of – love of – love of—' But it needed another word to wake Father Tom and he could not think what it was. 'Let me in beside you,' he whispered. Father Tom continued snoring, only a shade restless in the bed. His appearance seemed to be fading, losing its clarity as the light outside the cave grew stronger.

'Don't leave me Tom,' Gombeen screamed, but it was only the sound of a seagull in Father Tom's dream.

'Give me a glass of whiskey, damn you, didn't I give you enough of mine in my time?' And the whiskey was in his hand. Not much of it. A mean measure in the bottom of a dirty glass.

'Drink it up,' Moishe said kindly.

He drank, and the whiskey scorched his throat like fish hooks being dragged downwards.

'You should have had a biscuit with it,' Moishe said. 'Drinking on an empty stomach.' And again he went 'tsk, tsk, tsk,' reprovingly. There was something terrible to Gombeen about the sound, and the apparent concern. An iron mockery. He would have almost welcomed true reproaches, curses even, rather than that kindly tone that had no kindness in it. He wept with pain and hopelessness. The last transparent hint of the image of Father Tom had vanished.

'I'm so cold,' he wept. The boy had got down from his neck but he felt no better.

'Maybe we should go on, then,' Moishe said. He stood up and put his hand on the rock behind him. A doorway had become visible and it opened, slowly. A kind of vapour coiled from the opening. Gombeen looked at it and his heart froze.

'There?' he whispered.

'Yes,' Moishe said.

'I'm – I don't think I'm so cold after all,' Gombeen pleaded. 'I wouldn't mind staying here at all. Let me stay.' He looked longingly at the Bay, at the sky outside the cave. He saw in that moment what he had never seen in all his haunted life, that the world was beautiful. 'Let me stay,' he whispered. But Moishe was beckoning.

'Come with me then,' Gombeen begged the boy, who was standing to one side. The boy shook his head.

'I have to wait for someone else,' the boy said. Moishe beckoned again and Gombeen covered his shadow face with his hands so that he should not see that stairway beyond the door. The vapour coiled about his feet. The door closed on him and the shadow of the boy went out into the morning sun.

It was at that same moment, in the dank Victorian house on Knuckle Street, that Gombeen Mulcahy's body became a corpse.

*

The Little Sister of the Crucifixion stirred in her prayers; heard the dry whisper in the throat, sensed the ending. She came like a dark wing and threw her shadow over the yellow, corpse face, the nose jutting out of the wax mask, the cheeks suddenly sunk in. She crossed herself, Rosary beads clicking, a prayer for the newly dead slipping on worn words through her mind. Her fingers drew down his eyelids. She did not need to feel his pulse, felt no need to call the doctor. She looked at her watch that hung from a large safety-pin on her robe. Ten minutes to five. Best to let the family sleep a little longer. She stood by the bed, thinking. She had watched by many corpses and rarely felt uneasy. But something about this corpse made her look away. She decided that it would be much the best if she used the next hour or so to fetch other Sisters from the Convent for the laying out. Without looking at Gombeen's remains again she went out of the bedroom and down the stairs, taking the last few steps almost at a tiny, tripping run. The front door opened and shut and it was not until she was in the street in the new washed brightness of the morning that she felt the weight lift off her heart. She began to be frightened that Mother would be angry at her leaving her post, and she walked quickly on her small hidden feet through the sleeping streets towards the Convent, rehearsing her reasons in her mind.

In the house behind her Mary Mulcahy slept exhausted in her truckle bed, next door to the best bedroom where Gombeen lay. Although he was no longer Gombeen, no longer anything. Only a corpse, the deceased, the departed, the relic, the mortal remains of our dear brother. In the second best bedroom that had once been Kathleen Mulcahy's, after she won at least the freedom of that much privacy from her marriage, in that second best bedroom Benedict Mulcahy lay sound asleep, his face red and his hair black on the white pillow, his two fat, hairy hands gripping the covers as though to demonstrate even in sleep that nothing would ever escape him if he wanted it. He was dreaming of Clara Mulcahy, of her big bosom and her plump thighs and her cow eyes like pools of blue water waiting for him to jump in up to his middle. He peeled off her dress like peeling a banana, a plum, a peach, an ice cream, all delicious things wrapped into one. Down over her white breast, her smooth, rounded stomach, her amphora hips.

'Grush glewsh mushwish,' he mumbled in ecstasy. In the dream they were in the back of the State Mercedes, but a more

178

commodious Mercedes than is given to junior ministers for State affairs. Leather seats and deep carpets and convenient handles spread round them in luxury. Clara said nothing, did nothing, only looked at him with admiration, which was all the eloquence he wanted.

Nothing under her dress, the strumpet, only the white skin of her and the black hair and the rosy tits. 'Gwosh glush,' he gnashed in a climax of longing, his thick bull body wrestling with the sheets, his own black body hairs like fur, his pink flesh bursting with good meat and drink, his thick little feet on their sturdy ankles pedalling at the bottom of the bed as if he was running a race with time. 'Don't wake up,' his brain commanded, while his Catholic conscience cried, 'No, no,' in a very small and stifled voice from somewhere inaudible. Down on the seat with her, one hand gripping the inside door handle to give him purchase, her soft splendour giving under him like the finest upholstery. 'GRARRHH.' His dream exploded, woke him, his arms clasping nothing. But for a fading second she was still there, the taste of her in his mouth, the warmth of her against his barrel chest and swelling stomach, his knees between her soft legs, and he drew a deep breath of triumph and satisfaction as if he had really taken her as she needed to be taken.

He lay thinking about her for a few minutes and then rolled out of bed. He did half a dozen knee bends and smacked his bare chest at the open window, staring across the roofs of the town that descended towards the Bay. His town. His. He scooped his fist as if he was physically macerating these small, miserable houses and replacing them with factories, skyscrapers, warehouses, docks and oil tanks and workers' flats. Smoke floated over his vision like the smoke of Birmingham or the Ruhr. He stared at the Bay with his hard brown eyes like glass marbles, and saw it covered with a silken sheen of oil, glitteringly beautiful, opalescent, the shore lined with wharfs and piers and mobile cranes. Railway engines shunted and huffed and screeched of wealth. Iron clanged. The shape of a million-ton oil tanker nosed between the two heads, dwarfing them with its bulk. Its blunt mast and white bridge house rose above the surrounding ridges. On one of those ridges there was a low cliff of rock, and in the face of it a cave that showed as a patch of dark on the pale grey stone. But Benedict never noticed it.

And yet he thought suddenly of his father and went next

door to look at him. Something about the waxen face and the lie of the knotted yellow hands on the turned-down sheet seemed different, and he looked closer. He lifted a fallen eyelid and the eye stared back at him without life or recognition.

'Dead,' Benedict said, his mind clenching on the word and fact like teeth closing on a bone. Lawyer. Will. Doctor. The necessities appeared to him in that order. Wake Mary. He'd have to tell John. Will. Reading the Will. All round table downstairs. Fight. The hardest of smiles stretched his firm, full lips and his fists unconsciously clenched. Let Johnno run the shops, and good luck to him. He'd have the land. Devil a matter what the Will said, he'd have the land. He opened his fat fist and hooked his stubby fingers round the whole of The Ross. Money. Capital. No problem there. Curtains of gold descended from the roof, heaped themselves on the floor into piles and hillocks. Their image scented the air and he drew in breaths of gold. Power. He went and woke his cousin Mary.

'Christ have Mercy,' she cried, rising up in bed in her curlers. 'Blessed be God.' When the fact of her uncle's death penetrated her prayerful mind she cried out, 'The villains, the I.R.A. did it, they killed him, the fish, it was the fish.'

Benedict, who had heard nothing of the fish being allowed to escape, thought that Mary had lost her mind and stared at her for a second at a loss of words. Chastity. Mad for a man. A horrid thought occurred to him and he backed away.

'Easy now, easy,' he said. 'Sure he had no fish, did he?' Fishbone? Stuck in throat?

'The fear of them,' hissed his cousin, enjoying the drama. 'The terror that walks by night! Oh the poor saint, dying on us alone in the dark night and never a soul near him! Where was Father Tom? Where was the Church at the hour of his Calvary?'

She had risen by then, being safely wrapped already in her dressing gown and they both went back into the death room. It was only then that either of them remembered the Little Sister of the Crucifixion. Where was she? Why hadn't she called anyone? Where had she gone? But within moments the Little Sister herself answered that question by returning to the house and to the room with three companions, and all the necessities for a laying out, from candles to Holy Water. The four Sisters stood with their burdened hands and downcast eyes.

'Leave everything to us, Miss Mulcahy,' said the eldest in a hushed whisper. For chastity's sake they did not so much as speak obliquely to the man in the room. Their white hands lifted and deposited, their Rosary beads clasped at their sides, their robes rustled like shadows of death. Benedict found himself uneasy and after muttering, 'Fine, fine,' hurried out of the room and took a deep breath on the landing. The Will. The Will. Telephone. Lawyer. What the devil had she meant about the I.R.A.? Fish? Fish?

But it was only after he had woken Martin O'Loughlinn the solicitor out of his pleasant Saturday morning lie-in and told him to be up double sharp to the house that midday with the Will that he found time to clear up the mystery. Fishponds. The Norwegians. An I.R.A. terror squad. Sabotage.

At the word 'sabotage' he felt the skin prickling and goose-pimpling at the back of his thick, bull neck, as though some hostile foot was treading on his grave. Sabotage! The Development! It wasn't possible, there couldn't be any connection, nobody knew— But there could, they did, and if they didn't they would. A slow – for him slow – smoulder of anger consumed his peace of mind for a full five seconds before erupting, like a volcano boiling out of its crater to destroy a countryside. THE DEVELOPMENT!

He rang the Guards.

'Sir,' said Sergeant McMenamin in both official languages, instantly recognizing the voice of greatness, of the Heir to the Throne.

'This fish business!' Benedict shouted. 'Have you arrested anyone yet?'

'We are pursuing—' Sergeant McMenamin began, and then, remembering the Superintendent's reaction to that innocent remark, substituted, 'We have our suspects, Minister, and—'

'Suspects?' Benedict roared. 'Don't you know? How many men are there in a place like this who could possibly do a thing like that?'

The sergeant would dearly have loved to answer truthfully by saying, 'A couple of hundred, Minister, if not more,' but instead, with a solid foundation of twenty-four hours' slow but fruitful thought supporting his answers, he said, 'Very few, Minister, of course, and we are watching them all. It's simply a matter of gathering all of them at the one blow, Minister.'

'All of them?' Benedict said, his voice dropping almost to a croak. Words that the sergeant had intended to soothe had

struck instead like a salvo on the waterline of a heeling galleon.
'How many are there?'

'About half a dozen activists in the area, Minister, no more
than that. But dangerous men.'

'Dangerous?' Benedict Mulcahy saw his dreams stopping
before their foundations were dug, let alone laid; dynamite
gangs of the I.R.A. publishing threats of death and destruction
for any foreigner who set foot in The Ross with an idea of
developing it; ruin and desolation. He gripped the telephone as
though it was a throat. 'Do you need more men? Permission to
carry arms?'

'I think everything's under control, sir. We're in constant
communication with Headquarters, and as soon as we apply for
warrants—'

'You haven't applied for them yet?' Benedict yelled.

'We want to be sure we're getting the right men, sir.'

'I hope you know what you're doing,' Benedict said in a voice
that carried subtle threats of banishment to the western islands,
or a return to point duty in some unspeakable part of Dublin
for any man who didn't know what he was doing.

'Have no fears, Minister, we have them under our eyes. The
Sons of Ireland, this group calls themselves. We've been—'
again he pulled himself back from incautious boasting. 'We've
had trouble with them before.'

'The Sons of—' Christ above, Benedict thought. Here we are
trying to pull this place up by its bloody bootlaces and make it
something, and people like that trying to destroy the country in
front of your eyes, the whore's gets.

'More or less Communists, sir,' the sergeant said, pressing
his advantage. And then, to nail it home, he said, 'and there's a
known Communist labour agitator in the district as well, sir.
We think he may be connected in some way. He was a close
associate of some of the men we're watching, and he was in the
neighbourhood of the fishponds at the time the crime was committed.'

'You can bet your bloody life he's involved.' Communists, by
God! At the bottom of everything. Atheism. Immorality. Destruction of property.

'A man called Carmody, Minister. He has a record the other
side for labour agitation and violence against the police.'

'Why the hell isn't he inside already?'

'Just giving him rope, sir.'

'Make damn sure you don't give him too much. And keep me informed. And not a word about this to anyone who doesn't have to know officially, you understand? Not a word to newspaper reporters, outsiders, anyone. That's my personal instruction as a Minister and you'll be getting confirmation of it from your superiors. Have you got that?'

'Absolutely, Minister. You can rely on me. Not a word.'

Benedict Mulcahy put down the telephone. The sergeant lowered his own receiver gently into its cradle with a hand that was close to trembling. He felt like a man who has crossed a river full of crocodiles on a series of unsteady stepping stones, any one of which could have plunged him to a most unpleasant end. But out of his trial by ordeal he had, he thought with a touch of complacency, done himself a modicum of good. A man on top of his job. Alert. Reliable. Thank God he had had his preliminary skirmish, his blooding, with the Super. He tried to imagine offering the Minister Peadar and Matty Power as credible saboteurs, and shuddered.

It never occurred to him for one second that he might have done himself a world of instant good by being honest, or at least simple and uncomplicated. Sergeant McMenamin, in his unworldly, Ross Harbour induced innocence, thought that the interests of all great men, from the Superintendent in his Belcorrig bungalow, to Minister Mulcahy in his suite of Government Offices, must be identical, and that if the Superintendent wanted the guilty parties to be Republican activists, then so must the Minister.

With equal innocence of heart, it never occurred to Benedict Mulcahy that there might be any other explanation for the crime. Everyone said it was the I.R.A., using that as a blanket term for any kind of violent and subversive persons, and the I.R.A. it must be, or at least the Communist section of them. Benedict, after all, had grown up in a world in which political violence was commonplace and almost admirable, and unlike an English politician who would be truly surprised to find that a crime of industrial sabotage had a political background, Benedict Mulcahy would have been truly surprised if it had not. He was conditioned by years of experience and the Sunday newspapers to believe that it was the I.R.A. that was behind it. But all the same he would have been a delighted man if the sergeant had suggested to him convincingly that they were not.

Meanwhile the sergeant was mulling over his limited list of

possible suspects. Michael Carmody, Johnny Conroy, alias Seagrun Ó Maelchonaire, Franky Murphy that was going round calling himself Proinsias Ó Murchu. Willie Carney that was calling himself Liam Ó Cearnaigh. Who else?

It was not that Sergeant McMenamin was a bad man. Nor even a bad policeman. Left to himself, unbothered by the Benedict Mulcahys of this world, or the Superintendents, or the Guard O'Neills, he would never have arrested a living soul except he found him committing violence. No woman listening to the wireless without benefit of licence need have feared his evening knock. No home-goer unlit by bicycle lamp need have looked for his booted shadow to step from the dark hedge with a summons. No distiller of poteen need have taken too much trouble to hide the whisp of smoke from his mountain still if all he had to fear was Sergeant McMenamin's determination to enforce the laws against poteen. No late night drinkers in The Angler, or any of the less inhibited drinking places of the town need have held themselves ready to leap out of the lavatory window to escape arrest and ignominy.

But a man is what life makes him, particularly if he is in constant dread of losing his pension, and Sergeant McMenamin had to do what life required of him. At the moment it required of him the makings of a conspiracy large enough, and crushable and exposable enough both to satisfy all authorities concerned that the emptying of the fish ponds was beyond the powers of any one sergeant and a constable to prevent; and also to impress on the highest authorities that a man capable, almost single-handed, of coping with such a crisis, deserved not only to have his pension when it fell due, but to have promotion into the bargain. Left to himself the sergeant would have been happy to stay a simple sergeant in Ross Harbour for the length of his active days. But in the modern world that was overtaking even The Ross, a man might rise, or he might fall. The one certainty appeared to be that he could not stay still. So be it. If he must choose between the two evils, let it be the lesser. He would rise.

As for Michael Carmody and Seagrun Ó Maelchonaire, he wished them no evil. But if they were not guilty of this they were undoubtedly guilty of something, and probably something just as bad. Michael had either been helping the old men to empty the ponds, or much more likely had been seducing Jenny Kershaw, for which he would ripely deserve whatever sentence was passed on him. In fact, as the sergeant thought of it, it was really God's Act and Judgment. There was no law against seduction, worse luck to the country for it, but if a man could be fined ten shillings or, God save us, fifty pence as it was now, for not having a lamp on his bicycle, and decent men like himself were obliged to haul other decent men into court for not having lamps, or licences, or for drinking a small glass of something after half eleven at night instead of before half eleven, then by God and his Mother it would be no harm if a lusty ram of a boy did a few months inside for fornication with an innocent young girl, even if the reason given on the charge sheet was something else. Let everyone's conscience be at rest about Michael Carmody, and let him cool his blood for a bit. As for Seagrun, as sure as an egg had a mother with feathers that boy would end in gaol soon. It might as well be sooner.

CHAPTER FOURTEEN

IT was already light when he woke. He could make out her features, the shape of her eyebrow, the curve of her cheek, the darkness of her hair. He touched her hair, stroked it softly. 'Wake up,' he whispered. 'You'll have to go.' The words hurt his heart as he said them. Suppose she didn't go, stayed here, suppose they told her ghastly father and mother that she would always stay here? Suppose they ran away together? Where? Over the Gap? Get lifts along the road? To where?

'You have to go back to your room,' he whispered heavily.

She opened her eyes, wide and frightened, not knowing for the second where she was. 'Michael?' She lifted her head and shoulders, put up her hands to cover her breasts and found that she was still dressed. And then she smiled. Because of that? Because of seeing him? He never knew. But she smiled, and bent her head on her thin neck, like a pony stretching its head sideways, and down to sweet grass, like a beautiful young animal, her eyes shy and pleased and then ashamed. He leaned forward, and put his face against hers, warm from sleep, her thin breast warm, and her hair against his forehead, against his cheek and ear, like skeins of warm silk and she put one hand on his shoulder, not pulling him against her but only resting it there, still too asleep to do anything else. She leaned her head on his, and his face was surrounded by warmth, by the warm nest of the bed and her body, and in that moment, those few seconds of warmth, he knew that this was why men were born, why he existed, that nothing else in the world mattered except this warmth, this love, this tenderness of possession. This was his reason for existence. And hers, and everyone's. If it could go on.

The light grew slowly stronger, and birds who had long ago sung their dawn chorus now sang irritably about food and worms and enemy intruders, competing with one another in sharp bursts of challenge. A pair of pigeons churred and called in the gutters of the stable roof. It was day. He had to tell her to go, but he stayed still and her hand stroked his cheek and she bent over him as though she was much older than he was and much wiser, her bent head and protective body saying clearly, 'we could have had this happiness long ago if only you had listened to me.' His hand crept into the bed and touched her waist, went round it, held on to her.

'Michael,' she said gently, for the pleasure of saying it. He put both arms round her and kissed her, their hearts touching, beating against one another, the warm softness of her mouth against his, her eyes shut.

'You'll have to go,' he said between kisses.

'Yes,' she said. If they had been listening they might have heard the town clock striking five, across the Bay.

'You're cold,' she whispered.

'Yes,' he said. He touched her skin and it was warm against his hand.

'Get in beside me,' she breathed. 'Let me warm you.' Her hands undid the buttons of his shirt.

If, much later, they had been listening, they would have heard the town clock striking six.

They even slept a little, for ten minutes, a quarter of an hour. This time when they woke they could see each other clearly. They had grown much older in the past hour, much wiser, more mature. 'Michael,' she said. She had been crying in her sleep and tears made a path down her cheek, like silver.

'Why are you crying?' he whispered, but only for the pleasure of saying something, because he knew exactly why.

'Because I'm happy.'

'Did it make you happy?'

'Yes.'

'What will we do?'

She shook her head at that, as though she knew that they would not need to do anything, that life would take care of such unimportant matters as that. She put her arms round his neck. 'Are you happy?'

He nodded, not able to say the word, and kissed her softly. 'You really will have to go.'

She smiled and stretched, yawning, her teeth white and the inside of her throat dark as a cat's, a beautiful, beautiful long, tawny cat, a gentle panther, its claws well-sheathed, its mind content.

'One, two, three—' he counted up to ten, and again. 'We really must – God,' he looked at his watch, 'it's twenty past six, Jesus, if they—'

'They don't wake up till eight,' she said, stretching her head and throat and closing her eyes, 'and they don't expect me to be in my own room then, they'll think I'm out getting mushrooms or something.'

'But—'

She put her arms round his neck and pulled him down to her. 'Tell me you love me,' she whispered.

CHAPTER FIFTEEN

ALL morning Michael was singing as he worked and every time that Angela Kershaw heard him it tightened something inside her, as though she had suddenly been forced to remember bad news, or had a premonition of evil. She hated the sound of it, instinctively, felt the same shiver of unpleasant fear that she felt whenever she saw pictures of hippies in the newspapers or on television, heard stories about them. Always, automatically, she thought of Jenny, and she thought of her now. Like a threat to her, like a lewd, dangerous animal prowling round, rampant, filthy. She was in the dining-room and the singing, the humming, passed the door, went on towards the kitchen. The tune was 'Spanish Lady', but she did not know that. She heard only the insolence, the challenge, and her heart seemed to tighten and she felt suddenly threatened, as though she were alone in the darkness and horrible, dreadful things were happening. What did he want in the kitchen? And behind that surface question the unaskable question; why was he singing like that?

She went out into the corridor. The singing had stopped. He must be talking to – Jenny. Asking her for something. But there was no sound of voices. It was absurd. There couldn't be – it— She'd just walk in, casually looking for something for the dining-room. Jenny didn't understand, she was so young—

There was no one in the kitchen. Her heart seemed actually to stop beating for as long as it took her to search the large, rather dark kitchen with her eyes. Pots boiling on the range. Bowls half-filled with things on the long table. The smell of roasting. No one. It couldn't – she – not Jenny – not with – she didn't know what she was thinking. As though she had been wounded under her breast. She even put up one hand to her ribs, held herself. 'Jenny!'

The kitchen girl, Eileen, came into the kitchen from the scullery, carrying her bucket, her apron filthy, her face red, her bare

189

arms pink and wet to the elbows. The sight of her added the last twist of pain to Angela's mind. She wanted to scream at her, smack her face, that stupid, vacant, Irish face. For that second, more than Michael Carmody, more than her fears for Jenny, more than everything else in the world that face summed up for her everything she feared and hated in her life. And the fact that she couldn't scream at the girl, couldn't afford to tell her to take herself and her filthy apron home to her slut of a mother, made it ten times worse.

'Where is Miss Jennifer?' Angela said, her voice unnatural, afraid to look at the girl for what she would see in her eyes.

'In the yard, I think,' Eileen said, astonished at Mrs. Kershaw's face. Like she had a terrible fright, she told her mother afterwards. Like a ghost.

Angela went out into the yard, and even the sunlight wounded her, seemed to conspire against her. As though there was nothing but sex in the world. She felt suddenly old, with no strength to fight any more. Jenny was coming out of one of the stables. Coming with a swift, hurrying step, looking back over her shoulder, her face alive, as it was never alive when—

'What on earth are you doing out here?' Angela said, the possibility of asking a straightforward question, of being legitimately irritated at having to ask it, at having to come out to find Jennifer, at seeing the kitchen empty, neglected when there were guests, when there was so much work, when they needed, when – all of this gave her back her strength, made her herself again. Jenny looked round at her, her step checking for a second, her face – but she couldn't see her face properly, the sun was in her eyes – she wanted for that second to cry out to her, Jenny, please, please, tell me there's nothing, nothing – and the thought of that ultimate treachery was like poison, unendurable. Her mind was saying, 'In the stable, look in the stable, walk in and look, see what she was doing, he's there, he's there behind the door, they were kissing—' but her legs wouldn't obey, she could only stand in front of Jenny and try to read her eyes.

'I came out for a breath of air,' Jenny said, and brushed past her.

'It seems a very odd place—' But against her will, or perhaps it was not against her will, she turned and followed Jenny, back into the hotel, into the kitchen, leaving that gaping, arrogant shadow of a stable doorway behind her. And behind it? In the kitchen Jennifer went instantly to the stove, making herself the cook, banging the lids of the pots, opening the oven doors, calling for Eileen.

'Jennifer—'

'I'm busy Mummy. At least, if you want lunch ready at one.'

Angela stood in the middle of the kitchen, watching Jennifer's back, bending, moving, the thin white cotton shirt clinging to her skin with damp, her hair tied in a green scarf, Eileen standing like a lump beside her, futile, useless, and yet somehow closer to Jenny than— It was so unfair, so terrible, that it was like a death. Like watching an enemy. Not even a stranger. An enemy. You brought them into the world, you suffered all that agony, loved them, kept them from harm, spent your whole life for them – a flicker of uncertainty crossed her consciousness – had she really spent enough, of herself – her life? – she had, she had – and all they wanted in the world was to destroy you, hurt you in the most terrible way possible. But that momentary flicker of doubt had brought her back to the surface of things, to the ordinary world in which she could act. She thought of saying something else, but Jennifer's moving back was too threatening, too much in command by the stove. Angela went out and down the corridor to Hubert's study.

He was drafting a letter to Alloway, Barnacle and Truett, telling them that 'on mature reflection – in the long term interests of the district – needs of the country – progress – serious unemployment—' At least he was trying to tell them these things. The wastepaper basket beside his knee was already full.

She opened the door so violently that his pen skidded across the page, leaving a trail of small blots like bullet scars across the lapidary phrases.

'Damn,' he said, and then seeing who it was, 'Really Angela! Must—'

'Hubert. I've simply got to talk to you. About Jenny.'

He tightened himself into the leather chair, like a hare into its form. His adam's apple jerked. 'I'm trying to write an extremely important letter—'

As she looked at him he seemed to be visibly hiding behind the letter. As he always hid, behind something, anything, rather than face any kind of reality. She clenched her teeth, her hands so tightened into fists with nerves that she felt the pain of it in her shoulders, at the back of her neck. Like trying to get support from a revolving door.

'You've got to listen to me,' she said. 'And you've got to do something. Jenny – she – I was looking for her just now and – I went into the kitchen and she wasn't there.' Even as she was saying them, trying to say them, the words became unsayable, and she was filled with a cold, piercing rage at being forced to say them; that he couldn't see without being told, that he couldn't relieve her even of this. She stood on the worn, the very worn Persian rug in front of the empty Adam fireplace with its cracked marble caryatids, unconsciously in the man-of-the-family's position, looking at Hubert with a painful, naked clarity; thinking how like a hare he looked, how – how trivial – how *Irish*. And yet once that same look of half-helpless Irishness had been what had attracted her. She had thought of it as romantic, endearing; a kind of warm sweetness about it after the cold efficiency of her girlhood. She had thought that at one and the same time she would be able to mould him, and that he would love her in a way that no one else—

All this was so familiar that it no more than flashed across the screen of her mind, subliminally, barely touching her consciousness. All she was really conscious of was anger. And frustration. And yet she had loved him once, given, offered him a devotion that he had never been able to recognize, because it was a controlled, disciplined devotion that hid inside her waiting to be discovered, like a child in a shrubbery playing hide-and-seek, like a jewel in a mine. While he walked on the surface, in the open, looking for something cheap and meretricious that he might find lying in the grass. Until the unused, unnoticed devotion turned into a cold impatience and finally into contempt. And all the stages between had been so camouflaged by self-control, by her conception of what was right, of what one could say, show of oneself, that he had hardly noticed that she was changing, and what he did notice he put down to 'marriage' and to 'women's things', and more sadly to his own mature realization of what she was 'really like', of what he had done in marrying her.

'She was out in the stables,' Angela was saying, her voice high and hard with self-loathing for having to say it. And at the same time shaking. That tremor of the voice was the only signal that she allowed herself, a half-concealed cry for help, for what she had longed for when they were first married, a husband who— She no longer remembered what it was that she had wanted from him. But at least understanding, at least—

'It must get pretty steamy in that blasted kitchen,' he was saying, jollying, soothing, even his tone of voice a charade, a mask. ' 'Spect she wanted a breath of air. Can't keep her too close to the grindstone y'know.'

The echo of Jenny's actual words made something explode inside her head. And yet even her explosion seemed cold, like ice breaking under unendurable pressures.

'Can you understand nothing?' she cried. She wanted to scream, to do something violent. But she could only stand there, raise her voice, stare at him with hatred. She lowered her voice to a slow, deliberate whisper, like the long cut of a whip through wintry air. 'You will have to get rid of him.'

'Him?' For a second he was genuinely taken aback, bewildered, and then instantly, as he caught her leap of meaning, the charade came back, he began to pretend, to act. 'Jennikins? And – that – and – Carmody?' Half act, half genuine. 'Dammit, Angie, you can't – I mean, you can't seriously think—'

'Of course I can seriously think. I only wish you could. I should never have allowed it, never, I had an instinct – I'd only to look at him. Hubert, you've got to get rid of him.' He had his mouth open to answer and she went on as though she was stamping on him. 'I'm not going to be talked out of this. I want him out of here and I want him out at once. Today. I don't care what excuse—'

He was staring at her, his mouth still slightly open, hunting in his mind for an escape, for something that would deflect her, prove to her that what she was thinking was ridiculously wrong, or that what she wanted was impossible, undesirable. He did not think of what he was looking for as either pretence or escape. Only as a way, the proper, gentleman's way of avoiding that cardinal sin against the gentleman's code of allowing a woman, one's wife, to take the controlling hand in a serious matter (and that not because it might be humiliating for the man, but because it was unfair to the woman, would put too great a strain on her delicacy, allow her to fall into errors which would hurt and humiliate her when inevitably she discovered that she was wrong). And this need was so much in his mind that it was several seconds before he realized that there was another, even more serious crime against the code involved; the possibility of having to tell her something that would frighten her, allow her to see the unplumbed depths of danger from which her husband, as always, was protecting her.

But in this case the truth was so close at hand, so convenient, so clearly shaped as the best means of preventing her from trying to make him do something damn silly, that he had no real choice. And behind the gentleman's façade a whisper of genuine malice breathed 'and a bit of a bloody shock might do her good'. 'I didn't want to have to tell you about this,' he said, staring huntedly at the door, 'but—' He told her. The I.R.A. The Communists. Sergeant Mac. The charge the sergeant had left with him to say nothing and do nothing to alarm Michael Carmody.

And for the length of time he spent in telling her they were almost close, each of them almost stripped of their pretences and protections – like two uncurtained windows facing each other's naked light across a dark and frightening nothingness. Yet two people from behind those lit windows cannot really touch one another. Only gesture to each other across the dark.

'Oh my God!' Angela whispered. 'And he's—?'

'One of the ring-leaders,' Hubert said. 'If not *the* ring-leader. So you see, I can't—'

The appeal to reason was a mistake, and he knew that it was a mistake as soon as he had made it. He tried to think of a way of drawing back what he had just said. But the closeness, the sense of an overwhelming reality was dispelled, and she was a mother again, faced by a husband who could not, would not, was incapable of playing a husband's role.

'And you mean to say that you expect me to—'

'M'dear, it's not me, it's the bally Garda chaps, it's Sergeant Mac.'

'Jenny is not Sergeant Mac's daughter. She is yours. Are you going to leave her in the same house with—'

'God damn it!' Hubert cried, smacking his hand down on his desk. The nib of the fountain pen went into his palm and he shot upright, much as Sergeant McMenamin had done the previous morning after impaling his foot on the drawing pin. 'Bloody hell! Ooooh, oh, damn, my hand, I've gone and stabbed my bloody hand, oh blast.' He pushed the chair back so violently that it fell, and stamped round the room holding his right hand cradled in his left.

'Now look what you've made me do.'

Angela drew in her breath. 'If—' She let her breath out again. He did these things on purpose. She felt as if she was going to be really ill. 'I'll get some Elastoplast,' she said in a tightly controlled voice. She went to the door.

'I'll need some iodine,' Hubert called. He had stolen a swift glance at his wound. There was more ink than blood but what blood there was had given the ink a strange and frightening colour. Thoughts of blood poisoning came to him. He sat down in the leather armchair on the far side of the fireplace. 'And some hot water. We'd better sterilize it.' He made the sounds of a man enduring close to unendurable pain.

'Jenny!' Angela called, her voice grating with anger, and when Jenny answered, 'Bring some hot water and iodine and things. Your father's hurt his hand.' She came back into the study. 'Hubert, we've got to decide about this thing. I simply can't—'

'Not now,' Hubert said, allowing his eyes to close and leaning his head back. 'Damn thing went in rather deep to tell you the truth.'

'I can't stand any more,' Angela said.

'You won't have to,' Hubert said, his eyes still shut.

Before Angela could ask him what he meant, Jennifer was there with iodine and bandages. Behind her came Michael, carrying an enamel basin of hot water. Angela stared at him as she might have stared at a snake suddenly appearing in her bedroom. For a second she felt completely paralysed, her whole body locked. Her jaw wouldn't move, she couldn't speak.

'Here you are,' Michael said. Out of the corner of his eye he saw her face, saw the locked fear and hatred, knew that she knew. Or thought he did. He stood for a fraction of a moment stooping forward, his eye glancing sideways, the basin poised above the small table beside the armchair, conscious of Jenny near him, afraid to let his eyes move, to look away. Very carefully he put the basin down. Jenny was saying, 'Which hand is it, Daddy?'

Hubert put his finger-tips in the water, testing the heat, let his hand sink in. 'Ahggg,' he said very softly through his teeth and then, 'Thanks Carmody, no need to keep you.'

Jenny gave the bandages and iodine to her mother. 'I'd better get back,' she said coldly. 'Or things will boil over.'

Outside the door Michael was waiting for her. They moved down towards the kitchen, out of earshot of her mother. Touched hands.

'Your mother knows,' he said.

'I – she can't really know.'

'I'd like to tell her.'

The fingers tightened on his, she began to say 'No' and changed it to 'I know.' She glanced back up the corridor, and the other way towards the kitchen where, with luck, Eileen was looking after the stove and the vegetables and the two different roasts and the three kinds of soup. There was no one staying in the hotel, but a couple had arrived in a car a half hour ago and were walking down by the bay until it was lunch time, and a party of five in a Minibus had come by earlier and said that they would be back at half past one.

'Meet me this afternoon,' he whispered. 'I'm off from half two.'

'I can't. We're going to the Eagans for tea – it's a huge do for some people who are going away.'

'Say you've got a headache. You're going to bed.'

'She'll suspect.'

He took both her hands and held them against his chest. 'We've got to talk,' he said. 'I could wait for you at Stukeley's Pool—' Everything was gone, pride, sense. And he was glad. It made him feel light, as though he had flung weights overboard, and was suddenly free. He lifted her hands to his face and kissed them. For that second as she looked at his dark head bent over her finger-tips he seemed so beautiful that she was willing to die, it seemed impossible to contain so much happiness and love and fear in one body without dying.

'They'll come.'

'Half four. Four.'

'I'll try,' she whispered, now only frightened, her breath catching. She did not know why she was frightened. Of her mother? What could her mother do? Nothing. Just shout, say ugly things. But in reality she was afraid of herself, of him, of the path they were following, going – she hadn't meant to follow it, to go anywhere. And now it was no longer possible to stop, she no longer belonged to herself. 'Please,' she said.

'Four o'clock,' he said again. 'I'll be waiting.' He walked quickly along the corridor and was gone. His going left her feeling as if she was no longer complete. That in the kitchen she would be walking in her sleep.

In the study Angela Kershaw was bandaging her husband's sterilized hand. Once the ink had been washed away there was almost nothing to see, and out of a furious sarcasm she made the bandage enormous, as though he had broken his wrist.

'Steady on, old girl,' he said. 'No need to overdo it.'

'Isn't there?' she said through her teeth. She had had Red Cross training in the Sunningford Ladies Sports Club, and before that in the Girl Guides, and even in malice there was a hospital efficiency about her bandaging which made him feel momentarily queasy when he looked down at his imprisoned right hand, the fingers pushing out helplessly like the ends of something broken, maimed for life. Another woman would have felt a bit of blasted sympathy, he thought bitterly. Like a damn matron in a hospital.

'And now about that – boy,' Angela said, lowering her voice on the last word and nodding towards the door, as if she suspected hidden listeners.

'For God's sake,' Hubert said. 'I've told you. We can't do anything—'

'You never can.'

'Don't be so damned unfair.'

He got up and stamped across to his desk, wondering again whether to add to the truth about the fellow outside the even greater, if less immediately urgent truth that he was going to sell up.

'Unfair?' she was saying, her voice shivering with contempt.

'Christ, Angela!' He lifted his bandaged hand to bang it on the desk for emphasis, and caught himself only just in time. 'Do you *want* him to burn the place over our heads?'

She let her breath out helplessly, defeated. She couldn't go on. He was so hopeless that— For a few moments she had almost believed him. That it was really as bad, as urgent as he said. But there had been too many pretences, too many charades. Barmen didn't burn down hotels, not even here. And typically, that was the danger that Hubert wanted to face. While the real one—

'The one thing that really matters in all this is the one thing you seem determined to ignore. Jenny – and that – that—'

'For God's sake!' Hubert shouted. This time he did thump his bandaged hand on the desk and the pain – caused by the bandage being too tight rather than by the minuscule wound in his palm – the pain actually stiffened him in mid-cry and he stood with his mouth open, his bandaged hand lifted like a ridiculous dog lifting its paw, pretending to be hurt. But the hurt was real. 'Oh my God!' he whispered.

'Please stop acting the fool, Hubert. My head's bursting. I'm going to lie down upstairs. And when I come down again I want you to have settled things with that boy. It's his afternoon off. You can simply tell him his work is unsatisfactory and he's not to come back. I want him out of here by tonight.' She went before he could answer. And for a moment he was brought back by helplessness and rage and something as close to hatred as he was capable of feeling for a woman to something equally near to reality. Like soft mists dissolving for a moment on the mountain side and showing the edge of a ravine. Driving him over it. Bloody well driving him over it to disaster.

But in reminding him that it was Michael's free half-day she had given him the way of escape that he needed. The chap'd be out of the way all afternoon, most of the evening. Before he came back he'd think of something, persuade her, get her to see— He might ask Sir Philip to talk to her, she'd listen to him (he brushed aside the fact that she disliked Sir Philip even more than she disliked Lady Eagan). She'd have to listen to him. Lady E. might talk to her as well, tell her a bit of Irish reality, although God dammit, after twenty years—

The filled wastepaper basket caught his eye, reminded him of the letter to Alloway, Barnacle and Truett. He looked at his bandaged hand. He couldn't even write a blasted letter now. The thought of taking off the bandage came to him and was rejected. He held the hand close to his chest, slid it into the front of his jacket, said an 'Ah' of relief. Might be just as well he couldn't write. Letters were chancy things. Much better to talk to them. The thought of driving up to Dublin, a race against time, came to him and hovered in the back of his mind. If they weren't going to the Eagans this afternoon— Telephone. He took half a step towards the hall where the telephone was. Saturday, blast. They wouldn't be there. He went to the window, staring moodily at the trees, the stretch of unkempt paddock that had once been lawn, sloping gently down to the shore of the Bay a few hundred yards from the house. He saw the two lunch-visitors walking aimlessly along the narrow stony beach. A youngish chap and a girl. The man stooped, picked up a stone and flung it into the water. By God, it was all right for them.

There was the sound of a van driving over the cattle-gate. He looked to the right and saw the Mulcahy Supermarket van leaving, and Michael walking back into the stable yard, carrying something. Mulcahy. Of course! The very man! Go straight to him, put his cards on the table. 'We all know you're behind this Development thing, Mulcahy. Well, why don't we talk business? These solicitor chaps—' He pulled his affectations of folly round him like a warm coat against the wind, an addict gasping for his drug. He looked at his watch. Half twelve. He'd catch the fellow just before his lunch. Have a whiskey together. 'A chap doesn't usually say these things, but I've admired you for a long time, Mulcahy. You're the type of chap this country needs. And if you need my place for this Development—'

He went out to the courtyard, trying over phrases in his mind, much the same phrases that he had tried and retried in the draft-letters to the solicitors. '—Unemployment – progress – industrialization—' But with a freer swing to them, fitting an easy, man-to-man confrontation. Damn sight easier than writing blasted letters to faceless fellows up in Dublin. Glad to get down to brass tacks. I know you people think we – my – our sort – Anglo-Irish – no, better not introduce any stuff about class – just a business thing – a straight deal. 'You want my land, I want your money, eh? Ha!'

He was fumbling with the bolts of the doors to the Bentley's share of the stables. 'I'll do that for you,' a voice said behind him and he jerked as though a gun had been pushed into his spine. Bloody fellow, creeping about. Christ, he'd be glad to get out of this place.

'I can manage,' he said sharply. Why the hell couldn't the chap just cut and run for it? Didn't he know the damn guards were on to him? For a second he thought of warning him. You'd better get out while the going's good, Carmody. God, what a blasted mess.

Michael was unbolting the doors, swinging them wide. The Bentley gleamed. And on the instant he felt better, in command. Even to see it gave him strength. He rested his bandaged hand on the high green sweep of the mudguard. My old friend. The thought of his loneliness pierced his heart. Nobody understood, nobody cared. Angela! Even Jenny – a chap gets older – wears himself out – faces the most fearful odds – some chap on a bridge, who was it? He was climbing into the Bentley's bucket seat, heroism flowing into his legs from the contact, from the very floor of the cockpit. That was it. How can man die better, than facing fearful odds? By God, he was facing some pretty fearful odds, but he'd come through some rough times before, and he'd come through this lot.

The engine chuffed, whirred, caught and roared, the big body shook inside the stable like an aeroplane straining to be off the ground. Ease her. Roll forward. He looked down at Michael with a hard dislike, the horseman's for the peasant. Let the blighter try anything on. His hands caressed the wheel, or at least his left hand did. With his bandaged right he could only steady it between thumb and gathered, immobilized fingers. Out into the sunlight. He should have stuck out for becoming a racing driver when he got back from the war. Wasting his life in this blasted place.

Out of the courtyard, engine growling, power under his hands. Fangio at Le Mans. Nuvolari. By God, they're away. Roaring across the cattle-gate, Coca lifting a dreamy head to look. Round the curve, sparse gravel spurting, tyres sliding, bit of axle tramp on that lap chief – no, no, can't afford the time to whip it out for a new one, we'll soldier on. First or burst, eh?! On to the main road. The archdeacon's Morris 1000 missed disaster by inches, pulled into the hedge twenty yards ahead. The archdeacon said things which he had learned long ago, when he was an army chaplain. Hubert was already round the curve in the road, the vroooom of his exhaust hanging on the summer air. Round the next corner a horse and cart, bloody tinkers, blocking up half the damn road. 'Look where you're going you silly swine!' Hubert yelled, but his yell was lost in the huge unsilenced VROOOOM as he accelerated, offside wheels lifting on to the far grass bank of the narrow road, the horse shying, pots hanging, the King Gallagher lurching sideways, grabbing at the reins.

'The eighth curse of God on you you bloody heathen banshee, Christ rot you,' yelled Gallagher in fury as the great green rump of the Bentley vanished round the corner ahead. 'May your woman give birth to a cat and it clawing her gut. May you die roaring. Hold up you brute,' he shouted in a different tone, dragging at the reins of the frightened pony, more frightened by the King's voice than by the Bentley.

'Aisy, aisy,' said the Whisperer who was on the seat beside the King. 'Let me down to him, you have him frit with the cursing.' The Whisperer, a lanky stoop-shouldered man with a squint and tow hair and a scrawny throat like a chicken's, slid down from the high seat and went to the pony's head.

He did whisper, blowing gently into the pony's ear and nose, stroking her shoulders with the flat of his hand, and yet barely touching the hairs. The pony quieted instantly, blowing in her turn and snuffling and shaking her head. The Whisperer came back and climbed on to the seat again. The King looked at him sideways.

'It's uncanny,' he said, as he had said a thousand times before.

The Whisperer said nothing. The pony trotted forward, her ears going this way and that, puzzled and delighted by what she had just heard.

'It'll be a bad job if we're cott,' the Whisperer said.

'The devil we'll be cott,' the King said impatiently. 'Who'd catch us? The old man aself? The girleen? And if they cott us? Will he go roaring to the polis that we're after stealing his stachy that he stole himself? Will he?'

'I dunno,' the Whisperer said, whose talent lay all in the one direction. It had brought him fame and a lorry, but outside of taming horses and making the horse that thought it belonged to one man quietly follow the Whisperer away until it could be nicely painted and belong to another man, outside of that he was no more than middling.

'Lave the thinking to me,' the King said. 'Do you bring your lorry where I tellt you and Stofirt and me and Stan will see to the rest of the gruber. And the sheer-legs. Bring the sheer-legs wit' you.'

They had come back to the Whisperer's camp by then, a semi-permanent scatter of rusty iron and scrap metal that ran for fifty yards along the side of the road. There was a traditional caravan, with a half door and a hooped roof, and painted wooden sides, a dog tied underneath it; and a camp fire, and a woman, and several children, and a kind of shelter built in the ditch; and a newish, trailer-caravan made to be drawn by a motor car, with plastic flowers in the windows. It housed his mother and father. His mother had been the Whisperer before him.

'We're agreed then?' the King said. He spat in his palm and held his hand out for the Whisperer to take it. The Whisperer shook hands reluctantly.

'Midnight, so,' the King said. The Whisperer got down to rejoin his family and the King drove away.

CHAPTER SIXTEEN

HUBERT stood uneasily in the tiled porch of the John Mulcahys' ranch-style bungalow. He was already half-sorry that he had come. Behind him, filling the short driveway, the Bentley stood enormous, glittering, grotesquely out of place, like a horse in a shop. The chimes of the doorbell rang musically inside the hall, died away. Clouds drifted across the sun. On the freshly sprinkled lawn a green and red plaster leprechaun held a tiny yellow shoe in his lap. He had, Hubert thought, a most sinister expression. He began to hope that no one would answer.

But behind the coloured lozenges of glass in the hall door a shadow moved, came closer, became the Picasso-like fragments of a woman. The door opened a few inches, and the housekeeper, dressed in black, her face at once grief-stricken and vaguely suspicious, stared at Hubert. It was not that she was suspicious of Hubert. It was simply that living here, a mile outside the town, after a lifetime in Knuckle Street, any ring at the doorbell filled her with alarm.

'Mr. John in?' Hubert said, making his voice cheerful, as though he and John Mulcahy were on the most intimate of terms, always dropping in on one another. In fact, he had only been to this house once in the five years of its existence, and then by a kind of accident. As old Mrs. Cecilia Barton, niece of the last Lord Medmenham, had said when someone, probably Lady Eagan, had suggested inviting the John Mulcahys to a largeish garden party – 'They may be very rich and very nice, m'dear, but his father started life as a pack boy to a Jewish pedlar, and I'm simply too old to alter m' mind about certain things.'

It was the sense of this gulf that he was now going to try to cross, and as a suppliant, that had struck Hubert in the moment of dismounting from the Bentley. The red tiled roof, the white-painted Spanish plaster, the wrought-iron decorations of the porch, the imitation ship's lantern, the leaded glass of the front door, the plaster leprechaun, had filled him with gloom. The idea of appealing as man to man to the owner of all this appeared to him with naked clarity as ridiculous and, if he had not already made so much noise in arriving that anyone inside the bungalow must have heard him, he would simply have driven away again.

The housekeeper was saying something in a tragic whisper. '... arrangements ... Knuckle Street ... funeral ...'

'Funeral?' Hubert said, his mind caught back from unhappiness. 'Not—' he stopped himself in time from saying something inappropriate. 'Not the old gentleman?'

The housekeeper bowed her head. 'This morning, sir. Half past five.'

'Ah,' said Hubert, 'I see. I'd better – terribly sorry – if you'd give m' condolences—' He saw to his surprise that the woman was actually sniffling. She was, in fact, the only person in the entire countryside who had shed a genuine tear for the old man. Not that he had ever treated her well, or even tolerably, beyond securing her her present employment with his son, whose nurse she had once been. But when she had been John's nurse, a girl of twenty, with the thickset body and a plain face and an obedient nature yearning to love and to be loved, the old man had taken her as his mistress.

There had been nothing romantic about it. He had taken her as he took medicine for his other natural needs, and he always went to Confession afterwards, like a spoonful of jam after castor oil. She had been his shame and his disgrace, grabbed hastily in the dark three or four times a month over a period of a few years, before the sap sank in his veins for ever, and by the end of it he had hated her for what she had allowed him to do, made it possible for him to do. The only reason he had gone on employing her was for fear of her telling. Until the passage of time helped him to convince himself that none of it had really happened, or at least not in any sinful way, and she was simply part of the furniture. He passed her on to John on John's marriage much as he might have passed on a clock.

For the girl herself, there had been so little pleasure in it that it had never seemed like a sin; more like a rather strange extension of her duties, and as the years went by and she never married she had consoled herself by thinking that if 'that' was all that was involved it was little enough that she had missed. But the fact remained that those few scufflings in Knuckle

Street had been all that she had ever had of romance, and when she knew that the old man was dead it affected her to an extent that had surprised even herself. And so she stood at the half-opened door staring down at Hubert Kershaw's well-polished, well-worn brogues, and actually cried for Gombeen. (A long, long way off, as he trod down the iron stairway in the burning dark, it seemed to Gombeen that a fine mist fell like rain about him, cooling the iron.

'It's raining!' he whispered wonderingly to Moishe Gavron descending before him like a great leather shadow, darker than the dark. 'I felt a drop!'

'It won't rain for long,' Moishe said.)

'Terribly sorry,' Hubert said again. And at that moment Clara Mulcahy came into the hall from the drawing-room. She had heard the Bentley arrive, peeped through the net curtains to see that it really, truly was Mr. Kershaw; seen him step down with his long, elegant legs, seen him lift his hand to the knot of his tie, brush the hair over his ear with a gesture that brought a kind of tremor to her nerves, and had run to compose herself in one of the armchairs, waiting for Nanny to show him in. She had heard their voices and recomposed herself, picked up a magazine, and put it down again, not sure whether to find her reading would create a good impression or not. Mr. Kershaw! Come to express his sorrow! Whoever would have thought? And she was practically in a négligée! It crossed her mind to run and put on something else, but there was no time, and – it was not really a négligée, more a – more a housecoat. A morning coat. It came to her that with John out Nanny might simply send him away.

Hurriedly, or at least hurriedly for her, she went out into the hall. 'Oh Mr. Kershaw! How very kind of you to call. Isn't it terrible? So sudden! All right, Nanny. Do come in Mr. Kershaw. John *will* be vexed he missed you.' Chattering vaguely she led the way back into the drawing-room, and Hubert followed her, not even intending to at first, but merely trying to find the right words in which to tell her that he was not going to come in. 'Thanks – er awfully good of you – I—'

But as he followed her, words and intention died away. He knew Clara Mulcahy as everyone in Ross Harbour knew everyone else, and like most other men who saw her – had seen her ever since she was sixteen or seventeen, walking in demure crocodile with the other pupils of the Convent of the

204

Crucifixion, her young bosom and her creamy throat and wonderfully rounded knees transforming the grey flannel gym slip and the black stockings of her uniform in a way that caused sharp pangs of anguish to the Sisters – he had had his occasional thought about her. She had a way of walking in the street, down the hill to the Supermarket, or simply standing gazing into a shop window, her ripe, perfect mouth half open, her dark blue eyes half hidden by their black velvet lashes, her bosom seeming to make her bend forward slightly, an air of half consciousness about her, that suggested somehow that something quite staggering had happened to her recently and she was about to fall down.

But she stood, or lay, so far outside the very narrow range of women about which Hubert's ideas of what a gentleman thinks and does allowed him to fantasize that he had never thought of her seriously. She was neither a lady nor a wench, and he had long ago pigeonholed her simply as that jolly handsome little Mrs. M. And if he had thought about her any further than that it was to pity her vaguely for being hitched up to that awful feller Mulcahy. But it was all money with these people of course. Like the French. For wenching one went to Paris, not that he had ever been, or for something a bit more serious one found someone of one's own set, someone fastish but discreet like that Loach girl who'd married the American. Although here again hearsay had to take the place of experience.

Yet at this moment, following Clara Mulcahy into the Mulcahy drawing-room, his eye first caught and then almost hypnotized by the slow, dreamy sway of her hip as she moved ahead of him, all these barriers of prejudice seemed suddenly insubstantial. She was a damn fine looking girl and no mistake. The idea of approaching John Mulcahy no longer seemed ridiculous. It was damn stupid to be prejudiced, a chap couldn't really help how he had been brought up. He looked round the drawing-room, determined in advance to approve of it, or at least not to condemn it.

It was a big room, furnished from ceiling to floor from the Mulcahy Furniture Emporium in Belcorrig, a newish annexe of the Belcorrig Supermarket. The moss green carpet was as sparklingly new and clean as if it had never been walked on, the gold tapestry upholstery of the Chesterfield suite looked as though it had never been sat on, the deep-foam cushions plumped up like down; the reproduction Sheraton occasional tables and upright chairs and the slope-fronted escritoire looked as though they had never been used.

And as Hubert turned from looking at the drawing-room to looking again at its mistress, even to his eye there seemed to lie about her splendid shoulders, her yearning bosom and full-throated neck, something of the same newness, a strange, un-natural untouchedness. Her flowing nylon housecoat with its scalloped, frilled neckline; her rich black hair; her ripe, longing mouth; they had one and all the same look of the shop window about them; brand new and exposed for sale, but not yet bought.

This was not entirely true. She had been bought, by John Mulcahy. He had bought her with his name and prospects, and what he had got in exchange was the future ownership of Glennon's Hotel when her childless aunt died; four houses in Knuckle Street, some land on Lir Head, and twelve thousand pounds immediately in cash. He had also got Clara of course, and been happy to have her, at least at first. But Clara had been brought up by her mother and her aunt, and the Little Sisters of the Crucifixion, to believe that sex was something extremely unpleasant which only happened to servant girls, and when John had attempted to teach her differently on the first night of their honeymoon in Torremolinos it had sent her into hysterics. Such ferocious hysterics that the hotel management had come running and had with difficulty been persuaded by John not to throw them both out into the street at three in the morning.

Since then their sex life together had gone from difficult to non-existent. John relieved himself with one or another of the girls in the Supermarkets, paying them off with free groceries, and Clara lay in bed until midday and then sat in her drawing-room waiting for something to happen. It was not truly that she was against sex, and certainly not against the idea of it. It was simply that her idea of it, and John's, were at opposite ends of the spectrum. His was a compound of guilt and brutal lechery. Hers was True Romance. And lying in bed of a long morning, or sitting in this drawing-room of an even longer afternoon, she had daydreamed an enormous number of genteel fantasies in which sex played a genteel and romantic role – not under the heading of 'sex' of course; a manly hand grasping her wrist, an eye gazing deeply into hers, a masterful voice whispering, 'I adore you. Come!' the scent of pipe tobacco on a rough tweed coat as she buried her face— These fantasies, bloodless as they might be, had reached such a pitch that once or twice in the market square or walking down by the Harbour or up Knuckle Street, a drift of pipe tobacco had reached her and she had almost swooned, only to turn her head and see some horrible rough sailor or labourer puffing away and she had shuddered all the way home.

Hubert himself after his one brief visit here had played a part in her day-dreams, but just as she had always lain outside his arbitrarily chosen area of 'reality', so he had lain outside hers, and he had had to surrender his place to Clark Gable. And now here he was, really here in her drawing-room! A few minutes ago there had been nothing to look forward to except the funeral, and now she was actually entertaining a gentleman visitor! Mr. Kershaw himself!

What could she offer him? What did ladies offer gentlemen before lunch? Her bosom lifted gently under its loose sheath of nylon, the pink frill like the mouth of a voluptuous flower. Her lashes drooped, her lips were parted in thought, she looked like a magnificent courtesan of the Belle Epoque about to surrender to Guy de Maupassant.

A number of half-formed emotions stirred in the deeper recesses of Hubert's mind. She really was a stunner. Seeing her outside didn't give you an idea. A real – a real stunner. His adam's apple swallowed and rose again, like a float. By God she was. 'Jolly nice little place, eh?' he said.

An echo from her reading came to Clara's aid. 'Can I offer you a sherry?' she breathed. John had been extremely vexed the time Father Tom had called, soon after they were married, and she had opened a new bottle of whiskey and Father Tom had had three glasses. But the sherry was already open, she knew it was, because John had opened it at Christmas.

'Ah, well, if you're having something,' Hubert said. 'A jolly nice place.' He waited for her to pour the sherry, but she stood where she was in the middle of the drawing-room, not quite swaying, but giving the appearance of it. She was thinking with a mixture of excitement and alarm, 'Suppose he expects to stay to lunch?' What would she do? He'd have to have John's chop. The thought of having him sit opposite her at the dining-room table made her head swim.

'Not if it's any trouble,' Hubert said. 'The sherry—'

'Oh. Oh. No, not at all.' She moved herself, going to the dining-room, leaving Hubert standing, and only thought of asking him to sit down as she reached the connecting doors. 'Do sit down Mr. Kershaw.' She put her hand up to her bosom, held the frills together. She thought sometimes she must have something wrong, the least excitement and it was as if her heart was going to burst out of her chest. She ought to see a doctor except that Dr. Halpin was so grumpy and didn't ever believe anything. If only there was a doctor like Mr. Kershaw. The thought of that possibility accompanied her breathlessly to the sideboard. The cupboard where the whiskey and the gin and the sherry and the bottle of lime and the Australian Port were kept was locked, but the key was in the biscuit barrel on top and she had it open in a moment, her hand shaking so much that she spilled some of the sherry on the carpet. Nanny would be furious. She scuffed it in with her slipper and rebrimmed the Waterford glass tumbler. She wondered for a moment if she had the right kind of glass, it looked rather a lot, but it wasn't every day— In her mind she was lying in bed and Doctor Kershaw was opening his black bag and taking out his stethoscope and—

'Here you are,' she whispered, handing the filled tumbler to Hubert like a chalice. He took it from her, trying not to look startled.

'By Jove,' he said. 'Full measures, eh?' Her bosom as she leaned forward seemed on the point of unprisoning itself from the nylon. Perfume reached him. 'Cheers,' he said, watching as she sat, and again that strange sense of her untouchedness came to him as though that feller Mulcahy spent so much time totting up his damn profits he didn't have – by Jove, if she was his. He lifted the glass and tasted, cautiously, but not cautiously enough. The sweet brown liquid coiled its vapours round his tongue, enveloped his tonsils in a wet fog of stale, sticky sweetness. His eyes widened, and his adam's apple leapt up and down.

'Is it all right?' Clara said, alarmed at his expression. 'It ought to be.'

'No, no, splendid stuff,' Hubert whispered. A tumbler of it! He looked round the room for a potted plant. Not a bloody one. Some kind of Spanish galleon on the mantelpiece, two frightful looking china angels with red candles on one of the side tables. But no blasted aspidistra. Absent-mindedly his bandaged right hand slid down into the depths of the couch, behind the deep-foam cushion. Could he – but of course he couldn't, not even to get rid of this. By Jove, one paid for one's pleasures, all right. 'Not having anything yourself, eh?' he said hopefully. If he could get her out of the room again—

She shook her head. 'John doesn't like me to,' she said. She imagined the stethoscope on her – on her – ice cold, moving here, there – She put her hand again to her bosom. 'I never thought,' she said dreamily. 'The last time you were here – the accident—'

'Accident?' Suppose he – just a bit of it – it'd be bound to soak in, no one would ever know – what the hell did she mean, accident?

'The water for your motor car, the engine.'

'Oh, ah, yes. The radiator. Boiled over. Yes. Of course. Not an accident really, y'know.' She wasn't very bright, poor little thing, but you could have too much damn brightness, sometimes. A bitter flash of remembrance came to him of Angela bandaging his hand. Gripping it like a blasted golf club. 'Had a bit of a damn silly accident this morning,' he said, holding up his bandage. 'Stuck m'self on a fountain pen.'

She looked amazed.

He imagined her bandaging her husband's hand. Her own hands were like – he searched for a comparison but he had never been much for poetry reading. Like – little white rabbits, by Jove. He imagined saying that to her, and his cheekbones turned a dull pink under the bronze and the tiny network of reddish veins. A woman ought to be like this. All soft and scented. Even Harriet Loach – like a damn jockey in bed from the look of her. This lassy'd be more like a Dunlopillo bally cushion.

'Nice old ship that,' he said, nodding at the galleon on the mantelpiece. He had never seen one made of plastic, and from where he sat it looked like the genuine article.

'I brought it back from Spain, actually,' she said. 'A place called Ibbytha.' As she said it the holiday came back to her, the heat, the sun, the white, dusty road. 'It's a kind of island.'

'Ibbytha? Oh, ah, yes, yes I know, I've heard of it.'

Sunlight burning her skin. A boy riding a donkey. He had looked at her – looked at her with such eyes, it was like being touched. He couldn't have been more than fifteen. But such a look. She parted her lips, remembering. The bus tour had stopped and they had all got out to have wine at a place with gypsies serving at the tables, and music, it was all included, and

209

she had had no one to talk to and she had walked up the road and there had been a farmhouse, all tumble down and deserted, and this boy on the donkey. Almost every night since the holiday she had remembered him, remembered the look. He had said something that she hadn't understood, it had been in Spanish, but even the sounds had seemed like fingers touching her. And the heat melting the bones inside her body, her dress clinging to her skin with damp, like wet leaves, her hair heavy and hot so that she had wanted to lift it up from the back of her neck.

As she remembered, sitting in her drawing-room with the galleon she had brought home as a souvenir, she did lift her hands in the same gesture, lifted her hair, and without her knowing it, or Hubert recognizing it, the gesture was that of every woman born in great heat, a slow voluptuousness of surrender, letting a suspicion of cooler air flow under the hair, around the bared nape of the neck. Her eyes were faraway, drowsy with sun. Through four centuries of the climate of The Ross her Spanish forebears whispered in her blood, taught her wrist and arm to curve bonelessly as she lifted them, her head to bend forward like a camellia too heavy for its stem.

'If I had my way,' she said dreamily, 'if I had any money, I'd buy that farmhouse. I'd like to live in Ibbytha. Always.'

'Would you, by Jove?' he said. Even he thought that he said 'By Jove' too often, that even once might be too often, but he could not stop himself. Like a nervous tic, like lifting the corners of his moustache with the knuckle of his forefinger, like touching the knot of his tie to make sure it was in the right place before he went into a room, it was part of his mask, and futile as the mask might be at least it hid him from the world, like dark glasses, like a hedgehog's prickles.

While she was thinking that 'By Jove' was an immensely attractive expression. She had never read boys' stories, or P. G. Wodehouse, or heard of Bertie Wooster or Jeeves, and she lay back in her deep-foam cushioned chair thinking of that farmhouse, white and burned in the sun like a bone; of the olive trees and the dusty road and the donkey, and the boy. But now there was someone with her, and the boy receded, was no more than part of the backdrop to her day-dream. Someone like – Mr. Kershaw with her, gentle, tender, whispering in her ear 'By Jove, you're beautiful.' Her eyes half closed. Her skin seemed to tighten all over her body and relax again, in a kind of shiver.

A stunner, Hubert thought miserably. He saw himself, his

ideal self, walking across this ghastly carpet and – and what? What the hell could anyone do? Kiss her? She'd scream for that bloody housekeeper. Her husband'd walk in. But somewhere inside a dark devil of alter ego sneered contemptuously, 'Talk to her, you imbecile. Soften her up. Tell her she's a stunner. Ask her out for a drive some time.'

'D'you – d'you go out much?' he managed.

Her eyes widened. 'No,' she breathed. She thought of the Bentley. Ten thousand generations of womanhood told her what he was going to say next.

'Ah,' he said, touching the knot of his tie. 'Ummm.' He thought of her husband. Of why he had come. It gave him a strange sense of relief for a moment. How could he – how could he – dammit, when he wanted to sell his blasted land to a chap he couldn't very well start by asking the chap's wife to come out for a spin. He sat mute, relief giving way to disillusion, to dulled regret. It was always the blasted same.

The door opened, not quickly, but with a sense of suddenness about it, as though Nanny had half imagined that there might – 'If you wouldn't mind coming to the kitchen for a minute, ma'am,' Nanny said.

Clara woke from her trance. 'Oh. Oh no, yes, yes Nanny. If you'll excuse me, Mr. Kershaw.'

He got up, struggling out of the deep-foam, balancing his still brimming glass. She made becks and awkward nods and smiles to indicate that he mustn't get up, that he must sit down again, that he musn't think, that— She was gone, the door closing behind her, and before it was shut he was by the window, struggling one handed with the fastenings, the glass on the windowsill. He had it open, the glass emptied, the window almost shut, when she was back.

'Oh Mr. Kershaw!' she said, wondering what he was doing. Nanny had just warned her against any thought of inviting Mr. Kershaw to stay for lunch. 'There's only the one chop left, and that's for the Master when he comes home,' and 'Of course not, of course not, Nanny.' The same relief, the same dulled regret, followed one another in her mind as they had done in Hubert's. For a second she had thought – she had been afraid – she had almost thought he was going to— And there he was by the window, what on earth—

'Oh I say,' Hubert said, flushing a turkey crimson. 'Ah.' The empty glass in his hand seemed to swell into the size of a flower vase. Inspiration came. 'Thought I saw a – a chap prowling about outside – just went to have a decko. Must've – nobody there at all – could have sworn–' He floundered, seeing her face change to alarm and terror. 'Just a shadow or something. Or a gardener. Ha.'

'The gardener doesn't come today,' she whispered, her throat contracting until she couldn't speak properly. She put up her soft small hand to it, her eyes filled with a smoke of fear. The I.R.A. The fish. The old gentleman dead. Prowlers. In the garden. She wanted someone to put his arms round her. She shut her eyes, allowed herself to sway slightly. 'Oooh,' she breathed.

'Oh I say,' Hubert said. 'There's no one. Just a silly mistake – I mean–' He gave her elbow a reassuring pat. His hand seemed to stick to the soft flesh through the nylon like iron filings to a magnet. Her eyes opened, blue as midnight, sudden, immense, great blue holes through a mask and he was looking into them, seeing things that scared him out of his wits. Like looking through the innocent eyepiece of a microscope and falling into another world. He opened his mouth and shut it, burned. He didn't know what he was seeing, passion, hunger, the coils of serpents, Eve, seeing how far he could fall if he – if he– The burning was so intense that even his folly melted like a wax mask and left him naked. His adam's apple jumped and fell. He tightened his hold very slightly on her elbow. He felt drunk, dizzy, he was going to fall down. By Jove. He grasped instinctively for the ruins of his mask, his melted folly, crammed it back between them as a shield.

'Better – I'd better be toddling – mustn't – lunch waiting–' Warm scent. The feel of nylon. That white throat. Her bosom. By God it wasn't fair, a chap could stand— He swallowed, wrenched his hand away. She didn't say anything. He stood helplessly, the moment gone. 'Don't worry about that – that – I mean my seeing a chap – no one, that – there was no one, really. Just imagination.' What a frightful thing to have done, worried this poor little girl. He tugged at his collar with a hooked finger. 'By Jove it's late,' he said, looking at his watch as if it had suddenly appeared on his wrist. 'I'd better dash. Don't – see myself out – no need–' He went as though he was being pursued. She followed slowly, her feet almost dragging on the moss green carpet. When she reached the door he was already climbing into the Bentley. He turned and waved, his face—

Like a pirate she thought suddenly, having recently seen a pirate film on television.

'Cheerybye,' he cried. She lifted her white hand. Spasms of regret shook him and were lost in the shaking of the great machine. The drive filled with noise, the Bentley moved, roared, eased itself out into the road. His hand waved again, he shouted something that was lost in the vrooommm as he accelerated, his pirate head rode for a triumphant second along the box hedge and was gone. Clara turned slowly back to lunch, and the afternoon.

CHAPTER SEVENTEEN

MICHAEL CARMODY sat on the blanket that he had brought from his room, a dark grey square on the pale spread of sand, arms locked round knees, staring across the steel mirror of Stukeley's Pool as though the surface, the reflection of the surrounding trees, the cloud drifting overhead and underneath the stilled metal of the water had hypnotized him. He had been there for half an hour and it seemed like half his life. He had come with his heart beating, after a long detour in case anyone was watching him from the hotel, and for the last few hundred yards through the woods he had run, sure that she was already there, waiting, that she would think he was not coming. He had flung himself forward to the brow of the small bluff, like a miniature cliff of stony earth overlooking the Pool and he had been so certain that she would be there that a shadow on the pale, level apron of sand *was* her, and he jumped down the few feet of the bluff ready to touch her, put his hands over her sleeping face. And in mid-jump he saw that there was nothing there, the shadow of a tree.

And in that second his feelings changed from a wild excitement to a chill foreboding, like the change of a day from bright sunlight to a threatening coldness with the feel of rain and dark, as a cloud covers the sun. She would not come. She did not want to come. This morning – last night – she had been playing. Seeing if she could—

Since that first moment of arriving at the Pool he had swung back and forwards between the two poles of happiness and something close to despair like a compass needle. Of course she was going to come. And what on earth was there to feel forebodings about? That old fool Sergeant Mac and his informer? Suppose anyone had really seen them. Then they had seen them doing nothing. Suppose Sergeant Mac wanted to fix it on him that he had let out the fish. Wanting to fix it and getting a jury to agree were different things. It'd be a very queer Ross jury that sent a Ross man to gaol for letting out a

214

few bloody fish from a fish farm. Even if they believed he had done it, and the likelihood was that the jury would know damn well who had really done it and would be having the best laugh of their lives at the whole thing. There was nothing to worry about.

Of course she was coming. He stood up and listened. The wind, no more than a summer breath, rustled the leaves. A squirrel ran chack chack chack through dry grass and climbed a tree. A bird called. In the middle of Stukeley's Pool a fish jumped, fell flat on the water like the smack of a hand. Ripples ringed out. He climbed on to the top of the bluff again. No sounds.

And Seagrun. That clown. What could he do? Or if Sergeant Mac went to Mr. Kershaw and told him, 'Your daughter was seen with Michael Carmody—' Suppose he did? What then? What could anyone do? If they loved—

He went back down to the sand, sat, locked his arms round his knees, stared at the fading ripples, faded, gone. Loved. Two days – two nights ago he despised her. For herself. For her class. For her parents. For her ignorance. And now— Things don't happen like that. And he felt her mouth against his, waking up, in that narrow, uncomfortable bed, looked down into her face. It had happened. It had. He did. Love. He lay on his back, stared at the sky, a grey white sheep of a cloud, drifting, grazing on blue sky. The tops of trees. Love. He did. But – she hadn't come. Half past four. He had said four. Half past. He sat up, listening. Perhaps she had thought – her bloody father and mother had—

She'd come. You couldn't fake this morning, not that. Not the best actress in the world could fake that. It had been real, real, real. She'd come. Late, breathless, afraid that he was gone, that *he* had been lying and had never come, that he was taking his revenge on her for – for what? Trying to climb down from the bluff, afraid to jump; he'd get up— He got up and there was nothing. He sat down again, determined not to move, not to look, not to turn his head until she came. Look at the water. If the fish jumped again she'd come, everything would be perfect. The water stayed like steel. Stukeley's Pool. Stukeley the pirate, the privateer, hiding there on a summer's day like this in 1564 from the English ships out of Cork and the Spanish, and God knew who else who wanted him. Driving east from Bantry with the world against him, slipping past Cork and Sir Peter Carew in the short darkness, but his sails seen, and the pursuit up, twisting and turning like a sea fox, and on a sudden turning north, darting into Ross Bay where he had secret friends and in the Bay striking all sail and pushing his barque like a rowing boat into the narrow, winding channel between great summer trees that led to this hidden secret pool, known to the Irish as the Pool of the Massacre, because of some legendary killing of the Danes by the Irish there. The channel so narrow and twisting that the naked spars brushed leaves on either side. Until it opened out into a natural harbour. A hundred yards across, deep enough to turn the barque, even at low tide, present a broadside of guns that would cripple any boat foolhardy enough to follow them if they had been seen.

But Carew had not seen them. Later that day he searched Ross Bay as he searched every bay and inlet from Cork to Waterford, but he never noticed the small, impossibly narrow break in the wall of trees along the east flank of the shore, never conceived that his quarry's masts were hidden in that depth of Irish wood, and he sailed out again to beat back to Cork and another admission of failure to enrage his Queen and the Spanish ambassador. And Stukeley lay where he was, taking on meat and water and fresh powder, paying for it with Spanish velvet and French brandy and a bag of Mexican silver. A lad of the Ó Cearmada flying from some local trouble about a girl swam out to him and begged to be taken with him when he sailed and because the boy had fine muscles and a knife and looked as though he knew how to use both, he took him on. The boy would stay with him to the end, that ending like a saga in the desert sands of Morocco when three Kings died.

Michael knew of this story as he knew most of the stories of The Ross, and although he was not thinking of it, it still formed, a sub-conscious background to his thoughts.

Or rather, helped to shape them. His own life was like the Pool. Closed in. Trapped. And yet the way out was there, there, as simple as water flowing. Out into the bay. The Sea. The whole world. Why had he come back? To a place where it mattered what a cretin like Sergeant Mac was told, thought, wanted. Where people spied, whispered, told lies for the fun of destroying anyone who might be happy.

But if he hadn't come back, he would never have met her, never have ... Well, he had. And now? They couldn't stay here. And the weight on him had been the feeling that they had to stay, that there was no escape. Of course there was. Just go.

Together. Over the Gap. Out there into the bay. Out into the world. London. Anywhere. Where class didn't – Class, by Christ! What class did the Kershaws think they were with their stinking failure of a boarding house and their phoney antiques and their overdraft? Because his own father was a roadmender did that make him a roadmender? He was what he made himself. What would he make?

He sat and thought of that, his mouth hard, his eyes narrowed, staring at the bright water, the dark trees. And again he had that feeling of a force inside him, stirring, unfolding, preparing to be born. And the trees and the Pool and the sky seemed for a second to belong to him, to be in some strange, complete way his; to be telling him something, something of ultimate importance, and he tried to capture it, to understand, so that he could tell everyone. Everyone. It's here, it's here. This is why life is. Like a woman feeling her child move inside her when the movement is still strange, miraculous, a thing that has never happened to a woman ever before in history, since the world began. My child. My *child*! My truth, my truth. It slid in his mind, changed shape, was no more than smoke and shadows. And yet it was there, he knew that there was something there and that it was why he had been born. It was a most strange experience.

He lay back on the blanket as if the experience had exhausted him, and yet he wanted to laugh aloud, to exult. Like a vast achievement. He knew, he knew. He did not know what he knew, except that life was fantastic, magnificent, he loved it, loved. Loved everyone. And again that white face that would stare from ten million record sleeves, stare down with hidden eyes at invisible, mysterious truths, at love, at life, at death, at the tragedy of being born; that white Renaissance princely face cast its as yet unborn shadow on him, gave him foreknowledge, made him feel for a second that he had been chosen, as indeed he had, to speak for an entire generation. All over the world children were waiting to grow into adolescence, to hear his voice tell them why they existed, why there was no reason that they should exist, why they should laugh because there was no reason. And those now-children become adolescents would love him like an elder brother, like a teacher, like a young father who understood. Priest, guru, singer, poet of their hearts. Love me, love me, love me. Save me from the dark. And he would say, 'The dark is *there*. It *is*. Accept.'

And out of the acceptance, the dark, would come now and then like a fountain, like a birdsong, the voice of Ireland. Not the Ireland of the nineteenth century, the middle classes, the Celtic Twilight, but that deep spring of Gaelic Ireland; the blackbird singing on a tree; a sword lifting; a king, a hero dying; the Morrigan croaking, death of kinsfolk, smell of blood. And over the blood the blackbird singing, hard and careless and alive and singing. How wonderful the morning world, bright with beauty.

A rivulet of earth fell, rustled down the bluff on to the sand, her shadow covered him.

'You're asleep!' she accused him. He lay and looked at her, spent with his vision, guiltily feeling that he had indeed been asleep, he must have been, he must have dreamed. He looked at his watch. Almost five.

'Where have you been?' he said, trying to sound angry. 'I thought—'

She was down beside him, touching his chest with her hand, pouting. 'Did he get frightened, den, all by his self in the lonely wood? Poor poor Michael.'

He caught her hand and held it against his face.

'I thought they'd never go,' she whispered. 'I said I had a headache, I was expecting my thing and felt awful. And mummy actually came up and looked into my room to see if I was really in bed—'

'Were you?'

'I heard her coming.' She laughed, imitated her mother's voice. 'I don't know *what* I'll say to the Eagans.'

'Kiss me.'

'I'm supposed to be the one who lies down looking all helpless and you're supposed to be the one who leans over looking masterful.'

'Kiss me.'

'Tell me what you were dreaming about.'

'You.'

'I don't believe it.'

He caught her by the hair and pulled her face down to his. They lay together kissing for a long time. He began to undo the buttons of her shirt. She lifted her head, alarmed. 'Not here!'

'Why not?' He had it all undone, pulled out from her belt.

'Someone may come.'

'Sergeant Mac?'

'Anyone.' She tried to push the ends of her shirt back into the top of her jeans. But he undid the fastening of those, tugged at the zip. The thoughts of making love under the sky, the faint sense of danger, of recklessness, had made him suddenly excited, so that he was almost brutal, held her roughly by the shoulders, pushing her down. 'You mustn't,' she whispered, her eyes wide with alarm, and yet with an answering excitement that made him want to cry out with triumph, with possession.

They made love as though they were playing, as though they were drunk, like two cubs playing in the sun, twined and rolling, almost clawing one another, shameless and half-ashamed and laughing and mad with love. Sand in her hair and on his shoulders, falling in his eyes, in his mouth, taste of sand and salt and warm skin and tang of hiddenness, the dark warmth under her arm, the soft beginnings of her breast, thinness of rib. Love love love his body shouted, take take take, she's mine, she's mine. They let go and fell apart, rolled on to their backs, side by side, gasping for breath, dazed and helpless, the sun blinding them, warm sand under their spread arms, warm blanket under their naked bodies, whisper of water, singing of a bird. The fish jumped, high, flicking the water with his tail, fell like a pistol shot, flat and echoing in the wide quiet of the Pool.

'Fish,' he said. 'Love's fish.'

She didn't know what he meant but it was too much effort to ask. She touched his hand. 'Always?'

'Always.'

'I'm so happy,' she breathed.

'And m—' he began. The chill came like a cloud, like a cold hand. 'And me,' he said, but his voice echoed in his ears. No no no. Echoed in the dark. Only now, only this, never again.

He sat up, brushing off sand, furious with himself. 'What are we going to do?' he said, his voice unintentionally harsh. She looked at him in surprise.

'Do?'

'Yes. About us.'

She lay and looked at him, but he felt that her mind was looking over his shoulder at things that she would not tell him about. 'What – do you mean?'

'Well, we can't go on like this.'

'Why – not?' Her face had begun to seem drawn, frightened.

She wanted to reach out and touch him again but she could not move. His face frightened her, the tone of his voice, the words he was using. And just when everything— 'Please—' she whispered. She meant, 'Not now, not just when we've made love, not this one minute that we'll have—' and the feeling came to her too that all would not be well and perfect, that a shadow had fallen. But she could not think why.

'What do I say to your father?' he said. 'How do I look at your mother? Do we sneak in and out of bed waiting for them to find out? For someone to tell them? For them to guess?'

'We can be – careful,' she whispered in a small, lost voice. He didn't bother to answer, scooping up a handful of sand, letting it fall from inside his closed fist like sand from an hour glass. Time passing. Ending.

'I don't want to be careful,' he said in a measured voice.

'What do you want?' she breathed.

He thought he could answer immediately and found that he couldn't. He had to say something, and to say it this second at once. 'I want to marry you, I want us to be married, for ever and ever. Live happily ever after.' And he couldn't. He wanted to and he couldn't.

'I want you,' he whispered. But that wasn't the right answer, even though she pretended that it was.

'I know,' she said. Why couldn't he say it? He did want to – he thought of it, and it was impossible. How could they marry? How could he keep her? He couldn't keep himself. Where could they go, where could they live? He saw her in a back room in Camden Town, saw her face grow tired and yellow. Saw himself. 'That's all that matters,' she whispered.

'I know.' He took more sand up, held it, not releasing it. 'Except that it isn't all. You have to live. How—' He let go of the sand, not slowly, but all at once. He wondered if he should tell her about Camden Town, if he could. The rooms he had lived in. Dirt, and bad food, and the smell of last year's cooking, and the sounds of trains all night, men fighting. Bottles breaking. He was thinking of the last room he had had before he was arrested. At least he had had it to himself. 'When I began in London,' he said, 'ten of us shared a room. Five on day shift, five on night. There were only five beds.' But it didn't mean anything to her, she couldn't conceive of a life like that, it was only a story. Men relieving themselves on the stairs. Children crying all night because they had worms, or lice, or both, and their parents didn't care. A baby with both arms broken and a fractured skull, blackened eyes staring out of a grey, old-man's face. The father nineteen, dazed by ignorance and fatherhood and no sleep, the mother seventeen, already five months pregnant again. The police taking them both away.

He thought of the Indian, old and quiet and slow, going from dustbin to dustbin every night, filling a plastic shopping bag with scraps, his dog trotting behind him, sitting down waiting, cocking an eye at its master, at passers by, at each new dustbin, hoping for a bone. The Welfare State. He tried to imagine Jenny sharing that room. Pregnant. With a child. How long would she last? Before she ran screaming, back to her own world. If she wasn't pregnant she'd run sooner. He spread his hands and shrugged helplessly.

'What are you trying to tell me?' she said in a strange, distant voice. He felt her going away from him, as if she was floating away in the air, like two capsules in space, away and away and there was no connecting line, no means of getting back. He wanted to look at her and he couldn't, he wanted to say something and he couldn't. And five minutes – less – two, three minutes ago they had been – He looked down at the sand, beat his hooked fingers into it, hurting the quicks under the nails. Damn damn damn.

'Try and understand,' he said in a dull voice. Understand what? That it wouldn't work? Why not, why not? Because his father was – her father was— Christ, how stupid. People made bigger jumps than that all the time, all the time. White girls and black men. White men and black girls. Indians, Chinese. Dukes marrying chorus girls since choruses began. Duchesses marrying – marrying what? What am I? He plucked sand and let it run in thin, dry rivulets from his closed hands. What am I? What will I be? And the vision of that grey room in Camden Town surrounded him, he could see her standing in it like a ghost, body heavy, pear-shaped, sluggish, her eyes bruised with despair. It doesn't have to be like that, it doesn't doesn't. He tried to think of her running, laughing, along a street, towards him. Lying in a warm room, in a wide bed, lifting her arms. 'I want her,' he thought. 'I want her more than I want—'

'You're trying to say that it wouldn't work?'

'I don't know what I'm trying to say.'

'I haven't asked you for anything. It was you that said—'

'I know.'

'Or are you saying that you don't – that you don't—'

'I don't know. No. No, you know that isn't true.' He turned to her, made himself turn, look at her, recover the thing that he had felt this morning, last night, just now; the wanting, the pain of loving, the fear of losing. And now he had no fear, and there was no pain, only a heaviness, like handcuffs. And yet she was still beautiful. She lay on her back, staring at the sky.

'I knew it would be like this,' she said. 'They say— If you give in to a boy he won't respect you. He'll despise you.'

'Don't.'

'They all say that and they're right. You think they're not, that they're old and cruel and they don't know what life is like any more, that when it comes time to love someone, when you meet someone – you'll see it in his eyes. That he's different. He won't feel like that.'

'I don't feel like that.'

'Maybe in England it is different. I know lots of girls who've had – affairs. They loved someone and they went to bed together and they still loved each other. Maybe it's only here that it's horrible, that they talk about "giving in" and "respect" and "despising". Don't worry, I'm not going to cry, I'm not going to make scenes.'

'None of that is true,' he said. He wanted to touch her hair, touch her face.

'Isn't it?' Her eyes seemed to take their colour from the sky, now green, now almost blue. Looking at him from an immense distance of understanding, of calm motherhood. And even that made him feel trapped and imprisoned, like a very small animal beneath a huge net. What had he done to deserve it, what in hell's name had he done? He beat his fist softly against the sand.

'You want to go away,' she said. 'Alone. Isn't that it?'

'No.'

She smiled, and when she smiled she was so wise, so beautiful that the pain came back and he knew that he didn't want anything, anything in the world except to hold her again. If it was only once, if he died for it.

'It's my fault,' she said. 'When they say "giving in" what they really mean is "telling the truth, showing the truth about one's self". You mustn't ever do that. And I showed you myself. I've been a lie so long that I wanted to do it, and I thought I could. I thought you'd understand.'

'I did.'

She shook her head, as though she was a thousand years old.

'I've never seen anyone so beautiful,' he said. What held him back? Some failure in the blood? Why couldn't he grasp, take what was given him, believe in the future, believe in luck, in fortune, that God would provide, take what was in his lap and enjoy it?

'I've never seen anyone so handsome,' she said. She reached up and traced the line of his cheek with her finger tip, down to his jaw bone, across to the corner of his mouth. 'Every time I've seen you,' she said, in that same distant, calm voice, 'my heart has sort of tightened inside me, I've felt it couldn't ever be true. Not for me. Not for Jennifer Kershaw who's so reliable, such a help to her mother. And she speaks beautiful French and she was terribly good at games. Love doesn't happen to sensible girls, does it?'

'I love you,' he said with a dry throat, like saying words in a strange language. He didn't know that he was going to say them.

She shook her head and smiled.

'I love you,' he whispered, bending towards her, shutting his eyes as his face touched her face, their mouths touching. But he didn't want to kiss her, only to touch, to be close, to say over and over again, 'I love you, I love you,' in every kind of tone, amazement, wonder, fierce certainty. And her arms were round his neck and when he moved his mouth her face was wet with crying and yet she was laughing.

They lay together. A small cloud floated its shadow on the Pool like the shadow of a boat. The squirrel came back above their heads and cried, 'Chack chack chack,' stuttering with irritation about some concern of his own.

'I love you,' Michael said aloud to the sky. She put her hand over his mouth.

CHAPTER EIGHTEEN

THE Eagans' tea-party-cum-garden-party was the last in a series of farewell celebrations for the Daly-Browns, who were returning to Africa again, this time permanently, having sold Castle Daly. There had been lunches and dinners and cocktail parties from one end of the county to the other, and even further afield, because the D-Bs as everyone called them had been extremely popular and would be missed. No one had yet quite brought themselves to face the plain fact that the D-Bs had let them down, and that Castle Daly was going to become a hotel. Everyone still spoke to and about the D-Bs as though the Daly-Browns had suffered a great personal loss and were bearing it very bravely.

'The only answer is Portugooses,' Mrs. Verreker said. 'We've brought a couple back from the Algarve and they're absolutely marvellous. Of course, we don't understand a word they say.' She trilled off into her rather stupid laugh. Hilda Gauntlett-Smith looked at her with the contempt of a clever woman of forty for a stupid woman of thirty.

The Kershaws were in the dining-room, because that was where Sir Philip was, and George and Flora Daly-Brown, standing with their backs to the great marble fireplace with its hansome *Famille Verte* rose jars and its Lantern clock by Peter Garon, and its split logs piled in the big-bellied, wrought iron basket-grate. Hubert stood with one foot on the leather kerb and one hand on the mantelpiece, trying to look casually at ease, while his mind took refuge in that green drawing-room like the shop window of a furniture store, and the memory of Clara Mulcahy threatening moment by moment to spill out of her nylon frills. He should have asked her out for a spin, by God he should.

He was caught back to the present by Angela's voice asking Flora Daly-Brown about the auction and what she had got for the Louis Quinze chairs, had she *really* got four hundred each?

Christ why couldn't she shut up? She was visibly setting the D-Bs' teeth on edge and absolutely bloody oblivious of it. Even Lady Meg was showing strain. He tried to imagine the little Mulcahy thing talking to Flora D-B or Lady Meg – she'd probably never heard of Louis Thingummy and a damn good thing if Angela hadn't.

Suppose he had asked her out? Settling her into the bucket seat, patting her knee. He caught his breath. The warmth of nylon came back to him like a wave running up a tropical beach, great ripples of foam reaching into the grains of his mind. By Jove what a—

'—and someone was saying that the Sheraton bookcases went for—'

Vroooommmm. Hitting them both in the back like a rocket. Seventy. Eighty, ninety. Her mouth open, giving little squeaks of fright. 'Hold tight, we're going over the ton on the next straight.' One arm round her shoulders, hand on her – snuggling up to him – quivering with bally terror. Hedges streaming, telegraph poles flashing by like blasted fence posts, feeling like God. By Jove—

'—of course I didn't dare go myself. I knew I'd be tempted. But Mrs. Herzberger said she was going to bid up to seven hundred for—'

Pulling into a lay-by – jolly good name that, he'd never thought of it before—

'If you go on like this Mrs. Kershaw you'll be bringing the tax people down on us before we escape,' George Daly-Brown was saying. He said it with a heavy humorousness like a steam-roller, flattening the remainder of Angela's story. He had a way of flattening things and people that he didn't care for. He was in every way a most impressive man, with that kind of sleek stoutness which it is almost impossible to achieve under twenty thousand a year – and the D-Bs had very much more than that. His grey moustache and thick grey hair breathed to those who could appreciate them the weekly attentions of the best barbers. His firm red cheeks had never known the touch of a safety razor, let alone an electric shaving machine. They were attended to every morning by his Spanish manservant, armed with the cut-throat razor of that particular day. The razor case had belonged to Louis XVI. And seemed by no means to have come down in the world by passing into the possession of George Daly-Brown. There was truly something of the ancien régime about him. His suit had the discreet shimmer of silk woven into the wool, his shirt and underclothes and handkerchief and foulard tie were all of pure silk and his gold watch was on a band so thick and heavy that it looked like half a pair of handcuffs. The top of a gold and platinum cigar case for holding two tremendous cigars glittered behind the red silk handkerchief in his breast pocket.

Although, if he had not been so rich, there might have been the hint of vulgarity in some of this, and there were indeed people who recalled at times that his great-grandfather had been a cattle jobber. Mrs. Barton recalled it most often. But if his great-grandfather on the father's side had been Patrick Brown, cattle-dealer and Catholic, D-B's mother had been a Daly and the Dalys had held Castle Daly since the year dot. And of course old Patrick's son had turned, and got a Knighthood, and *his* daughters had been presented and one of them had married one of the Glenalmond sons, the one that got killed at Ypres, and his only son Thomas had married Augusta Daly when the Dalys, who had no son and no money, were on the point of having to sell up. Thomas and Augusta begat George.

And now the Daly-Browns *were* selling up. Had sold up. Within the month they would be in Rhodesia.

'We've found a place near Umtali. Flora hasn't seen it yet of course. Rather a nice countryside.'

'How are things out there?' Hubert said, his voice assuming a man-of-the-world, far-travelled tone.

'Oh, absolutely calm. Calmer than here. They've just taken petrol rationing off and everybody's sure that by the end of the year they'll have everything patched up with Britain. Under the rose I should say everything is pretty well patched up already. Too much money involved for it not to be.'

'Hear you've got an enormous place,' a newcomer said.

'Well,' D-B laughed, with embarrassed modesty. 'By Irish standards I suppose it's big enough. Twenty thousand acres or thereabouts. But that's small by their standards,' he added hastily. He turned to Hubert with ducal condescension: 'You're jolly lucky to be able to hang on here.' They had been talking about the Kershaws at the much more intimate lunch-party which had preceded the tea-party for the generality of county neighbours. There had only been the Eagans themselves, and the D-Bs and the Bartons. The Verrekers should have been there but had arrived late because of a puncture. And at lunch

Margaret Eagan had explained, in case anyone was wondering why their closest neighbours the Kershaws were not also there, that they were indeed coming to tea.

'But not to lunch. I'm sorry, but I simply cannot stand that woman at close quarters for more than five minutes. She always makes me feel that she's valuing the silver, or measuring the lawns for putting greens or something. And poor Hubert, he really is such a fool. Of course, his father was too.'

'The Kershaws have always been fools,' Mrs. Barton had said, stirring her prune soufflé with a disapproving spoon. She liked sponge pudding with her lunch and if she had stayed at home she could have had it, instead of this silly mess out of some book. It'd have her running to the lavatory all night. 'Yer don't have any sponge pudding?' she croaked in a loud aside to the maid, Maureen Carmody, who was passing with the soufflé bowl. 'Then I'll have some cheese.'

'But you have to give Kershaw credit for holding out against this Development scheme,' Sir Philip had said, loyalty to a neighbour stiffening his voice slightly. And then, in case George Daly-Brown should misunderstand him he added, 'Of course, it's quite different in your case. You were right out in the middle of nowhere and your selling up doesn't affect anyone else—'

'Except that we're all so terribly sorry to lose you,' Margaret said quickly. Poor darling Philip trying to be tactful was a worrying thing.

'We're sorry to go,' D-B said heartily. 'But I'm not really sure that any of us are going to have a choice very much longer. This fish thing—'

He came back to the same point again, having spread his condescension on Hubert like a dab of butter on a rather uninteresting biscuit. 'That sort of affair casts a nasty shadow just now, given what's happening in the North.'

'Oh, I don't know,' Sir Philip said, more for Margaret's benefit than because he thought it was true. 'It may have been just a few of the lads out for a bit of sport.'

Hubert's mind had left the conversation again, but this time in a much less pleasant direction. George D-B's casual praise had been like walking into a tree in the dark. Jolly lucky to be able to hang on here. Luckier than George D-B. Braver, more obstinate, more loyal. More rooted in his land. And today, tomorrow, sometime very soon – he was going to have to come here again and tell Sir Philip that he was pulling out, that he was running. In the atmosphere of the party he had almost forgotten. Had forgotten. The familiar voices, faces, the cries of welcome, recognition. Like the atmosphere of an officers' mess on party night. On an outstation, a frontier. Outside, the dark and the tribesmen. Inside, the uniforms, the wives, the mess silver, the laughing courage. For half an hour he had been drawn back so thoroughly that it had seemed to him that he belonged here as a hand belongs in its glove. Even Angela had not completely broken the spell. How the devil was he going to break it to Sir Philip? And the same wave of irritation that had swept over his mind because of Angela, came back now because of Sir Philip, George D-B, the lot of them. The voices seemed imbecilic, like birds screeching in a bloody tree and he thought this time of that green and Spanish plastered drawing-room like a refuge, that soft white breast as somewhere to bury his face, shut out the future.

'You can get frightened of shadows,' Sir Philip was saying. Lady Eagan's face tightened with pain, her eyes trying to smile with warm intimacy and woman-to-woman understanding at Flora Daly-Brown.

'Maybe,' George Daly-Brown said, his voice, his full, florid, handsome face conceding by its expression every position that Sir Philip might wish to take up, and at the same time by some alchemy of tone and twitch of the corner of a lip conveying to Lady Eagan his complete understanding of her husband's congenital and hopeless lack of tact, his amused mock-sympathy with her for being tied by marriage to such a terrible fellow, his full and hearty understanding that the old chap hadn't meant anything, and behind all that, like a Rolls-Royce drifting over a bump in the road, that he didn't give a damn what any living soul in the room thought or said.

'Maybe you can,' George D-B repeated, allowing his smile to spread, firm and commanding. 'But there's some pretty rough customers about and the way things are at the moment it doesn't take much to turn a small incident into something quite nasty. Did you hear about that Belgian feller over in West Cork? They ran him right out inside twenty-four hours.'

People gathered closer to be told the story.

'Well this Belgian chap bought this little place over here, sort of holiday bungalow I suppose—'

Some of the tensed expectation went out of the listeners.

Belgians with holiday bungalows were not the kind of people they cared much about, one way or the other.

'Anyway, this Belgian chap found the locals were walking across his land to get somewhere or other, a beach probably. So he put up a fence. The next day he finds a chap climbing over it with his dog, and he tells him in no uncertain terms to get off his land and take his dog with him, or else he might find the dog getting shot. So next day it happens again, and by Jove, the Belgian ups and he jolly well does shoot the dog, with a twelve bore.'

There were murmurs at this.

'Wait a minute,' Daly-Brown said. 'Let me finish. Suddenly, out from behind a hedge, or whatever it was, come about twenty local chaps at the double, and the head man gets hold of this Belgian, smashes his twelve bore across his knee and says to him, 'This is Tuesday. And it's four o'clock in the afternoon. Tomorrow is Wednesday. By four o'clock tomorrow afternoon, you'll not only be out of West Cork. You'll be out of Ireland.' And by Jove he was, you know.'

The murmurs were repeated. Nobody felt quite sure how to take the story, although most of them had heard somewhat similar stories before. On the one hand no one much cared for Belgians and Frogs and Huns and people like that unless of course they happened to buy a decent place and knew how to keep it up. And there was an element of patriotic pride in the thought of Irishmen throwing out a foreigner who had shot a dog. On the other hand – it was not so much the simple feeling that property was sacred – everyone knew that it would be suicide to try and stop local people crossing a bit of land that they thought they had a right to cross. It was the knowledge that once violence started, for almost any reason, there was no telling where it would stop.

'It's like the fish ponds here, the other night,' someone said, who had joined in the middle of the telling. 'Did you hear about that, D-B?'

'Yes,' D-B said shortly. He didn't care to have his stories capped. 'And yet, you know, I'm really sorry to be going. But what can one do?' He allowed his beautifully shaven smile to spread, show his strong white teeth under the clipped, sculptured moustache. 'You might be able to manage some sort of *modus vivendi* even with the bomb throwers but you certainly can't live without a cook.'

229

Everyone laughed. In the doorway there was a great cry of 'Hodi?' as the Farleighs and the Stephens and Mrs. Marriner and the Frobishers came in to see how many people in the dining-room could speak Swahili. In the drawing-room they had found a total of fourteen out of thirty-one. '*Kumi na mbili, kumi na tatu, kumi na nne. Mwaweza kunena Ki-Swahili,* anyone?' They had all lunched very well on the way to the Eagans, and now that somnolence had worn off they were quite hilarious. For all of them it was an outing, a break in a rather boring period of the year. With the edge of excitement sharpened by that feeling that was always there, 'perhaps this is the last time, the last party, the last year'. Just as it had been in Kenya before the end of the good times.

Sir Philip had moved away from the dining-room fireplace group and was going from room to room and out on to the terraces seeing that everyone was happy and fed. Tea cups were beginning to disappear, collected and taken away by Maureen Carmody and Lady Eagan, and the wife and elder daughter of the gardener, pressed into service for the occasion and looking extremely awkward in caps and aprons borrowed from Maureen. Whiskey glasses were beginning to appear and voices were rising higher.

'There you are, Philip, been looking for you all over.' Mrs. Barton caught at his sleeve with an imperious claw. 'I've been trying to find *someone* who can remember the name of the Tim Parfitts' place up in North Tipp. Don't tell me *you* can't remember. It's just on the end of me tongue.'

'Sydneystown,' Sir Philip said.

'Of course! Sydneystown! Gettin' senile. Forget me own name soon. That boy of mine, John—' she sought for his plump figure across the room with a venomous eye. 'Not like an Irishman at all anymore, all stocks and shares, telling me to sell War Loans, wanted me to invest in something out in Australia – Poto – Possy—'

'Poseidon?'

'That's it. Tin mines or something.'

'You'd have done very well if you'd taken his advice.'

'I don't know that I want to do very well. Not in that sort of way. Of course, the world's changing, I know that. Leaving us old fogeys behind.'

'I'm afraid it is.' He steered her towards the study, where the whiskey was, and left her. Most parties depressed him rather, forcing him to realize again how little he cared for his fellow man in quantities, but there was something more than that depressing him now. The world leaving them behind? The D-Bs going? They really meant nothing to him. And he thought with an ache in his chest that nothing any longer meant very much. He was going through the motions of caring, writing his book, looking after this place, taking part in the life of the county. He supposed he'd go on going through the motions, as long as he had to. But it was as though a long time ago his real life had stopped.

And the terrible thing was that he knew to the second, knew the exact moment that that had happened. In Canton, in '46, saying 'Goodbye' to her. 'I know that you must go home, Pi Li. You must go to your own people.'

'Come with me, Kim, please.' They had been in the hotel room. She would not come down to the docks.

'You are better seeing me in shadows, Pi Li. I am grown old, and wrinkled. I am no more young.' There had been no wrinkles. She was as beautiful as she had always been. Only her eyes had grown older.

'You know what I mean. Not just to the docks. Come to Europe with me.' And then, for the first time, he had said, 'Marry me, Kim. I'm not young any more, not much of a catch. But I can give you peace.'

'I am not looking for peace, Pi Li. You know that I must stay here.' But she would not ask him to stay with her. Why hadn't he said he would stay? What was there to go home to? 'You must go to your own people.' Had there been irony in her voice as she said that? No, none. But if there had been it would have been justified. What people was he returning to? The Daly-Browns? The cemetery where the Eagans lay under their leaning headstones, their cracked vaults, their smooth, indecipherable slabs? What was left for him to return to?

Nothing. And in his inmost mind he had known that there was nothing. No part for him to play, no one who needed him. And yet he had gone, driven by what, by some bird-instinct of migration home? And, so terrible that he did not want to acknowledge it even now, even to himself, he had been relieved that she was not willing to leave China for him, go home to Europe with him as Lady Eagan. Twenty-five years later it hurt to think of that shameful, horrible instant of relief, and he had wondered painfully, many times, countless times since, whether that relief had shown for a fraction of that instant in his eyes.

She had wished him happiness, and Ten Thousand Years, and given him a small piece of porcelain, an ox-blood vase, that she had found for him as a parting gift. And he had had nothing for her, only money that he could not give her, and love that was too thin.

A month later, in Singapore, he had met Margaret again, remembering her from a couple of years before in London at a party, very cool, and English, and beautiful in her uniform, going home on the same ship as himself. Just north of Suez, in the Mediterranean, the first night of Europe, they had got engaged. Like closing a great door that he would never be able to reopen. China. Kim Suan. Half his life. Sometimes in the TV programmes and newspaper pictures of Peking, and demonstrations and marching crowds, and rows of identical officials on identical platforms, he had wondered if he was seeing something that she had seen. If that dark dot of head or that, or that, was hers. She would be sixty now.

And he was sixty-six, and he had chosen this, and there wasn't anyone whom he knew who would think for a moment that he had chosen wrongly; who would even guess that there could be doubt about it. They all had their certainties. Why had he never had them, and yet had acted as if he had? As though his stock was so old that it had grown hollow at the heart, and each new generation was born old and withered without any chance of being young. That had been true of his father, looking back. A man who had done no more than go through the motions of duty, an outsider wherever he went, looking at the world with cool, cynical eyes. It was from him, really, that he himself had learned to be an outsider with dignity, to watch without passion, never allowing himself to recognize that this is the most inferior of gifts.

And grandfather? Who had served in India as he himself had served in China? But at least served more constructively, as a magistrate, an administrator, kept things going. But still without passion, without criticism, without engagement.

Had there been some Indian Kim Suan in his grandfather's life? A memory of her behind those drooped eyelids, the white moustache, the fierce nose? A sense of hollowness at the heart? But what could we have done? How could we have altered things? Taken a share, a part, here or somewhere? What have we done, we who have had all the gifts of Fortune poured into our laps, and have sat for generations holding them, or throwing them away, but never setting them to use. We have deserved destruction.

He shivered.

'Hullo old man,' Farleigh said. 'You're looking a bit peaked. Penny for 'em?'

'Oh, I suppose I'm thinking of the D-Bs. They've probably made a wise choice.'

'I'm jolly sure they have. As a matter a fac' Sausage an' I are thinking of potterin' out to the Cape this winter to have a look round. Hire a car you know. Drive round a bit. When you add everything up it's damn near as cheap as stayin' at home. Spendin' the winter out there, I mean. And of course, Sausage's cousins are in Natal and we can stay with them for a couple o' months. If you ask me—' he lowered his voice to a shout, 'didn't want to say it in front of the girls, but we might all be lookin' for somewhere to trot off to pretty soon. I remember when the old Admiral was shot – I was only a boy at the time, but I remember the feelin' everyone had. The servants not lookin' you straight in the eye and never quite sure who was goin' to be next. Well, I'm gettin' that feeling again.'

'Nobody's been shot this time,' Sir Philip said, wishing that Farleigh would go away.

'Not yet. But this fish business, that's a damn nasty thing. They don't like us, Philip. They never have liked us and they jolly well never will like us. Factories. That's what they want. You see. Ten years time this blessed place'll be full of factories. Like Brummagem. And they want to get us out o' the way first. Like clearin' weeds. Let alone all this damn business in the North.'

'You think Rhodesia'd be any better?'

'It'll last our time, anyway. There's more space for one thing.'

Margaret came out on to the terrace. 'The D-Bs are off, Philip. Tom? Are you coming?'

They all walked round the house to the front, and the main terrace and gravel sweep. There were at least a dozen cars there, and twenty or thirty more, parked down the edge of the drive for a couple of hundred yards or so, under the elm trees. But a space had been made for the D-Bs' Rolls right in front of the steps, and the chauffeur in his plum coloured uniform and black boots was standing by the rear door with a rug over his arm. Sir Philip made himself smile and look like a proper host as D-B turned to shake his hand and say good-bye.

' 'bye George, 'bye Flora, safe journey to you both.' Everybody shouting, 'good-bye', 'good-luck'; an air almost of a wedding, of new beginnings, festivity. The chauffeur reverently closing the heavy doors of the great maroon car. The silver lady shining in the sun on the long, glittering bonnet. The car inching forward, the engine inaudible, only the sound of the gravel under the wheels, the voices, the calling. D-B waving through the back window, Flora waving, the chauffeur's immobile silhouette. Down the drive, past the parked cars.

People stood around on the gravel, some with glasses in their hands and the air of intending to stay as long as there was anything to drink and anyone to talk to, but most of the guests already thinking of going home, saying good-bye to each other, looking round vaguely for Margaret Eagan to thank her for the party, making arrangements with one another to meet at the Cattle Show, or the Horse Show, or at so-and-so's shindig next month, or at Bella's wedding on the 8th. Mrs. Barton was looking for her son to take her home. 'Never know where he is. Anyone seen John? Me son. Someone said he was out here. Are the D-Bs gone, eh?' She sniffed as much as to say that this was not the loss that some might think. 'John, there you are. Been looking for yer everywhere. Get the car, I want to go home.'

He had already fetched it close to the door. It was a Mini. He had got rid of her ancient, enormous Daimler the year before. He eased her into it.

'Like a damn sardine tin. Hate this blessed thing. Mind my hat, you stupid boy.' She was tired and cross. ' 'bye Philip. Lovely party. Don't let Margaret bother to come out.' They drove away and Philip went inside, wondering how long it would be before his study was his own again. It was still full of people. They were drinking whiskey and talking about Bella's wedding. He didn't even know who Bella was and he was too tired to ask. He wondered if Margaret would take it very badly if he went upstairs and lay down.

CHAPTER NINETEEN

'I HAVE to go,' she said, not moving, lying on her back, watching him from under the shadow of her hair, her mouth half smiling, smiling, filled with tenderness. He let sand run from his closed fist on to her breast, her stomach, making small sand dunes on the warm ivory of her skin.

'Why don't we never go back?' he said.

'I know.' They had decided nothing. Only made love again and lain half asleep for a quarter of an hour holding each other, and tried to believe that they had decided, or that there was nothing to decide. Only that they loved each other. And for that short space of time it had been enough. The world surrounded by these trees. Adam and Eve. The sun quite still in the sky. Late afternoon for ever, quiet, golden.

'I have to go. They'll be back.'

'And I have to go up to my mother. She'll be waiting.' He thought 'Suppose she says Let me come with you. Let me meet your mother.' What would he say? How would he feel? It was strange. It was not his father that worried him. His father would look at her with calm, accepting eyes as he accepted the weather, the weight of his broom. He would shake her very gently and carefully by the hand and make her sit down in the place of honour at the fire's corner and within an hour's slow, easy conversation he would have made up his mind what manner of girl she was and whether she was fit for his son. But his mother—

And her parents.

But she said nothing, only smiled that wise half smile that made her seem to know things that he would never understand. And strangely, as she smiled she herself was thinking 'If I only knew what he's thinking. If I could reach him.' Her smile no more than a self-protection, a rebuilding of the same lie that had protected her since she first left home to go to boarding school, Jennifer the Wise, the balanced, the self-contained. The

Sensible. Don't take any notice of my smile her inmost mind begged him. Touch me, hold me, let me break down and cry and be weak. Let me be frightened. Tell me what to do. But she smiled and said 'I have to go.' Because if he let her go it would not be quite so painful if she had smiled all the time. And what else could he do but let her go? She had to go. It was true. It was no good his saying 'Why don't we never go back?' Unless he said more than that. And inside her her small, frightened self wept in the dark 'Don't ask me anything, tell me, tell me, take my hand and lead me out of the dark.'

She brushed the sand off her breast and stomach, sat up, shook her hair; 'If my mother sees my hair—'

He helped her brush it, combing it with his fingers. Their hands and voices were as tender, more tender, than they had been for the past hour. And he had said 'I love you.' Everything was perfect. Perfect. Except that the tenderness rang hollow and the heat had gone out of the sun. They stood up and dressed, fastening their clothes with quick, slightly embarrassed hands, brushing more sand from their shirts, their jeans, feeling it dry and rough at the back of their necks.

The Pool had changed from steel to pewter. A fox came out on the far side of the great circle of water, stared at them in surprise. He vanished again between two bushes. The squirrel behind them cried chack chack chack, from high up in a tree, and dropped a nut on the ground. The air was cool. When they had finished dressing and had shaken out and folded the grey blanket, they looked round them on the sand for anything they might have dropped, like guests in a hotel room checking out. They felt awkward and didn't look at each other.

'We'd better not go together,' he said.

'No,' she said.

They stood for a moment trying to smile at each other, not wanting it to end like that even for the few hours before they saw each other again. He wanted to say 'What the hell does it matter? Let's not worry who sees us—' But he didn't say it. She made her smile very bright, put her hand again through her dark red tangle of hair and turned to the bank, the miniature cliff. He cupped his hand for her like a stirrup and she scrambled up. 'I'll take the blanket for you,' she said.

'We could—' he began. But she was running. Gone.

When he followed her she had already disappeared among the trees. He wanted to run, and yet he went on walking. From the edge of the wood he thought he would see her still crossing the meadow at the back of the hotel, the meadow that had once been lawn, parkland. But there was only Coca there, standing under a tree, grey white, like a statue. She must already be inside, in the kitchen.

He began crossing the meadow himself, not towards the hotel, but leaving it on his left hand. It would take him the best part of an hour to get to his father's cottage, even cutting straight across fields and up the mountainside. He walked fast because he was very late and his mother would be angry and he felt that on top of everything else he couldn't stand very much of that. He took off his jacket again and slung it over his shoulder. Beside the Pool, enclosed and shadowed by the wood, it had seemed almost cold, evening creeping among the trees, across the surface of the water. But out in the fields, and as he began to climb the first gradient of the mountain, it was still afternoon, and warm with sun. He wiped his face with his shirt sleeve. What was he going to do? What was he going to do? And behind that question the one that he didn't want to ask, let alone answer. What do I want to do?

He stopped and looked back. He was already quite high up the slope. The hotel lay small in its parkland, its trees scattered like outriders, scouts from the main body of the wood. In the wood itself Stukeley's Pool lay like a round shield, its metal dulled by shadow. The Kershaws' Bentley was crossing the Canadian gate.

He turned back to the mountainside and the steepest part of the climb. And as he climbed it was as though the hotel, all that part of his life, fell away from him, and he was a small boy again, climbing back home to tea after a long afternoon of freedom; half afraid of the welcome he would get, the raised voice, the skelp on the ear for tearing his trousers, for being late, for something he had done that morning and long forgotten. And yet in a strange way glad to be back. Or not 'glad' perhaps, no positive feeling about it. Simply one of rightness, that this was how a day ended. Home. He tried to keep the thought of Jenny, the feel of her hand touching his face, the sound of her voice; tried to keep those things with him, in his mind. But they seemed unreal. What was real was the grass, the stone wall he climbed, the blackberry hedge with the unripe berries beginning to show, the clump of furze. What was real was the house he was going to. He could already see the high, ragged hedge that stood in front of it, cutting off half the view from its small close windows, unless you went upstairs.

His father sitting in his stockinged feet as *his* father used to, boots beside the fire. His mother rattling about. His sisters, maybe a neighbour. Fall back into it like a nut into its shell. Only he couldn't. Even as he climbed towards it, felt that it was reality, he knew that he couldn't, that he had changed shape, so that he was as out of place, as uncomfortable there as down below, as in London, as anywhere in the world, as much a stranger here. Worse. Because it was more painful to be a stranger here. And yet he went on climbing towards the cottage almost eagerly as though his mind was in two halves and one half was still naively saying 'This is home, this is where you'll find comfort, where you can hide, where the questions can't follow, where everything will be quiet and easy, where you can gather your wits and your strength before you go back into the world again.' For even that half of his mind was not so naive as to think that he could stay there long, have a place there for more than an hour or two, a night. It was that half of his mind that had brought him back to Ireland, back to The Ross. And had refused to think 'If you cannot stay long in your own home, with your own mother and father and two sisters, where in The Ross can you stay, where in Ireland can you belong? What has happened to you?'

That was what the other half was already thinking. Trying to cling now to Jennifer, to escape. And now just to escape. He came through the gap in the hedge with his face sombre, in no mood to talk to anyone. If it was only possible just to go in and sit down and find his father there alone, sitting quiet and smoking, saying nothing. There had been times, very rare, but ones that he remembered above all others, when he and his father had been alone for hours together in the house, or out walking, looking for hares with the pointer, and they had neither of them said anything at all and yet they understood one another more completely than he had ever understood his mother, let alone his grandmother. His father like a rock, solid, immovable. All the way through the same. No lies, no pretence, no vanities, no illusions. He knew exactly how the world was, and accepted it, and knew that in spite of everything it was right for the world to be like that, it could be no other way. Like a rock facing the sky.

But there was no chance that his father would be alone. From the road he could hear the voices through the open doorway, see someone moving. His mother. He came to the doorway, bending his head a little under the lintel. The same small, cramped kitchen with its smell of turf smoke, of old coats wet by the rain and dried by the fire; the same soft glint of white and blue delft on the dark painted dresser against the back wall; the two short wooden benches, the chair, that had been his grandfather's, the stool made out of a butter box; the framed prayers hanging on blackened strings above the mantelpiece, and the china plaque with its blessing.

'God save all here,' he said.

His father by the fire, Peadar Power, Matty, Jamey the simpleton with his hat crammed on his head and his eyes wide at the sight of Michael coming in. Mary Jack, and her daughter Sheila who was a good way simpler than Jamey; and Timmy Pat of the Gap and Sean the Post. All of them looking at him except Sheila Mary Jack who was playing with her fingers.

'Come away in, boy,' his father saying. 'We had you given up for lost altogether.'

'Welcome to you Michael boy, welcome.' This from Timmy Pat and Sean.

'It's easy seein' the great haste he has on him to be home to his own.' This was his mother, not looking at him, but stamping about the fire, huffing and billowing the embers to get the huge, black iron kettle boiling again, and covering all near her in ashes and turf dust. The kitchen filled with smoke.

'Will you hold easy woman,' his father shouted. 'God a'mighty, you'd think you were trying to blast the fire out of the hearth itself instead of raise it.'

'It's very thin you're looking after your travels,' Mary Jack said, coughing from the smoke. She hadn't seen him since he was back, living as she did five miles along the side of the mountain. Sheila blushed scarlet and giggled and put her thumb into her mouth, snuggling close to her mother. Michael had brought up an ounce of tobacco and he gave it to his father. In the other pocket of his coat he had a half a pound of tea and he put that on the corner of the table. When his mother backed away from the fire with the brown teapot he pushed it towards her.

'The fine times you're having down there and grudging the hour you'd be away from it to come and see your own people.'

But she took the tea, grumbling to herself, and went and put it on a shelf of the dresser. 'I suppose you wouldn't be wanting tea and soda cake like anyone else, but only grand things, and divil a grand thing we have here.'

'Leave him alone woman and hould your whisht for a bit. Come here son and sit by the fire and tell us how the world is going. We've been hearing great stories about the fish escaping on the foreigners below, millions upon millions of them.' His father cocked an eye at him, over the bowl of his pipe. 'You wouldn't be knowing anything about that I suppose?'

'What would I be knowing about it?'

'Sean the Post here was saying that there was talk in the town that politics was behind it, and you're the most political divil of any boy I ever heard tell of. I just thought you might know.'

'The politics is at the bottom of all things,' Peadar Power said cunningly, shooting a look at Matty. Matty sat staring into the fire, nursing his mug of tea. Jamey looked at the roof and then at the door and then at the fire.

'I mit a man,' Peadar said, 'who told me that politics is the most awful class of a disease to catch hold of a man and destroy him until he hasn't a splink of sense left in his body only politics aself. He'd be waking in the night an' the first thing he'd be talking of what would it be only politics, politics, like a man with a fever would only be sweatin' or else he'd be shiverin'. It was politics surely that 'scaped them fishes.'

'Well, it wasn't me,' Michael said shortly. He had known as soon as he saw all of them there in the kitchen that they would be getting at him, and that only half of it would be in fun, and he had braced himself for it, but it was still unpleasant. As though they resented him for going, resented him for coming back, resented him for daring to break the mould, the pattern that they themselves had accepted. 'I don't know a thing about the damn fishes.'

'And if you did, boy,' Peadar said, 'who'd blame you? Sure them foreigners has us all destroyed wid their fences and their hedges and their little ponds that a Christian would fall into and get drownded likely, if he had the smallest bit of drink on him.'

Matty, who had been watching Michael's face, nudged Peadar softly to urge him to stop talking about the fishes but Peadar was in the vein to hold the floor, and if he hadn't been,

Matty's nudge would have made him go on. 'I did hear tell,' Peadar said, 'that there is a class of a fish and if you fell into them they would eat a Christian from his buttons to his backbone before you could be pulling him out of the water. A red kind of a fish I did hear they were,' he said, cocking his eyebrow at Michael. 'Would you ever have heard of a thing like that and you across in England?'

'I heard of a lot of things over there,' Michael said, taking the soda cake and the mug of tea from his mother. 'I even heard of a kind of sheep whose tail gets so fat he can't move around with it, and they have to put a small bit of a trolley under it so the sheep can pull his tail behind him.'

'That's a strange kind of a sheep, it is, faith,' Peadar said, not sure whether he ought to be angry or not.

'No stranger than your red fish,' Michael said.

Peadar took his pipe out of his mouth, visibly searching for an answer, but as he was not quite sure what Michael had meant, the answer was slow in coming. Timmy Pat of the Gap came into the awkward silence with a quick clearing of his throat. ' 'tis not right nor Christian,' he said, ' 'tis not lucky to be havin' God's creatures cooped up like that in holes in the ground only for eating. They take them out in little boxes and send them away to foreign places and there isn't a bit of nature in it like you'd be catching them in the sea or in the river. It's against all reason.'

'There is a story,' Peadar said quickly, before Timmy Pat could go on; 'there is a story,' he said, fixing Michael with his eye for a fleeting second and then looking steadfastly into the red heart of the fire as if he was finding the inspiration for the story there, 'that the beasts of the field did be in rebellion once.' He let the sentence hang in the air like a challenge. Michael stared at the china plaque on the chimney breast above the fire, with its legend 'Bless this house'.

'Why for,' Peadar was saying, 'why for, the beasts said to themselves this day, should we be living only to be ate by man, and we stronger than him, and bigger than him, or else able to run faster than him? Don't we be living on grass, they said, and couldn't men be livin' on grass and leaves too, and drinking spring water, and maybe we'd give them a sup of milk now and then as a neighbourly act. But the divil take us, they said, if we'll put up with his butchering, and his meat eating, and his ferocious ways any longer, they said, robbing us of everything from our eggs to our lives. So, didn't they go on strike the beasts, and off with them up into the mountains where a man would run all day without catching them, and men were starving here and starving there, and not a morsel of meat to put between a man's teeth if he had the grazing of twenty cows and gold in the bank. The hens was gone out of the yards, and the donkeys theirselves out of the fields along with the cows, and the sheep off of the mountainside. Mwirra that was the sorrowful time for a man that liked eating.'

Sheila Mary Jack began to cry.

'Whist,' Jamey said softly. 'Don't mind, don't mind, 'tis only a story.'

'The divil mend me if it is only a story,' Peadar said, outraged at the Boy daring to put his spoke in. He cleared his throat and spat into the fire. 'How would any man be telling stories at all,' he said, 'and nothing but interruptions?'

'No harm no harm,' Sean the Post said. 'He's only after quieting the girleen. Let you go on with the tale.'

'Well so,' Peadar said after he had let a pause stretch on long enough, 'maybe I'll be let finish if the humour is in Jamey there to stop his whispering.'

Jamey hung his head miserably. Peadar looked sideways under his eyebrows at Michael to see how he was taking the story. Michael seemed occupied only with his tea and a cigarette. Peadar cleared his throat again.

'Well now, where was I at? At the beasts striking, and they off in the mountains and mankind starving to skeletons from trying to digest the grass and the leaves that was all they had. So the men that was in it didn't they get up a deputation and off with them to see God Almighty on His Throne and complain to Him about the conduct of the beasts in bein' on strike.

' "Mwirra," says God, "but that is a hard one, and how can I be telling the poor beasts that they must submit to being slaughtered and ate and they my own creatures as much as yourselves?" Do you go and look after the matter says He to His Son, for, says He, I'm gettin' too old to be bothered with this class of thing, and 'tis time you were taking over some of my burdens.

'So the Son of God Himself went to the animals and said to them Yerrah, He said, and what do you think you do be at gallivanting and play acting this way and the men below starving for a bite to eat? What do you think you are in the world for at all, He said, do you think it's for pleasure entirely, He said?

'And at that the beasts were most of them downright ashamed and were for going back, but a young ass that had been among the leaders in rebelling against men ups and says "Mwirra Your Honour," he says, "but that's a one-sided kind of a bargain. Does Your Honour know," he said, "what it's like to be carrying turf on your back day in and day out and be left in a field all night with the wind whistling round your legs and the ghosts fleering at you out of the ditches and the rain lashing your back? Does Your Honour know any of that?" said the ass, and the Son of God had to admit that He did not.'

'The creature!' cried Mrs. Carmody scandalized, and banging the teapot down on the table.

'Yerrah damn,' said Peadar, carried away so far by his story that he had forgotten why he had begun it and whose side he was ultimately on. 'And why wouldn't he speak up for himself, the poor ass, seeing the life that he'd had behind him and saw in front of him? Wouldn't you speak up for yourself now?'

'I would not, and the Son of God talking to me. You mind yourself, Peadar Power and you telling blasphemies. Let Father Culhane get hold of you and he'll mend your music. It's the Rosary beads you should be telling and not lies and roguery.'

'The devil blast the lie it is woman. Will you let me finish or not?'

'Go on with your story and don't mind her,' Donal Carmody said. 'If she told her own Rosary instead of shouting and roaring when a man would like to be sleeping or thinking his own thoughts it might be better for her. Will you not see that Michael here has another sup of tea and a cut of cake and he after walking from below after a day's work?'

'Day's work, day's work! Stravaging about and making sheep's eyes at females and blinding himself with little books is his day's work. Am bostha! If it was my work that you were both doing the two of you between you it isn't telling stories by the fire you'd be, it's stretched flat as planks on your two beds you'd be lying and not fit to rise a croak out of you till morning. Work!' She slammed things about on the dresser while the men looked at one another with mutual sympathy and waited for the flurry to die down.

' 'tis a hard job for a man to be telling a story in this house,'
Peadar said. He poked the fire with a twig until the end was
reddened so that he could relight his pipe. 'But do you want the
end of it or do you not?'

'We do,' said Timmy Pat, 'so long as you're sure there is no
badness or sin in it. It has a doubtful sort of start to it to my
way of thinking.' He was a solemn man, who took his religion
more seriously than the Powers had ever done, apart from Jamey.

'God mend your head,' said Peadar contemptuously. 'How
can there be badness in a story, man? Sure didn't my father tell
me this story when I was no higher than his boot, and didn't his
father tell it to him and so back into the old times to the man
that heard it with his own ears?'

'Divil the sin,' said Sean the Post, 'get on with it Peadar.
What happened the ass and he speaking up for himself and his
fellow creatures?'

'Divil the thing happened him but what I'll tell you if I'm
let,' said Peadar. 'There is the ass standin' there obstinate as an
ass can be the one side of a wall, and the Son of God standin'
t'other side, and they looking at one another like you might look
at Sergeant McMenamin and he tryin' to discover did you have
the piece of paper for the wireless or a light on your bicycle,
and the rest of the animals standin' about on this foot and that,
embarrassed to be causing so much stir and furory, and the ass
said, If we was to be going back down he said, would we get
conditions?

' "What conditions?" says Our Lord.

' "Well," says the ass, "the first thing is that You let men
start to eat bread as their chief sustenance and support," says
he, "and porridge or stirabout. And make cheese out of their
milk, and not be depending on meat and eggs for breakfast,
dinner and tea," said the ass, "which is the lazy man's way of
eating and enriches the blood till it does harm to their vital parts
and their tempers. Let that be the first condition," he said. For
until that time you see there was no such thing as bread.'

'No such thing as bread?' cried Mary Jack. And Mrs. Carmody, who had come and sat down with a bad grace to hear the
rest of the story, got up again and began rinsing delft in the
bucket in order to have no share in such rubbish.

'The divil fire you,' cried Peadar, 'will you let me be talking
and not be interrupting me till I forget is it Tuesday or
tomorrow?'

'Don't mind them,' Donal Carmody said.

'Go on,' said Sean.

'Well now,' said Peadar, 'Our Lord said He saw no harm in that condition. And the ass said, the next condition is just as easy. 'tis the way the cows and the horses do be getting the rheumatics standing about in the rain and the wind he says, winter and summer. Do you tell the men below he says, to be building little houses for the beasts, he said, like they have for themselves. But at that the sheep, that had a great gradh for the free life of the mountains, set up a terrible bleating and said divil a bit they wanted little houses, only that the wind be not let blow so cold when the men were after shearing their wool in the spring weather. Well enough, said the ass, if that's what they want, let You have an angel or two attend to that, and Our Lord said He would, and no difficulty there.

'Well at that didn't the cats and dogs set up a great barking and miaowing, for they saw themselves getting nothing out of this at all, except stones thrown at them when they went below again. So the ass made a condition for them that they might lie by the fire at the end of every day, and have a share of the little houses that would be built for the beasts, and another share of men's houses aself.

' "Mwirra," says Our Lord, "and that's a fine string of conditions you're after making. But you've left out yourself."

' "I have so," the ass said, "for I would not want it to be thought that all this was for my own benefit. Let you think of a condition for me."

' "Well now," said Our Lord, " 'tis not so easy as you might be thinking, for with all the rumpus and the reeraw that you're after making, there's not many below would be glad to be troubling themselves building you a house, and many's the skelp of a stick you're likely to be getting in times to come, and you staggering under two baskets of turf that would break the back of a big horse and he under them for a quarter of a morning."

' "I know," said the ass sorrowfully, "but that's the way of things, as Your Honour aself may be after discovering in a bad day, if You don't mind my mentioning it." And at that they both looked sorrowful and a kind of friendship was struck up between them in that moment.

' "I'll tell you what," says Our Saviour, "divil the bit I can do for you in the way of saving you skelps and the weight of the turf and the odd kick in the ribs that you'll be getting from this out, but there'll come a day," says Our Lord, "when I'll be needing someone to carry me," says He, "and I going into Jerusalem. Let you be there that day," says Our Lord, "and we'll go in together. There will be fine horses will envy you that Honour and I going where I shall be going." '

Peadar stopped for a long moment, reddening his pipe with the twig.

'And you may see proof of that story to this day,' he said quickly, as Jamey opened his mouth to say something. 'For in sign of His promise didn't Our Lord lay His hand on the ass, like he'd be giving him a friendly pat, and from that out hasn't every ass carried the Cross on his back in memory of the event.'

'And all honour to him,' Sean the Post said.

'Maybe, maybe,' said Peadar, allowing himself a small knowing smile without looking at Michael. 'But maybe too he'd have been a long way better off without the Cross, and he minding his own business, without worrying about the rights of sheep and cows that don't mind him a bit, or going off interfering in Jerusalem in an affair that was above his understanding.'

'Glory be!' said Jamey, although he had heard the story before.

Timmy Pat crossed himself and looked uncomfortably towards Mrs. Carmody, whose good opinion he valued. 'I wouldn't be in agreement with that class of story at all,' he said in a loud voice.

'And what class of story would you be in agreement with?' said Sean the Post. 'Pishogues and fairies?'

'I like a story out of the papers,' said Timmy Pat defensively, 'out of the *News of the World*, now, that does be true and a thing that has happened in our own time.' His sister in Leeds sent him the *News of the World* now and then wrapped round a jersey or a shirt or some small present for Christmas or his birthday.

'Naked women,' said Mary Jack. 'I wouldn't have a newspaper in the house,' she said. She looked at her daughter beside her who was playing with her fingers again. 'How would I be explaining that class of thing to her?'

Sean the Post began telling a story that his father had told him about how a woman fell into the Devil's Well one night and was drowned, and ever after whenever there was no moon wouldn't she come out and be walking about the edge of the Well all dressed in white and beckoning to passers by that they should come and be keeping her company.

'Ring a Dora!' cried Mary Jack. 'Passers by! By the Devil's Well? What passers by would you find there by day, let alone in the dark of the night?'

'Amn't I telling you this was in the old times?' Sean the Post said impatiently, for he had little patience for women of any kind, and less for Mary Jack. 'There were more people in those days as your own sense might tell you, and half the cottages and better than half of them from here to the Head with their roofs fallen in. Well now, wasn't my father passing there one night—'

Michael sat letting the story-telling pass over him like water flowing, his mind still on Peadar's story, trying not to let it irritate him. There had been no malice in it, not real malice, and he imagined for a moment the same kind of argument in London, in one of the committees on which he had wasted half his life and most of his strength when he was in England; tried to imagine any man there making a point in an argument with a story like that. And he sensed for a moment the depth of history behind the kitchen, behind the voices round him, the story-telling, reaching back and down into the deepest layers of man's mind, felt the depth of strength of their simplicity. Like a tree. Roots deep in the ground, down to the living rock. As though the kitchen was reclaiming him, Peadar's story was reclaiming him, saying 'Where have you been, boy, that's so important? What have you achieved with your gallivanting and your reading, and your arguing and your fighting? Who do you think you are to raise yourself up above us, where do you think it will get you? Standing by the roadside like the ass, with a cross on your back and skelps for your dinner, and let all the fine memories of Jerusalem warm you when the wind blows.' The bitter reality of poor men who know that whatever happens they will stay poor. The terrible cynicism of poor men, who will shout Hosanna for the entry into Jerusalem, and within the week cry Crucify him, give us Barabbas. Why had he come back?

He sat with his elbow on his knee, his hand shading his eyes from the heat of the turf fire. What was he going to do about Jenny? Suppose she had come up with him now? What would they have said?

'—and didn't he have the mark of her four fingers on his wrist to the end of his days, and I seeing them myself with my own eyes?' Sean the Post was saying, ending his story. Mary Jack and Matty and Jamey crossed themselves, and Sheila followed suit, clumsily copying her mother.

'—'tis unlucky to be talking about such things,' Timmy Pat said. He had a long walk in the dark to reach home.

'I heard a different ending to that story, and it not concerning your father at all. Are you sure that you have it right now?' Peadar said, displeased at being out of the centre of things for so long.

Sean the Post drew in a long breath to give him time to find the right crushing answer.

What was he going to do about Jenny? They would have to go away.

' 'tis like the story of the seal woman,' Peadar was saying scornfully. 'Divil the family that doesn't claim that one time a seal woman married into it.' As he said this he allowed his eye to meet Donal's for the briefest of moments, for indeed it was a story that the Carmodys claimed to have happened to themselves. The words caught at the edge of Michael's mind, and he was a small boy again, sitting by this same fire and for once his grandfather telling him a story and not his grandmother. Looking back he had often wondered how much and what had underlain his grandfather's appearance of oxlike humility. A big crag of a man with worn fingers like the stumps of roots worn out of the soil, all his bones huge, his eyes sunk in the deep pits of his eye-sockets. Usually saying nothing, half bending his head at some whip-lash remark of the grandmother's. But when he did talk his voice was full of a harsh music, slow and struggling as though he was unused to talking, and yet at the same time compelling.

He had been six or seven, crouched on a box close to his grandfather's knee, hoping for a pull from his mug of tea. All the others out. Perhaps he had had a cold, that was why he was left in the cottage alone with his grandfather. And his grandfather had seemed to unfold in the unaccustomed emptiness of the kitchen, in the firelit quiet, grown huge and different, as though with the weight of his wife's contempt off his shoulders, and for this hour relieved from having to earn bread, he had become for a moment what he might have been always.

'Did you ever hear tell, child, that there was a seal woman in our family?'

'A seal woman grandpa?' His eyes wide, and yet wider for the mug of tea than for the seal woman.

'Aye aye. No less. Wet and dripping out of the sea. My grandfather's grandfather, or maybe it was his grandfather, found her and he a young man. Naked as a fish she was. He had been gathering seaweed for his fields and he hears her crying like a lost soul, moyee, moyee, little and small and lost and he takes pity on her and puts his coat round her and his soft shoes on her feet and he leads her back to his house.'

'This house grandpa? Here?' The story had him now.

'No boy! What class of a house would this be for a seal woman, and it built by the council for my father when he came back to The Ross? No, a proper house with a thatch roof and thick walls and an earth floor and the pot never off the fire. Out along the Head. The house my father was born in till they pulled it down round his mother's ears for having a son a Fenian.' He had stopped, holding the big china mug clasped in his huge, gentle hands, his eyes lost, as if he was searching the fire for words. Perhaps, Michael thought now, he had been seeing that destruction in the grey ashes round the hearth, that fear of starvation and the weapons of the powerful that had ruled his life, turned him into an ox.

And as he remembered, the story, his grandfather's telling of it, like finding an old photograph in a drawer, Michael felt himself almost overwhelmed by the memory, as though his body was stiffened where it sat, could not move for a second and the present was gone, vanished, not yet happened, nothing of his life had happened, had all been dreaming, and he was back, he could feel the heat of the fire against bare shins, feel his body small, thin, the rough serge of his grandfather's trousers against the inside of his wrist, as he hung on his knee with locked hands. Could feel the longing to taste the cool, sweet thickness of the dregs of the tea in the mug. Could see the mug, cream yellow, with a blue line round it just below the rim. Even the brown chip inside the rim. See the bristles on his grandfather's jaw, bright silver in the firelight.

'Go on with the story, grandpa.'

'Aye. Aye. Well, that was the house the young lad brought her back to and presented her to his mother.' The voice growing easier, more fluent as he entered the worn, familiar path of the story. 'Mwirra and all the saints, a she-weasel would make more friends with a rabbit than that mother of his made with the seal woman. She did not know what she was except that it was a queer unchancy class of a female would be coming back to her house dressed in nothing but her son's old coat and pampooties and the sea still dripping from her like rainwater on a wet day. Yerrah, the reeraw that she made, but nothing would do her son but marry the seal woman, and marry her he did.' He stopped again. But this time for story-teller's effect, supping his tea.

'And what happened then, grandpa?'

'What would happen, boy, and they two married, and young in themselves? They fell to making small lads, what else, and your own grandfather's grandfather or maybe his grandfather, the first of them. And all went like a June day with them until one night there's the queer kind of calling outside the house and the seal woman sits up in the box bed and cries, "I'm coming, I'm coming." '

'Ooh, grandpa!'

'Well, her husband catches tight hold of her and won't let her go, for he knows well what's happening, and who it is that's calling her. It's the seal-king has come to claim his own again, and the boy has no mind to be deprived of the mother of his sons and his own bedmate, to let her go back to the cold sea. But the next morning doesn't he find one of his two cows stretched on her side and a great smell of the sea round her corpse as though she had been drowned?'

'Drowned!' Luxury of fear with the door shut and the fire burning and his grandfather to guard him.

'And the next night isn't it the second cow that is killed on him and he sees that there is no help for it. For if any more is done to him he will be ruined entirely and he is close enough to ruin as it is with the two cows dead. And so when they go to bed that night he lies on the inside and pretends to be fast asleep when the calling begins. Sure enough, up gets his wife in her shift and cries out, "I'm coming, I'm coming." And off over her head she takes the shift and lets it drop on the earth floor, and there she stands in the middle of the kitchen as naked as the day he found her, and the roaring outside getting closer and closer until the bones shake in his body and he's feared for his life.'

'Oooh, ooh! Was it the seal-king grandpa?'

'It was so. And doesn't the seal woman catch up the two small lads out of their cradle by the fire, for she doesn't mean to be going back into the cold sea alone. And at that my grandfather's grandfather leaps out of the bed, for if he's feared of the seal-king he has no wish to see his sons drowned.

' "Hould ye divil!" he cries, and grabs the first one out of her arms. But before he can get holt of the other isn't she away out of doors and down the mountainside, and divil the chance he had of catching her and she with her fairy father, even if he had had the courage to follow them. And that's why none of our family from that day to this has gathered sea weed for its fields or gone fishing, or had any truck with the sea, for fear of his own kin coming up out of the water and catching tight hold of him and drowning him. And my own grandfather told me when I was as young a lad as you are now, that the seal-king and the seal woman would still come crying round the door at nights, calling for their lost child. Yerrah, the sea is a bad place.'

His grandfather had shivered then, as though he had frightened himself, and young boy and old man had bent together by the fire, the boy listening for the roars of the seal-king, the cries of the seal woman, imagining her crying for him, coming to take him, out of his bed with his baby sisters sleeping, no one hearing, no one coming to save him.

'Would I drown in the sea?' he had whispered.

'Yerrah child, the strongest man in the world would drown in the sea, and he the champion of swimmers.'

He had got the dregs of the tea then, burying his face in the mug, inhaling its safety.

And yet even in his fears he had been restless, and the story had stayed with him not only as his grandfather would have interpreted it, if he had ever thought that a story required interpretation – as a warning against strangeness, against stepping out of the safe and ordered world of one's own; but as a challenge, as a promise of wonders. That there *were* seal-kings and seal women, and they were powerful and beautiful and armed with magic. Here inside the cottage was safety and bread and jam and tea and bed, and a corner of the fire. But out there was the whole mysterious world. And he had listened at night not only with a warm shiver of teror, as he burrowed down into his bed, but also with a kind of trembling hopefulness. Suppose they came? Where would they take me? Oooh!

They were talking now of wishes. Not believing in what they were saying; only as a kind of game; and yet with a foundation of belief behind the talk.

'Divil the bit it's hard,' said Timmy Pat. 'Bedam but I know what I'd be asking her.'

' 'tis not as easy as that, now,' Sean the Post said. 'I mind hearing of a man that got asked that same question by a Fairy that he met along the road one night, and that was the most woeful bit of business he ever got mixed up in. Fairy wishes have a troublesome way of turning out.'

'I'd be asking for my fields above to be as flat as a table, and for them to be tended to without my stirring hand nor foot from the fire,' Timmy Pat said.

'Be all that's Holy,' Sean the Post said, 'you wouldn't be asking for much in that second wish that you don't have already. What would the third one be?'

'It isn't right nor Christian even to be talking of such things,' Mary Jack said. 'The old people knew better than to be taking certain names in vain.'

'I'd wish my pipe never to be empty,' Peadar said, 'and always lit.'

'There's trouble for you for a start,' Sean the Post cried triumphantly. 'How would you sleep, man, and your pipe never out? How would you eat, how would you drink your tea? Sure, you'd be dead in a week from your foolish wish. If that was Jamey there, or Sheila aself made such a wish, who'd blame them? But yourself that sets up to have his five wits active in his head! God mend you, Peadar Power.'

'It fails me,' Mrs. Carmody said savagely, 'it fails me to know how grown men can sit talking and talking for an evening and a night and say nothing that has any point nor sense in it.'

'I've lost my roots,' Michael thought, 'and got nothing in exchange. I can't get back and I can't go on.' And he knew in that second what his own wish was; to get as far from here as he could and not come back. Take Jenny with him, forget The Ross, and politics, and everything that had ever happened to him and start again. What would they start? Damn you, he cried to his questioner, what does it matter, anything, anywhere. It's always been done. I'll get a job. I'll sing.

I'll sing. Even as he thought it it seemed ridiculous, a mad conceit. Because he had sung a few times in the Bar, because a few of the locals came to listen, a few tourists shouted for more. Where else would they let him sing, who'd listen? And what would he sing? My Lagan Love? He'd get hellish fat singing that, or anything else he sang on Fridays in the bar.

And yet behind these shocked humilities, these reflex contractions of his mind, that were not so much humility as fear of the unknown, like someone touched by a hand in the dark when they believe they are alone, there was excitement, almost a kind of breathless certainty. He could see it, see himself, hear himself. He knew that it must happen.

She had said it. You could get a job singing in a pub. Why not? And again the kitchen shivered, faded, the voices faded. For that moment he was alone. I wish it, he thought, above all the world. As though he was holding himself in with his hands, holding his heart, his stomach inside his body, because they were threatening to burst out. He knew what he wanted to do, what he wanted to be. Not yet how he would do it, what he would sing. What he would tell. He still did not know that part of what he would have to tell would be this kitchen, these stories, things that came out of this simplicity. But he knew what he wanted to be and suddenly he felt an immense gratitude to all of them, because they had been there when he found out, when he discovered his inner self. He wanted to tell them something but he had no stories that they would understand, no way any more of reaching them.

'My wish,' Jamey was saying shyly, 'would be to have understanding of the beasts' talk. I would love dearly to be able to talk to the cat and to the hens in the yard. You and Matty do have each other,' he said, 'but I do be alone often. Or I'd be up on the mountain and there is only the sheep and the wind, and the old dog. And maybe the ass. If I was able to understand his talk he might tell me about Our Lord.'

'The divil break your legs,' cried Peadar. 'Tell about Our Lord! Did ever a man have such a brother?'

' 'oo said aself,' Matty broke in accusingly, ' 'oo said aself that all the beasts themselves had the power of our speech once, and lost it. Why for should Jamey not learn theirs?'

'I'm for going home,' Peadar said. His triumph over the Guards had been so sweet that he had wanted to savour it, hearing men talk about the fishes and the great wonder of their escape, and maybe himself helping to turn their thoughts in other directions if they were looking for who might have done it. But not at the expense of Matty and the Boy upsetting the order of things and taking up every blessed word he said. 'Come,' he said, settling his hat on his furze bush head and creaking to his feet. Normally leave-taking could occupy a comfortable hour of proposing that it was late and being assured that it was no such thing, that the night was barely dusk yet and what harm if it was, sure it wasn't every night they had the chance of a bit of good crack, and sit down man, and another fill of the old pipe and let herself wet the tea again. But the divil fire him if he was going to sit here and have his blood and kin in rebellion against him.

It was at that moment, as Peadar stood settling his hat, and his two brothers looked at him in alarm at the note of rage in his voice, that Sergeant McMenamin and Constable O'Neill arrived outside the house in the sergeant's car. Peadar had his face to the door as it opened, and the doorway was instantly filled with the dark, massive shape of the sergeant.

'God a'mighty!' Peadar whispered, and sat down again, his face going white under the dark patina of dirt. Timmy Pat, who saw everything and put the worst construction on most of it, drew his breath in with a sharp excitement.

Why for would Peadar Power be getting a weakness at sight of the sergeant coming into Donal Carmody's house? If it was Donal himself sitting down sharp and losing his heartbeat, little surprise in that, who wouldn't when it was his own house the Guards were at. But Peadar? A bad conscience lay behind it, as sure as there was a tail on the cat.

Donal had stood up to make the Guards welcome, his mind searching his own conscience as he did so. 'Come away in Sergeant dear,' he said, and, 'Guard O'Neill. Here's a seat by the fire for you.'

'We'll not be troubling you that much,' the sergeant said uncomfortably. Now that the actual moment had come he had neither heart nor stomach for arresting the boy. But it had gone beyond the possibility of turning back. Far beyond it. His own position, job, career, pension, were at stake, not, he thought hastily, that that would have weighed with him in the face of an injustice. But what injustice? If he himself in the first flush of the thing had thought that it was indeed the old men that had done it, and that Guard O'Neill was right, blast him, what certainty had he now that he mightn't have been wrong? In fact sure to God he must have been wrong. But even so the words of the formula for arrest stuck like a bone in the sergeant's throat and he only beckoned to Michael, who was looking at him as if he knew already why the sergeant had come. Michael stood up slowly while equally slowly every eye in the kitchen except Sheila's turned to look at him.

'I'd like to be having a word with you if you don't mind,' the sergeant said. At his shoulder Guard O'Neill coughed contemptuously. 'Have a word with him.' By God, he knew what kind of word *he'd* have with him. Might have yet when they got him below in the barracks.

'All right,' Michael said.

'Jesus Mary and Joseph,' cried his mother. 'What is it? What is it?'

'Nothing too much, ma'am. If you wouldn't mind stepping outside, Michael. No need for disturbing yourselves now.'

'Is it the fi—' Matty began, his mouth trembling. Peadar kicked his ankle and Matty cried out, 'Oo, ooh.'

'What have you done now, boy?' Donal said in a choked voice, supporting himself with one hand against the chimney breast. Sean the Post was looking this way and that, in agonies at being involved in such a situation and he with an official position and his uniform on. Mary Jack had a protective arm round Sheila and was staring at Michael furiously as though he had already been found guilty of rape and murder.

'I've done nothing,' Michael said. Guard O'Neill caught hold of his arm. 'Don't touch me,' Michael said. 'If you want me to come quietly don't touch me.'

'So you know we want you to come with us?' said Guard O'Neill in triumph. He had chosen to forget his suspicion of the Powers and was doing all that he could to make Sergeant McMenamin forget it too.

'Don't try and be clever,' Michael said, his temper beginning to shake inside him. 'You might be sorry yet.'

'Threats is it?' the guard cried. 'Did you hear that, Sergeant? It's my business to tell you that you're under arrest and that anything you say may be taken down and used in evidence against you.' It was not his business, but the sergeant's, but like a Peeping Tom at the glimpse of flesh he could not restrain himself.

'Arrest?' said Mrs. Carmody in a fainting voice.

'Lord save us!' cried Mary Jack. Sheila began to blubber and stamp her feet and her mother threw both arms round her and pulled her close, putting the greatest possible space between her and that villainous boy that was nothing but trouble to his good mother and his father since the day he was born, not that she'd think much in favour of Donal Carmody if it came to that, the great loose-tongued galoot, doing nothing but cast bad glances at a woman if she so much as passed along the road before him. Mary Jack's husband had died of despair many years before.

'Go with them, boy,' Donal said. 'Don't make it harder for yourself.'

Timmy Pat had already made himself small in the back of the kitchen, and Sean the Post was twisting his hands together, his posture saying as clearly as he could make it that he was really there for no more than a kind of business, inquiring was there a letter that he could take anywhere, or maybe a parcel.

'No trouble now, I hope?' the sergeant said uncomfortably. 'Sure maybe 'tis all a mistake and will be cleared up in the morning. But you'll have to come down with us now.' He was feeling worse and worse about the business. Hadn't he seen the boy grow up, nearly, and his father as decent a poor man as ever swept grit.

'Don't lay a hand on him!' said Mrs. Carmody in a savage voice. 'Lay one finger on him either of you and—'

'Threats and threats!' said Guard O'Neill. 'Have you a note of that, Sergeant? Maybe the whole family is in it, and more beside them.' He cast round the kitchen his Committee of Public Safety look, that by itself alone would lift him into the Special Branch in a short while.

'I'll go with you,' Michael said. 'Whatever it is that they think I did it will be sorted out soon enough. Try not to worry about it.' He kissed his mother and touched his father's arm, and without looking at anyone else went out of the house with the two guards, the one in front of him, the other behind him. When they got outside he took a deep breath of the night air, that was not yet dark, but only a deepening of the evening, a red ragged banner in the western sky beyond Lir Head, the clouds like black islands stretched across it, and to the south gathered into a deeper mass like a volcano. It was very warm.

'Get into the car, Michael lad,' the sergeant said. He was thoroughly ashamed of Guard O'Neill. But it was Guard O'Neill who got in the back beside their prisoner. He smelt of hot woollen uniform and sour breath in the cramped interior of the little car.

'We've a way of fixing hard lads,' he said.

'And there is a way of fixing soft policemen,' Michael said. 'And don't you forget it.'

'Go on, go on,' Guard O'Neill said, 'dig your grave with your tongue. 'twill all go down in the book.'

Inside the cottage Donal Carmody was holding Mrs. Carmody back from throwing herself outside to catch a last glimpse of her son. 'Be easy, woman,' Donal said in agony. 'Don't make it worse for him.'

'Worse for him, is it?' she hissed at last, when she could not free herself. 'And for myself? Am I not to be considered? Let you be easy, Donal Carmody, 'tis only your son that they've arrested, 'tis only the boy that carries your name. But it is the flesh out of my own heart that they are carrying away to shame and imprisonment, and am I not to see them do it, even, am I not to see the last sight of him going down the road and wave my hand to him for comfort?'

'Yerrah God 'tis a fright,' said Peadar, uneasily. 'May they have no luck, the divils, for taking him on you.'

'May God diminish them,' cried Mrs. Carmody, 'and if I was a man they would not have taken him. But there are no men here, it is easy to see that.'

'Now, now, hould hard,' said Peadar. 'How could we be stopping them, and they acting in the course of their duties and in uniform an' all?'

'Aye, aye,' Sean the Post said. 'You couldn't be going against them and they in uniform.'

'We'll be getting home,' said Mary Jack, eager to be out of that house of sin and illegality.

'I'm sorry for your trouble, ma'am,' Jamey whispered, unconsciously speaking as if Michael was already dead and they were at his wake, Sheila had stopped blubbering and was stooping down to play with the red embers of the fire.

'Holy Mother of God the child is at the fire!' screamed Mary Jack. She darted a look of fury at Donal Carmody as if it was his fault that the fire was there in the first place, which in a way it was. It was as though something terrible had entered the room with the two guards that had poisoned all neighbourliness.

Mrs. Carmody was standing by the kitchen table, the cold

teapot in her hand and the tears running down her face. 'What has he done?' she was whispering to no one, 'what has he done that they should take him away?'

' 'tis the politics,' Peadar said hopefully. ' 'tis the scourge of man.' Matty tugged his sleeve, wanting to be let say something, and Peadar kicked him again. 'What are you tugging me for you omadhaun, you're as bad as Jamey and I breaking the heart in my breast to be putting bread in your two mouths. What would you be doing and saying if it was me that was took, leaving the pair of you on your lone up there beyond? What would 'oo say then, eh, boy?'

'Ooo, ooh,' cried Jamey, and Matty sank his head in his shoulders, afraid of a skelp across the back of the neck from his elder brother.

The evening broke up in unhappiness and awkward leave-takings. Timmy Pat and Sean the Post walked together a few steps of the way.

'I have a strange feeling on me,' Timmy Pat said in a low voice, 'that there were maybe others back there just now who knew more than they said.'

'And maybe they were the wise people if they didn't say it,' said Sean the Post.

'Aye,' said Timmy Pat doubtfully. 'Maybe so. Maybe so.' They walked on a bit, between the scented hedges. 'But if a man knew something and did not say it to the right person, maybe that would be a sin for him?'

'The guards do know what they be doing,' said Sean the Post. 'They do have information.'

'But where would they get that information if people that knew things were not for telling them?'

'It would be a terrible thing for a decent man to be giving information to anyone,' said Sean the Post not sure where this conversation might be leading him. Nor even sure where he wanted it to lead. He had his own suspicions of Peadar Power, but a complex of feelings prevented him from expressing them. The simple, basic feeling of not getting mixed up in things; the only slightly less fundamental feeling that whatever you knew it couldn't be right to tell it to the guards; while against that there was the uncontradictable fact that he too wore a uniform and was an employee of the State, and might be expected to have a different relationship with the State's Guardians of the Peace than other men had; and giving information, not that he had any, or sharing suspicions, admitting privately inside himself for this one moment that he had any suspicions of anyone, which was not a thing that he would be prepared to declare aloud; admitting so much – where was he at? – well, on the one hand there was Michael Carmody and on the other there was Peadar Power, and if one came out of gaol, the other must go in.

Now, which would a man choose? Young Michael, that had been in gaol already, and was mixed up in politics, and might well have done whatever it was anyway, not to speak of having no one depending on him, and being young and strong and well able to bear such things, having his health and strength and all his life before him; and on the other hand, Peadar Power, with his two brothers half foolish – one of them in fact as completely foolish as you needed to be, short of being locked up in the County Home, and as Peadar himself had just said, what in the name of God would those two do if Peadar was taken? What would happen to his farm?

'I wouldn't be for getting mixed up in things,' Sean the Post said at last, as if this was a solution. 'Faith and I wouldn't.'

'Maybe so,' said Timmy Pat.

'Let you be sure it is so,' Sean the Post said enthusiastically, delighted to have the problem solved. 'What way would your conscience be and you maybe sending an innocent man to gaol? And what way might you yourself be, and you meeting him afterwards? 'tis many a belt of a spade men got for less.'

'Maybe I could tell it in Confession? That would ease me.'

'Arragh damn, Timmy Pat, but you're the divil for making a hard road for yourself. Let it go, man.' Their roads forked at that point, Sean the Post going down to his cottage on the edge of Ross Harbour, and Timmy Pat turning up towards the Gap.

Michael Carmody was already in his cell. Or what in that peaceful part of the world passed for a cell, being no more than a back room in the barracks, with a lock on the door, and three bars on the small window. There was a bed and a chair and two grey blankets and a pillow almost as hard as the floor. On the floor there was nothing but dust, and a dark and apparently irremovable stain where one of the Walshes had tried to cut his throat with a piece of glass from the window. It looked vaguely like the map of Ireland.

CHAPTER TWENTY

THE Garda Siochana Barracks in Ross Harbour was no more than a middling small house with a Garda Siochana green plate above the front door, the two main rooms downstairs turned into Charge Room and Waiting Room, the three upstairs rooms serving their natural purposes of bedrooms, exactly as the kitchen and bathroom served theirs, and the one miserable small return room at the back built out into the garden, with three iron bars on the window, serving as a cell, into which Michael Carmody was roughly shoved by Guard O'Neill at twenty minutes past ten that Saturday night.

Three hours later Michael was the only one still awake. Upstairs Sergeant McMenamin slept the sleep of a widower, tranquil and easy, spread out to the four corners of the bed, his dreams untroubled by matters of conscience, or doubts or fears. No man could do his work properly, Sergeant McMenamin held, unless he got his proper share of sleep. And so he slept.

Next door, Constable O'Neill also slept, his fox-face made not much less foxy by unconsciousness, his uniform hanging on a wire hanger on a nail driven into the door, his dreams a turmoil of arrests and promotions, of reports and intrigues which in turn slid into a most satisfying dream during which he went down to the 'cell' and gave Michael Carmody a most unmerciful going over with boot and truncheon. Take that you insolent wee villain, you, you dirty Communist rat. Thud, bang, scrunch, womp.

He woke with a start. What was that? Knocking. Knocking on the door below. His heart thudded. Trouble? Drunks? Michael Carmody in his cell? Was he kicking the cell door? Be the Holy, be Cripes and he'd kill him, he'd kick him senseless, he'd use his testicles for hurley balls. Wait till I get down to you my beauty, he promised the air, pushing his bare feet into his black regulation boots and stamping them twice to get a good grip of them round his ankles for kicking. He'd teach him to be giving smart answers in front of the sergeant. He went out on to the landing and met the sergeant there ahead of him, because the sergeant hadn't troubled to put on his boots.

' 'tis someone knocking,' the sergeant said. The noise had stopped for the moment.

'It's that Carmody boy kicking up ructions,' Guard O'Neill said, 'and I'm just in the humour to go down and teach him what's what.' He was fastening his coat round him over his pyjamas.

The knocking began again, and this time there could be no mistake about it, it was from the front it was coming and not the back.

'Jasus,' said the sergeant, 'it's them from Dublin. Or the Super.' He remembered the drawing pin and ran back into his room to put on his boots. As an afterthought he put on his trousers. The knocking continued, more furiously than before. The constable had hung uncertainly at the head of the stairs, wondering whether to be prompt in his pyjama bottoms, or belated in full uniform. It was the kind of indecision at crucial moments that would dog him all his life and rob him of the fullest fruits of his dedication to his career. The sergeant came out of his room in his boots and trousers, and so the two of them went down more or less together, one full uniform between them.

'God above, have patience,' said the sergeant under his breath as the knocking climbed in a crescendo of impatience. ' 'tis Dublin surely.' He had an image in his mind of squad cars outside filled with large men in grey-blue senior uniforms, all of them cursing him. 'Divil take the bolts.' He drew them at last, undid the lock, and only then thought to ask, 'Who's there?'

For answer the door opened with the weight of a man's shoulder behind it, the edge of it took the sergeant between the two eyes and he staggered back the length of the hallway to collapse at the bottom of the stairs.

'What the—' Guard O'Neill began to shout, and the muzzle of a sub-machine gun took him between the flaps of his coat and the flies of his pyjamas, four inches below the navel. He doubled forward and the muzzle of the gun lifted sharply and did his nose a severe injury. He clapped his hands to it and Seagrun O Maelchonaire kicked him in the crotch.

'Ye dirty wee Donegal rat,' Seagrun cried happily, 'this is a raid. Where is he? Where have you put him, ye bastards? MICHEÁL? MICILÍN AVIC, WE'RE COMING FOR YOU!' Two hearty young men had shoved in behind Seagrun's shoulders. One of them had a pistol and the other a bomb. The one with the bomb tossed it up in his left hand and caught it again like a hurley ball. His name was Proinsias Ó Murchu, having been christened Frank Murphy, and the ambition of his life for the time being was to explode that bomb. He had only been admitted to the ranks of the Sons of Ireland the week before and had spent the last few days with Seagrun and some others training on the heathery shoulders of Slieve Clogher. Increasingly he had felt that training was all very well but that it shouldn't be allowed to interfere with action. And here, thank God and His Blessed Mother, was action at last.

'Imperialist Swine,' he said to the sergeant who was tearfully mopping blood from his split forehead. As soon as he mopped it it ran down again into his eyes, blinding him. The third raider, Liam Ó Cearnaigh, younger son of the Ross Harbour chemist, pushed the muzzle of his British Army Webley (stolen from a British Army post in Belfast many months before, and reaching the trembling hand of Liam Ó Cearnaigh at several strange removes); Liam pushed the barrel of his gun into Guard O'Neill's face and said in a shaking whisper, 'The first noise and I'll sh-shoot.'

'God above,' whispered the constable, 'don't be putting that thing near me. Sure what harm did we ever do you?'

"D – d'you know me?' whispered Liam.

'I do not,' swore the constable. 'I wouldn't recognize you if you were the only man on the parade. I swear it. He's in back there. D'you want the key?' This last to Seagrun rather than to Liam.

But keys were no more in Seagrun's mind now than when he had scored to get in the Barracks' window five minutes before. Although scorn is not quite the word. He hadn't thought of it. He had already rampaged through the Charge Room and the Waiting Room. He came back to the sergeant. 'Ye have five seconds to tell me where he is,' he said. 'One—'

'Holy Christ, where could he be?' said the sergeant. 'He's in the cell. Will I open it?'

Seagrun hissed, 'Mark them, lads. One move and you can blow their heads off. I'M COMING MICHEÁL!'

In the cell, where he had been lying on the bed in a slow red smoulder of rage, Michael had come to his feet at the first sounds of conflict and was now standing by the door, his mind upside down. If there were two last things in the world that he wanted least, one was to stay in that cell, and the other was to be rescued from it by Seagrun. But the choice was going to be out of his hands.

'Are you there, old comrade?' Seagrun cried in a tremendous voice.

'I am, you bloody lunatic,' Michael said. 'What are you at?'

'Stand back from the door till I blow it open,' Seagrun roared. 'STAND AGAINST THE WALL, MAN!'

Michael had hardly time to fling himself flat against the dingy green and brown paint separated by an orange stripe, that was some previous sergeant's idea of suitable decoration for a place where drunks would wake up with hangovers, when a small salvo of sub-machine gun bullets blasted the lock off the door and the door off one of its hinges. The bullets smashed their way on through the back window. The door fell at a wounded slant into the room.

'ARE YOU ALL RIGHT?' Seagrun yelled, having deafened himself with the gunfire. Michael was slightly pale and his hand shook as he put it up to his head where a splinter of the lock had hit him.

'I think so.'

'Did they torture you?'

'No.'

'God is good. Then you can still walk?' He reached out his left hand and gave an emotion-charged grip to Michael's arm. 'By God, old friend, you had me fooled yesterday. I had half a mind to go back and shoot you.' He pulled Michael out of the room. 'We'd better get moving.'

'Where?' Michael asked, playing for time. But then, as they came into the hall, and he saw the two guards sitting on the linoleum, each of their heads pouring blood into their cupped hands, he saw that it was too late for playing, probably too late for anything. 'Christ,' he whispered, 'what have you done?'

'These are a couple of new lads since your time,' Seagrun said. 'But you can trust them to the death. Lie flat you bastards,' he ordered the two policemen. They lay as flat as planks without protest. 'The first one of you that moves can be buried by the other one,' he said. 'WITHDRAW!'

The three Sons and Michael went out of the front door. A van with DOYLE FOR FISH written on the side of it was parked and waiting, a boy crouched over the wheel. They all climbed in the back, to be enveloped in a smell of fish and to find their feet slithering on fishscales. There were empty fish boxes turned upside down for seats. Michael was thrust in head first with Liam Ó Cearnaigh after him. 'Operation Destroy,' whispered Seagrun. Proinsias Ó Murchu went back to the front door, kicked it wider open causing the two policemen to cover the backs of their heads with their bloody hands, and tossed his bomb into the Charge Room. It had a ten-second fuse and the van was already moving with Proinsias being dragged into the back by Liam and Seagrun when the bomb went off. It was a Mills Hand Grenade and while it did little enough damage apart from knocking down the counter and blowing the window in fragments into the street, it made a very satisfying noise.

'Oh Christ save us,' wept Constable O'Neill. 'Holy Mary Mother of God intercede for us. Blessed Saint Joseph pray for us. Most loving Father I have sinned against Heaven and Earth and am no more worthy—'

'Shut your bloody wee snivelling trap,' snarled Sergeant McMenamin, who realized that the bomb was obviously the end of the raid, and that if he was still alive he was not going to be killed now. He staggered to his feet and ran to the telephone. But that was one of the casualties of the bomb and it lay in several pieces on the floor. In the event it was a full fifteen minutes before the sergeant had managed to dress himself properly, staunch the wound in his head, and get the night porter of Gennon's Hotel to wake up and let him in to use the telephone in Glennon's Reception Office.

During those fifteen minutes a number of neighbours had peeped out of their windows to learn what had happened, and some of the bolder ones, seeing the street empty and nothing remarkable at all in sight except that the Garda Barracks had its front window broken and its front door open at half past one in the morning, had come out to investigate. But none of them had telephones, and they did little more than obstruct the two unfortunate policemen with foolishly repetitious questions such as 'What happened?' 'Who was it?' 'Did they kill 'oo, Sergeant?' or cries of dismay at the sight of blood.

'There's been a raid,' the sergeant gasped into the telephone when at last he had the attention of the Belcorrig Barracks. '—eight men – sub-machine guns – getaway cars – bomb attack – wounded men taken by companions – casualties – blood all over the place – destruction – set up road blocks—'

But Doyle's Fish Van, driven by Seamus, son of Doyle the Fish, without the knowledge of his less politically-minded father, had long ago hammered up the road leading out of Ross Harbour towards the Gap, swinging from side to side, throwing the Sons and Michael into one another's laps, against the doors, back again as Seamus braked violently to crush themselves against the back of Seamus's seat. At one violent lurch the sub-machine gun went off again and eleven shots ripped holes in the roof of the van.

'Jesus!' screamed Liam Ó Cearnaigh, 'is it an attack?'

'For the love of God put on the bloody safety catch you half-wit,' Michael shouted.

'That was a great bloody bomb,' Proinsias exulted. 'Be the Holy, I'd like to have seen those two and it raining half the barracks down on their backsides, be Jesus so I would.'

The van hurled itself round a hair-pin bend, bounced on to a bog road, and went leaping like a hare over the ruts and heather tufts of the track. They had already been driving on the parking lights, and now Seamus extinguished even those, trusting to the stars and the bit of moonlight that filtered through the gathering clouds. After a minute or two of being tossed about in the interior the four passengers managed to wedge themselves with stretched feet and hands and at that moment Seamus mistook the track and hit the side of a boulder. The back doors of the van flew open, the four men inside it shot forward against the driver's seat, and were slung back from it like four stones out of a catapult to land one on top of the other in the heather. Seamus lay stunned in the van, wedged between wheel and seat. There was a heavy smell of hot metal and spilling petrol.

Seagrun came to his senses first, tottered on to his knees and levelled the sub-machine gun which had landed across his chest. He would have loosed a burst at two sheep running away from them only the safety catch prevented him.

A lick of flame ran up the side of the van. Seamus inside it began to scream, 'Help, help!'

The four of them ran to him and pulled him out and away from the wreckage. It seemed to burn for a long time before the petrol tank exploded.

'Me da's van!' Seamus said in sad wonder. 'Be God, what will he do now?'

'It's a small price to pay for the Republic,' said Seagrun. 'It won't be forgotten him when we're hanging the other gombeen men from lamp posts.'

'He is not a gombeen man,' Seamus said in a small, wicked voice.

Seagrun turned a cold face towards him, the muzzle of the sub-machine gun swinging in the same direction like an after-thought. 'He is,' Seagrun said. Seamus said nothing more.

'This is where we said we'd be splittin' up,' Liam Ó Cearnaigh whispered. 'I'd better be gettin' to bed. I have to open the shop up in the morning.'

The van continued burning, its pieces scattered over thirty yards of mountainside. Subsidiary fires had started among the heather, like signal beacons of revolt.

' 'twill destroy the evidence,' Seagrun said with satisfaction.

Liam Ó Cearnaigh saluted. 'I'll be going home, so.'

'You'll be getting your orders,' said Seagrun, jerking the barrel of the sub-machine gun in acknowledgment. Liam and Seamus went. After a few yards of soldierly striding they began to run.

'We'd better get out of here, too,' Seagrun said. 'The bastards will see the fire.' He slung the sub-machine gun on his shoulder by its strap. 'We've a good three miles in front of us.'

'Where are we going?' Michael asked. He had hurt his knee when they were thrown out of the van and it was painful to walk on.

'Your sister's place,' Seagrun said. 'The old Bishop.'

Michael stopped and stared at him. He had already made up his mind that at the first convenient second he was going to leave these criminal lunatics to go their own way, and would try and look after himself, but that convenient second was not likely to be yet. He had no illusions in the world about the ease with which Seagrun would turn the gun on him if he tried to leave him now. 'My sister? The Bishop's place? Are you right out of your mind?'

'It's a perfect hide-out,' Seagrun said, torn between a desire to be coldly commanding, and an even stronger desire to ex-plain how perfect the hide-out was. 'Wait till you see it,' he said more warmly, and then, as he noticed Michael limping, 'You're hurt man? So they did torture you? By God, if I'd known that—'

'I banged my knee on a stone.'

'You're the close-lipped divil. Relax, man, you're among friends now. I hereby appoint you my Lieutenant and all that old stuff's forgotten, eh?'

Michael said nothing.

'God,' cried Seagrun, unable to contain his ecstasy. 'Isn't it grand to be out on the hillside, a gun in your hand, action behind us, the whole bloody world against us, more action in front of us, and none with us but tried comrades. I know how the men of '98 must have felt, and the Fenians in '67. Better three days like this than a hundred years on your knees. What do you say, Proinsias?'

'I wish I had another bomb, Captain.'

'Maybe we'll get some, yet. There's a quarry out beyond Belcorrig with a dynamite store. We might raid there tomorrow night. D'you know much about dynamite, Micheál?'

'Only enough to leave it alone.'

'God, you haven't changed. Listen to the man, Proinsias. To hear him you'd think he was a bloody school teacher. And he spreadin' revolution from Cork to London. But we'll leave it till we're safe in hiding before we get you properly acquainted. My soul to the divil but you're the two finest comrades a man could wish and he on the run. You couldn't ask for better men to die with.'

The air was close and still and before they had walked a mile they were damp with sweat, stumbling over heather tufts, sinking to the ankle in soft patches of bog, following a sheep path for a hundred yards to find it ending in nothing.

'But why my sister for Heaven's sake?' Michael had already said. 'Why drag her into it?'

'She's a better Republican than you know, Micilín. The second I heard about them arresting you—'

'How did you hear?' There seemed to be a dreadful naturalness about what was happening, as though he had slipped back four years in time. It seemed to be a night for time travel, for going back.

'There isn't much I don't hear, boyo. The postmistress's son is one of ours, for one thing. But this hidey hole. I got word to her that we'd be coming and to have food and bandages and places to sleep and she has it all fixed for us in the Bishop's stables. You can stay there safe for a few days till we can get things fixed for you.'

'Fixed? Haven't you fixed enough with that bloody nonsense below?' It was difficult to talk connectedly, stumbling through heather and across the broken ground of the mountain, at least Michael found it was, but nothing seemed to stop Seagrun talking.

'God! Listen to him! You'd think he'd wanted to stay nice and snug in that cell like a drunk gettin' rid of his hangover. 'tis lucky I know you better. Of course we'll get things fixed. False papers, dye your hair. Canadian or Australian passport maybe. I could send you to America to raise funds.'

'Thank you very much.'

'Don't be thanking me, boyo. You'd do the same for me. One for all and all for one, and our lives for the Revolution.'

Now and then they stopped to look back. The fires started by the van had died out and there were no lights visible except the few street lights of Ross Harbour, and far out to sea the lights of some ship passing the two Heads. Michael looked at them with a terrible longing. What wouldn't he give to be on that ship? As though some part of himself, his future, was being carried away from him – to where? And he was left trapped and helpless in this nightmare. He thought for a second, 'maybe this really is a nightmare, I'm asleep and I'll wake up in a minute, below in bed, or – or down by the Pool'. And at that thought a pain twisted inside him like broken glass and he wanted to catch Seagrun by the neck and kill him.

'We're nearly there,' Seagrun said. The mountainside was indeed flattening, levelling off into a plateau that had once been the outer portion of Lord Medmenham's park. Within another ten minutes they were at the back of the Bishop's Palace.

'The stables,' Seagrun whispered.

They crept forward among dark buildings, found a door, and Seagrun whispered, ' 'tilda? Are ye there?'

There was no answer. They went inside, since the double doors of the stable were not only not bolted but could not be shut, the hinges having rusted solid. Seagrun struck a match. Matilda Carmody, fully dressed, lay stretched on several bales of mouldy hay like a human sacrifice on an altar. She was fast asleep, her pleasant red face rosy in the matchlight, her mouth open, her young breath snoring softly, her young bosom rising and falling like two happy balloons. Seagrun shook her awake.

'Holy Mother of God!' Matilda began to scream, until Seagrun clapped his hand over her mouth.

'Murder, rape!' she screamed again, having bitten his hand to free her mouth. Then she realized who it was and quieted herself. 'God, the fright!' she whispered, her voice shaking, and her hands hastily rearranging her skirt that had worked its way up to her waist in the struggle.

She had been having the most marvellous dream in which she was the only girl in the entire, boy-crammed reaches of the Panoramic Ballroom in Belcorrig, and every boy in the place including the band and most especially including the trumpeter (the band of her dreams still being the fabulous Steeplejacks, no other band having come to Belcorrig in the meantime), every male hand in the place was attempting to seize her. And then to wake up and find this eejit Seagrun trying to throttle her. Seagrun's naïve belief that Matilda was a Republican had sprung from a misunderstanding. She had thought at first that the Sons of Ireland were a new dance band, and that the absence of instruments at what she took to be a rehearsal was due solely to poverty. She had imagined saving up and buying them a trumpet and a saxophone and a set of drums and becoming their singer, and had seen herself, a cross between Raquel Welch and Dana, creating male havoc the length and breadth of Ireland.

By the time she realized it was about politics rather than music, the secret meeting to which Seamus Doyle had brought her because he hoped to seduce her on the way home was over, and her next contact with the Sons was when Seagrun had come to her that afternoon to command her as an enrolled Daughter and Michael's sister to have a safe place ready for him that night. Because she loved her brother and had had a pleasantly vigorous time in the back of the fish van on the last occasion, she had agreed. But she still thought that Seagrun was a right eejit and a gom, and the whole thing would worry His poor old Grace out of his keeping if he ever came to hear of it.

'I'll be dead in the morning,' she said. 'I haven't slept a wink.' She gave her brother an embarrassed nod of welcome, and a toss of her head to Proinsias who she thought was even more of an eejit than Seagrun, and pointed behind the bales of hay and the old, collapsing carriage and the pony trap. 'In there,' she said. 'There's a loose board, if you push it. Squeeze in and if you're smoking cigarettes don't set light to the straw or you'll have us all burned to the ground. There's a chicken and some bread and butter and some eggs for you and some milk. And mind the old stachy.'

'The what?' Michael said. But she had already gone, tip-toeing across the yard in the warm darkness. Pitch dark, for clouds had covered all the stars by now, and even more than warm, as though a storm was gradually lowering its hot mouth towards The Ross.

In the stable Proinsias had fumbled his way past cart and carriage to the boards and had found the entrance to the hidey hole. Seagrun gestured with the barrel of the machine gun for Michael to follow him. Proinsias struck a match and dropped it.

'We should have brought a torch,' Seagrun said as the match went out. They felt around them in the dark, that smelt of straw and rats and mice and chicken droppings and dust, and rotting timbers. Things scuttled near their feet. They found the cardboard box with the provisions and places to sit. Michael eased himself down. Seagrun lit another match so that Proinsias could divide the food and for a few seconds shadows leaped this way and that and then steadied. Michael was looking at the food and realizing that in spite of everything that had happened he was very hungry. His hand stretched out to take what Proinsias was offering.

'By God,' Seagrun cried, 'drop lads!' The match curved away as he flung it. Darkness fell on them like a cloak, stifling. Michael threw himself flat just in time. Shots crashed in his eardrums. There was a ringing sound of metal being hit and the whine of the ricochets until the bullets buried themselves in timber. The echoes seemed to go on for minutes. Michael felt himself to see if he was hit. When he was sure that he was still alive he began cursing Seagrun with detail and savagery.

'I got him,' Seagrun whispered. 'Will I light a match?' The match flared and steadied. When they could look they saw the dark and terrifying figure of a man dying on a cross.

'Holy God,' whispered Proinsias.

'Jesus,' breathed Seagrun and crossed himself, in danger of firing more shots from the sub-machine gun as he did so, having forgotten that his finger was still on the trigger. Michael reached out a hand and touched the bulging, contorted thigh that was less than two feet away from him when he turned to see. Bronze. Patrick Carmody's lost bronze. Crucifix, Christ the Sufferer, hidden here for more than thirty years. His great-uncle's legendary lost masterpiece.

But they did not think of its origin or how it had got there, or how long it had stood in that place. They could only stare at it, shivers of fear turning their skin cold and prickling the hairs at the back of their necks.

The Face hung sideways, and outwards, as though all the pain in the world, all the pain of that Crucifixion burned in the dying Man's back. Not in the nailed hands or feet, or the bloody side, or the head gashed with thorns as big as nails, but in the back. Lacerated with rods, torn with the weight of death, straining the raw flesh away from the rough timber of the upright beam, the whole body arched outwards from that dreadful contact with the wood. There was no tranquillity in this dying, no resignation, only agony.

And the Cross itself was strange, hideous, frightening as a gallows. The upright beam was squat and thick and had obviously been used for many deaths. It was not possible to say how anyone could know this from looking at it by matchlight in the stuffy dark of a stable. But all three of them knew it, knew it as the soldiers knew it who played dice at its foot. These were in low relief, and yet they lived. The faces of professional soldiers, indifferent to all but duty and time off. Their God Rome and their Mother of God a tavern whore. Their Faith was in their eyes, in their hands shaking the dice. And the upright was so squat that God's feet were no more than an inch above the rock where they played. Nailed by the ankle, between bone and tendon, and roped tight. The feet alone would have said 'Death'. The legs twisted in their pain like boughs breaking from the tree, the muscles knotted, ivy-thick, contorted, veins bulging with blood.

The crotch rested on a blunt peg driven into a hole in the upright and the peg caused such pain that the tormented body tried to lift itself, tried to hang by the arms that lay along the crossbeam, elbows and one thickened shoulder hooked backwards over it. It was not possible to see the nails driven through the wrists behind the beam but they knew that they were there. Ropes fastened wrist to beam to take the body's weight. A soldier's spear leaned casually against the cross-beam.

'Give me the matches,' Michael whispered. He felt for the

271

box and lit two together with a shaking hand. He felt shocked out of himself, out of his own nightmare into a greater nightmare. He stared at the face, and the mouth seemed to move in the flickering shadows of the flaring matches. For a moment it reminded him of the crucifix hanging in his bedroom in the stable loft. But it was not possible to remember anything, make any comparisons for longer than a moment looking at this terrible reality of execution.

'I don't want to stay here,' Proinsias said in a trembling voice.

'The man that did that must be in Hell,' Seagrun said. 'Christ curse him.'

'Let's go down to Eagan's Tower,' Proinsias said. 'I never wanted to come here in the first place.' The matches died.

'Maybe,' Seagrun said, his voice struggling for coolness, for the commander's tone. 'It might be no bad idea to go back on our tracks. What do you say, Micheál?'

Michael shook himself awake. 'Why don't we split up?' he said. 'The bloody place will be alive with guards – if we're one by one—'

Seagrun's hand gripped his arm, half comrade, half gaoler. 'By God no! I know what you're thinking! Play decoy, and sacrifice yourself for us. No, no, we're with you to the death, man. We'll go down to Eagan's Tower and spend the day there sleeping. Wherever they look for us it won't be there.'

They crept out of the boarded-up hidey hole into the welcome of the ordinary stable, and then of the night. It was still dark, but wth a livid darkness as though somewhere light was trying to break through the thick covering of cloud.

'No harm if there isn't a living soul outside of ourselves who knows where we are,' Seagrun said, casting a look up at the attic window behind which Matilda Carmody slept and dreamed of being manhandled by regiments of trumpet players in a ballroom like a Cathedral. The three fugitives crept out of the yard, Michael between the other two. A cockerel crowed in triumph, preparing himself for a day of hens.

CHAPTER TWENTY-ONE

IT was four o'clock in the morning rather than midnight before the King Gallagher and the Whisperer, and the King's sons and the Whisperer's two brothers-in-law (not that there was much law about them), arrived at the Bishop's Palace in the lorry. They had spent the night arguing and drinking, and arguing more, and drinking more again, and they were all feeling middling young, swerving between hilarious carelessness of what might happen or who might stop them, and gusts of rabbit-timidity when one or the other of them said, 'Whoooa, Whisperer, hold her now, aisy man, and let's consider things.'

'Yerrah, you mosheen,' the King would say, 'considerin' is over. Now for the stachy.'

But for the weight of cloud above them it would already have been light. As it was they moved through a leaden, smoky dawn, unhealthily, stickily warm, a feeling in the stilled air as though rain was yearning to fall in great splashing tears but was unable to release itself. The Palace was in darkness. The cockerel that had crowed a half hour earlier had gone back to sleep. In the trees about the place one or two birds sang in the desolate certainty that before midday they would be soaking wet and possibly struck by lightning. Trees, Palace, dawnlight, lurching lorry with its lights and engine switched off, rolling forward on its bald tyres, all together had the gloom of a Victorian etching in a massive book that no one would ever read.

'Down my ducks,' the King said, jumping from the cab of the lorry. They all got down, whispered, cursed. A chicken clucked in alarm and ran about the yard. The cockerel woke and crowed.

'*Oooh gami gra dhi il, gretin.* Be quiet you villain or you'll finish in a pot, with an onion.' The King flung a handful of mud at the cockerel and caught it behind the comb. It ran for its life crying 'Chuck chuck chuck', trying with all its tiny might to warn the chickens that here was murder.

The six men went into the dark of the stable. 'I know where she is,' the King said. He had a candle stump and lit it. The shadows bowed and swayed around him. 'Be God, the board is asthray,' he said alarmed. But the Crucifix was there. 'Me beauty,' he said, slapping his hand on the beam of the Cross. 'Me darling stachy. Dere's a hunerd poun' locked up in you, my sweet one.'

'A hunerd poun'?' cried the Whisperer. '*Tom tul guksta!*'

'Mebbe fifty,' the King said quickly. 'Let you lads heave her up softly now. Arragh damn, don't be dropping her or you'll wake the girleen. Aisy, aisy.' And half pulling, half listing, sliding the leaning base on a bulk of straw, the six of them got the Crucifix to the gap in the boards of the partition, kicked out three more of the boards and heaved their prize through into the stable itself. Force still further open the stable doors, roll the lorry backwards into the wide opened doorway, set up the sheer-legs. In half a sweating hour the Crucifix was loaded. Put the boards back in place, roll the lorry out, and who would know they had been there?

They manhandled the lorry to the top of the sloping drive-way, let her roll downhill, only starting the engine when they were close to the gates. 'Be Cripes we have her now,' cried the King. 'A day's work with the hacksaws and a satleen burner and 'tis the handiest load of scrap you'll ever see. But little bitteens she'll have to be cut into, not a bit you'd recognize or Rinty Flynn will be asking the divil's questions about where she was got and slicing the price on us.'

They roared along the quiet road into the first drops of heavy rain. Within minutes they were driving into a dark sheet. The rain drummed on the cab roof, danced on the dirty boards of the lorry, pelted the bodies of the four men crouched about the Cru-cifix, fell on the bronze itself with smacking kisses, hissed on the engine and the radiator. The windscreen wipers had not worked for several years and the Whisperer peered into nothingness.

He was on the road block before he saw it. A wooden trestle, the dark figure of a guard, a car parked by the roadside. If the guard cried halt they never heard him. They hit the trestle and smashed it to matchwood. The guard leapt out of their way like a stag and fell in the ditch on his back. His companion jumped out of the car, levelled his pistol and fired. Bullets hummed high and low about the vanishing tailgate of the lorry, hit the road, lost themselves in the air.

'Holy God!' cried Stofirt, the King's elder son, 'dey're firing at us.' He beat on the roof of the cab. The lorry hammered faster.

'What is it?' the King yelled through the cab's rear window.

'Guns. Shaydogs.'

If that was possible the lorry went faster still. It never stopped until, far past the Whisperer's camp, far past the ruined cottage where they had planned to cut up the stachy into unrecognizable lumps, they were deep among the turf cutters' tracks on the high slopes of Slieve Clogher. Far far, far behind them the two guards were trying to get the back wheels of their Cortina out of the ditch, into which they had backed it as they turned. The unspoken thought between them was that it might have been God's Act that immobilized them, preserving them for future duties. To chase dangerous terrorists armed with bombs and machine guns mounted in an armoured lorry, themselves equipped and armed with no more than one pistol and a clapped-out Cortina, was asking more of them than the State had a right to ask.

Higher and higher the lorry drove, bumping now over a lost and stony track that had been laid down a hundred years and more ago by a Lord Medmenham obsessed with the belief that Slieve Clogher contained an ancient gold mine. He had also believed that the Ancient Irish were the lost tribes of Israel, and that the Queen of Slieve Clogher was no other than the Queen of Sheba. 'The apparently quite usual Irish word "Slieve" or mountain,' he had written in a learned paper for the Royal Dublin Society, 'is in this instance an obvious corruption of "Sheba", and by their use of this name, in this connection, I am convinced that the Ancient Inhabitants of our fair Isle intended to signify that the mountain was Sheba's Rock, the word Clogher meaning in the Antique tongue both a stony place and a rock.'

The learned article continued in much the same vein for thirty pages of close manuscript on folio paper, and the learned Lord was extremely angry when the Royal Dublin Society conveyed to him, as politely as it could, that the days of such speculations were over, and the reign of a colder-minded science had begun. But if the article never startled the learned world in print, the road remained. Well into the present century there had been locals who spoke of 'Queen Sheba's road' following Lord Medmenham's desire.

In fact it was all that did remain, out of the spending of large fortune. Lord Medmenham had opened the Fort, looking for the entrance shaft to Sheba's gold mine, and when he had not found it he had closed up the Fort again, and it was said locally that the ill-health which struck him soon afterwards was the Queen's punishment on an intruder. No one else went near the place for close on a hundred years, and it was not until the King Gallagher wanted a safe place to hide poteen and maybe a strayed horse or so that the Fort came into any further use. It was going to come into use now.

'The Seven curses of God on the shaydogs,' the King kept repeating all the way up the Queen's Road (the name Sheba had fallen out of local use with the old lord's death), a 'road' that by now was so overgrown with turf and heather that no one who had not explored and tested it would ever have known that a road existed there. They came to the Fort and still in the pelts of rain, split now and then by bolts of lightning far away to he south over the twin Heads of Ross and Lir, they manhandled and manoeuvred the Crucifix on to the ground at the concealed entrance of the passage that led deep into the mound.

The mound itself towered about thirty feet high at its highest point, and was about eighty yards long and sixty or seventy at its broadest; for all the world like a great boat turned upside down and then covered with stones and earth and green turf. But greater than any boat of that long vanished building time can ever have been. And running deep into the fort, like the secret chambers of an Egyptian pyramid, there was a stone passage way, a shaft running straight in and lined on either side and roofed overhead and paved underfoot with great slabs of stone; a number of them carved with the owl-eyes and maze patterns of that older Queen than Sheba who had been brought here from the south by the small dark farming men who worshipped her as Mother of All Things, Giver and Destroyer. At the far end of the passage, some twenty-five yards long, there was a stone chamber, twelve feet across and as many high, with small recesses, to left and right and on the far side. There was something of the church about it, nave and transept, side chapels and even a kind of altar, a dished slab of stone that always had water gathered in it, dripped from the high, corbelled vault of the roof.

'Bring her in lads,' the King panted, and they struggled into the mouth of the passage, the bronze weight of the Crucifix grinding a groove in the stones. 'Heave her again, lads.'

'By God, 'tis far enough,' gasped the Whisperer.

' 'tis not so,' said the King. 'Get her up to the big room beyont where we had the still and we'll work on her dere wit' the saws and the burner. I have a lad beyont in Belcorrig will give us the lent of a satleen burner and all, and no questions.'

They sweated further. Simon himself could never have sweated more and he carrying the true Cross to Calvary.

'By God she's a heavy brute,' Stofirt said, winded. The others were beyond talking. But at last they got their stachy into the central chamber of the Fort and because they had heaved it in upright for ease of manoeuvre they left it like that, arms spread, head thrust down and forward as though the figure on the Cross was looking down the passage for who might come.

'We'll be back, my beauty,' the King said, giving a fond smack of farewell to the hunched shoulder. 'Wit' de satleen burner.' But not for a while they all agreed. If the shaydogs were on to them they had all better disappear for a month or two until things had quietened. 'We'll go Limerick way,' the King said, and the Whisperer thought he would take his mother over to Liverpool for a bit to see cousins there. They drove back to the Whisperer's camp in the downpour and by ten o'clock that morning there was no trace of any of them beyond rags and bottles in the hedges where they had been, and a few bits of rusty iron not worth their while carrying away. They were gone like birds on the wind and even if the police had been searching for them they would have had a hard time laying hands on the fugitives. But in truth, of course, the police had no more interest in them than they had in sparrows out of a hedge, and even the small interest they might normally have had, to move them on to another parish, or inquire after a strayed horse, had been swamped and drowned that day in the excitement of hunting for the Sons of Ireland and the escaped Republican Left-wing terrorist Michael Carmody. By God it was no tinkers the guards were after that day.

And on the crown of Slieve Clogher, three thousand feet above the leaden, rain-lashed surface of the Bay, the Crucifix stood in its new hiding place, rainwater from the stone roof dripping on to the outstretched arms and the beam and the hunched shoulder and the thorn-crowned head. The rain water dripped into the dished altar stone and formed a pool like a dark mirror to reflect the Cross above it, except that there was no light for the reflection. The darkness of the grave. Wet dark. The water worked among the stones, ran earth away from them. The six thieves had banged the great weight of the Crucifix against this stone and that, and unsettled a side-stone of the passage half-way down. The water worked behind that stone, carried away earth, a pebble, a last handful of support. Nothing held up one of the roof stones now except old habit and inertia. The weight of water gathered heaviness above it until slowly, grinding like two millstones one against the other, an end of the flat roof stone tilted downwards, pushing a side-stone outwards and away. The last fraction of support vanished and the roof stone fell, closing the passage to the chamber. On the surface of the mound earth and grass shifted slightly, settled into a small hollow. Nothing. But no thief would get back into that now-sealed chamber without machinery and days of time. No Gallagher would ever lay hand again on that hidden stachy. In fact for more than a thousand years no human being would lay hand or eye on it, and when they did the world would be a different place and the discovery would cause great bewilderment, leading to all kinds of theories. None of them involving the King Gallagher and his two sons, nor the Whisperer, and his two brothers-in-law, nor even Patrick Carmody nor the Bishop, nor the Princess, nor Matilda, nor the guards, nor Michael Carmody, nor the Sons of Ireland. By the deprived nature of their calling archaeologists lose much of interest. But how can it be otherwise?

CHAPTER TWENTY-TWO

WHILE the King and his companions were stealing and hiding the Crucifix, Seagrun Ó Maelchonaire and Proinsias and Michael were finding their way down to Eagan's Tower, that stood, a ruined stump, in a corner of the park at Eaganscourt. The first drops of the rain began falling as they clambered over the high stone wall surrounding the park, and ran, tired and stumbling, for the shelter of the wood and the tower itself. Michael was so tired by this time that he was no longer capable of thinking of escape from Seagrun's insane helpfulness or of anything except lying down in some kind of shelter. And at least the Tower promised that. The dungeons under it were half-filled with fallen masonry and earth and rubble, but they all knew from childhood explorations and later exercises as Soldiers or Sons that there was room and to spare for men to hide. And no sooner were they in shelter than they stretched themselves on the soft, collected mould of centuries in a dry corner, and fell asleep. Outside, above, the rain lashed down with summer fury, pelted on stone and ivy, bounced like bursting silver coins on the great flagstones of the interior, right over the sleepers' heads. Lightning broke the black sky, thunder grumbled in the south, birds in their nests crouched mute and sodden, spiders hid under ivy leaves, the sky seemed a leaden water spout intent on drowning The Ross entirely. The three of them slept as if they were dead.

While on the surrounding road in their patrols and road-blocks the guards were blinded by the rain, turned into dark sponges, felt the rheumatism grind its crystals in their joints, coughed and sneezed and cursed the Sons of Ireland and Michael Carmody, the Government, The Ross, the climate of Ireland, the rain, the road, and their superiors, in every conceivable combination. Two-way radios kept them in unwilling contact with the planning headquarters of the operation in Belcorrig.

Anyone else who found themselves awake early that morning took one look at the rain, remembered that it was Sunday, and unless they were extremely religious went back to bed. Most people, guided by an instinct that worked unfailingly even in sleep to warn them of unpropitious days, simply continued sleeping. The sounds of the rain and the distant thunder lulled them like lullabys. Only Timmy Pat of the Gap found himself awake in his small cottage unable to go back to sleep. The vision of Michael Carmody arrested, and Peadar Power's guilt-shadowed face, refused to let him sleep.

'What will I do?' he kept wondering. He got himself groaning and creaking and grumbling out of his bed, stood in his long johns and his socks while the cat made a furious outcry at the window to tell him she was drowning, and to let her in, scratched himself, drank some milk and ate some bread, thought of the rain, thought of going back to bed and forgetting all about it, and finally dressed himself, put on his boots, put on an ancient mackintosh, threw a sack over his head, and leaving down a saucer of milk for the cat closed the door behind him and started down the hill to Ross Harbour.

'Mwirra 'tis damp,' he said at intervals, his boots squelching as if he was walking in the sea or wearing them in a bath, not that he had ever seen a bath, let alone taken one. 'Mwirra 'tis bloody damp. 'tis wet, bad luck to it.' Squelch squelch. Rain running down his face and into the collar of his shirt, carefully fastened for Sunday with a stud.

'I will get Mass while I am at it,' Timmy Pat consoled himself. 'And a pint or two after.'

He came at last to the Presbytery in Knuckle Street about ten o'clock in the morning, just as Father Culhane was sitting down to breakfast after nine o'clock Mass. Father Cooney, who had taken seven o'clock Mass, and was due to take the final Mass at eleven thirty, was having a cup of coffee. Mrs. Cleggan came into them, bristling with indignation.

'It's one of them,' she said, meaning by that one of the children of darkness who lived outside Ross Harbour. 'He says he must see you on a matter of life and death and he's dripping water all over the linoleum.'

'Poor fellow,' said Father Culhane mechanically. And then as the enormity of the fact impressed itself on him, 'Could you not stand him in the porch?'

'He walked in on me,' cried Mrs. Cleggan. 'In on me!'

'I'd better see what he wants,' Father Cooney said.

'Finish your coffee,' said Father Culhane. 'Whatever it is it'll get neither better nor worse in the next five minutes. You'll get indigestion the way you leap about.'

'I think I'd better go, Father,' Father Cooney said, showing by his winks and frowns and quarter nods of the head towards the furious Mrs. Cleggan that if he did not go and do something about the linoleum, if not the man, Mrs. Cleggan would have it in for them both for the rest of the day.

'As you like,' Father Culhane said, buttering himself a corner of toast and putting thick cut marmalade on to the golden butter with a connoisseur's care. 'It's your stomach after all. But you'll never get another one.'

Father Cooney went out of the room, smiling placatingly at Mrs. Cleggan, his smile saying to her 'We are God's humble servants, both of us, you in your kitchen Mrs. Cleggan, I at the altar or on this small errand. We have much to put up with here below, but trust in God, Mrs. Cleggan, trust in Our Holy Father above, to make it up to us. There we will sleep late every morning, and there won't be so much as an inch of linoleum in need of polishing.' All this his smile attempted to convey. Mrs. Cleggan though he was a half-wit, the way he gave in to people.

In the hall Timmy Pat was by now surrounded by a shallow pool. 'God bless your reverence,' he said on seeing Father Cooney approach. He looked down at his leaking feet and was embarrassed. 'It's a damp sort of a day,' he said in explanation. 'Saving your presence.'

Father Cooney saw in front of him a big, wet, bean-pole of a man apparently dressed in a sack and running water from every seam. Timmy Pat became aware of the sack at the same moment, and took it off with a quick snatch which sprayed rain water as far as the walls, and splattered Father Cooney from head to foot.

'Ooah and I'm sorry your reverence. Have I wet you?'

'It doesn't matter,' Father Cooney said, beginning to wish he had taken Father Culhane's advice. 'What do you want?'

'Ah,' said Timmy Pat and got stuck. What did he want? He had thought of almost everything on the way down the mountain except that exact question. What did he want?

'Is someone dying?' Father Cooney asked. He knew Timmy Pat by sight and would know his name when he was reminded of it, but he had no idea whether Timmy Pat had an aged father or mother or both who might be at death's door. He thought of the rain and found himself hoping that Timmy Pat was an orphan.

'Nooah. Not dying exactly.' And then in a rush, 'It's in prison they are.'

'In prison?' Light flashed. 'Is it Michael Carmody?' The few who had been to early Mass and the few more who had been to nine o'clock Mass had gone there in the rain almost as much for the urgency of gossip about the night's excitements as for religion. The two priests had been talking about it up to the moment of Mrs. Cleggan's entry into the dining-room. 'Is he wounded?'

Timmy Pat, who alone of waking men had not yet heard of the escape, shook his head in bewilderment. 'Wounded? How would he be wounded? What it is your reverence, is that he's innocent.'

After that the remains of the story came fluently enough and with such conviction that Father Cooney had no doubt in the world that it was true. Hadn't he thought himself as soon as he heard of the matter that it was the old Powers who had been at the fish ponds?

'So it was Peadar Power?' he said. He told an even more furious Mrs. Cleggan to let Timmy Pat dry himself at the kitchen fire and to give him tea and some bread and a piece of bacon.

'So it was Peadar Power?' said Father Culhane when his curate had told him the story. But he said the words with an entirely different intonation. Sarcasm, irony, disbelief, something close to anger and contempt. 'Peadar Power!' He snorted, feeling so put out that he could not enjoy his third cup of tea. 'Do you think that Peadar Power is Chief of Staff of the I.R.A.? Do you think Matty Power is his adjutant? Was it Jamey Power who blew up the police station to free an innocent prisoner? My dear Father Cooney, I can put up with a great deal, but stupidity I cannot abide.'

'I am sorry Father.'

'Well you might be.'

'But, Father—'

'There is no but in the matter, Father. Murder and wickedness are abroad in the land, the very Prince of Darkness has manifested Himself among us, and you come burbling to me about three poor simple old men who are as innocent of this

matter as three beads on your Rosary. As innocent of anything,'
Father Culhane said, his voice rising, his emotions taking wing
on the inspiration of the Powers' innocence and simplicity, 'as –
as–' It failed him for the moment to find a suitable metaphor
or simile for the Powers' angelic innocence and he snorted contemptuously as a substitute. 'We could learn much from such
humble members of our flock,' he said. He poured himself more
tea from the tea pot, inspected it, and pushed it away from him
with an expression of distaste, a St. Anthony in the desert putting aside the things of this world.

Father Cooney took this as his dismissal and went off with
himself. He might only be the curate, but at least the hours
between lunch and tea on a Sunday afternoon were his own to
do as he pleased in. And what would please him this afternoon
would be to go up to the Powers and see if he could persuade
them to tell the truth to the Guards.

And so, after lunch, Father Cooney rode up the mountainside on his bicycle like the Angel of the Lord, except that
much less than half-way up he had to get off and push. Half-
way up he left his bicycle under a furze bush and climbed the
steepening track with his coat over his arm and his handkerchief sodden in his hand from drying his forehead and mopping
his face. The morning's rain had vanished as though it had
never fallen, except for a green freshness on the grass, a jew-
elled look to the wildflowers in the springing turf and an added
softness under foot. The sky was like blue enamel and the few
white puffs of cloud like small sheep. He stopped and looked at
the Bay spread out below him. The two peninsulas, the fretted
coast touched here with gold sand and there with silver as small
waves broke on rocks, the land grey and blue like the colours of
worn Irish tweed, white cottages tucked into folds of ground,
the ruler-straight line of a dry-stone wall, the curving line of a
footpath. 'May God protect it,' he thought. He was, in principle, in favour of Development, but there were times when he
had his doubts. He shook his head and went on and up until the
barking of a dog and a curl of smoke told him that he was
almost there.

Jamey saw him coming first and went in breathlessly to
where his brothers sat drinking tea by the fire. 'The priest!' he
whispered.

'Himself?' said Peadar, alarmed.

'Nooah. The priesteen.'

283

'Arragh God,' said Peadar irritably. 'What would he be wanting?'

'Collections? ' Jamey suggested. 'Money, surely.'

'The fishes,' Matty whispered. 'They know.'

'The divil fire you,' Peadar shouted, 'how would they know?' But he looked very thoughtful. 'I don't feel well,' he said suddenly. 'I think I'm for bed.' He stood up and took first one foot and then the other out of his boots, leaving them standing in the hearth like memorials.

'Bed?' Matty said in wonder, and then repeated it joyfully. 'I think I'm sickening too, so.'

'He's on us,' Jamey whispered by the door. Outside the dog barked furiously, and a hen squawked and ran.

'Hallooooo,' cried Father Cooney, slightly at a loss faced by a closed door and silence. Inside the cottage the two older brothers crept on stockinged feet into the back room and climbed into their bed. They pulled the covers round their ears to shut out all danger and fitted themselves into their shaped places like two old stones into sockets of earth. Through the layers of blanket and greatcoat and sacking and the shut door they heard Jamey calling out, ' 'oo's dere?'

'Father Cooney. Let me in. The dog—'

'Oooah.'

The door opened. Father Cooney stepped in, was smitten in the face by the smell as if a fog had been released, choked, stepped back, felt his eyes begin to run, and tried to say 'Is Pea – Pea – Peadar—'

'Oooah,' said Jamey.

Father Cooney tried again and this time ducked his head, held his breath hard, and got inside. It was like a deep cave, like a fox's earth. He had the sense of living creatures in the dark about him that were not human.

'Your brother Peadar?' he whispered, his hand feeling his throat.

'A bed,' Jamey said, backing away from the priesteen and twisting his face into a sickly smile of welcome. 'Sit 'oo down, Father.'

'No, no,' Father Cooney said. He had been up here before, although not often, and never inside the house. He wished now that he had simply commanded Peadar to come out to him but it was too late to retreat. 'Tell your brother I must see him. Urgently.'

284

Jamey waved his hands.

'Urgently,' commanded Father Cooney. He became aware of two boots looking up at him from the hearth, and although it was quite impossible that he should distinguish their particular smell from all the other smells in the cottage it seemed to him that he could and he felt distinctly faint.

'I'll ask him,' Jamey had said, and had vanished through an inner door. Father Cooney went back to the half open outer door behind him and drew in gulps of fresh air. Voices whispered and seemed to quarrel in the inner room. Father Cooney took a last breath of fresh air, held it in his lungs and dived inside again, this time going straight across the kitchen and into the bedroom. Here it was so dark that he could see nothing. If there was a window it was blocked up. His knees seemed to be against the edge of a bed, and in fact the room was so small that there was no space in it beyond what could hold the bed and a cupboard. In fact the cupboard was jammed so tight against the end of the bed that the doors could not be opened, and both Matty and Jamey had often speculated when Peadar was out of earshot what might be in it. But they had never had the courage to move the bed out and open the doors and look. Now, with Jamey standing crushed in the corner and Father Cooney in the doorway, it was not possible for anyone to move at all, beyond Peadar or Matty sitting up in the bed.

'Peadar Power,' Father Cooney said, 'do you know that Michael Carmody was arrested last night for a crime that he didn't commit?'

'Oooogh oogh,' Peadar croaked in a dying voice. 'I'm terrible bad, Father. 'twas good of you to come up the mountain to me.'

'I say, Michael Carmody was—'

'And Matty near as bad as myself.'

'Hugh gah,' Matty said, rasping phlegm in his throat. A dreadful fear seized Father Cooney that the old man was going to spit over the side of the bed. He moved his feet back.

'Do you understand what I say?'

' 'tis the rain Father, ant the frightus. I can hardly move.'

'I command you to tell me the truth.'

'The divil blast the lie it is, Father. The legs is locked on me. And the arms too. It's the frightus.'

'Wooo ooogha,' cried Jamey by the cupboard. 'Ooogh.'

Matty had already covered his head entirely in layers of

clothing so that his holey socks stuck out at the far end like grey foot-mittens, not that they were visible to the keenest eye as more than shadows in the thick dark of the stifling small room.

'I command you as a priest!'

'Me voice,' whispered Peadar. ' 'tis gone on me.' He croaked and hawked until it sounded like a death rattle and Jamey began to keen, 'Och oooogh.'

'You will bring a curse on this house,' cried Father Cooney, beside himself, and at that Jamey raised such a wail of terror that it was not possible to talk or think for a full half minute.

'Will you be quiet!' shouted Father Cooney, every liberal priestly idea that he had cherished since long before his ordination flying out of his head like moths from an old fur coat that is shaken. If he had had a blackthorn stick he would have raised lumps with it on the three of them. 'Do you not know that you are in mortal sin, all three of you?' Jamey began to weep, gabbling in a frantic whisper, ' 'twas not me, Father. I wasn't in it at all, I never touched the fisses, never a one, Father, 'twas them two did it, Father, don't curse me, Father.'

'What are you whispering you bosthoon?' shouted Peadar in a tremendous voice, and then, remembering, he croaked 'Oh me frightus, me frightus is after destroying me back.'

Father Cooney returned to the attack. 'Are you going to tell me the truth of your own free will?' he said. 'Or shall I go down to the Guards? An innocent man is being hunted this minute—'

'The Guards?' whispered Matty, shoving his head up like a badger out of its black earth.

'The Guards.'

Peadar rolled the whites of his eyes, and with sudden cunning fixed his stare on the priest, for his ancient eyes were well used to the dark of the cottage and he could see in it like a cat. 'All right, Father. Get out of the bed, Matty. GET OUT OF IT!'

Matty rolled himself out on to his hands and knees, and without much straightening up scuttled out of the way into the kitchen, where Jamey was already crouching by the ashes of the hearth, rocking himself to and fro and reciting the Rosary.

'Let me make me confession to you, Father,' Peadar wheezed.

'To me?' said Father Cooney, seeing the trap he had dug himself, but too late to get out of it. 'It's the Guards you have to confess to.'

'I won't live the week out,' Peadar croaked. 'I want to confess to a priest. Bless me, Father, for I have sinned.'

'I won't hear you!' Father Cooney shouted.

'I'm dying, Father,' Peadar whispered in a terrible voice.

'You are not, damn you.'

'I confess to you Father—'

'I won't listen—'

'—dat since my last confession—'

'It isn't under seal. It isn't a true confession. I haven't any stole. I'm not listening.'

' 'oo must hear me, Father. Suppose I died on you this minute? I'm an old man, Father. Think of your conscience.'

'*MY* conscience?'

'Hold my hand, Father. Are you too proud to hear the confession of a poor old man? Is it only the rich people in the town you'd be willing to listen to? Sure, wasn't God aself a poor workman a one time?'

'The devil is in you, Peadar Power.'

'Then hear my confession and wash my soul, Father.'

'You'd be better washing yourself, you old villain.'

'I confess before God, Father—'

A hundred thoughts struggled for mastery in the poor priest's mind, and while they were struggling the ancient, terrible voice wheezed out the story of the fishes.

'Give me absolution, Father.'

'I will not. Go down and tell this to the Guards and then ask me to absolve you.'

'How could I go down and I locked in the bed?'

'Then I'll send the Guards up to you.'

'You wouldn't break the Confessional, Father, you wouldn't tell what I told you between you and me and God aself?'

'May you die roaring,' shouted Father Cooney, stamping out of the room, or turning to stamp out. He struck his forehead a dreadful blow on the low lintel of the door and for a second he thought that he must have concussion. His skull seemed to be full of Catherine Wheels and his knees were giving way.

'Mind your head, Father.'

He felt his way forward.

'Did 'oo hit 'oo's head, Father?' Matty said.

'Get out of my way.' He ducked his head into his shoulders and felt gingerly for the outer door that Jamey had pulled shut. Sunlight struck him, fresh air met him like strong perfume, making him feel almost drunk, and he stood in the yard drawing it deep into his choked lungs. 'I'll go mad,' he thought. 'I can't stand any more of this.'

Could he still go to the Guards? What could he say to them? Had it been a true Confession, had he listened to it as a true Confession? Of course it wasn't. Of course he hadn't. But . . . It went round and round in his aching head and all the time he knew that there was nothing, nothing that he could do. He went furiously down the mountainside, seeing now in all the beauty spread before him nothing but malice and cunning and deceit and invincible ignorance.

CHAPTER TWENTY-THREE

NEWS of Michael Carmody's arrest, and escape, reached The Old House Hotel together, by telephone, from Sergeant McMenamin.

'No need to be alarmed, sir. We have everywhere well covered and he'll be back in our hands before too long, you can be sure of that. But if you *should* happen to see anyone prowling about—'

'Of course, Sergeant,' Hubert said in a dull voice. He sat staring at the wall of his study.

'And if Miss Jennifer should happen—'

'Jenny?'

The sergeant coughed, and changed his mind about what he had thought of saying. There was no way of saying it without saying too much. 'I don't think it's likely that he'll be your way at all, sir. If he isn't over the Gap already, that's the way he'll be heading. Alone or with the others.'

'The – others? How – how many?'

'Now don't be worrying about anything, Mr. Kershaw. We have it all under control.' The sergeant barely managed to conceal his contempt behind the comfort. By God that one was shaking in his breeches, and good enough for him. But the sergeant was doing Hubert less than justice. It was not any ordinary kind of fear that was keeping him sitting there, staring at nothing. It was something infinitely more complex and interior. As though the walls of his mind were dissolving, losing their shape and substance. The walls of pretence.

Only a few days ago, almost a few hours ago, he could have met the sergeant's news as he had met every crisis for twenty odd years, holding up his mask of folly, crying 'By Jove, let the blighters come! They may get more than they bargain for eh!' And behind the folly, behind the schoolboy words, he would, in a sense, have meant what he said. He was not a coward. He had not been a coward in the war. Except that the war had invited that kind of unreality, had allowed it, at least to Hubert. It had taken him out of his safe world of home and family in Ireland, and friends and flings in London, and cast him into total unreality. And all the crises since, the small crises of debts and Angela and the hotel, had also had a kind of unreality for him. He had been able to face them through the mask, keep himself intact. His protective image of himself intact.

But in the last day or so he had begun to dismantle the image, strip away the protection, in order to free himself. Perhaps he had been doing it for much longer than that without realizing what he was doing. He had wanted to free himself so that he could at least act for this once in his own real interest, sell the hotel, the land, get out of here, this place that had nothing for him, never had had anything for him, and remake the remainder of his life in some other, comfortable place. Like a man changing out of fancy dress so that he can leave the party and go out unnoticed into the street, and while he is standing naked in the changing room the door burst open and burglars rush in.

It was an image that Hubert saw in almost exactly those terms. A gang of desperadoes breaking in here, for money or for drink. Or – Jenny. What would he do? And he saw with a terrible, new clarity that there would be nothing he could do. He hadn't so much as a shotgun. And he sat facing a reality which he had ignored all his life. It wore Michael's face, sneering and cruel, filled with hatred. As unreal as the other unreality he had just discarded, but behind the face there was a kind of truth and it was this that sickened him, kept him sitting nerveless and helpless in his chair. That Ireland itself hated him.

Angela came in and he told her in the same dull tone what Sergeant McMenamin had just told him. 'What are you going to do?' Angela said, her voice rising. Again, it was not fear that made her voice rise, it was outrage, a fury that this kind of thing could happen, a surge of anger against Hubert for allowing it to happen, for sitting there like a stick and doing nothing about it. Jenny – and then there came real fear and she sat down in the armchair behind Hubert and stared at the back of his head with the same wide-eyed dullness with which he had just stared at the wall.

'I'm going to take Jenny over to London. I'll take her down to Sunningford,' she said.

'That's a good idea. I – I only hope we can still get a price for this place. These Development people— Not that there's really anything to worry about. Sergeant Mac said—'

'Sergeant Mac!'

'I know. But they'll have extra police. They won't let—' He was still staring at the wall, not wanting to turn and face her. Violence walked through the room like a cold presence. 'It's just damn bad luck from a selling point of view—'

They had both come to believe that they had always intended to sell, that they had only been waiting for the right moment.

'I thought of slipping up to tell Sir Philip this afternoon,' Hubert said. 'Didn't get a chance yesterday.' Before Angela could say anything he went on quickly 'The Maces'd stay with you while I'm out. I'll ask him to bring his shotgun. Not that—'

'I'm perfectly capable of looking after myself,' Angela said. 'But if you really think it's essential to consult Sir Philip about our future why not do it on the telephone?' She sat tight with anger in the chair, and they began a circuitous, meaningless argument about the rights and needs of informing – consulting – I simply want to inform him – and *I* call it *consulting* – of telling Sir Philip that lasted for half an hour until Jenny came looking for her mother on kitchen business and they had to tell her what had happened.

She stood and looked at them, from one to the other of them, without saying anything, and they both knew in the same instant as she looked at them, that she was Michael's – that Michael was hers – and they both crushed the ends of those phrases inside them as unthinkable, horrible. And strangely enough it was Hubert, with his new nakedness of mind, who found it the harder to deceive himself. Angela had looked quickly at his face to see what he was thinking. He couldn't be – couldn't have – it was only she – only a mother who could— She had looked at his face for at least that much comfort; that he, Jenny's father, fool and failure that he was, at least had that much faith in his own daughter, and his faith would strengthen her own, tell her that her suspicions were vile, unnatural, they couldn't be true. And she found nothing of that in his face. She saw her own certainty reflected there.

And Jenny wanted to say 'Why are you looking at me like that?' and at the same time to cry 'Where is he? Tell me the truth, what have they done to him, where will he go?' She wanted to press her hands against her heart, she wanted to support herself. All she could say was 'I don't understand' in a very small, unnatural voice. They would have to tell her over again, repeat it, contradict it, give her a new detail that would make it better, easier. She had already had so much pain all night that she couldn't bear any more. Waiting all night to hear him come back, to see his light go on, see the crevices of light in the slate roof of the stable. Twice she had crept over to the loft to find him and the room had been empty. The second time she had stayed for half an hour, with the light on, almost challenging anyone to find her there. She had taken one of his books and sat on his bed and tried to read. 'For my own part I cannot positively say whether Xerxes did send the herald to Argos or not; nor whether Argive ambassadors at Susa did really put this question to Artaxerxes—' The words meant nothing and she went on reading without seeing, without taking in any meaning an all. 'Afterwards, on the death of Cleander—' Where was he? What was he doing? Why didn't he come? 'Thus spake the envoys; and Gelo replied—' He was gone. He would never come back. But he'd have taken— She looked at the dozen books, his working clothes hanging behind the door in the place of his good suit, tried to believe that he would never have left them behind. The guitar—

She touched a string. If she lay down and fell asleep he'd come and find her and . . . But in the end she had been afraid to do that and had gone back to her room, and had fallen asleep in her own bed at five o'clock in the morning.

And now this. She half lifted one hand and let it fall. 'I – don't understand.'

'There isn't anything to understand,' her father said in a harsh voice. 'He's just a damned bad lot and we're lucky to be rid of him without—' He ran out of breath in mid-sentence, the breath robbed from him by the horror of what he knew about her. His daughter! Jenny! His own daughter. He looked at her as if she was a stranger, someone he had never seen before. He felt Angela's eyes on his face and that drove him to fury too. If she – if – how could she have? As though she had betrayed them not simply like – like – but with— And the depth and horror of the betrayal was like looking down into a pit. Like having one's body cut in half. You couldn't go on. Like having the meaning taken from everything. How could you go on? Say things? Do things? Knowing that—

'Jenny!' Angela said. 'What – I have to – I want–' And she in her turn found herself without words, because again, this was not any simple betrayal of parents by child, of finding that the child is a woman, that she has – these things – today – one reads – hears – she felt for words in her mind to cover up the wound, tell herself that if it had been another kind of wound – but with *that* boy – that– And like Hubert she stared at Jenny as if she could not recognize her. A boy like that. She wanted to shut mind and eyes against the thought of Michael, as though the inmost bestiality of this country had taken shape and attacked her in the one place where she was defenceless, helpless.

But already Hubert was feeling his way back to safety. He had had more reality than he could bear. He reached for his rags of Pierrot costume and pulled them round his nakedness. 'Jennykins.'

Her face twitched.

'A bit of a shock, eh, old thing? But no harm done. They'll have him locked up safe before the day's out.'

She turned and ran.

'Poor old Jennykins,' Hubert said, turning to Angela. 'Sooner you get her out of here the better. If I were you I'd get off next week. Pair of you go on a shopping spree, eh? Bright lights and all that.'

'Hubert!'

He faced her down, faced the knowledge in his wife's eyes with blank surprise, with cunning amazement. 'Don't say you won't go, old thing. I'll be able to manage. There's only a few bookings and I can get old Mrs. Hegarty to come in an' do some plain cooking—'

'You know it's not that. Jenny—'

'She looks thoroughly done up, poor kid. Bin asking too much of her, I think. She's only nineteen after all—' The truth was receding, fading. He had never seen it. Never seen it in her eyes. 'It's not like her to get so nervous about things—'

Such rage shook Angela that she couldn't speak. When she had wanted help, when she had wanted to see trust in his daughter in his face, to cancel out her own horrified certainty, he hadn't given it. And now that the least she could ask of him was that they should talk, that for this once they should be honest with each other, face this terrible knowledge together, he was slipping away from her, like a clown tumbling about a circus ring. And she felt in that second that he too was Irish, in the full, alien, most beastly sense of the word; that Jenny, her own child was Irish, that nothing in the world belonged to her, there was nothing in the world that she could trust. She felt sick and cold and withered.

'I'm going upstairs to lie down,' she said. 'Don't – I won't – want anything—' She couldn't face her, couldn't even eat food that she had cooked. Just to be alone.

CHAPTER TWENTY-FOUR

HE had no intention of stopping outside the Mulcahy bungalow. Had never thought of it. It was simply, as he roared in the
Bentley up the long road that would lead him past it to the
cross roads, and the turning uphill to Eaganscourt, that the
urgency of his feeling that he had to talk to Sir Philip, had to
tell him that he was going to sell, began to fade, to vanish. Why
had he got to? His foot eased on the accelerator, the big green
car with its headlights like enormous, insect eyes, slowed,
drifted, grew quiet. He saw the box hedge, the red roof of the
bungalow, the gateway. Why had he got to tell him anything?
Drifting to a stop. Why? Half the reason for going to
Eaganscourt had been to get out of his own house, not to have to
face— He would not even admit to himself what it was, who it
was, that he could not face, that there was anything— He just
had to get out.

He had rung Colonel Mace and the Maces had said they
would be over in a quarter of an hour or so and Jenny could
look after them, give them a couple of snifters. 'Got to hang
together these days, eh old man, or we'll all hang separately,
hah?'

He had left the hotel before the Maces arrived, shouting to
Jenny that they'd be along in a few minutes. He had felt that
this afternoon he couldn't stand even the Maces.

And now he knew that he couldn't stand Sir Philip either. He
dreamed for a second of simply going away, leaving the damn
hotel with the agents, closing it up, seeing nobody, ever again,
no one that was part of this whole blasted mess. If only he
could. Instead of which he'd have to go back and talk to the
Maces. He looked for a turning place. And still he had no
thought, no conscious thought, of the Mulcahy bungalow, of
Clara Mulcahy.

He turned the great bonnet into the drive, and the door
opened, was flung open, and she was there, still in her nylon

housecoat, holding it across her breast, her black hair falling in wild, tormented curls and waves on to her shoulders, her small, plump white hand lifting, agitating, catching his eye. He stopped the car moving, switched it off, and sat with his mouth opening, staring at her. She came running on to the tarmacadam of the driveway, running with little, uneasy steps, her high-heeled pink slippers threatening to overbalance her at every moment. She came and clung to the side of the car, looking up at him, her face lifted, her bosom heaving.

'Oh Mr. Kershaw, I couldn't – believe – it was – when I heard – I ran to the door–' She patted herself above the heart, stretched her throat up, tried to smile. 'I've been so frightened.'

'Frightened? By Jove! What – what's happened – is–'

'I'm all alone. Nanny – John – they're out – I'm alone – people – outside – in the – bushes–'

'By God!' He clambered out, took a tyre lever from the tool box, and made as though he was about to search the garden. She caught at his arm and held it.

'No no. It's just – I was afraid – yesterday you said – you said you saw someone. I've been frightened ever since. And last night, the bomb, the I.R.A.' She went on holding his arm. He became conscious that if anyone went by it might look rather strange. 'I've been terrified,' she whispered, as if she was so frightened that she could hardly breathe. 'Nanny's gone to see her aunty in Belcorrig, in the Home there, she always goes on Sundays, and John was going to come back this afternoon and he rang to say that he couldn't, he's in the Supermarket doing the books and he couldn't get away and I'm so frightened–' Her weight was on his arm. 'I couldn't believe when I heard you coming. And then – you were stopping–' She had both hands on his arm. He felt the Bentley at his side like a warhorse, like his greater self. By God. Throw her up into the seat and – off! But he was already out of the car and standing on solid, unimaginative ground. It wasn't possible. But by Jove, he couldn't leave her like this. Damn fellow Mulcahy, leaving his wife terrified, all alone, the bloody swine.

'I could come in for a bit,' he said. He cast another look over his shoulder for passers by, not that any were likely on this road at this hour of a Sunday afternoon. She was already drawing him towards the porch, still holding his arms. Half way there she seemed to realize what she was doing and let go of him, putting up both hands to touch her hair instead.

'Oh you are kind,' she said. 'I don't know what you must – you must think I'm terribly silly – it's – it's just that – all alone – and you said – I daren't even look out of the window—'

They were in the polished hall, the door to the drawing-room open with its vision of green carpet and tiled fireplace and plastic galleon floating serenely before the big frameless mirror over the mantelpiece.

'If you'd like me to telephone someone – y'r husband? Tell him—'

She put up her hand to the opening of her housecoat. 'Oh no – he'd be angry – he really would – he—'

'Ah.' The poor frightened little thing. He still had the tyre lever in his hand. He looked at it, gave an embarrassed laugh and searched for somewhere to put it down. He placed it with exaggerated gentleness beside the white china angels with their red candles held in their joined hands.

'Do sit down,' she breathed. 'Would you – can I—' She stood looking at him. The way his coat fitted his shoulders, the way it – and his – John's legs were so *short*. And fat. She could still feel the roughness of the tweed jacket in the palms of her hands. Like prickles. Like – as if she had touched nettles and— She knew that if she looked at them the palms of her hands would be quite red. 'Sherry?' she whispered.

'No, no thanks,' he said quickly. 'Don't want to put you out.' Such a gentle little thing. By God if— It was bloody ridiculous. Silly as the day was long, a mind like a white rabbit – and yet – there were times when what a man could do with was a bit of soft silliness. If she was his— She went on standing there, looking at him, and he went on standing.

'I was going to make some tea,' she said in a small voice. 'If – if you'd—'

'That's a jolly good idea,' he said, at once relieved, and yet far back in the back of his mind disappointed. 'The cup that cheers!'

'Yes.' She gave an embarrassed laugh. 'You'll think I'm terribly silly but I was afraid to go out to the kitchen. But I won't be now. If you'd like to sit there—'

'Mebbe I can give you a hand?' he said. 'I'm quite a domesticated sort of chap y' know.'

They went out to the kitchen and he felt the excitement in his throat like a lump. It was damn stupid. The last thing in the world – and John Mulcahy's wife! Good God! It wouldn't cross his mind, even if – and if a chap did try anything she'd scream her bally head off, not, by God, that it'd be him that would try it. As if he hadn't enough on his plate. But the rustle of nylon, the scent of warmth and youngness – and frightened youngness – the thick softness of her hair like masses of black silk and velvet, the feeling that under that nylon there was—

By Jove, he thought, if she tries to reach anything off a high shelf the whole shooting match will fall off. 'Better let me,' he said gallantly, fetching down the tea pot.

'You're so tall,' she said, her voice beginning to purr in her throat with happiness and relief. 'If you hadn't come—'

They made tea, and found bread and toasted it, and sat together in the cool, pleasant kitchen, an intimacy growing between them, like two people in a railway carriage, or sheltering somewhere from a storm. He wondered what she would do if he patted her hand, just to reassure her. He wanted to say 'What pretty hands you've got.' He swallowed his toast. She had burned it on one side, and it must be some kind of margarine she had spread on it instead of butter, funny stuff out of a little plastic tub which tasted rather like cooking fat, or what he imagined cooking fat to taste like, but even that didn't matter. It seemed to add to her helplessness, her softness. You'd even have to make toast for her, buy things for her like butter and the right kind of marmelade. He did pat her hand.

'Not to worry, eh?' he said.

She didn't answer. His hand rested on hers, and she looked at him, and he remembered with a lurch of his heart that look she had given him yesterday, as they stood facing each other in the drawing-room through there. By God. He swallowed, wanted to take back his hand, was afraid to, couldn't. Playing with bloody fire. And yet— As he looked into her great shadowy eyes a world opened, a whole life, spread out instantaneously like a map. Love and bed and softness and warmth. He swallowed again, his adam's apple seeming to swell, fill his throat.

Her hand fitted into his like a bird into its nest. He knew that he only had to move his hand, touch her wrist. Say something. He couldn't breathe.

CHAPTER TWENTY-FIVE

MICHAEL woke suddenly, the dream fading out of his mind on the instant that he woke, that he was being strangled, stifled, couldn't breathe. And behind that dream another dream – Jennifer – the Pool – all of it fading, gone. He sat up in the unfamiliar, baffling dark. Smell of earth. Damp. His hands touching earth. The night came back to him. He could see. Not really see. Only filterings of light, a narrow shaft of light across one corner of the cellar, the dungeon, falling on broken stone, a paleness of growth, weed, a pallid, clambering thing reaching up towards the light.

'Be quiet,' a voice whispered. Seagrun.

In another corner of the cellar Proinsias groaned himself out of sleep. They were all sitting up. 'Sssh.' Clink of metal as Seagrun eased the gun across his lap, with its loose shoulder strap and buckle.

'What time is it?' Proinsias said.

'Past eleven.'

'By God I'm stiff,' Proinsias whispered, stretching, creaking. Michael sat still, trying to think, to gather the night and the present moment into a coherent whole. He felt as if too much had happened to him too quickly to grasp it, to know what it meant. Like a man who is hit from ten sides at once, or one blow after the other so that the next blow catches him before he has shaken his head clear from the first. Jennifer. The sergeant's suspicions. The arrest. The rescue – God, rescue! He put the heels of his hands against his eyes. If he could get away from Seagrun, give himself up? He tried to calculate his chances of being believed, that he had had nothing to do with it. His chances were nil. They were not very good even as far as getting away from Seagrun was concerned. Why the hell had he slept? Slept so long? He flexed his knee that he had hurt when the van crashed and they were flung out on the ground. It was stiff but he could move it. Could he run? He flexed it again. His

eyes were growing accustomed to the dark and he could make
out the shadows of Proinsias and Seagrun. Proinsias might not
count, but Seagrun was sitting under the hole in the cellar
roof that seemed to be the only way out. Overhead it was concealed by bushes and sheltered by a ruined wall.

'Who's got the food?' Proinsias said.

'You have,' Seagrun said.

There was a rustling of cloth as Proinsias touched each of his
pockets in a demonstration that he had not. 'I thought you—'

'Christ Jesus,' Seagrun said. 'Haven't I the bloody gun? Do
you expect—'

'There was a whole chicken,' Proinsias said accusingly. 'And
a loaf of bread. I was sure— Why the hell didn't he take it?' He
jerked his arm towards Michael.

'Then we do without,' Seagrun said. 'Until it's dark.'

'Is there any water?' Proinsias said.

'Do you think this is a hotel?'

'My throat's parched.'

Seagrun cursed him.

'One of us could go and scout for something,' Michael suggested. If he only had one of them to deal with— His own
throat was dry enough too, now he had been made to think of it.
He tried not to think of the chicken, the mouthful that he had
been going to take just as Seagrun fired at the statue, and that
he had never taken. He imagined it lying on the floor of the
Bishop's stable, the chicken, the bread. It became immensely
vivid in his mind.

'My other sister works for the Eagans,' he said, trying to
sound indifferent.

'I know,' Seagrun said. 'And I know her. The second she saw
one of us she'd scream her head off.'

'If it was me—'

'No,' Seagrun said. Something had happened to him during
the night. It was in the sound of his voice, the way he sat. A
kind of coldness, a distance from his companions. The furious
emotions, the wild, romantic grandeur of the attack on the barracks, the escape across the mountainside, had gone. Like a girl
losing her virginity when she's drunk, looking forward to losing
it, dreaming of being seduced, of love, getting drunk to let it
happen. And when it has happened, it is not what she thought it
would be.

It was not what Seagrun had thought it would be. The drunkenness had gone. And he was at last committed, and had to face it in soberness, hiding in a cellar with two unwilling companions, with no food, no water, a handful, a small handful of bullets left in his gun, no action left to him that had any meaning. Unless he could give it meaning. He had woken much earlier than the others and had sat for an hour thinking of that meaning, what it could be, what he could do. The Sons of Ireland, the Manifesto, the speeches, the training in the hills, the talk of revolution, a new Ireland had become one bomb explosion, a burned out fish van, this. And the Crucifix had weighed on him. He had given up his religion so long ago that he had thought that he had none. Last night it had come back like a wound, not into his mind but into his heart. Not the religion of prayer and penance. But of sacrifice.

He had sat thinking, the face of the dying Christ that was in reality the face of the suffering Patrick Carmody scarred into his feelings as though a force had reached out and struck him, a voice had said, 'This is truth. This is the only truth.' Sacrifice. He felt as if he had grown older during those hours. Been drawn away from everything that until then had seemed important. He sat with his knees drawn up and the gun lying across them and looked at his life and what had happened from a great distance, like looking down from a mountain top on a land spread out. Sacrifice.

That was the only meaning.

He did not think in immediate terms, 'I will die today, sacrifice my life as a symbol,' nor, although it was also somewhere in the back of his thoughts, 'It would be better for everyone of Micheàl was killed instead of retaken. Then he too would have a meaning.' He did not allow himself to think that openly, but already he felt detached from Michael, saw him as a piece on the board, to be moved, and used, and – well, pieces on a board must, in the end, be sacrificed. If they cannot be, then either they have no place there, no meaning, or they mean defeat.

It took him a long time to think these things out, and he thought them reluctantly, prevaricatingly, because even to himself he seemed a stranger, he was not yet sure how this new Seagrun Ó Maelchonaire would think, how he ought to think. But he felt at the same time a cold and determined certainty that this was his true self, and that everything he had been until now was no more than preparation.

Without knowing any of this, Michael sensed it in the new tones of his voice, even when he was saying the most commonplace of things, if anything said in those circumstances could be commonplace. He imagined that Seagrun had come to realize that he had made a mistake, that he had rescued a man who didn't want to be rescued, and put the three of them at a terrible and imbecilic risk for nothing. He wondered if he could make Seagrun begin to admit it, and then to let him go.

'They'll be looking for several of us together,' he said tentatively. Seagrun said nothing. 'I was wondering if – we separated – one at a time we might—'

'We're staying together,' Seagrun said. 'They won't get you back.'

'What are we going to do?' Proinsias said. His voice sounded half tearful in the dark of his corner.

'Go north,' Seagrun said. 'Across the Border. They'll have a use for us there.'

'I don't—' Proinsias began, and stopped. After a minute he whispered, 'If I don't have something to drink soon—'

'The new Ireland is in the North,' Seagrun said, as if Proinsias hadn't spoken. 'That's where we should be. It was a mistake to start down here. The people aren't ready. There has to be blood spilled first. A lot of blood. We've grown too soft down here to know that any more. Pearse knew it, and Connolly. We have to learn it again.'

The shaft of light that had been slanting between two stones overhead narrowed gradually and vanished. It was midday. It was one o'clock. Two. Proinsias's complaints became urgent, tearful. Michael held his bruised knee between the palms of both hands and rubbed it gently, trying to massage the stiffness out of it. If he could get across the cellar and disable Seagrun, get the gun from him.

It was becoming difficult to think of anything except his thirst. Every time Proinsias complained it seemed to become worse. The hunger was nothing compared to it. He tried to think of Jennifer, of the future. But there was none. Once or twice he tried to talk to Seagrun, to reach him on the level they had once occupied, when they were in school together, in College, in the Soldiers. Do you remember— Trying to re-establish his position as Seagrun's teacher. But when he thought of that he wanted to hold his head in his hands and laugh with despair. That he had created him! Oh God, oh God. And if he was lucky he'd only get two or three years in gaol to think about it. If he wasn't lucky—

Seagrun's answers were 'yes' or 'no', until all three of them were too dry in the throat for talking at all. Proinsias, who was very young, began to cry. 'I've a pain in my stomach,' he whimpered. Until a short while before, until yesterday in fact, no day had gone by for him without its three good meals, and cups of tea in between. He had sat there hour after hour thinking of his mother, thinking of his father, of the kitchen at home and food, and his bed, and of great steaming cups of tea, of cocoa, great slices of currant cake, mounds of meat and potatoes. Until, oddly enough, as the hunger became worse and the thirst unendurable, he thought more of his mother and less of food and drink. His mother baking bread, making tea. His mother in an apron, holding out her arms to him. He was only eighteen, and a very young eighteen. He had thought that the Revolution was what Seagrun had seemed to teach them that it was; a mixture of speeches and running across the hills stooping low with a pack on your back, and getting home just in time for tea with an appetite on you like an elephant and a huge feeling of importance.

And now, as Michael had hours earlier, he was sensing that Seagrun had changed, gone an immense distance away from him. It was nothing that he could understand, nothing that he could put in words. Even the way he held the gun. The sharpness of his voice. As though – as though they didn't matter to him. It was like being betrayed, and it was that, rather than the thirst or the hunger or the pain in his stomach that made Proinsias cry. He bent his head on his knees and wept as he hadn't wept since he was ten, like a child lost in a forest.

'Be quiet,' Seagrun said. His mind had indeed gone a long way from them. He had hardly heard Michael's questions. He was seeing a long path. He was walking down it, down it towards – at the far, far end of it the Crucifix. There are feelings that cannot be put into words, and if they are they change their meaning, become something else, cheaper, or unreal. There was nothing cheap about Seagrun's thinking as he sat in the mould-floored dungeon of Eagan's Tower nursing his submachine gun with its six remaining bullets. Nothing unreal.

He saw the sacrifice ahead of him. Saw his own unworthiness, acknowledged it as he might have acknowledged a lame leg or a squint or a stammer in his voice. It was all that he had and he would give it. He did not say, which would have been true, I will die in a gun battle in a dark street in Belfast, on the night of the eleventh of December of this year, this winter. I will die crying for a priest because of the pain, but in my soul I will be crying, 'Ireland, Ireland.' He did not say like St. Paul – 'I have put away childish things.' But like St. Paul on the road to Damascus he felt that a great thing had happened to him, a great darkness had fallen from his eyes even within the new darkness. As though he had been chosen. He had been chosen. As any man may be chosen if only he opens his heart and soul generously enough. And even that he did not think. He felt humility. And at the same time a cold and terrible arrogance of isolation. In the months to come that arrogance would give way to warmth, even to a kind of love. He would remember Michael before he died, would love him again. Love him as his teacher, as his friend of boyhood. But now he could not allow himself to think of that or he might lose this sense of purpose, of reality. He could not think now that he owed anything to Michael because he knew that Michael no longer believed in him, in what he believed in, in anything that mattered. He knew that Michael wanted to escape from him, wanted to escape even if it meant going back to gaol. He owed him nothing. Except to use him, not to let him ruin the little that had been done, destroy their gesture.

At least it had been a gesture. Some good would come of it, if not immediately, then in time to come. It would be a legend. If Michael could be prevented from destroying it. Even to himself it seemed strange that he could quietly think, 'If I need to I will kill him. I will kill him before I let him be taken, before I let him give himself up.' He would have thought it even stranger if he had guessed that Michael had known that from the beginning, long before he knew it himself.

'It's not going to be dark for hours,' Michael said. 'And when it is, that's when they'll be really looking for us.'

Seagrun sat thinking. It was true. And if he didn't get water and food for Proinsias very soon he was going to be useless, worse than useless.

'If I could slip home,' Proinsias whispered, hope rising between his dry lips. 'Maybe nobody recognized me—'

'If there was a cottage near where we could trust them—' Michael suggested.

'That is the cottage that would be being watched,' Seagrun said. An idea was already coming to him. 'There's a house that belongs to John Mulcahy about a mile outside the town. It's by itself in a big garden with a hedge. If we went straight downhill from here through the wood we'd come out at the back of it in a field with a high hedge that'd give us cover.'

Again, it would be very hard to put his real thoughts into words. He wanted food, and something to drink. And they needed money and there might be money in the house – it was no good being squeamish about taking money when it was needed for a real purpose – he wanted all these things, and there was a kind of truth in the argument that going down by daylight in the quiet of a Sunday afternoon might be as safe or even safer than doing it in six hours' time by twilight, or eight hours' time in real darkness, when they were already in danger of being careless from hunger and thirst. But behind the reasoning there was another kind of truth. That he was impatient for the reckoning.

Proinsias went first, as scout, to look and listen. Then Seagrun. Michael had expected to be told to go second, after Proinsias, had thought of running immediately. Proinsias had no weapon. But Seagrun went up through the opening above his head with a sudden, quick scramble, a kicking of the legs, before Michael could move. He waited for Michael to come up and join him.

'We'll go down through the wood,' he said, a strange, almost dreamlike contrast between his eyes, which were as sharp as a gaoler's, and his voice, which seemed remote, not indifferent, not indifferent at all, but giving a quite other, greater significance to his words, beyond their ordinary, workaday meaning. As though for him the wood was not merely a means of approaching somewhere in concealment, but a place set apart from the ordinary world. Like a man creating a legend.

It was a quality that was to stay with him, and recur at unexpected times during the remaining half year of his life, and when it did it would disturb his more earthbound companions very much. A man whose speech is ordinary, but sometimes betrayed by fanaticism or idealism or mysticism in the eyes, is bad enough and not a man one wants beside one in an ambush or a street battle. But a man whose eyes seem quite ordinary but whose voice has echoes of another world, a totally different set of values, he is a very frightening creature. Without understanding why, Michael shivered suddenly, telling himself that it was the cold of the dungeon and the coming into the sun. But he felt as though someone had walked over his grave.

CHAPTER TWENTY-SIX

THEY lay side by side in the great, dishevelled bed, with its satin coverlet and its flowered sheets from the Supermarket; the magazines lying half open on the blue nylon carpet; the box of chocolates with all the soft ones eaten from the bottom layer as well as the top, lying beside the pillows. They had not even put that on to a side table. Had not even got properly undressed. He lay in his shirt tails and his socks and his suspenders, she in her housecoat, opened all the way down the front.

They lay stunned. Very slowly she turned her white face, encased, enclosed in its great silk cloud of midnight hair, on the satin pillow, stared at him. She wanted to say something and was prevented by the most absurd of reasons. What could she call him? Not Mr. Kershaw after – after – what had just happened. She put up both hands to her ravished housecoat, began to hold the two edges of it together, and with a kind of luxury of lost innocence allowed them to stay apart. Not Mr. Kershaw. But how could she – how – she couldn't say Hubert. Darling? Wonderful words drifted through her puddle of a mind, like the reflections of clouds, rose-pink in a summer sky, lamb-white. Love. Beloved. 'Ooh,' she breathed. 'Ooh.'

He knew what she meant. He was staggered at himself, and at the same time drunk with triumph. By God! He lay looking at her, the black eyelashes, the curve of plump, soft cheek, the dark, parted mouth like a – he felt for similes, flowers, caves, rosebuds, oh by Jove.

How had it happened? Like a damned electric shock. Touching her hand like that. Looking at each other, looking into each other's eyes. What had they done after that? Got up? They must have. Come in here? They must have done that too. Stuck together. He drew in a long sighing breath of happiness, of astonished pride, of possession, of wonder. He had never known anything like it – never in his life. God above! He wanted to touch her and remind himself of the feel of her skin, and held himself back, half afraid that it would seem different now, half tantalizing himself.

'Whew!' he said. And then, some seventh sense alarming him, 'You're sure – he – he won't–' He was a fool, a double-damned fool to say it, he knew that the second he had said it. Remind her. God what an ass. But to his surprise she did nothing. No starting up in alarm, in shame, in recollection of her status as Mrs. Mulcahy. She lay looking at him as if he was God. After a long pause for thought she whispered:

'He won't be back for hours. It's the funeral tomorrow. He may not come back at all. And Nanny won't be back till ten.' She nestled her cheek more softly on to the pale blue satin curve of the pillow, her hair astounding, a black treasury in which a man's face could drown, cool, perfumed, a harlot's hair, a wonderful, stupendous harlot out of Nero's Rome, her voice slow and dark, fulfilled, dreaming. Even her eyes seemed to have changed, to have grown larger still, darker still, great wells of drowsy passion. Hubert's nerve ends quivered as he looked. What was she thinking? What for that matter, was he himself thinking? He tried to gather his thoughts. Angela. Jennifer. John Mulcahy. The sale of the Hotel. Solicitors. Sir Philip. The Bentley – Christ! – the bloody Bentley out there like a damned advertisement. God Almighty! He started up in the bed, and as he started the door opened. Proinsias Ó Murchu looked into the room, his face drawn with terror, his hands shaking on the door handle, peering round. When he saw a man in his shirt sitting up in the bed he staggered, holding on to the door for support, his mouth falling open, clicking shut, opening again.

'S-ss-sorry—' he croaked. And then, remembering Seagrun's cold contemptuous orders when he had asked what he would do if there *was* anyone in the apparently empty house, he croaked again, 'The house is ss-ss-surrounded.'

'My God,' Hubert breathed. Clara lay beside him rigid, in her first agony of terror that it was John. In that second of the door opening, of seeing it opening out of the corner of her eye, all that had happened, the hugeness of it, the overwhelming, life-changing nature of it, had fallen on her like a stone wall, and what had been almost a day-dream, a strange, amazing extension of a day-dream, a bursting into flower, into coloured ecstasy of her imprisoned, sepia dreams with their strong hands and smells of pipe smoke and words of magazine emotion that led her to brinks she was afraid of, thresholds she could not cross by herself, the nuns' teachings hobbling her feet, enclosing her mind, whispering no, no, no, just as the sepia tones promised to flame red and orange, take real fire, all this that had been a kind of innocent dreaming revealed itself as a most dreadful reality. And more dreadful still, she was caught.

Even when she saw Proinsias's white, frightened face she still thought that it was John She lay paralysed, too terrified to cry out, to sit up, to close her housecoat over her breast, over her – she did not think of what she was revealing, and to do him justice, Proinsias, who had never seen such a sight in all his eighteen years, did not take it in. All he could see was that there were people, people in the bed.

'The house is ss-surrounded,' he said again, his voice rising. He was supposed to whistle now for Seagrun and Michael Carmody to come running in. He pursed his lips, puckered them up to whistle. No whistle came. The man in the bed stared at him, his hands plucking his shirt in this direction and that trying to do up the buttons.

If Hubert had had his trousers on, even his underpants— But in his shirt, unbuttoned, in his socks with suspenders – he had always had a horror of showing his suspenders, his bare legs, his knees; even dressing with Angela he had always gone to the bathroom or the dressing room to put on his socks and trousers, even when they were young. Surrounded? He didn't take it in, that this was the I.R.A., the Son of Ireland, guerilla war. Like Clara he had thought that it was John Mulcahy. When he had seen through the mist of shock that it was not he had thought nothing at all, except that he was lying in bed with a woman who was not his wife, on a Sunday afternoon, in his shirt and socks, and someone was staring at him from the doorway. Automatically, not thinking of what he was doing, his fingers began to do up his shirt buttons.

'If you make a s-s-s-sound we'll sssh-shoot.'

He began to understand.

Behind Proinsias there was a noise, footsteps, voices whispering. Proinsias was pushed further into the room. Michael Carmody behind him. A third man with a gun. Beside him Clara gave small whimperings of fear, clutching her housecoat round her now, pulling the soft, formless edges up and over her bosom, her throat, up to her chin, trying to hide inside the flimsy folds of nylon.

'The gentry,' Seagrun said in a bleak voice. Hearing nothing from his scout he had decided to follow him. (They had come out of the wood on to level ground behind the bungalow, and the Bentley had been hidden from them. They had listened at the back door for a long time and there had been no sound. 'What will I do if I find anyone?' Proinsias had whispered, helplessly, 'will I run?' 'You will not, you fool. Do you want them to ring the Guards? Tell them they're surrounded, that if they make a sound we'll shoot them. But there's no one here. They'll be out playing golf.' His tone made 'golf' sound vile.)

'Go and rip out the telephone,' Seagrun ordered Proinsias. The strain of keeping both Proinsias and Michael under control, preventing either of them having any possibility of running away, was tearing at his nerves. And although there had been food on the kitchen table he had not touched it for fear of seeming to show weakness in front of Michael. Michael had already taken a slice of bread and eaten it and drunk from the jug of milk. Now he Seagrun stood looking at the couple in the bed. It had taken him a second to recognize his employer, his greying hair, usually so carefully arranged, dishevelled, standing on end, his mouth open, his bare legs—

'Get out,' Hubert shouted, but his voice cracked on the word. Michael Carmody! The – The—! Oh God! 'Get out of here at – this is a—' he was going to say 'lady's bedroom' and changed his mind. '—an outrage.' He couldn't take it in that it was Michael, his barman; the boy who – although in another fragment of his mind he had expected him, known. But it was the monster he had expected, not the thin, familiar face with mocking eyes. The boy he knew.

'—outrage,' Hubert whispered, his voice shaking.

'Yes,' Seagrun said. 'But we won't shoot you for it if you stay quiet. Although if I was the husband I would shoot you both.' He knew both Hubert Kershaw and John Mulcahy well by sight, and he was genuinely sickened at the thought of the immorality. He kept his eyes turned slightly away from Clara, his mouth twisted, as if he had tasted something nauseous. 'Tie them up,' he said to Michael. 'Tear a sheet in strips.' Michael hesitated. 'Do what I tell you,' Seagrun said in that strange, dangerous voice he had acquired. Michael went towards the bed, his face apologetic. When he had realized who it was he had wanted to laugh, felt at the same time an almost furious contempt for this man that was Jenny's father and was sitting allowing himself to look more ridiculous than any man should ever permit himself to look. But approaching the bed he felt a kind of sickened pity. This man who had unconsciously humiliated him a hundred times in the past three months; this man with his stupid affectations of superiority, his life built on the pretence that he was set above men like Michael by Divine destiny – this poor ignorant fool sitting there with naked, hairy legs and sock-suspenders, his woman weeping beside him, and neither the guts to get up and fight to protect her and himself, nor the dignity to – but what could he do? What could he do but what he was doing, sitting there saying 'outrage' in a cracked, frightened voice?

'I'm sorry,' Michael said, mumbling, looking away from Hubert's eyes.

'—police – gaol – ten years – monstrous—'

'Be quiet,' Seagrun snapped. And to Michael, 'Hurry up.'

Michael took the edge of the sheet, pulled it half off the bed. It had been covering Clara's legs. They lay naked now, plump, unbelievably naked, under the pulled up edges of the housecoat with which she had tried to cover her head. She seemed like a fantastic bird of paradise with nylon feathers and a woman's legs. The whimper grew in her throat to a cry of horror, she was going to be raped, raped, they were going to rape her, one after the other. 'Oooooohhh.'

'Goddammit!' Hubert shouted.

'For God's sake shut up,' Michael whispered. 'He'll shoot.' It was impossible to tear the sheet. It slipped out of his fingers, seemed to stretch without tearing. He saw a nail scissors beside the bed and cut the hem. The sheet ripped.

'Lie face down,' Seagrun said. Proinsias had come back. He had thought of running away, peeped out of the window at the giant green car, at the hedge, at the pond, at the pottery leprechaun, looked with longing at the Sunday sky, the quiet. And yet he had not dared go out of the front door and run, or steal to the back door and run. He had come back to Seagrun as dogs come back to be kicked. He wept inside his soul for his mother, for his foolishness, his madness in ever listening to Seagrun, ever getting involved in this. But he still came back. It seemed even worse to go out there by himself, to face unknown dangers alone.

'Face down,' Seagrun repeated. He had his back to the wall, the gun covering Michael even more than Hubert Kershaw. He said to Proinsias, 'Go back to the kitchen and make a parcel of food.'

Hubert had reluctantly lain back, almost flat, but he could not bring himself to turn over. Clara had not understood the order. 'Please,' Michael whispered. His eyes and Hubert's met. There was such an agony of humiliation behind the surface anger in Hubert's that Michael had to look away again. He wondered what he would do if it was he who was lying there. Hubert rolled on his side. Michael tied his ankles together, quickly. He found it horrible to have to touch the man, to touch his skin. When it came to tying the wrists he had to take each one and pull it into position.

'Gag him.'

He slid a strip of flowered sheet round Hubert's head, pulled it tight. 'Open your mouth,' he said. Pulled it tighter, knotted it. Clara still lay like a dead bird. He tied her ankles as gently as he could.

'Tie her properly you fool,' Seagrun said.

When he tried to take her wrists she began to fight him, not trying to hit him, only to hold her wrists and hands where they were, covering her breasts. She opened her mouth to scream. Feeling like a murderer Michael stuffed a corner of sheet in her mouth, twisted the strip swiftly round the back of her head and tied it. He took her wrists again and pulled them away. The housecoat fell open. 'Turn on your face,' he begged her. Her eyes stared at him, wild with terror. She was going to be raped, hard, terrible hands – mad eyes – passion – the filthy beast – she would die, die—

As gently as possible Michael rolled her over, grabbed one wrist and then the other, and tied them.

'Cover them up,' Seagrun said.

Michael drew the satin coverlet over them. Hubert groaned through the gag. 'Ahgggg.'

Seagrun remembered that he had been going to take what money he could find. He thought very briefly of ungagging them so that he could ask where it was kept, but he did not really want to take anything except the food. He felt the same shiver of disgust at the idea of taking money that he had felt on glimpsing the woman's nakedness.

'Are they secure?' he said. Michael nodded, not wanting to

speak. He felt sick. And at the same time felt ironic contempt for himself. The Communist. The revolutionary. And tying up a woman, seeing the humiliation of a fool, made him feel physically sick. And at that he felt such an anger against Seagrun that he turned on him with a swift tightening of his muscles like a man preparing to leap in a fight. There were three yards between them and the gun was levelled at his stomach.

'You go out in front of me,' Seagrun said, with that dream-like, distant voice. But his eyes filled with quick, alert suspicion, a gunman's eyes.

'I want to go altogether,' Michael said. 'I won't stay with you.'

'Later,' Seagrun said gently.

They stayed facing one another, and Michael felt for the few seconds that the confrontation lasted something of what Hubert Kershaw had felt. The humiliation of the unarmed man before the gun. A kind of rape, that no argument, no clear conscience, no superiority of mind could alter. The only answer for the unarmed man is to be willing to be killed rather than humiliated. And Michael knew that he was not willing to be killed in that stupid, absurd moment, and the humiliation was like the taste of iron. He learned something in those seconds that would stay with him for ever, like a scar.

'Come,' Seagrun said, as if he was talking to a lover. The gun seemed to move in his hands of its own accord, like a living thing, like a part of his body. His eyes misted, filmed, seemed to take on a new quality as if they were looking not at Michael but into him, into his soul. What he saw seemed to fill him not with anger but with pity. 'Come,' he said again. And it was not clear even to himself whether he meant, 'Come, throw yourself forward, come to me and be killed,' or simply, 'Come, it's time to leave, hurry.' Half one meaning, half the other. His eyes looked into Michael and saw corruption. The corrupted saint. And what is more terrible? Judas Iscariot. There is only one way to cure that corruption. He could see the small scarlet flowers that would come on Michael's shirt. One, two, three, four. Could see himself holding Michael as he died. 'Come,' he said for a third time. Michael moved slowly, his body slackening, turning towards the door. Seagrun sighed deeply, like a man with a lover, postponing love.

They went out to the kitchen where Proinsias had found a basket and loaded it with what food there was. There was not

313

much. A couple of eggs, some raw sausages, a dryish strip of bacon, tomatoes, some milk, some bread and butter, a pot of jam. He had not thought of a knife or cups and neither did Seagrun. They went out the way they had come in.

'Michael will carry the basket,' Seagrun said. 'We will go back to the Tower and eat.'

'As soon as those two are discovered they'll know we're still in the neighbourhood—' Michael began.

'Yes,' Seagrun said. He had no plan in his mind beyond the certainty that he would not let Michael go. Something would happen. He did not know what it would be except that it was something he had been moving towards all his life. It was that certainty that had brought the dream-quality into his voice. Like a sleep walker. A man hypnotized. He felt that he no longer needed to plan. On the small level, for details, to keep Michael covered, and at a safe distance, to keep his eye on Proinsias, to take cover behind the hedge as they made for the wood, to climb quietly among the trees; all those things he did carefully. But the longer term, the great things; those would be taken care of. There were no more words said between them as they climbed back to the Tower, scrambling up through the wood, over the park wall of Eaganscourt where tree roots had broken it and its eight-foot height had tumbled down to three or four with rubble on either side like steps, and bushes growing. He made Michael drop down first into the cellar, then Proinsias. 'Push him to the far side,' he whispered to Proinsias before he let him go down. Then he dropped down third, and settled himself against the wall. Proinsias shared out the food.

CHAPTER TWENTY-SEVEN

THE sight of Hubert Kershaw's Bentley in his driveway, almost blocking the path to the porch and the front door, as well as to the garage, astonished John Mulcahy. He had swung his Ford Corsair into the gateway and almost crashed into the enormous green rump before he accepted that there was something there. He had his fist poised angrily over the horn ring before he took it in that the car was deliberately there, not simply turning, that it was empty, that it was Hubert Kershaw's, that therefore Hubert Kershaw must be calling on him. He sat still, lowering his hand. Hubert Kershaw.

Thoughts of his father's death, the funeral, condolences, flashed through his mind and were discarded instantly. The Development! The Old House Hotel. The seventy-two acres. The fish being let out. The I.R.A. The bugger was frightened, scared out of his wits. He had come to do a deal as fast as he could, before everyone behind the Development could start drawing back.

A soft smile creased John Mulcahy's face. His cheeks were already developing dewlaps, and folding forward round his mouth. His smile, when he thought of money, took on a peculiar sweetness, like a plump old nun thinking of her Saviour. How lucky he had come back. He had been going to stay late in the Supermarket – there was a new girl helping him with the accounts, she had long legs and silly eyes and a passion for marshmallows – and he had been going to stay until about ten o'clock and then look in at Knuckle Street. But the girl had seemed shocked that he was thinking of that kind of thing the day before his father's funeral, and since he didn't know her very well yet he had been shocked too, and told her that he was so prostrate with grief that he hardly knew what he was doing, he just needed a sympathetic shoulder to cry on, and he had given her a small case of marshmallows and they had finished the accounts and locked up. As for Knuckle Street, the thought of Benedict being there had driven him home. He'd have his tea first. It crossed his mind that having failed for the moment with Eithne Gallagher Clara might – he might – God damn, if a man couldn't – with his own wife – what the bloody hell was marriage *for?* – but of course the funeral – she'd probably say it too— And here was Hubert Kershaw! Looking for a deal.

His smile folded and vanished. He put on the appearance of a man who has had a severe loss, a grievous shock, and squeezing past the Bentley let himself gently in. 'Clara?'

No answer. He looked into the drawing-room. Odd, no one there. He stood puzzled. She must be showing him the garden, although what she knew about the garden wouldn't grow weeds. No drinks out, no tea tray. The dining-room— The sideboard still locked. He looked out of the dining-room windows at the lawn. Not there. 'CLARA?' The kitchen? What on earth – 'CLARAAA!' Not in the kitchen. He began to get vaguely alarmed. Not for any specific cause. Just alarm. He went out into the garden and looked about. The thought of the I.R.A. came to him and was rejected. Nonsense, rubbish, ridiculous, idiotic. He had said all those things to her when she 'phoned yesterday and again on the 'phone this afternoon, when she was gabbling about 'prowlers'. 'Prowlers in the garden.' He looked at his garden with a nervous constriction of the heart. The bushes, trees, the hedge. Cast a look at the fields beyond, uncomfortably rough, with gorse clumps and stone walls. At the wood. The mountainside. He turned quickly and went indoors.

'CLARAAAAA!'

He went finally into the bedroom not so much to look for her as in bafflement. Half formed ideas of notes left on mirrors flitted through his head, without logic. He actually looked at the mirror before he looked at the bed. She was asl— He took in the second form lying almost concealed by the coverlet, the untidy grey hair, the head lifting, the sounds – 'Ahhhhh —gguggguuggh.' Whereas to Clara no thought had come at the sound of her husband's calling voice and searching feet but to lie quite still as if she was dead, Hubert had had time to think. Panic, terror, had slowly given birth to cunning. 'Ugggh.'

John Mulcahy came on unbelieving feet towards the bed, touched the coverlet, hesitated, let go of it. He couldn't, couldn't—

'Ughhhhgugggh.'

Slowly, piece by piece, he took in the scene. Side by side, gagged – in bed – BED! – but gagged – the I.R.A. – but in BED! In a frenzy he seized the coverlet again and tore it away. Naked. Naked legs. He shut his eyes, swayed, literally swayed where he stood.

'Uggghuggg.' Hubert Kershaw lifted his head still higher, twisted his neck to allow him to look at John Mulcahy, his eyes filled with explanations, readiness to make everything plain. He twitched his bound hands up and down, lifted his heels. Clara sobbed. 'Argghhhh.'

With fumbling, inefficient fingers John Mulcahy pawed at the knots, failing first with the gag and then with the wrists. After a second or two he felt that it was wrong to attempt to free the – the – oh my God – his wife! Clara! in bed He ran round to the other side of the wide bed, that was like a great untidy raft, with two drowned sailors on it, and began to pluck at her knots, his fingers unconsciously rougher, angry, yearning to slap and beat as well as free. The stupid – how – what had she – my God – he left off trying to free her and jerked the housecoat down as far as possible towards her feet.

'Stop crying!' he shouted. Oh my God. He ran out into the kitchen for a knife, and was suddenly struck by something that he must have seen a few minutes earlier without noticing. A kind of – a kind of strickenness – as if— He wrenched open the door of the refrigerator. Empty. Stark. Eggs – bacon – sausages – butter – milk – all gone. He looked in the bread bin. None. His desk! He ran on tottering feet to the small morning room that he called his study. Not touched. Everything in place. His heart quieted, but his hands still trembled as he opened his desk, opened the secret drawer, the cash box, saw that all was well. He locked box and drawers again and went back with an easier heart to the bedroom, still without a knife. But he saw the nail scissors put back by Michael beside the bed and with many stabs and jerks and grunts of exertion managed to free Hubert and then Clara. Clara still wept, covering her head with the pillow. She expected to be killed. What did men do to wives who – who – oooooh she cried, half smothered by down and satin, oooooh.

'SHUT UP!' cried John, distracted by his thoughts. She went quiet like a gramophone with its needle lifted.

'Ahh. By Jove,' Hubert said mechanically. His voice trailed away. He chafed his wrists, wriggled his toes, stretched his ill-used mouth and swallowed. 'Water . . .' he croaked. He looked so ill that John actually went out to the kitchen and filled a glass. Hubert drank half of it, thought suddenly of Clara, and carefully avoiding any glance towards what might be exposed held out the remainder to his left. Clara, her head still hidden, stifled her sobs. Hubert drank the rest of the water and gave a long sigh, as if it had been whiskey.

'By God,' he said. 'Thought I was – thought we were – I was–' he felt his throat. 'Jolly nearly strangled,' he said.

John Mulcahy had been twisting and untwisting his hands, in a kind of reflection of his state of mind, questions forming themselves, only to reform or seem unaskable before he could shape the words.

'My wife,' he said at last. His voice rose to a cracked squeak of indignation. Why the devil didn't this man – what had he – how could he ask–– In desperation he went savagely round to Clara's side of the bed again, ripped the pillow away and struck her across the side of the head. His hand was very soft and it hurt him severely, since he hit her on the bone of her skull. He wrung his hand, shouting, 'Stop being hysterical, you've got hysterics, stop crying, you're hysterical.' Even as his hand was descending he was ashamed of what he was on the point of doing, particularly in front of Hubert Kershaw. But in his bed. His BED! He hit her really hard and thought that he had dislocated his wrist. His soft palm burned like fire and having wrung it in sympathetic agony with the other hand he thrust it under his armpit and stamped back to Hubert's side.

'I say, I mean old man, dammit–' Hubert said.

Clara, who had stopped crying before she was hit, was now sobbing at the top of her voice.

'SHUT UP!'

'I mean to say,' Hubert said, 'we – I mean she – we, we've had a damned rough time. These I.R.A. chappies–' He gave John a carefully reshaped version of what had happened. Just passing – saw something suspicious – turned in to the gateway – heard cries – stepped out – tyre lever – rang bell – fellow with a gun – Mrs. M. in the grip of this frightful looking chap – not a chance of fighting 'em – made him strip – sadists – perverts – damned monsters – most frightful moment of his life––

John Mulcahy listened. He did not know whether he believed it or not. On the surface he did, he had to, it was clearly true. But beneath the surface? He saw without wishing to see; the bed, his wife still lying face downwards, crying more quietly now, Hubert Kershaw's clothes, his underclothes – my God, his trousers, his underpants – John Mulcahy shut his eyes – his shoes, scattered across the carpet in a – a *particular* way – the way a man – it wasn't possible – of course it wasn't possible – obviously it was the I.R.A. – and yet—

Clara, who had slowly taken in the immense cleverness, the astonishing invention of Hubert's story, was beginning to take courage. When John had hit her she had thought that that was the beginning of the end. But now— She rolled on to her back, sat cautiously up, holding her housecoat across her breast. She sniffed and risked a swift glance from under wet eyelashes at her husband. He looked so – so *stupid*. So – *fat*. She lifted her head, her face filling with dignity, with suffering, too noble to express reproach.

'Mr. Kershaw saved my life,' she said.

John Mulcahy's shoulders seemed in the last minutes to have taken on a stoop, as though he had aged ten years. He lifted his hands and let them fall. He felt that in some strange way he was being compared to Hubert Kershaw and found inferior. And yet for years he had despised Hubert Kershaw as the worst kind of fool; an imbecile, nearly bankrupt, taking months to pay his bill in the Supermarket, with nothing in the world to back up his bloody gentry nonsense; half English, half nothing. At least old Sir Philip had money. But this fool – and here he was sitting in John Mulcahy's bed in his shirt tails and his socks – and it was John Mulcahy who was being put in the wrong. God above! He wanted to go and hit Clara again, just to prove that he had the right. But she was looking at him now as if everything was his fault. Because he hadn't come back when she asked him to. Because—

'You'd better get dressed,' he said to Hubert.

When he got her by herself— When – but it did not take even the threatening thought of her aunt, Mrs. Glennon, to tell him that he would not do anything. He did not consciously understand that a distinct change had begun in their relationship, but already he sensed it. He could not even turn round to see if she was looking at – at – as – that swine – put on – John's mind dropped to a whisper – his trousers. His face turned a mottled red and he clenched his hands. It was only then that he thought of going to the telephone to tell his brother – the Guards—

'I'd better telephone Sergeant McMenamin—' he said to the window.

There was a long silence behind him, the rustling of Hubert dressing. And then Hubert said in a cautious voice—

'I wonder – of course old man it's absolutely up to you – but I wonder if – you know what damn gossips people are in this place – but of course, if you think—'

John Mulcahy went on staring at the window. In the end he decided not to telephone. It was as though he was no longer completely master of anything.

CHAPTER TWENTY-EIGHT

ALL that afternoon Sir Philip had done nothing, only sit quietly at his desk and remember. It made it easier to remember knowing that Meg was out. She had gone to play bridge with the Bartons and she wouldn't be back until midnight. He let his mind drift. He felt too tired, too heavy about the heart to work. As if the weather had— He sat in his study chair staring at nothing, his fingers touching the bronze mirror that he used for a paper weight.

The garden in Changsha, that first year. Every detail. As though there was a necessity about remembering it. The Judas trees, and the white lilac, and the jasmine bushes; the La Mei flowers like gold dust, and the Gingkos, and the bamboo, and the tall, feathery Lan mu trees.

'They are our wealth,' the Professor had said, with his small, self-mocking smile. Eight years later he had passed through Changsha again and all that had been left of that garden had been the black stumps of the trees, ashes. It had not even been possible to know for certain if the stumps had been in the Khoo garden or in a neighbour's. Everything had been ashes. But by then the Professor had been dead for several years, killed in an 'unfortunate incident' by 'unknown attackers'. Which meant that he had been beaten to death by Blueshirts, by a terror squad of the Kuomintang.

'Let me get you out of China,' he had begged her then. 'To Singapore, to Hong Kong, anywhere that you'll be safe.'

She had only lowered her eyes.

'What good are you doing?' he had shouted at her. 'What good did—' He could not say to her, what good did your father do, what point was there in his dying? And yet he was furious with her. Furious with her for making him concerned. Drawing him in. They had not seen each other for a year after that. Until the time when a friend rang him in Shanghai, and said, 'If you could come for her. She will be safe with you, I hope. It is very bad.'

She had been tortured by the Kuomintang police and she could neither walk nor stand, only lie on the bed and look at him, her face swollen and raw from the red pepper they had used on her, her nose like blood. When he and the boy Chang who had telephoned him tried to pick her up she had not screamed, only wept softly as though there were things in her heart and mind rather than her body that were broken. And yet she had recovered and gone back to Peking, and to her secret journeys to one Red base or another, one city and another.

He tried not to think of that side of her life that he could not share, except to report to his superiors in carefully guarded, carefully anonymous form, the things that she told him. There had been no breach of trust in it. She told him only what she was willing to have retold. She had teased him about it once.

'I make use even of you, Pi Li. I make you act.'

All that he wanted to remember now were the times when neither of them had been concerned with outside things. Only with themsleves. An October afternoon in Peking. The roadside stalls selling great scarlet slices of Hsiang-san melon. They had come to a cake shop and she had said, 'We must buy Moon cakes, Pi Li. It is Festival time.' And he had bought her a little painted hare, the Hare Gentleman who lives on the Moon, and she had carried it with her everywhere like a talisman. 'He will bring you back to me.'

But that he had not done. He sat all afternoon and evening in his study, thinking of how it might have been if he had gone back – stayed–

He had realized with a kind of distant surprise that it was half past nine, and that he had had neither afternoon tea nor a drink, nor dinner. He wondered where the girl had got to but it was too much effort to go and look. What had she said to him about her mother? Maybe she had gone to see her mother. It was pleasant in a way to feel that the house was his own. Even the dogs— He remembered then that Meg had shut them in the stables before church and they had both forgotten to let them out.

He went to the kitchen and got food for them and took it out to the stables. They woke from their bored sleep and jumped all over him, spilling most of the food in the straw.

'Down,' he said. 'Down.' He sat on a pile of firewood and

watched them eat. Even they were part of the emptiness. He would have liked another kind of dog, but Labradors were what one had. Meg had always had Labradors even as a child. So had he. And they were after all pleasant enough dogs. He felt ashamed and made a fuss of them to make up for not loving them as he should. They obviously believed that this was the prelude to a walk and would not stop barking and jumping up at his hands and sleeves, trying to pull him out of the stables with them. After a few minutes he gave in and got a stick from the boot room across the yard. He'd walk over to the Tower and watch the remains of the sunset and when he got back to the house the girl might be back. Or he might cook something for himself.

The dogs jumped round his legs in delight.

In the dungeon the three fugitives had finished all their food, all their cigarettes, even their matches.

They had also run dry of talk. There was nothing to talk about. Seagrun sat still and quiet, not moving, like a man deep asleep while sitting up, and yet whenever Michael moved, Seagrun's hands moved the gun, very slightly, but enough. Proinsias sat huddled miserably in his corner, thinking of his mother, of his bed, his tea, the future.

Michael sat thinking of escape. And increasingly, as the hours went by, of Jenny. If he escaped. When.

He thought also with a shiver of self disgust about that moment below in the house, in the Mulcahy bungalow, when he had faced Seagrun. But what could he have done? Nothing. Nothing. And Jenny— When he had been first arrested she had gone out of his mind as if she had never existed. A man who has been in prison once expects – in some irrational part of his mind always expects – to be imprisoned again. And as they took him down to Ross Harbour and the barracks it was like something continuing that had never really stopped. Everything between his release from prison in London a few months before, and this moment sitting wedged in the back seat of the Cortina beside the sweating bulk of Guard O'Neill, vanished. This was reality. The rest was dreaming. Even in that imitation cell in the barracks the smell of real prison was back with him; stone and cocoa and iron and urine and carbolic.

And after the attack on the barracks there had been no time to think quietly. Before they went down to the bungalow hunger and thirst and rage had made his mind sharp and jagged, cursing Seagrun, himself, Sergeant McMenamin, Guard O'Neill, whoever it was that informed on him; up and down, up and down, like a man pacing a cell. Half forming plans for escape, rejecting them, coming back to them, massaging his knee, trying to ease his throat as the thirst got more unpleasant. But now he had had something to eat, and drink, and he was tired of cursing, and he knew that the only chance he would have of escaping from Seagrun was when they left the cellar after dark. In the dark he must – he must have a chance. And then?

A fishing boat. There was no other way. If he could get into the town without being seen. They wouldn't be looking for him there, wouldn't be expecting him to try – there were two or three men who'd help if he could reach them—

It was then that the thought of Jenny began to come back to him, not as the past, but as the future. What was he going to do? Nothing. What could he do? The question was so stupid that it maddened him. What could he do? And she wouldn't – what was she thinking? Imagining? How did she feel? What was she doing now? His mind followed her through the hours. In the kitchen. Dinner. In the bar. It was difficult to think of life going on as usual. Her life— As the darkness in the cellar grew thicker and it became impossible to tell one shadow from another, she seemed to be in front of him, a small figure moving about within a frame, like a picture on a television screen with the sound switched off. Sometimes doing the things that she would really be doing at that moment, taking meat out of the oven, bending down, wiping her forehead with the back of her wrist; going through into the bar, untying her apron, pushing her hands backwards through her hair to tidy it. He had never thought of how beautiful her hair was until now. Had accepted it as part of her. But it came suddenly close, the tiny figure came forward, closer and closer, until all that imaginary frame was filled by her hair; dark red, tangled. Not beautiful at all, not really. Just red hair. But he had to shut his eyes against it and it was still there, she was still there, inside his eyelids. What was he going to do? He didn't remember, think of the moments he – not the moments anyone would imagine he'd think of. But in the bar. Passing her in the corridor, her eyes lifting, looking at him. Her mouth wanting to smile.

He moved sharply at the memory, and from across the cellar

an invisible Seagrun tapped the stock of the gun with a dry, metallic sound.

'It's time,' Seagrun said.

For a second Michael clung to the image of her, could almost feel her hair against his face, and the bitterness of what had happened was like a pain in his ribs, like cramp. Across the cellar there was the rustling sound of movement, a shuffle of feet, the knock of a shoe against stone, metal against stone. Michael tried to move quickly, but his left leg had gone to sleep as he sat and he had to take his weight on the other leg, hobbling and stumbling to keep his balance. Before he could move properly both Seagrun and Proinsias were up and out of the cellar and in the open air, crouching down, waiting for him. He felt his way forward, climbed the low slope of fallen masonry that made it possible to get out of the cellar without a rope, felt for the opening and hauled himself up.

When he was kneeling on the thin turf that grew inside the broken walls of the tower he stayed where he was, breathing heavily. 'My leg,' he said after a few seconds. 'My knee. I can't—'

'Get up,' Seagrun said. There was still twilight, and they could see each other, grey against the stone walls and bushes of the ruin. Seagrun well back from the hole in the ground over the cellar. Proinsias beside him. 'Get up, it'll be all right when you move.'

'I can't get up.'

Seagrun whispered. Proinsias came forward, bending down to help. Michael let Proinsias lift him by the arm, putting his whole weight on Proinsias. The boy staggered.

'I hurt it when the van crashed,' he said. 'It's stiffened up.'

'You used it this afternoon—' Seagrun came forward, still half suspicious, but unsure. One step nearer, two, three – cradling the sub-machine gun now rather than aiming it, peering forward at Michael leaning on the unsteady Proinsias. As Seagrun took the last step Michael drove his elbow into Proinsias's ribs, and Proinsias grunted, stepped back, and fell through into the cellar with a shriek of terror. The gun started to swing towards Michael and he leaned forward and kicked, as if he was kicking a loose, rising ball in a soccer game, kicking for touch. He aimed for Seagrun's wrist, but Seagrun had already begun to sway backwards, and the toe of Michaed's shoe only grazed his knuckles, struck the underside of the barrel of the gun, and half knocked it out of Seagrun's hands. But not completely out of them. Seagrun stumbling backwards. Losing his balance, falling. But still holding the gun, the webbing strap caught round his elbow. Michael ran. Over the lowest part of the ruined wall, crashing through the dry snarl of bushes, on to the open turf, trees to his left, swerving, running.

With every heartbeat he expected the crash of shots behind him, the huge, spinning kick of bullets hitting him. He was almost at the trees—

Sir Philip had heard Proinsias crying out and the thud of his fall, and sounds of running, and had thought, 'Boys – playing the fool – one of them fallen somewhere—' He began running forward, not very fast, but fast enough, the dogs bounding ahead, barking.

'Stop!' Sir Philip shouted. 'I can see you, I know your names!' The hopeless, ageless landlord's cry as boys run away from their trespassing. Nothing in the world was further from Sir Philip's mind than real violence. He saw the pale shape of one of the dogs bounding up over the wall, barking ferociously, thought, 'That'll frighten them a bit,' and didn't believe, didn't believe for a long moment what he heard, what his eyes saw, the hard smack of shots, two single shots from a sub-machine gun, the bright stitches of flame in the dark. He went on running forward, his mind refusing to believe – shotgun – poachers – the bloody swine, the dog – the dog— The shape lying where it fell, not moving, not whimpering, dead before it fell — oh my God— His brain already saying, 'lie flat you fool, throw yourself down, firing.' But it was so long since he had heard real gunfire. His legs continued, went on running, carrying him forward, his mouth opened to shout, began to shout, 'You damned swine—' He was at the wall—

Seagrun pushed the switch to automatic fire.

The four remaining shots took Sir Philip across the chest. It seemed to him as if they cut his body in half.

The young bitch who had stayed beside him while he ran howled in terror, ran off into the dark and crouched there, trembling, crying in her throat, death like a fog around her mind, the death of her father, of her master. Crouched there, blind with terror.

Behind the wall Seagrun stood holding the empty gun, standing upright, waiting. He had thought it was the police, that the dogs were police dogs. But even if he had known he might still have shot. He had come to a point where if he did not shoot, did not kill, do something that could not be undone, setting him apart for ever, his mind would have burst, he would have broken. And knowing that he had only a few bullets left he had carefully shot the dog with two of them and kept the rest for the first guard that came. And there was only one.

But even as he was shooting, as his finger was tightening, he half knew. That it was not a guard. That there was no one else. The man running towards him stopped running as if he had hit an invisible wall, lifted one arm, half lifted it, and quite slowly fell, knees crumbling, body leaning back. All in slow motion. Seagrun watched it happen, his mind detached. Part of it still waiting, acting out the charade for the other guards who already he knew did not exist.

And on the soft, short grass, five yards away from him, Sir Philip lay dying. Was almost dead. In a strange way he knew that he was dying. That something terrible had happened to him. But he was not sure what it was. Or even when it had happened. He seemed to have been lying there for a long time. He could see the dog that had died at the same time as himself and he wanted it to come to him.

'Come here old fellow,' he said. He wanted to comfort it, to tell it that he was sorry, that he would not for the world have had this happen to it. And at the same time he knew that if he had loved it it would not have happened. Or happened differently. He felt an overwhelming sadness because of the dog.

'Come to me,' he whispered. The dog seemed to look at him and half understand. He watched with a detached interest as the dog staggered to its feet and stood. And yet the same dog was also lying down. The dog that stood looked at the dog that lay still and put up its muzzle to the sky and howled.

'Poor fellow,' he said. 'He doesn't understand that he's dead.'

'Do you?' a voice asked him. He looked round and saw her, standing behind him. She was dressed as she had been dressed the first time they met, in a tight fitting Shan of the old style, but this time the colour was white. Over it she wore a soft white cloak with many folds.

'How have you come here?' he said. 'I was thinking of you—' She smiled, and yet it seemed to him that her smile was not as joyful as it might have been.

'I know,' she said, without making it clear what it was exactly that she knew, and not answering his question as to how she had come to be there at that moment. He found that like the dog a moment or two earlier he was standing up and yet his body still lay on the ground beside him. He was repelled by what he saw. Not the blood, the smashed bones of the chest. But at how old the face had grown, how much carved with a character that he did not like to see. Like a man who buys a new suit and sees with sudden clarity how shabby, how ugly his old clothes have grown. He could see in the grey lines of that face that was still, in medical and legal terms, that of a living man — he could see in that face a thousand lines whose causes made him ashamed, so that he hid his own face with his hands. She waited beside him.

'We have not much time,' she said at last.

'What must we do?'

'We have a long way to go.'

'I would have liked the poor dog to come.'

She shook her head.

'Then I suppose I am ready,' he said.

'Except that you must bring all your possessions,' she said. 'I am afraid that you will find them heavy.'

He looked and saw a great heap of things like luggage at a station. Family. Tradition. House. Prejudice. The comfort of things. He did not want any of them.

'I never loved them,' he said. 'I do not want them.'

'And yet you gave up everything for them,' she said sadly. 'I am afraid you cannot leave them now. Perhaps I can find you a cart.' There was a cart standing by the piled objects, its shafts tilted in the air. One of those two-wheeled carts of China, something like a rickshaw, in which peasants drag their possessions about if they ever need to, or take farm produce to the market. He had seen a thousand, ten thousand refugees dragging them along the dusty roads from one burned village to another, a thousand Li to the south or west. She held the shafts level and steady while he loaded up the cart. He found that he was dressed as a soldier, in a Colonel's uniform. His own. It still fitted him well enough. In his turn he held the shafts of the cart and she climbed delicately up until she sat perched on the piled belongings that already, before he had dragged them the first steps of their immense journey, he hated from the depths of his soul.

'Why must this happen?' he said. For although as yet he knew no more than that they would make the journey, and nothing of what lay at its end, his heart was leaden with foreboding.

'Because one chooses,' she said gently. 'It would be undignified if one's choices were meaningless.'

'I had to choose as I did,' he said, although he knew that he was lying. 'I had a duty.'

'One's duty looks forward,' she said. 'Not back. But you knew that always. Only you were afraid to look forward.'

'I did what was demanded of me.'

'By whom?'

'By my superiors.'

'Did they demand that you should turn your face away from life?'

'In a way they did.'

'Then you should have disobeyed, or chosen other superiors. Do you claim that all your life you were nothing, a leaf on the wind?'

'I did not know.'

'You knew all the time.' Her words were hard and cool, like jade, and yet behind them lay an infinity of pity, of compassion. So that the smooth oval of her face, the folds of her white cloak, were like those of Kwan Yin, the All-Merciful, who began Her existence as a young boy, and became a Goddess. It seemed to Philip much harder to bear the compassion than the coolness. He wanted to have the courage to say, 'Let there be only Justice for me.' But if he said that she would go, and leave him finally. Whatever was to happen, he would not make that ultimate mistake of pride.

Instead, he did the more courageous thing of humiliating himself, of continuing to plead with her. He wanted above all things that she should understand why he had done what he had done. And yet he knew at the same time that she saw into the bottom of his soul, and that was why she pitied him. Not for what was to come, but for what had already been. For what he had made himself.

She lifted one still slender, beautiful hand from among the white folds of her lap and pointed to the south and east. 'We must go,' she said. 'There is no time left.' And he felt in his body, by the strange pain in his chest, that that was true. And yet he still tried to explain to her. He was on the edge of saying,

'My ancestors are here. I had to return to them.' But that would have been so base a lie that he could not say it. He saw in a fraction of a second, like a tapestry hung before his eyes, all the vast emptiness, the nothingness of his ancestry for the past three centuries. Dead trees in the ground waiting to be felled. Perhaps it was impossible to strike new roots in this ground. The dead trees made it impossible. But he had been given the chance to strike root elsewhere, and he had drawn back from it, afraid. Afraid of the obligations of living, of real living. He had chosen to be dead while he still walked about.

She looked at him as if she knew everything that he was thinking. 'We must go instantly,' she said, and he sighed very deeply, feeling the pain in his chest become unbearable, rise up into his throat so that if he stood still for another instant it would spill out of his mouth and something terrible would follow. He turned quickly, fitting the smooth shafts of the cart along his forearms as though he had been born to be a coolie, to pull heavy carts. The wheels turned. Behind them, on the soft Irish turf, the last breath rattled in Sir Philip's throat, came up in a bloody frog of bright red foam. No doctor could any longer have said that he was still alive.

Far away the young bitch whimpered, longing to come back to howl beside her dead comrade, her dead master, but still afraid. She saw the cart trundling on silent wheels down the hillside, the shadows with it, one pulling, one swaying on top of its heaped load and the hairs rose on her back and her body shivered with fear. Then it was gone and she lifted her muzzle to the sky and howled and howled.

'What have you done?' Proinsias whispered. He had not been badly hurt by the fall into the cellar and had only lain on his back down there in terror, first at the fall, then at the shots, until the worse terror of the following silence made him crawl and climb back out of the hole like an animal, his body shaking with fear.

'Have you — killed him?' he whispered, thinking it was Michael the shots had been fired at. He twisted his hands together, his voice choking on the question.

'I have killed someone,' Seagrun said. 'I think it's Sir Philip.' He sounded as if he was coming out of a trance. 'We'll have to hide the body,' he said. 'And the dog.' His voice frightened Proinsias as it had earlier frightened Michael, making him so useless, on top of his existing terrors that he no more than stood there while Seagrun dragged the heavy corpse of the dog over the broken wall and dropped it down into the cellar. He had the gun slung over his shoulder but it kept falling and hindering him.

'You'll have to help me,' he said to Proinsias, his voice as gentle, as distant, as if he was saying, 'Carry these things for me across the room,' or, 'Have you a cigarette?' But his movements were quick and except for the clumsiness of the gun, efficient. Moving like a man in a nightmare, each foot, each movement of his hand weighing a hundredweight, Proinsias made himself bend down and take hold of one arm of the dead man. He dropped it again before he had lifted it.

'I can't.'

'You'll have to. I can't do it alone.'

In the end they hauled the body over the stones, let it fall as gently as they could into the cellar, letting it down by the arms. It crumpled down on top of the dead dog but they did not see that. Seagrun cleaned his hands with earth and grass and made Proinsias do the same.

'What will we do, Seagrun?'

'Go to the north. Once we reach Belcorrig there are people who will help us. It's nothing. It had to be done. There had to be – something like that.'

'What about Michael? Will he—?'

'He doesn't matter any more. Come on.'

They went into the wood, striking north towards the ridge of the mountain that separated The Ross from the rest of Ireland. So long as they kept away from the road they would have no trouble crossing it. While in the dungeon all the small creatures that lived there came to investigate the bodies and the scent of blood. And shadows moved about among the stones and the uneasy airs of the night sighed and whispered. An Eagan. An Eagan. Shadows that had died centuries ago in that harsh place, because an Eagan desired them to. But they looked in vain for this Eagan's shadow. That was far away.

Beside the opening above the dungeon the young bitch lay on the ground, whimpering in her throat.

CHAPTER TWENTY-NINE

SHE heard it strike two and sleep was further away than ever. Where was he? She had gone up to her bedroom as soon as she could and sat on the edge of her bed, thinking. It didn't matter what he had done, what he had done, what he had done. It seemed to her that in the last few days she had grown from a child into a woman, she had lived ten years, half a life. And now, if he was gone, the other half was useless to her. As though a door had opened in a blank wall and she had been shown a fantastic garden, promised it for her own, and then, without warning, it had been slammed shut in her face. What *had* he done, what could he have done? He had been with her when the fishes were let out, he had hardly been out of the hotel for an hour at a time since that night. Or for days, weeks before. What could he have done? And it didn't matter what it was. If she could only see him again. She thought of her mother and father asleep in the room down the corridor. They had spent the night talking about going to England, getting away from here. Getting steadily drunker, her mother in a genteel, golf-club sort of way, holding herself very stiff and upright on the padded leather bench in the Copper Room, hiccuping at intervals, her father talking endlessly, and half jumping out of his skin when the telephone rang. It had been the guards, asking them to keep a look out for prowlers.

'They say these chaps may still be in the district,' he had reported back to them when he had put down the 'phone. 'But they don't think it's likely. They've been combing the place all day and not a sign of them.' His hand had been shaking so much that he spilled his drink. 'They think they must have got across the mountains early this morning. There were some chaps seen in a lorry that didn't stop at a road block, and they're pretty sure that was them.'

'Thank God,' her mother had said.

'Best thing if they have,' her father echoed. But he had said it mechanically as though he didn't believe the police. He had been very strange ever since he came back in the car, earlier in the evening. They had closed the Public Bar very early and he had taken half an hour to check all the downstairs windows, make sure all the bolts were fastened. She had gone straight up to bed and left them still drinking in the Copper Room, with the Maces, all of them saying what they would do if any of these damn fellows showed their faces round the place. 'Shoot first and ask damn silly questions afterwards,' Colonel Mace shouted. 'Bloody swine. Like the damn Mau Mau.'

Half past two.

The Maces must have decided not to go home after all, but to sleep in the hotel.

'Lots of rooms, old man. Take your pick.'

'Jenneeeee?' Her mother's voice, seeing if she was awake. To get something or other that was needed for whatever room the Maces had picked. It had been one o'clock in the morning and she hadn't answered, sitting rigid with anger on her bed, where she had been sitting for the past hour. 'Jenneeee? Are you awake?'

'Leave her alone.' Her father.

'Please don't bother. Don't wake her up.' Mrs. Mace. A small, thin-mouthed woman who played bridge. God, I hate them, Jenny had thought. Hate them.

'Nothing ever gets done unless I do it myself,' her mother was saying, martyred. 'I simply can't cope, I simply can't go on.'

The voices faded behind a closing door. More drinks in the bedroom probably. Then her parents going to their own room. Silence. Where was he? On the run. The phrase had never meant anything before. Men on the run. What did they do? Hide? Sleep in a cave? What would they find to eat?

She had lain down at last, taken off her jeans and shirt and was lying naked, only the coverlet half over her because it was so hot. Even with the window open and the curtains drawn back it was stifling. As though the storm was gathering again.

Behind her the door opened, softly. So softly that she didn't hear it opening, didn't hear the tread of his foot.

'Jenny. Don't scream.'

She started to scream, breath drawing in, her mouth opening, her body twisting round.

'Michael!'

333

He looked like a ghost and for a second she thought that he was, that he was dead and had come to her.

They stared at each other. She held out her hands and he took them and sat on the bed. His hands were dry and hot and she held them against her body, against her skin.

'Your hands are hot,' she whispered, thinking how stupid a thing it was to say. He looked white and feverish and she felt at one and the same time that her heart would break with pain for him, and an overwhelming happiness that he had come to her, that against everything he had come to her, for help, for love, for hiding. 'Are you ill?'

He shook his head. He was swaying with tiredness, and yet it was not really tiredness.

'I'll get you something to eat.' She began to get out of bed and he stopped her, holding her hands tight.

'I ate something,' he said. 'I was in a house in the Harbour. One of the fishermen.'

She held her breath, not wanting him to tell her what she already knew, that he was going away, that he was going without her. She tried to tell him with her eyes that she could not bear it, that it could not happen like that, even life could not be as cruel as that. 'Let me get you something to drink,' she breathed, 'hot whiskey, you've got a fever, I'll hide you here, I'll . . .' Her words trailed away. She hardly knew what she had said. He went on looking at her.

'I have to go very soon,' he whispered. They were conscious of people sleeping, near, pressing on this moment, almost as though they were being overheard, watched through a keyhole.

'No,' she said. There were so many things to say, and there was no point in saying any of them. She realized that she had known from the beginning that this would happen, this moment would come. How long ago was it? The beginning? Seeing him? The first time she had thought – I like his face – the sound of his voice – the way he moves. How long? All her life. Lying in that hard narrow bed over the stables, waking up, seeing him. She felt it like a pain under the heart and began to cry, not making any noise. She put up one of her imprisoned hands and touched his mouth. As if life itself was going away from her, leaving her in a graveyard, with shadows; her mother, her father, the Maces. Shadows. They would talk to her, make sounds, want her to answer. She felt a tightness in her throat and moved her head from side to side, trying to push away that image of her parents. Even to be truly dead would be something. To be that much free. 'Take me with you.' And she knew that in his mind he had already gone, the goodbyes were over, she was a long way away from him, waving, he wasn't even looking in her direction.

But that was only half true. All of him that mattered was still there, holding her hands, looking. He held her knuckles against his mouth, kissed them. 'Try not to make it harder,' he said. She wanted to be angry then. And for me? her mind screamed. Who will make it easier for me? But she tried to stop crying, tried to smile, because that was the only way she knew, not to make things harder. Don't cry now, Jennifer, be a good girl, be a good sport, don't spoil things on your birthday, don't let the side down, let's have a smile now, it doesn't really hurt, does it?

But she couldn't smile and she bent her head down to hide her face. 'Where are you going?' she said through stiff lips.

'Wales first. They're picking me up at the Pool.'

'They?'

'Some fishermen.'

'Why can't you stay? If you haven't done anything—'

He didn't answer.

They sat, her face bent down, their hands linked. After a time he said, 'I have to go.'

It was her turn not to answer.

'And I need – money.'

Against her will her hands tightened on his and then let go. It wasn't true, that wasn't why he had come, not really, not the first reason. But it was as though something cold and hostile had entered the room, as though this was no longer her own private place but a waiting room, and the door had opened and a stranger had said, 'It's time'. There was no intimacy left, and as she thought of that the past minutes seemed to be going away from her at an enormous rate, like a comet, racing away from her in a dark sky, and she thought, 'a minute, two minutes ago I was happy, he hadn't said that'. She lifted her head and said in a heavy, old voice, 'I'll get you some. I know where he keeps the takings at night.'

'I'll send it back. I have to give the—' he stopped on the point of saying a name and said,'—the fishermen who're taking me – I'll have to give them something. And in Wales I'll have to buy papers, a discharge book—'

335

'Discharge book?' Like saying, 'Really, is it snowing?'

'A sailor's discharge book. I'll get one in Cardiff from a drunk. Then I can—' Already there was so much distance between them that he was afraid to tell her things.

'Let me put on some clothes,' she said. He even turned his head while she put them on.

They went down the stairs and she found the money in her father's study, the key of the cash box under a book on the top shelf, the cash box in the secret drawer of the roll top desk. Thirty pounds and some silver. He took it all in his cupped hands, not looking at her. 'I'll send it back,' he repeated. They went out into the passage, beside the kitchen, and she drew back the bolts of the door into the yard. They made small, dry metallic sounds. She had not put on any slippers and the tiled passage was cold against her feet. He opened the door and she thought, 'He can't wait. Not even for that.' The night was sudden and astonishing, sky and stars and the hint of morning, a bewildering freshness of the world itself after the closed passage and the house. She thought, 'I will die. When he goes I will die.' And she knew how stupid that was while she was thinking it, that she wouldn't die, that she would go on, she would get up and dress again, and go down to the kitchen and say good morning to the kitchen maid and her mother and father and the Maces. She would go through the whole day.

He was breathing in the air of the yard, holding the money in one hand, ashamed to put it finally and irrevocably into his hip pocket in front of her. While he held it like that it was still some kind of link between them. When he had been making his way down to the town and through the laneways, thinking about her, he hadn't known what he was going to say, how he was going to tell her, had tried to tell himself that seeing her was everything, that the only thing in the world that he wanted was not to have to go. But sitting in the fisherman's house had somehow broken that, and when he had reached the hotel it was already over. He was gone. The real part of his mind was gone. And yet the inner part, that takes no decisions, has no thoughts; that part had still been there, had sat with her, held her hands, had loved her. But he knew now, standing in the yard, already a thousand miles away from her, he knew that he had not really understood, had felt his own pain but not hers. He wanted to touch her again, tell her that he understood, explain, explain. But nothing can be explained. It simply is.

'They'll be waiting,' he whispered. She nodded. He pushed the money into a trouser pocket, pushing it in, trying to say with the gesture, 'It wasn't for this, I didn't come to you for this.' And the strange thing was that not now, but in an hour, a day, a week, a month from this moment standing in the morning dark, he would feel everything that he should be feeling as he stood there. It would come back to him like the pain of a tooth, sudden, like a nail driven into the bone, stopping his breath. He would feel her pain and his own, and everything that he had said and done, the wrongness of it, the stupid brutality of it. And he would begin to build in his mind a picture of her, a memory of her; would remember everything, the sound of her footsteps on the wooden stairs to the loft, her face when she was sleeping, the fall of her hair as she bent her head forwards, so that it half hid her face. The narrow thinness of her neck. And how many times he had hurt her. He would build up the image until he knew himself that it was becoming false, that she hadn't been like that, or that, and the pain would become worse, and he would be left with pieces, as if he had broken something beautiful and the pieces lay scattered on the floor, mixed with rubbish and dust and other, unwanted things.

'They have to catch the tide,' he said.

She didn't answer. It was as though he wanted her to let him go, tell him to go, and she was refusing. But she was not even looking at him, except out of the corners of her eyes. He put out his hand suddenly and took hers, shaking it and he knew that was wrong and wanted to kiss her, and that was also impossible. 'I'll write,' he said. 'When I can.' He turned and went quickly towards the open gateway of the courtyard, open because the huge timber gates had half collapsed years ago, and could no longer be closed. She watched him. When he was through the gateway he began to run. Almost out of her sight he turned and waved.

Into Stukeley's Pool the fishing boat came like a ghost. A dinghy swung away from the beach, and Michael could see the dark, steel water. Let down her anchor. The sound muffled and yet echoing, carrying across the Pool to the empty stretch of sand. Shadows moved on the deck, a small boat lowered away, men rowed for the shore. Michael came out from among the trees, down on to the sand, waited. And all the time that he waited he wanted to look over his shoulder, listened for her, for her footsteps running through the wood behind him. The keel of the dinghy touched the sand. One of the men stood up, held out his hand for Michael to grasp as he climbed over the gunwale.

Michael settled himself on a thwart. No one spoke. The dinghy swung away from the beach, and Michael could see the trees he had just come through without turning his head. Nothing moved. The stretch of rippled water grew wide, impassable. With a quarter of an hour of entering the Pool the fishing boat was gone again, the Pool was empty. It was then that she came. Walking slowly most of the way, only running the last few yards of the path, stupidly, breathless, taken with a sudden wild panic that he would still be there. But there was no one, no fishing boat, no sound. She stopped running and walked slowly again, coming to the edge of the bluff, climbing down on to the sand. She sat down where they had made love a lifetime ago, and stared at the water. After a while she lay back and stared at the sky. It was already light.

CHAPTER THIRTY

THE cellar was dark and smelled of wine and French tobacco and mould and stone and candle flames. There were candles on the tables, set in the necks of bottles, running their red rivulets of melted wax down the bottle sides, on to the heavy wood of the table tops. Long, trestle tables with benches, that ran the length of the stone walls. It was part of the atmosphere, or affectation, of La Chatte Grise to keep its old simplicity to amuse the rich. The rich who came and paid a hundred francs a time to eat labourers' food and drink Pernod and Algerian wine, and listen to Johnny Le Gallois. Johnny who sings.

It was three o'clock in the morning and he was going to sing. He sat cross-legged on the flat top of a wine barrel, cradling his guitar. His face very white, carved out of the shadows by the uneasy light from the two candles on a shelf beside him. Staring down at the guitar, touching the strings with absent-minded fingers, letting long notes echo and die away and reawaken before they had completely died.

He began a song that seemed to grow out of the reawakened notes, almost singing to himself, like a man listening to how words sound, trying their effect. He sang in French at first, good enough French after a year in Paris, after a year of washing dishes for food, helping in bars, beginning to sing again, coming to La Chatte Grise when it was already hoping to become smart, attract people looking for something new.

A journalist had heard him and written a paragraph about La Chatte and its new singer, the ex-sailor from Wales, Johnny, who sang Irish songs. People began to come there after the theatre, after parties or the cinema, or late dinners, sitting until three or four or five in the morning. The owner of La Chatte, who owned many other things as well, decided that it was worth his while to have his new singer's papers put in order, rather than let him go as soon as the police came round asking questions, and Michael Carmody became even more

339

officially John Williams of Swansea, ex-able seaman, with a residence permit and a work permit and a right to exist.

He sat now, cross-legged on the barrel top, and sang one of his own songs; of loss and loneliness and darkness like an empty world; and yet in the sombreness of the music, scattered here and there like two or three birds singing in a dark wood, one here, one there, a sudden ripple of notes, light and sinuous, rising like spring water out of rock, well-spring and birdsong and a white branch of hawthorn, all sudden, joyful things that say, 'Here I am! I live! A miracle!' He was singing of The Ross, although the words he was singing did not say this. Singing of a boy who had lost a girl, who would never find her again. Of a boy who had lost his home, and would never see it again. Of a house on a hillside. Of the wind crying as it has always cried, no sorrow in its crying. For how can the wind feel sorrow?

He sang the keening of the wind, and the cold darkness of the mountainside, the timelessness that saw tragedy as nothing. And the sunrise. Let her sleep, he sang softly of that girl who had lost her friend. Let her wake and see that the sun has risen. Surely that is enough. Let her see that life goes on. And maybe, maybe even the indifferent world is kinder than she thinks – not kind, that is not the word for how can the world be kind or unkind or even notice our existence – maybe even blind chance will allow them to meet again, maybe one morning she will hear his voice, for the foxes do not kill all the birds, nor the hunters all the foxes. Even love can survive.

He let the music die at last, the notes whispering away into the corners of the cellar. He had begun singing in French but he had finished the song in Irish and no one in the cellar had understood the words. But the song had still created its effect and there was a long stillness before anyone applauded. The owner was by the bar and a man he knew came over and said, 'He is not bad, your fellow. Not bad at all. Has he cut a disc yet?'

'Not yet.'

'Maybe we could talk business then.'

They began to talk the business that was the beginning of Michael Carmody's career. Michael touched the strings of the guitar again as though he was searching for another song. He was still thinking of The Ross, of Jennifer, of his mother, of Seagrun, of all that had happened. He wondered if his mother had got the letter yet that he had written to her. He wondered if there was any point, if it would be madness to write to Jennifer. Because he was thinking of her he began to sing one of the songs he had sung in the bar all that time ago, all that distance away. When he sang he could believe, half believe, that he would see her again.

'Not bad at all,' the man said by the bar. 'He has something different, this boy of yours.'

On one of the benches a woman who was drunk began to cry uncontrollably at the sadness of the song, and the man who was with her, who worked in the Foreign Ministry and prided himself on being very English and impassive, was pierced with an agony of embarrassment. 'For Heaven's sake, Mathilde, control yourself.'

'He is so beautiful,' she wept. 'So tragic and beautiful.'

The same journalist who had first taken La Chatte and Johnny Le Gallois under his wing heard the phrase, sitting just beyond the Foreign Ministry official, and the next day in his column he made a great anecdote out of it, the beautiful society woman brought to tears by the poor singer in the night club of the Grey Cat. 'A thread of tragic simplicity runs like golden stitching on black velvet in this singer's performance. And the sophisticated are touched by it, as though suddenly, in a world of false emotions, they had been shown reality.'

He went on like that for several paragraphs, and such is the power of the written word that long, long afterwards, when it would have been very difficult to find anyone more sophisticated, or further removed from poverty and tragic simplicity, this image of Johnny Le Gallois persisted, of the poor singer in his rope-soled canvas shoes and sailor's jersey, so poor that he could not afford to eat, so simple, so real that he reduced the rich to tears as soon as he began to sing, so close to nature that he sang as a bird sings; and people saw only the legend, only the image. Even Michael was affected by it. And The Ross in its humility and simplicity and stubborn endurance of history wove itself into all the singing of this particular one of its children, and through his singing spread something of itself throughout the entire world that listens to songs, had its infinitesimal yet actual effect in places and in people who had never heard of its existence. Like one seed from a tree blowing on the wind.

CHAPTER THIRTY-ONE

THE sun touched Lir Head like a warrior lowering his shield after battle, although in all the world of The Ross there were no signs of battle. A year gone by since the minuscule rising of the Sons of Ireland; the attack on the Garda Barracks, the death of Sir Philip. And to the tranquil eyes of Sean the Post, Donal Carmody and Tim Pat of the Gap, standing in front of Donal's cottage and watching the sun go down, no change in the world had taken place apart from the changing of the seasons. If there was fighting and tragedy and burning in the North, it had brought no changes to The Ross.

Sir Philip's death had brought changes, certainly, but at a level and a distance that left the simplicities of life untouched. The Eagans had gone and it was as though they had never existed. An Irish American, a man whose great-grandfather and great-grandmother had left The Ross after the Famine, had bought Eaganscourt and planned to make it a Stud Farm. He might succeed or he might not. The first evening of his ownership he had walked out of the dining-room in his black suède shoes and his dinner jacket, with his wife and his secretary-factotum, a fine perfume of cigar smoke wafting behind him, and the taste of good brandy in his throat, and they had walked towards the Tower to see where it had happened. On the way, below the stone supporting wall of the terrace, they had come on the great iron Famine cauldron, from which the Eagans had dispensed thin soup to dying tenants and beggars from the road.

Mr. Patrick O'Loughlinn gave it a kick. But it was too sunk in the earth to make any sound beyond a dull and deadened thud. 'Wonder what in hell the old guy used that for? Feed the pigs, I guess.'

They went and gave themselves a pleasant moment of macabre chill as they stared down into the dungeon where the body had been found.

'If people throw their weight about, that's what they can expect,' Mr. O'Loughlinn said. His secretary lowered his eyes. 'We're going to make these people real glad we've come,' Mr. O'Loughlinn said with sudden uneasiness. 'Find out if there's any poor kids around. We'll have a kids' party to warm the place up.'

It was arranged, and there were lots of children there and they enjoyed themselves, and their parents said polite and grateful things. But when they were home again they folded their mouths and thought that that was not the way real gentry behaved. And if they had met Lady Eagan in the street they would have said, 'Ah God, ma'am, milady, it isn't like the old days at all, and the family gone out of it.' And that would have been a lie as well.

The Kershaws had also sold up and gone. In the end Benedict Mulcahy had got The Old House Hotel for twenty-two thousand pounds, and he too planned to breed horses there, and keep beef cattle. He was not a man to spend much time unprofitably cursing Fate and weeping over spilled whiskey. He had done his share of cursing, but even while he was shouting his mind had been working, picking up the pieces, sorting out the salvage from the flotsam, grabbing what could be saved. The Old House was obvious salvage and with a cunning and brutal mastery he had grabbed it, while Hubert Kershaw's mind was still in a fog of terror at Sir Philip's death and at the possibility of word of his affair with Clara reaching Angela. He had started by asking fifty thousand in so weak a tone and his eyes so eager for a sale that Benedict, who had approached him direct, knowing his man, had offered him twenty in cold cash and sat and waited while Hubert walked up and down the Copper Room declaring that they were wasting each other's time, that if that was the kind of offer he had come to make he might as well go back to Dublin. Half an hour later they had closed on twenty-two and within the week the last male Kershaw was out of The Ross and out of Ireland, as though the family had never set foot there.

And within the same period Benedict had already begun to gather round his mental shoulders the tweed jacket of a county squire. The Development would have been a great thing, a very great thing, to bring to his own backyard, but – seeing the thing frankly now that it was no longer a possibility – it may be great to find oil in your garden but it's likely to make your house an

unpleasant place to live in. It might be no harm at all to have
The Ross remain the way it had always been, quiet and sleepy
and undisturbed, his own peaceful bailiwick, in which he knew
to a dozen votes what his majority would always be, as safe as
money in a mattress. And The Old House, living in it, walking
out of it of a morning to see his grooms lead the horses to the
paddock, his cowman coming from the milking sheds, would –
he sensed this rather than thought it – lift him to another level,
above his brother and his colleagues and enemies in the
government, with their rotten little suburban villas and their
eyes that couldn't lift higher than the gentry's boots. Why in
hell shouldn't an Irishman, the right kind of Irishman, *be*
gentry?

As for the Sons, Seagrun was dead, killed by an English
soldier's bullet in that dark and waiting Belfast street; in that
battle that he had almost foreseen, sitting in the dungeon of
Eagan's Tower, his knees drawn up, his sub-machine gun resting across them, thinking of sacrifice, of the Crucifix, of that
terrible bronze death they had discovered in the old Bishop's
stables. The poor Proinsias, he was still alive, working in Man-
chester as a bus conductor, feeling the hairs prick at the nape of
his neck whenever he saw a policeman. But for The Ross it was
as though he too, like the Eagans and the Kershaws, had never
existed. Like dandelion clocks that blow away on the wind.

'Yerra damn and blast the weather that's in it,' Tim Pat was
saying. 'The grass is burned on me with the drought.' It hadn't
rained for almost a week.

'There's no satisfying you,' Sean the Post said. 'Last week
you were threatening to be drownded if it didn't stop raining.'

'What do you know?' Timmy Pat said, spitting with
comfortable contempt into the dust of the road. 'And you paid
by the Government.' Donal Carmody pursed his mouth at the
sky.

'There's rain there surely,' he said. 'A small bit of it by
morning.'

None of them referred to the letter that Sean had brought up
with him that day. It had been addressed to Mrs. Carmody and
had been posted from England although quite obviously it had
not been written there.

'I'm a long way from you,' Michael had written, 'but you are
always close to me in my thoughts and I'm sure it won't be too

long before I can come back and see you. I'm having a friend make enquiries about everything that happened, and whether I'm held responsible for any of it, and if I am how it can be put right. Until all that's sorted out I'm in a very safe place with a good job and using a different name. Don't worry about me. Give my love to everyone, and to The Ross. I'll write again when I can, your loving son, Michael.' There was money enclosed for presents and a postscript. 'Buy something foolish for yourself and for father, and the girls.'

'Foolish!' Mrs. Carmody had cried in a rage, banging the letter down on the table. 'You'd think he had enough of foolishness.' Then she had taken the letter away into her bedroom to hide it in a secret place. Every now and then for a long time to come she would take it out and read it again, or simply sit with it in her hands, her spectacles half way down her nose and her eyes staring over the rims of them at the Sacred Heart on the wall. She used her share of the present-money to buy a small statue of St. Christopher with Christ on his shoulder, beautifully painted in red and cream and the Holy Child in blue, with bare feet and golden curly hair.

'Blessed St. Christopher mind him wherever he is. He hasn't the brains of a grown man to mind himself.'

But that night of the day that the letter arrived Mrs. Carmody was still in her rage with the folly of men and of life and she had made the kitchen uninhabitable.

'That was all a strange business,' Sean the Post said, coming as near as he would to any reference to the letter, or to Michael. He would not have it thought for the world that he was in any way curious about where Michael might be.

'Arrah damn,' Donal said. 'What Peadar said that night was true enough. Politics is the death of everything. If there was no politics the world would be a good place.'

They heard a voice calling a long way off, and looking in the direction it came from they saw Jamey Power running down the mountainside towards them.

'That's never Jamey,' Tim Pat said wonderingly. 'Running? This hour of the night? What for would he be running anywhere and it near dark?'

'The last bit of wit has gone on him,' Sean the Post suggested.

'Me brother, me brother, Peadar!' Jamey shouted to them while he was still a long way off. 'I'm running for the priest!

He's taken terrible bad in himself and is groaning and roaring up in the bed. Will the priesteen ever come d'you think, lads?' He stopped by them, panting and gasping for his breath, his old hands holding his heart from leaping out of his chest. 'Oh I'm dead from the running.'

'Easy man, easy boy, or it's you'll be needing the priest.'

'D'you think that Father Cooney'd come back up with me? He was terrible angry the last time he was up.'

'He might so, boy,' Sean said; 'He's a soft kind of a man, you have to say that much for him.' And then, 'Is he real bad, Peadar? Is it the frightus is at him again?'

'It's his soul he's screeching about. "I'm damned," he keeps yelling, and Matty there in the bed with him and he thinks Matty is the Old Black Fellow and he trying to kick him out on the floor, and Matty fighting for his life to stay in. What will I do if I'm left alone in the world?'

'Go down with him the pair of you,' Donal said. 'Or at least you, Sean.'

The three men, Jamey walking now, between Sean and Tim Pat, went down the road towards the fork, where Timmy Pat would turn up towards the Gap, and the other two could continue on down into Ross Harbour and Knuckle Street.

Donal watched them for a minute or two and then turned his eyes to the sunset. The sky was crimsoning, and the Bay was dark. Below him the ponds of the refurnished trout farm lay like rectangles of lead. Nothing had changed. His son would one day come back. Would find a job here maybe, although he would never be content with road mending, that was certain. And why would he, and he a scholar? And yet what was better in life than to mend a road, to keep its surface fine and smooth for the people who would pass? A road was a grand thing to be minding.

He did not think of anything much else. He certainly did not think that all that he looked at, the headlands lying like seals in the dark sea, the curve of the land, the small town, the life that he lived and that his friends lived; that all of that had been under sentence of destruction and had been saved. That in a filing cabinet in a tower block of offices in London all the files had been marked 'Closed'. How could he think of that?

He turned and looked up the mountainside towards the Powers' invisible cottage. The Old Black Fellow'll have a hard time of it if he takes that one, he thought. The dog came out of the house, driven out by Mrs. Carmody's furious sweeping, and nudged his hand. He remembered the story Peadar had told of the rebellion of the beasts. 'She'll be quiet soon old fellow,' he said. 'We'll go back in then.' He looked beyond where the Powers' farm lay, higher up until his eye saw the dark shape of the Queen's Fort on the crest of the mountain. He remembered his grandfather telling him that when he himself, the grandfather, had been a boy, there had been a big stone near the Fort and people had poured milk on it and smeared it with butter. And they used to light a bonfire between it and the Fort on John's Eve. Father Pusey had had the stone smashed and the bonfires stopped.

'He would have been right to do that,' Donal thought comfortably. It hadn't been a Christian thing that the old people did. And yet, it was sad if the old ways went. He took out his pipe and wondered if he had a match about him without going back in. There was nothing like the old ways. Nothing.

'Will you come in out of that, you bosthoon,' his wife cried in a fury, 'standing like a stachy to collect the rheumatics. Will you away into your bed, man, and you with work to do in the morning?'

He went in, and after a while fell asleep. It must have been two hours later that he woke briefly, hearing footsteps on the road, and voices. Jamey Power and Father Cooney no doubt. He fell asleep again.

Up in the cottage Peadar Power lay groaning in the pit of his side of the bed. 'Oh, will he come, d'you think he'll come, Matty?' And then, mistaking his brother again for the Devil, lashing out with his heels; 'Get out of this you Old Black One, by the power of Christ.'

Until Father Cooney came, holding his breath as he ducked into the dark cave of the cottage.

'Is it himself? Is it you, Father? Oh God be praised, may God reward you for a Saint. Give me absolution, Father, I'm dying, I'm killed. Give me my absolution for the fishes.'

THE END

CRY OF MORNING

This is a novel of the new Irish revolution – of money and expensive cars and towering office blocks among the Georgian slums. And of what this revolution has done to Ireland and the Irish, a country and a people torn out of the nineteenth century and thrown into the 1970s in a dozen bewilderingly brutal years.

It is the story of the developers against the Preservers – the old against the new: but in a conflict clouded by human emotions and weaknesses. It tells of Francis O'Rourke, a fighting bull of a man, whose vision of concrete, glass and stainless steel rising out the dirty hovels of Dublin brought a storm of protest from its inhabitants and 'Auld Ireland' Preservers. From Lady Honoria who, with the enormous, if unwilling wealth of the Gandon family behind her, also had a vision – that of herself as the uncrowned queen of Dublin. From Father Tracey, the dedicated rebel priest. And, unintentionally, from smooth TV commentator John Lennox who brought both sides together for a confrontation but found he could not remain impartial.

CRY OF MORNING is about the real Ireland and its folk, behind the legends, behind the headlines; about a country that is in the process of awakening, and a people striving for progress yet fearful of change – this is the Republic of Ireland today.

'A consummately professional piece of work, continuously interesting and amusing, its extensive cast intricately marshalled . . . a useful chronicle of the changes, the increasing prosperity, the increasing inequality, of Dublin since 1954 . . . enormously readable.' – *Irish Times*

'A hard, cool look at life over the border. An unglamorised picture, warts and all, of a republic hankering after the simple past as it thrusts into a complex future.' – *Daily Mail*

552 09104 9   45p

A KIND OF LOVING, the best-selling first novel by STAN BARSTOW

Written in the early sixties, *A Kind of Loving* is recognised with *Room at the Top* and *Saturday Night, Sunday Morning*, as one of the most important novels of that era – novels in which the ordinary unhandsome and conventional young man and his way of life were first investigated and portrayed in the modern idiom.

Now in the seventies, Stan Barstow's powerful novel emerges as one that surpasses all others of that genre; for in *A Kind of Loving*, the young Vic Brown, his attitudes and those of his family, his problems and the background against which he comes to resolve them, still have relevance to life today as many people know it. Moreover, Barstow tells his story with a realism and honesty that is rare and that put this, his first novel, into a class of its own.

0 552 09274 6   40p

JOBY by Stan Barstow

To Joby Weston that summer, the world was surely a strange and brutal place. It was the summer then he should have been swollen with happiness at the knowledge that he was going to Cressley grammar school in September but which was clouded by his mother going into hospital. It was the summer when he tasted the bitterness of injustice. And it was Joby's last summer of innocence in which, slowly and painfully, he learnt the hard facts of life and discovered the world of adults was also full of tragedy . . .

'In *Joby* Barstow has pared everything down to essentials, the essentials of reality. It is a considerable work of art.' – *The Scotsman*

0 552 092789   30p

A RAGING CALM by STAN BARSTOW

A Raging Calm is a study of conflicting passions, of loyalty and betrayal, in a vigorous and recognisable urban world.

'The affair between Alderman Simpkins and Mrs. Moffat, one of his constituents, would have made an interesting tale in its own right. So would the awakening of Andrea Warner by Philip Hart, grammar school teacher. Stan Barstow dovetails these together without skimping on plot, characterisation of theme. This is the core of his power as a writer; he *cares* about people. It needs more than narrative skill to manage this: it takes imaginative warmth and a rare balance of sensibilities.' – *Tribune*

'Stan Barstow is one of the very best of our younger regional novelists and *A Raging Calm* is a fine example of his work.

It is humane and it is perceptive. It never fakes feeling in the interests of drama, yet it remains dramatically alive.

Deeply felt and skilfully told, this novel will certainly enhance Mr Barstow's already high reputation.' – *Evening Standard*

0 552 08506 5   35p

A SELECTION OF FINE READING
AVAILABLE IN CORGI BOOKS

All these books are available at your bookshop or newsagent; or can be ordered direct from the publisher. Just tick the titles you want and fill in the form below.

CORGI BOOKS, Cash Sales Department, P.O. Box 11, Falmouth, Cornwall.
Please send cheque or postal order. no currency, and allow 7p per book to cover the cost of postage and packing in the U.K. (5p if more than one copy) 7p per book overseas.

NAME ....

ADDRESS ....

(NOV. 73) ....